MW00565961

CUTE EATS

CUTE
EATS
CUTE

C.B. Murphy

NORTH STAR PRESS OF ST. CLOUD, INC.
St. Cloud, Minnesota

Copyright © 2010 C.B. Murphy

ISBN: 0-87839-365-X
ISBN-13: 978-0-87839-365-7

All rights reserved.

This is a work of fiction. Names, characters, places, and incidents
are the products of the author's imagination or are used fictitiously.
Any resemblance to actual events or persons, living or dead, is entirely coincidental.

First Edition, September 1, 2010

Printed in the United States of America

Published by
North Star Press of St. Cloud, Inc.
P.O. Box 451
St. Cloud, Minnesota 56302

www.northstarpress.com

To Judith, Nicolas, and Lucas
who know where to find me.

CHAPTER ONE

THE TROUBLE BEGAN WHEN MY PARENTS sat us down and told us to call them by their first names. My little brother, Perry, who was eight, looked as if he might burst into tears.

"Even at bedtime?" he asked.

"Honey," Elissa—formerly known as Mom—said, "someday you'll understand and thank us."

Jeff—formerly known as Dad—was staring straight ahead. Elissa elbowed him, and he said, "It's true. El and I agreed to do this way back in college, but—" He stopped suddenly, as if he'd lost his train of thought.

"We just forgot how important it was to us," Elissa said. "We were so . . . busy. When you kids were younger, I mean."

"So why not just forget it permanently?" I asked.

"We just felt it was important," Jeff said, glancing at Elissa. "To clarify some things around here."

"It's about reaffirming shared values," Elissa said, looking back at Jeff. "For all of us."

"What shared values?" I asked.

They both opened their mouths, looked at each other, then shut their mouths. Jeff nodded for Elissa to go first.

"When we were in college," she started, then giggled.

Jeff looked like he wanted to roll his eyes, but he rubbed his forehead instead.

"We had all these ideas," Elissa said, "about why the world was, well, the way it is. When we talked about the future—and then it seemed impossible that we would ever have kids, given the pollution—"

"El," Jeff said, "cut to the chase."

"Oh, you," she said to him. "I was having fun. But, okay. We wanted to live in a world of . . . equality, where there were no hierarchies. Without hierarchies, there would be no—"

"Abuse of power," Jeff said. "Honey, this is way over Perry's head."

"No, it isn't," Elissa said. "You know about evil, right, Perry? Bad guys? The powerful ones who always want—"

"To take over the world?" Perry said.

"You see?" Elissa said to Jeff, "he's tracking perfectly." Turning back to Perry, she said, "Yes, absolutely right. Hierarchy is when the evil kings and queens make the servants—"

"Do all the work? Like Cinderella!" Perry said.

"Right," Elissa said. "That's abuse of power. And we thought, in our own small way, that teaching you from the beginning that we are all, well, just people—"

"So does this mean, being equals, we get to make our own rules?" I asked.

Jeff glared at me. "You know very well—"

Elissa restrained him with a finger on his forearm. "We work together. As a unit. We work things out. Love is greater than any difference of opinion. Isn't that right, Jeff?"

Jeff nodded, but he squinted as if he'd been yanked from an unpleasant daydream. He might have been thinking about those evil hierarchies, but the way he looked, I sensed it was something else. Something big was going to come down.

And I was right. The next day, Jeff's employer, the Department of Natural Resources—the DNR—announced that they intended to slaughter "excess" deer in Wirth Park. My family stopped saying anything more complicated than "Pass the salt" after that. Before the decision was made we'd listened to Jeff's explanations that the herd was vastly overpopulated. He even practiced his presentation to the city officials on us, using charts and graphs that were supposed to show how the deer were destroying the ecosystem and endangering the city's fresh water reserves.

"Like so many cows packed into a small pasture," he said. "These animals have to be managed."

According to Jeff, these sweet creatures had eaten everything green in the park and were now wandering through the city munching expensive flowers. He grossed us out with pictures of the parasites and germ-infested fleas they carried, then thrust a chart at us showing radical increases in deer-auto collision ratios.

"They're like giant rats on the prowl," he said.

Elissa asked, "What kind of people would send men armed with weapons of death into our beloved nature spot?"

I added that perhaps the DNR had missed some of the good things the deer were doing. I described watching a doe clean up the park by eating a whole carton of McDonald's French fries.

Jeff threw down his charts and graphs about then. You might say that was the point when the trouble shifted into second gear.

From that point on, nothing my mother or I said (or Perry, if he mattered) helped. The DNR set the hunt date to begin on October 31. This wasn't terribly bright, according to Elissa.

"Halloween was once called Samhain by the ancient Celts," she told me when Jeff wasn't around. "It was ruled by a stag-headed god named Cennunnos." She explained that scheduling the hunt on Halloween was their way of daring someone to stop them.

In the weeks that followed, we tried to pretend we were a normal family. Jeff went to work. Elissa went to her meetings. Perry and I did the zombie school thing. But we all knew something was brewing beneath the surface.

Despite our family's social life nearly grinding to a halt, Jeff and I continued to share our one peculiar ritual. On Friday nights, after Perry conked out and Elissa headed off to some spirituality meeting or another, we made popcorn and watched my favorite show, *Strange But True*. Just a cheap tabloid-style cable show, but I taped and cataloged it religiously. Mostly it rehashed stock monsters and unsolved mysteries, but it occasionally revealed information so significant people would call me a nerd if I tried to tell them about it.

That night's show was about a humanoid goat that walked on two legs. The chupacabra had vampire fangs and an appetite for blood. It haunted Mexican border towns spooking illegal immigrants and mutilating farm animals. But it could be the most serious threat facing our nation.

While we watched, Jeff and I stared at the glowing TV, stuffing our faces with popcorn.

"You know why we do this?" he asked.

"Eat popcorn?" I said.

"Watch TV."

I waited for his latest theory.

"Because cavemen sat in front of campfires for thousands of years listening to stories," he said. He took another handful of popcorn, talking and chewing at the same time. "Our brains mistake TV for a campfire. We feel comforted and safe."

"So the system lulls us to sleep so we'll buy anything they tell us to?"

This was how it went with us. Theories and jabs.

A clomping on the stairs disturbed us. I turned away from the TV, which was showing a drawing of a quasi-satyr hiding behind a giant cactus. Elissa was putting on her trench coat over the blue-gray robe thing she wore to her Women's Spirituality meetings. She'd told me not to tell Jeff it was called a Wiccan tunic, then asked if it made her look fat. Jeff had already warned me about women asking if they were fat. He said that in many parts of the world Elissa would be considered average, even small. If Jeff didn't look so much like a squirrel monkey, they might have fit together better.

"I like your hair," I said.

She looked at me funny, probably because she wore it medium length with bangs like she had in every picture since high school. "I was supposed to pick up Janine fifteen minutes ago," she said.

As she walked toward Jeff, she held her coat closed. "I might be home pretty late," she said.

Mouth full of popcorn, Jeff said, "Isn't it a little cold to dance around a maypole?"

"It's not . . ." Elissa clicked her tongue. "We're not . . ."

She sighed, shut her eyes and inhaled loudly through her nose, something she called a "centering breath."

"I want you to know," she said. "We're doing something . . . with Stewart Spiranga."

"What's he selling?" Jeff said.

"You haven't heard of him?" she asked. "I thought he might be on your villain list. He's the activist who wrote *Releasing Your Inner Wild Person*."

Jeff looked up as "Strange" cut to a commercial for a fishing lure. Bits of popcorn stuck to his beard.

"Isn't he that guy who lost his job at the university? The one who's into weird stuff like mercy killing disabled people?"

She forced a laugh. "I figured you'd know *that* much. Everything he says gets garbled by the media. He stirs people up, that's all. He said people would throw that at us." She stepped toward the door. "No, he's not into anything like that. Not at all. He loves the . . ." she searched for a word, "environment."

"Don't we all," Jeff said.

Elissa inhaled sharply. "We're doing something . . . in the park."

Since the deer controversy had begun, the word "park" in our house meant only Wirth Park.

Jeff jumped up. "Don't get me in trouble, El. You know the park closes at ten. I can't afford any hassles at work."

"Everything isn't about you," she said. "This is about me." She looked suddenly happy and alive, as if an espresso had just hit her blood stream. "Don't wait up," she sang happily as she disappeared out the front door. A cold gust of wind reached as far as the couch.

"Jesus H. Christ," Jeff said.

He watched from the front window while her white minivan pulled out of the driveway. Then he moved as if in a trance to our big picture window, the one that faced the park. He aligned his toes to a piece of tape on the carpet. If you keep your toes on the tape and your head perfectly still, you wouldn't see any other houses from this spot. People teased him about that, but I'd come home and find him standing on his spot, just staring.

I told him I'd tape the rest of the show, then headed off to bed.

Perry and I still shared a room. Mostly I hated it, but occasionally it was funny to see him all knotted up in his Batman quilt, dumb as a cat. The room was hot, so I cracked open the skylight. The cold night air made me think about Elissa and her ragtag band of witches out there in the forest doing desperate magic to save the deer. I was proud of her.

I shucked off my jeans and T-shirt and flopped onto my bed in my underwear. I picked up *The Grave Robbers of Arkkorn*, a book I reread for tips on guerilla tactics. Science fiction was comforting because it reminded me there are millions of intelligent creatures in the universe as unsatisfied with their lives as I was. They lay on their beds or cave floors or in their gelatinous pods, wishing they were somewhere else.

Perry shouted from a dream. "No!" He thrashed around and said something about his Mr. Hairy. I was tempted to whisper something nasty about his toy bear, but I didn't. Eventually, I heard Jeff thumping up the stairs. He poked his head in.

"Goodnight, Sam. Sorry about . . ." he glanced around the room, "everything."

"No problem," I said, following my rule: Never show adults they've gotten to you.

Then I just couldn't sleep. I kept thinking about Elissa out there in the forest. I knew more than she'd told Jeff. This Spiranga guy wanted them to communicate psychically with the deer. I'd sworn myself to secrecy when she told me this.

I studied a poster of Middle Earth left over from more innocent times. In maps of fantasy worlds, evil places are clearly marked with dark clouds or dragons lurking in caverns. In real life, you have to figure it out when you might be in one.

In half-sleep, Perry walked over and climbed onto my bed. He curled up at the end of it like a dog. In the old days, I'd kick him off when he did this, but that night I watched his chest go up and down rhythmically.

I don't know how much time passed, but a loud crash woke me. I jumped out of bed in my underwear. My light was still on. I heard a second crash and remembered how raccoons got into the garbage. Then an eerie noise like a human wail came through the cracked skylight. I knew cats in heat sometimes sounded like angry babies, but I wondered if a chupacabra might sound like a cat in heat.

Curiosity finally led me out of my door. A man in boxer shorts was running down the stairs. I knew it was Jeff, but in the dark he looked leaner and more muscular. In a minute, he was at the front door, putting on his boots.

"Something's going on out there," he said mysteriously.

I followed him out. Despite the weird thrill of being in my underwear, it was much colder than I'd expected. Jeff crouched down on the front lawn, moving his head back and forth as if scanning for animal tracks.

"What?" I said, crossing my arms for warmth.

"Look."

He pointed at Elissa's minivan parked in the street. It should have been in the garage. Something was wrong, something involving Elissa. Then he pointed to our garbage can rolling on its side. Another bumping sound came from our backyard.

"Someone's going up the attic stairs," he said.

Running to the backyard, he paused at Perry's sandbox and picked up a plastic shovel. I made a gesture that questioned his sanity, but he ignored me. He pointed at the open door of the stairwell, the only way to get to the unheated attic over the garage.

Our attic is a weird place, full of my grandfather's outdoorsy crap that Elissa couldn't get Jeff to throw away: mounted animals, old fishing tackle, ancient leather gloves, meaningless awards and plaques for hunting and fishing, a lifetime of outdoorsy loot passed to Jeff when his dad had died.

Jeff moved quickly through the darkened doorway, walking in a low martial arts crouch. I followed up the stairs, mainly out of fear of being left behind. I heard the sound of boxes falling to the floor. I was sure someone was trying to lure us up there to hurt us. It was a trap. I wanted to warn Jeff, but he was too far ahead.

As my eyes adjusted, I saw Grampa's trophy deer mount lying on the floor. Other stuffed animals were scattered about. I saw a pheasant, a fox, a northern pike frozen in its last lunge for a jig.

"Elissa?" Jeff said.

"Go away." It sounded like a little girl version of Elissa's voice.

I looked over Jeff's shoulder and saw Elissa sitting on the floor in the corner. Moonlight passing through a windowpane striped her with dark lines like an old-fashioned prison uniform. Her face glistened with tears.

"Hon? What happened?" Jeff said. "Are you okay?"

"I can't live like this anymore," she said, still a pouty child.

"Like what, hon?" Jeff said softly.

"This!" she shouted, kicking a mounted pike on the floor. "Live with all this!"

Jeff bent over and gently picked up the fish. He placed it on one of the piles of boxes.

"What happened?" Jeff whispered to her.

"Nothing *happened!*" she snapped.

Just then, hysterical screams came from the base of the stairwell. I grabbed my dad, completely spooked.

"Perry," Jeff said. "Go see. And turn on the light."

Perry sat at the bottom of the stairs clutching Mr. Hairy. When he saw me, he screamed again. I flicked on the energy-saving light bulb, which sent a pale yellow glow over us.

"It's okay, Pere," I said. "It's just Elissa."

He cried, "Momma!" opening his arms toward the attic, his hands open and closed, clutching at empty space.

"Don't be a baby. Just go to bed. Everything will be fine in the morning."

"What's she . . ." he was hiccupping and shivering, which made him hard to understand, "doing out here?"

"Working," I said. "Reorganizing the attic."

"Everyone . . ." hiccup, "was gone . . ." hiccup, "when I woke up."

"Just be quiet," I said as kindly as I could stand.

"Momma!" he screamed at full volume.

In a moment, Jeff was beside me.

"I think he needs you," I said in my best exasperated adult tone.

"Okay," Jeff said. "Stay with El a minute, would you?" He snatched Perry off the stair. "C'mon, kiddo. Everything's going to be fine. Let's put Mr. Hairy to bed."

This was my only chance to find out what really happened to Elissa. I was sure she wouldn't tell Jeff. I hurried up to the attic, which was now bathed in weird yellow light. A box full of her old cow-pattern tea crap was open next to her. She held up a black-and-white dappled teapot, the one that vomits tea into its calf cups.

"This is the only thing of mine that's up here," she said.

"Mom?" I whispered. "Elissa? What happened?"

"Sammy," she said, breaking into a smile. She touched my face with a cold hand.

"Who did this to you?"

She told me about Spiranga, how he went on and on about why the ancient religions required blood sacrifice.

"Can you believe he was saying this to a bunch of middle-aged women who won't even allow their kids to play with toy guns?" she asked.

Then she explained that she'd thought they were just going to talk about how they could help the deer, maybe have a snack.

"I didn't want to hear about it," she said. "I mean, if people chain themselves to trees and want to call that human sacrifice, fine. That I can handle. You know I'm against violence of any kind."

She'd wandered away from the group, she explained, and got lost. She said it was like that scene in the *Wizard of Oz* when Dorothy came across those mean trees that grabbed at her. It was all brambles and thorns. She'd lost her coat and begun crying.

Then she smiled strangely at me.

"But something really cool happened, Sam. I can tell you, but keep it quiet. Don't tell Jeff. Something really cool." She looked years younger.

"What?" I said.

"I saw him."

"Who?" I asked as a chill went through me.

"Big Buck. You know? The biggest buck in the woods? The one the DNR named Big Buck? I saw him. Just for a few seconds. He looked at me with these intelligent, loving eyes."

I began sweating. I was sure Jeff would pop up behind me.

"He sent me an image," she said. "Like the tarot card of the hanged man, only it was a buck deer hanging upside down from a tree, only . . ."

"Only what?"

"He was smiling, or at least peaceful. Like Christ on the cross, but upside down. It was like he was doing this on purpose, letting himself get killed this way. Spiranga would call it a sacrifice, I suppose." She shuddered again.

"What do you think it meant? He meant?"

She reached out and held my hand. Her hand was still cold.

"I don't know," she said. "That we all have to sacrifice ourselves to stop the hunt? I don't know. My spiritually group will help me with it."

I was buzzing inside with her unsolved mystery when Jeff showed up.

"Well, I got him to bed," he said as if Perry were the big problem of the night. "Sam got your whole story?" he asked Elissa. He stroked his beard with a weird smile on his face. "Heavy stuff?"

"Yes," Elissa said. "Heavy is appropriate right now, don't you think?"

Jeff all at once looked tired. "Yeah, it's been a big night for all of us. Let's not jump into anything . . ."

I was heading for the stairwell when Elissa screamed, "You don't understand anything, do you?"

I practically stumbled over Perry, who was once again lurking on the stairs.

"You don't understand how violence in one place creates violence someplace else," she said. "Go ahead, kill them! Go on! Take your stupid hunters in there and kill all the deer. Who needs them? They're nuisances. Cockroaches! Kill the ants, kill the mice, kill the squirrels, even kill the goddam raccoons. Kill everything!"

"I like raccoons," Perry whispered.

"Shut up," I said quietly as I crouched beside him.

"Are you finished?" Jeff asked.

"You know what my friends say?" Elissa shouted. "They say I married a murderer."

"And what do you say back?" Jeff was dangerously calm now. The eye of the hurricane.

"We should go," I whispered to Perry.

Instead, he put his arm over my shoulder, and amazingly I let him. His eyes were wide open.

"I say I'm starting to believe it," Elissa said. "Maybe you are a murderer."

"You're going over, El. You're really going over now. Your brain's so full of this New Age bullshit it's turning to mush. Christ, you need help. And I'm not talking about spirituality groups or action committees. I'm talking real doctors here!" Now he was yelling.

"Ha! Ha! Ha!" she yelled back. "Real doctors—ha, ha, ha."

"Oh, that's good," he shouted back. *"Ha! Ha! Ha!"*

Jeff made a halfhearted attempt to close the door, but one couldn't close that door without concentration. He gave up, leaving it half-open.

Then they really let it rip.

They yelled about the deer kill, about Grampa's stuffed deer heads and mounted fish, about Jeff taking the stupid DNR job. Why did he have to give up on his old business and throw in with "a bunch of right wing extremists?" she yelled. He yelled back something about her turning into "a goddam witch or Wiccan or whatever the fuck she called it." They yelled about hippies and rednecks, environmentalists, and lesbian daycare workers, hunting and animal rights. Finally they started calling names.

"Macho man!"

"Witch!"

"Murderer!"

"Bad mother!"

Something hit the door with a hard knock. The momma cow's head from Elissa's favorite teapot rolled into the open space of the door. As many video cow mutilations as I've seen on *Strange But True*, the decapitated ceramic cow was still a shocking sight. I felt Perry's arm tighten on my neck. We crouched down and held on to each other. He was sobbing quietly, but his body was jerking. I hate to admit it, but I was crying too.

CHAPTER TWO

A
T LINDBERGH HIGH, WE ALL WANTED TO LIVE in a Pepsi commercial where
every race wears dreadlocks and parties together. Ms. S-T was my home-
room and American Culture teacher. Her real name was Ms. Steinlicht-
Trakea, but she let us call her Ms. S-T. We pronounced her name "Mizesty," slurring
it together to sound as if we lived in a community of color. Sometimes we shortened
it to "Zesty," which usually reminded me of that soap commercial.

"Okay, guys, let's give the principal our complete attention," she said, the morning
after Elissa broke the cow. Our class stared at the TV. Mr. Katami, aka the Kat, was
making an announcement on our school's closed-circuit TV system.

Ms. S-T sat on her desk and began pumping her legs like an old lady at a swimming pool. This was her routine for the Kat's announcements. My friend Ryan said
she went into heat when Katami showed up for his daily message, even though Katami
was Japanese-American and pretty strange looking. Maybe it was one of those love-
him-for-his-mind things. Someone once drew a picture of their love child and sent it
around. It was E.T. with folk singer hair and fun glasses.

Thinking of love children sent my eyes to Megan's sincere face. She sat upright
with her hands folded, looking at the screen as if she expected important information
to come her way. Megan's of solid Scandinavian stock, strong and brave with slight
disdain for her feminine beauty. Dark hair framed her face—casual but sensible.

Megan had been established in my fantasies long before she entered my life as a
real person. In the real world, she first approached me because I'd written a poem about
how pheasant hunting grossed me out. When she hit me with her Council of Nations
idea, I jumped at the chance to be near her.

"Volume!" someone shouted. Ms. S-T pointed a remote the size of a shoe at
Katami's face, then frowned and hopped off her desk when nothing happened. She
fiddled with the set, which hung precariously over a green-tinged aquarium in the corner of the room.

Katami's voice came on mid-sentence. ". . . agreed that the term 'Earth Day' just wasn't accurate enough, we—that is, the Committee and I—thought that, in light of the challenges facing our regional environment, we ought to have what we used to call in the sixties a 'teach-in'." He paused long enough for us to roll our eyes at the reference to the sixties. The edges of his mouth turned up into something like a smile.

"Look at Zesty," Ryan pretended to whisper as he fished for laughs. "She's practically having sex with that desk."

"I can't believe you," his friend Holly said with a big smile. "You're so gross."

She slapped Ryan on the shoulder, then looked around to see if anyone had witnessed their flirtation. She and Ryan were the other two members of the Council of Nations.

"We are the first school to come up with this idea," Katami continued, "but we're hopeful it will catch on. We're going to rename Earth Day . . ." he paused and smiled, "Ecoday! We think Ecoday places the emphasis more firmly on science and the ecological problems the earth faces. Earth Day was a great and valuable concept for its time, but we—that is, the committee and I—found the name a bit too celebratory. If we're going to focus on the fragility of the earth's ecosystem only once a year, we ought to do it seriously. Don't you agree, students?"

"Yes, Mr. Katami," we answered in the mocking way that drove Ms. S-T nuts. This time she held up a stern index finger.

Megan beamed because Ecoday had been her idea. The Earth Day Committee was made up of her, Ms. S-T, and the Kat. Despite being such a radical, Megan mysteriously managed to maintain a brown-nosey relationship with teachers and administrators.

"Ecoday will be a chance for all of you to exercise the accepted environmental concept—'Think Globally, Act Locally,'" the Kat said. "Since the biggest issue to hit our area in some time revolves around the proposed reduction of the deer population in our beloved Wirth Reserve . . ."

All eyes turned on me, and I felt as if the Kat had just announced my parents were in the Ku Klux Klan.

Ryan leaned over and said, "It's not your fault your dad's an asshole." He winked and gave me the thumbs-up sign.

As usual, Ryan's support made me feel worse. I pretended to notice a hairline fracture in the linoleum. By the time I looked up, most of the other kids had lost interest in me.

"The specific theme will be Urban Ecology," Katami said. "Let's consider the question: Can we live with the animals? Let's think out of the box on this one, students.

If anyone can bring fresh insight to this problem, I believe the students at Lindbergh High can!"

He paused and took a sip from a Greenpeace mug. Once he had lectured us on the importance of hydration, though he's a living example of how hopeless it is. He swallowed his herbal tea and smiled.

"The excitement doesn't stop there," he said. "Our Earth Day Committee, now renamed the Ecoday Committee, of course," he laughed, "will be inviting dignitaries from both sides of this controversy to come here and debate. We hope the local news media will pick us up. Possibly even the national news."

Ryan kicked my chair for emphasis. Ryan claimed the most basic human instinct is a craving to be on TV. Then Katami disappeared into snow and static. Ms. S-T snapped off the set with her giant remote.

"Class, listen up," she said. "Your first assignment for Ecoday is to think about what you are going to do. I want everyone to commit to some project by next week. How about a little brainstorming to help you out? Let's generate options!"

"Yes, Mizesty," we answered in our mocking tone.

She ignored us, writing on the board. "You can either do a science project, a dramatic presentation, a theme paper, or an art piece." She wrote in first-grader handwriting. "Other ideas?" she asked, turning around.

I watched Holly write feverishly in her notebook. It was probably another poem about death. Suddenly she raised her hand. "Could I make a mix of my favorite ecological rock songs?"

"Hmm," Ms. S-T said with an insincere finger to her lips. "Class? Do you think that would constitute the same amount of work as, say, a real science project?"

"I think if she wrote a paper to go with it explaining the songs, it might be," Megan said with a smile at Holly.

"Good addition, Megan," Ms. S-T said. She wrote "Music Theme Paper" on the board.

Holly made a face at Megan, who looked hurt. Being raised by Unitarians, Megan thought very clearly, but she was constantly surprised that people didn't appreciate her efforts to help them.

Ryan raised his hand. "Ms. S-T, I would like to do, uh, a live performance? A street theater sort of thing?"

"That would be lovely, Ryan," she said. "Will you be needing volunteers?"

"People can talk to me after class," Ryan said with a smirk.

"That sounds very exciting, Ryan," Ms. S-T said.

Possibly because of his movie-star chin, female teachers always went easy on Ryan.

"Does anyone have any other questions?" Ms. S-T asked.

Megan glanced at me before she spoke. I recognized the dreaded Helper Gaze and held my breath. What followed was an example of why no friends are sometimes better than helpful friends.

"Do you have any suggestions," Megan began slowly, continuing to look right at me, "for any of us who . . ." she was chopping this up so much I hoped no one could follow, "might want to do something, say, against one of their parent's positions?"

All eyes turned to me. Again.

"Thank you for bringing this up, Megan," Ms. S-T said. "Is this a problem for anyone at home?" She drilled me with her eyes. "I realize that for some of you, this project might stimulate some lively dinner table discussions."

Ryan nudged me with his foot.

"We don't want to start World War III in anyone's home," Ms. S-T said with a forced laugh. "Have your parents call me if anything like that comes up. Okay? Did we process that?"

Cheese whip is processed. This was not.

After class, Ryan began signing up volunteers for his performance piece. It was the usual girls who thought he was cute.

"Sam? You in?" he yelled to me.

Before I could answer, Megan grabbed my arm and wheeled me down the hall. "I know what you have to do," she said.

"You do?" I said. Her hand felt good on my biceps.

"Hello?" She cocked her head to the side. "To convince your father—or Jeff, as you call him—that you have a mind of your own."

"Oh," I said. "And how am I going to do that?"

She slapped me playfully like Holly had slapped Ryan. Ecology was looking more interesting by the moment.

"You have to come up with something great. Scientific, but alternative-y. I had this image. A science project, you know the kind, an old-fashioned diorama?"

"The classic nerdy science project," I said.

"Right," she said, missing my irony. "I see little deer or something. Like maybe one side shows them getting killed and . . ."

". . . on the other side they're lining up to vote?"

She gave me a funny look. "I'm trying to help you here, Sam. Work with me."

"Sorry," I said. "I like it. I can picture it."

"I know where you can get the data. The university has a website where they post their research on deer contraception and stuff like that."

"Deer contraception?" I pictured a diorama of deer condoms.

She forced an exhale and placed her hands on her hips.

"Sorry," I said. "I'll come up with something. Something that'll blow Jeff away."

"Good," she said. "I can't tell you why just yet, but it's very important that you stand on your own two feet with your dad. The students need to know that you don't agree with him."

"What can't you tell me? And why would people care about that?"

"That's what I can't tell you. Yet." She smirked, cocked her head, and grinned.

I didn't like how that sounded, but I liked how she was playing with me.

"Great, then," she said like a politician, and then she ran down the hall as if she were afraid to be seen with me.

CHAPTER THREE

MEGAN HELPED ME SKETCH OUT MY DIORAMA, as she insisted on calling it. The baseboard would have two sides, one showing some intelligent and humane approaches to the so-called deer problem. On the other side, I would sacrifice some of my once-precious green army men by spray painting them Day-Glo orange and show them killing these tiny toy deer painted with red splotches. Behind all this, I would have a poster loaded with charts and graphs I got from the web.

Holly's sister worked for the deer research project at the university. She said they were cool people who cared about animals, despite their mysterious name: Experimental Deer Station #47. Their website pretty much gave me all the science I could handle.

Elissa suggested I should build this project at the Whole Child Daycare, where I used to go after school and Perry still did. "The Hole," as I called it, took up the bottom half of an old duplex. With its lights off, it could pass for the neighborhood psycho house. Elissa's friends Patti and Janine (who Jeff called the Marxist and the Witch) ran it and fussed over me like aunts. They were lesbians, so they were against all kinds of things. I was sure they'd be against the hunt.

Walking through the Hole was like walking through a compost pile of dreams. Patti and Janine named every nook and cranny after some way they had wanted to improve the world. Also, these weren't just rooms—these were Play Centers, and each had its own color scheme.

The Global Peace Play Center was purple and dark green. An inverted map of the earth was its main feature. An upside-down Africa and South America took up the space where America would normally be. Patti used to track liberation wars with little pushpins until the kids began sticking each other with them.

Our Animal Friends Play Center was part of that small room. It came equipped with an endangered species puppet set, circa 1980. I think Janine got too depressed adding species to the collection and abandoned it.

Next was the Diverse Universe room. Its walls were once painted in Dalmatian puppy spots, which Jeff cited it as an example of how you can't use soy-based, earth-friendly paint if you want color to last.

——— ▪ ——— ▪ ——— ▪ ——— ▪ ——— ▪ ——— ▪ ———

JEFF AND I WERE QUASI-COZY AT HOME WAITING for Elissa to return with Perry from the Hole when we got her distress call. Something was wrong with her van, and she needed us to meet her at the Hole to check it out.

"Christ," he said, slamming down the phone. "We gotta go pick them up." He looked out the window. "This weather will bring out the stupid drivers. You better come with."

Jeff was still dressed in his brown DNR slicker with the logo on the shoulder. The outfit included a matching hat, which I especially hated. He'd begun wearing this costume more regularly since the announcement of the deer kill. As he and I drove up to the Hole, we spotted Elissa's white minivan on the street, parked near the daycare, its rear-end stuck out so badly I was surprised it still had a left taillight. Jeff circled the block once and found a spot about six cars in front of it.

As I got out of the car, a BMW nearly hit me. Jeff stepped into the street and, shaking his fist, yelled, "Slow down, you steaming pile of shit!"

I walked up the slick sidewalk as Jeff went for Elissa's van. The Hole's door opened and closed as parents walked past me, herding small children toward the street.

The glass storm door had a big X-shaped crack bandaged with duct tape. A faded poster of a cartoon hound dog in a raincoat was taped onto the inside of the door, leftover from an ancient government program to save children from psychos. I couldn't help staring at it, remembering how the program was supposed to work. While a kid was running from a psycho killer, he was supposed to scan houses for a poster of Raincoat Dog. If he saw one, he could barge into that house for help. Without asking I assumed.

I shook myself out of my Raincoat Dog trance by remembering I had planned to get in, get Perry and leave quickly, before Jeff came in. Once Jeff was inside, he would find something to fix. The beat-up condition of the Hole was a constant inspiration to him. Whenever he came to the Hole he'd go straight for their pathetic tool set and end up fiddling with a mismatched storm window, a loose outlet cover, or a leaky faucet. He'd cut back on fixing things after Elissa had commented that he'd do that for Patti but not for her—but he still fixed things now and then.

I opened the door and took in a familiar smell of mildewed furniture and guinea pigs. Despite everything, I liked the place much better than I admitted. I brushed past a bulletin board cluttered with cards from Feng Shui consultants, masseuses, and people selling educational toys from their homes. Right in the center was a large poster of a black bird sitting in the middle of the universal 'No' symbol. Underneath it was the slogan: Support Prop19.

I knew that Prop19 was one of Patti's latest causes because she'd made a presentation at our school about it. I'd allocated minimal attention to it, but enough to know it was something about urban sprawl. The Prop19 people wanted our city to be more like Portland or Seattle, densely populated with the eco-minded, multiple coffeehouses and rock bands sprouting on every block. Megan supported it, and that was good enough for me.

I smelled patchouli, and there was Patti, her big eyes coming at me. Our noses nearly touched. "Sam-I-am!" she said.

She pulled me into a muscular hug. I could feel her breasts pressing through my jacket.

"Sam-I-am, you're getting so big."

"Hormones in the beef," I said.

"You da man," she said, pinching my cheek like a grandma would.

Patti's head had looked like a brown tennis ball before that look got too trendy. She'd started growing her hair back when bald girls with nose rings began selling cosmetics at Target. She retained huge earrings as part of her trademark look.

"I gotta keep Jeff away from my project," I whispered just as I felt a rush of cold air behind me.

"I was right," Jeff said as if we'd been waiting for him to come in and lecture us on his stalled car explanation. "She left the lights on."

"Jeff!" Patti said. They high-fived with a surprisingly good smack. "You da man!"

I said, "I thought *I* was," under my breath.

"Quick," Patti said. "Let me think. What's broken?"

Jeff said, "Men are still good for some things, Patti."

"At least until we finish the robot-technicians that'll replace them," she said.

"That the new Prop19 poster?" Jeff laughed.

"Careful," Patti said. "Janine designed it."

"Vote for Prop19, we're against birds?" Jeff said. "What have those nasty critters been up to now?"

"No, no, no," Patti said. "I thought you DNR guys would understand this. The poster is supposed to say voting for Prop19 is voting against developers who are the people reducing nesting space for birds."

"You got state funding to put a person next to each poster and explain it?" Jeff asked. "I'm impressed."

18

"You're just evil," Patti said.

It confused me that they could be so playful about this stuff. He and Elissa went tooth and claw over much less.

Patti lowered her voice. "Look, Janine's just getting into designing posters. Be nice."

"This *is* nice," Jeff said. "And don't start on me. I'm having a hard enough day as it is."

"You need a hug?" she said, wagging her head from side to side to jangle her trademark earrings.

"Your answer to everything," Jeff said.

But they did hug—and for a rather long time I thought. Despite my mission to get in and out quickly, I felt oddly rooted watching them hold each other.

A yuppie mom pulling her child by the arm bumped into us. "Coming through," she sang.

"Bye-bye, Jasper," Patti said to the scowling child.

"Where's Elissa and Perry?" Jeff asked.

"Lying down in the Think about It Loft," Patti said.

Shit, I thought. That's where my project was. I couldn't let Jeff go back there.

Patti spoke to me with wide eyes. "Sam, why don't you run back and get them?"

I nodded but couldn't stop watching Jeff and Patti tease each other. This was a "playful Jeff" I rarely saw.

"Isn't the loft some form of punishment?" he asked.

"Yeah," Patti said. "Perry called little Jasper a witch today."

"Perhaps he meant it as a compliment," Jeff said.

"I thought Elissa was better-equipped to tell the story of crones and witches and all that woo-woo stuff," Patti said. "Besides, I thought lying down would be good for her."

"What do you mean?" Jeff asked.

"She's exhausted, Jeff. Worrying too much. About, you know . . ." She hunched over and whispered something to him, then straightened back up. "Take her on a vacation. Someplace without animals—New York, maybe."

"They got cock-a-roaches," Jeff said in his cowboy dialect.

"Sam?" Patti said. "You might want to check around where you were working on my computer. I think you left it . . . a little messy." Her eyes glared wider this time. She was trying to remind me that I had left my project out for all to see. "I'll give this guy something to fix in the meantime."

"Right, lady," Jeff said, touching the brim of his ugly hat. "I've taken an oath to keep chaos from engulfing you ladies."

"Then take a look at the kitchen faucet," she said.

I plunged into the narrow hallway. There was hardly any room to move through the struggling children and their impatient parents. Mothers were forcing kids into expensive rain slickers in Crayola colors. Everything screamed Disney or the latest creature from a PBS "learning show."

One mother said through gritted teeth, "Well, Julia, if you're going to make that choice, you're going to cut into your transition time before dinner."

Another snapped, "Shosona, I'm counting to three. One, two . . ." Shosona glared at her mother with crossed arms, unafraid.

Someone was standing at the end of the dark corridor that connected Diverse Universe to the Think about It Loft. I could tell from the science fictional head shape that this was Janine. She had E.I.—environmental illness—which meant she was allergic to everything made in the twentieth century.

"Die, Dam," she said through her industrial strength Honeywell gas mask. "*Die, Dam*" translated as "*Hi, Sam.*"

"Hi, Janine," I said loudly.

She whipped out her little dry erase board from her Afghani purse. She printed out the strange word, "Formaldehyde?"

I nodded compassionately.

"Rug Center," she wrote.

This meant clueless suburbanites had once again donated a toxin-soaked rug to The Peoples Center where she worked. It happened all the time.

"Sorry," I said. "Hey, nice poster."

She raised her eyebrows, and I sensed enthusiasm.

"Elissa and Perry?" I enunciated.

She pointed, then touched my shoulder as I walked by. "*Dam-I-am,*" she said.

I called out, "I do not like green eggs and ham."

Everyone did the Dr. Seuss thing with me.

The Think about It Loft shared the room with a beat-up washer and dryer and a pile of clothes. The Loft was a bunk bed platform reached with a ladder. I'd spent many hours up there, thinking about sex and outer space mostly.

Beneath the platform was the Hole's ancient computer I had taken over for my project. Neither Patti nor Janine cared much for computers anyway, agreeing they were a patriarchal trap.

I glanced at my project with satisfaction. It was coming along nicely. I had glue-gunned little cardboard deer to a discarded board I'd found in their basement. I was in the process of pasting downloaded diagrams and smart-looking charts onto another board.

This will blow people away, I thought.

I ran to the back room and rummaged through a bin of laundry, found a sheet, and tossed it over the table. I felt myself relax.

"Who's that?" Elissa called from the Loft.

I growled, and they giggled.

Rising on my toes at the end of the bed, I saw two lumps, one large and one small, covered in a Hmong quilt showing rice paddies and oxen with curved horns. I remembered the Loft's peculiar smell—organic soap seasoned with a touch of petrified bagel crust. Or was it string cheese marbleized with green mold?

I growled again and clawed the smaller lump.

Perry's head popped up like a gopher. "Sam," he said with a squeal, and he disappeared back under the covers. Elissa's arm curled upward like a curious cobra. It waved once at me, then dropped down. I moved up the ladder and pulled the quilt off of them. They were curled together like fox pups. Perry had a blissful smile on his face that said "happy" though I don't really like that word. I felt compelled to climb up. Elissa looked unusually relaxed.

"Can this thing support all of us?" she asked.

Elissa thinks she weighs more than she does, and Jeff says all women think like this.

"Live dangerously," I said as the platform creaked.

I lay down, spoon-style, in front of Perry. He started singing one of his made-up idiot tunes, and I didn't stop him when he tried to hug me. Elissa reached over both of us, trying to stroke both our heads simultaneously. I closed my eyes for a moment and imagined how aliens on Arkkorn had sex.

"Where would you go if you could go anywhere?" Elissa asked. She was always coming up with questions like this.

"I'd live in a little village," I said. "Like the Amish. A farm village without cars, without pollution, without capitalism. Before we destroyed nature and tried to wipe out all the animals."

"Ah," Elissa said, "before the modern world."

"I would get a goat," Perry said. "I'd name him Binky."

I elbowed the little idiot. "*Binky?*"

"Ow," he sang. "Mo-om, Sam hit me."

Elissa's hand came back, patting the top of my head.

"Why couldn't I have been born Amish?" I asked.

Then I remembered an Amish carriage I saw on a road in Iowa two summers earlier. The strangely dressed couple turned their eyes away as if we represented something awful. I wanted them to know that I was good and on their side, that I wasn't like normal people. But there was no way to signal them as we whizzed by. In seconds we were a mile away, their carriage a tiny Hollywood prop.

"Boys," Elissa said. "I know Jeff's and my fighting has been hard on you. And lately, it's been a little worse than usual. Am I right?"

"Duh," I said.

She slapped my head gently. "Let's play good news, bad news, okay?" she said. This was another of her "let's communicate" games I hated.

"Don't you mean bad news, bad news?" I said.

"Maybe," she said. "I do have a little announcement to make. A surprise."

"Why do I think this doesn't sound like a good surprise?" I asked.

"I love surprises!" Jeff's upbeat voice boomed.

I stiffened with panic, thinking it had something to do with me and my project. Like in a thriller movie, the evidence was sitting right beneath us. I forced myself to remember how deliberately I had covered it up with a sheet just moments before.

"Let's go out to dinner since it's so late," Elissa said. "I'll tell you there."

"Already planned on it," Jeff said jauntily from below us.

"*Burger King, Burger King; I want to go to Burger King,*" Perry sang.

"I have an announcement too," Jeff said as his bearded face rose over the edge of the Loft. Elissa and I exchanged glances.

"Don't come up or we'll crash land," I said.

"I distinctly remember it was my turn to choose the restaurant," Elissa said.

"Let me guess," Jeff said. "Green Valley?"

Elissa always suggested vegetarian places, which Jeff usually vetoed since he was on the Back Country Diet. I don't know why, surely not to lose weight. Elissa called it the "DNR Diet" or "Lenny's Diet," which seemed to get to Jeff. Lenny, Jeff's boss, needed to lose fifty pounds.

Sometimes she called it his "Roadkill Diet" because there was a chapter in his book on how to determine the freshness of squashed animals. Jeff said he ate what Neanderthals ate, that our bodies weren't that different from monkeys really. Clearly his wasn't.

"Why not the Valley?" Elissa said. She turned to me. "You'd like it, wouldn't you, Sam? Isn't Megan a vegan?"

"*Megan a vegan, Megan a vegan,*" Perry sang until I elbowed him.

"Everyone's going vegan," I shrugged. "Except jocks and cretins."

"Okay," said Jeff. "Whatever."

This was not like him. I thought of Patti suspiciously. What had Jeff repaired that had made him so jaunty and agreeable?

CHAPTER FOUR

BEFORE DRIVING TO THE GREEN VALLEY, we had to go home and drop off Elissa's car. It was out of our way, but she insisted.

"Otherwise, it's not exactly a family outing, is it?" she said.

To drop off her car, Jeff and I rode home in his Ford pickup together. He insisted on listening to classical music. At least I thought that's what it was until I recognized it as German attack-opera made famous in a Vietnam War movie. The American helicopters used it to scare villagers they were about to shoot. But this was not classical radio. This was theme music for an AM talk radio show—*The Michael Blaine Show*.

Blaine's voice came on. It was deep and nasal. I'd heard it before, and it always sounded as if he were getting over a cold. His laugh rumbled with phlegm, probably from smoking.

"Oh, here's a good one," he said. "This one's from a Mildred Knutson of—where is it? Oh, International Falls, Minnesota. Mildred writes, 'Dear Mr. Blaine. How did you ever get on the radio? You are obviously in need of mental treatment.' She spells treatment as two words—treat and meant.

"She goes on. 'Are you supposed to be a comedian? I heard your show on re-enacting The Battle of Little Bighorn using live ammunition. It went way beyond the boundaries of bad taste. Surely you weren't serious. They should cancel your show and send you back to the loony bin or New York.'

"Well, thank you, Mildred. I take the New York thing as a compliment. But I'm also curious about those boundaries of bad taste you mentioned."

"Isn't this guy wild?" Jeff said, cheering up slightly.

I looked out the window, torn between dismay and playing up to Jeff. The city streets were narrow, dark, and busy. We drove in a surging stream of overpowered vehicles. They swerved, passed on the right, and generally took every chance to cut one tenth of a second off their scurry home. A Mercedes station wagon hopped a curb maneuvering desperately around a left turner.

"Yuppie trash," Jeff said.

"I'd like to see those boundaries of bad taste," Blaine said. "I'm picturing a faux rustic Scandinavian fence, you standing there, your troll dolls grazing like a herd of cattle. May I call you Milly? Kafka, would you send her one of our Chaos Forever T-shirts and an autographed mug shot of yours truly? Hey, Milly, use it for a dartboard. Live a little."

A second radio voice, a man speaking in a depressed German accent said, "Very vell."

"Kafka as a sidekick?" Jeff said, laughing. "I love that."

"We got another letter here I want to read," Blaine said, and he switched into a high-pitched, whiny voice. "'Why don't you speak out against the horror about to be perpetrated against the deer herd in Wirth Park? You claim to be an environmentalist, yet you have done nothing to save these sublime and inspiring creatures.' Whoa, deer— sublime and inspiring? Now cockroaches, there's an inspiration. Been around millennia before the dinosaurs and, believe me, they'll be crawling over our graves when our dear old sun goes supernova. But deer?" He made a sound like spitting.

"Shit," Jeff said. "He's talking about us."

"*Us?*" I said with as much breath and attitude as I dared.

"You know what I think they should do with that Wirth Park problem?" Blaine continued. "I had a dream about this. I saw the deer herd marching downtown, a whole mass of fat, poor excuses for wild animals. They were wearing these little signs of em-broidered yarn that said, 'We have rights. We live here too.' Human supporters marched along with them—PETA, Animal Liberation Front, various vegan societies, and do-gooders of all colors and creeds. Up ahead the NRA and your hunter types yelled at them from behind police barricades."

"I prefer ze kaka-roach," Kafka broke in. "Ze kaka-roach ees my powa onimal. But zees deer?" He made a spitting noise. "I care notting about zees deer." They cut to a commercial for a water filtration system called Pure Now.

"This show is completely nuts," Jeff said.

I knew he meant nuts in a good way, and I wasn't going to follow him there. "Then why do you listen to it?" I asked.

"What's happening to you kids?" Jeff said. "Don't you get it?"

"What's to get?" I said. "You said yourself he's just trying to make everyone mad."

Jeff clucked his tongue at me and swore at another driver.

"You want to know what I think they should do?" Blaine asked. "First of all, they should stop messing around with these fakey staged hunts. Can you imagine? Hunters won't solve the problem. We need cougars! Mountain lions! Forget your timber wolves;

they don't appreciate the taste of human flesh. We need to be reminded of our true place in nature."

"Fakey staged hunts?" Jeff shouted at the radio. "What the hell is he talking about?"

"Yes, cougars," Blaine said. "You heard me right. Let's work on this predator-prey thing. Tax the cappuccino shops for a species re-introduction. Cordon the place off for a season, let a couple of hungry cats loose in there, then send in some bird watchers to see who's king of the hill. Better yet, send in some of our homegrown eco-anarchists. Hell, send in supermodels armed with tennis rackets, I don't care. Reality TV, the local franchise. Maybe the DNR can even make some money on it. Let's get creative with this thing, people. *Let's take a call.*"

I had no idea who the real Michael Blaine was. As the corporate-promoted urban myth went, nobody did. The man kept his real identity secret, for obvious reasons, if you ask me.

"Yeah, this is Neil? From Maple Grove?" the call-in voice said.

"Hey, buddy, if you don't know who you are or where you are, why ask me?" Blaine said.

"Yeah, okay," the guy from Maple Grove said. "You know these deer? It's not their fault they're tame animals. We made them that way. We can't just let them get eaten by mountain lions. That's not fair."

"You, sir, are an idiot," Blaine said. "Animals eat each other. We eat them. Cute eats cute, the law of the jungle. Of course, cute eats ugly and vice versa, but the point is life isn't fair. Didn't you learn that in kindergarten? Hell, we even eat each other. What are you people thinking?"

A lion's growl came from the radio. In the background, Kafka started screaming, "Wait! Nice kitty! Help!"

"Whoops, we just lost Kafka," Blaine said.

"Cougars," Jeff laughed. "That's good."

"He's a chicken," I said.

"Excuse me?"

"Why is he afraid to let us know who he really is?"

I already knew the answer to this, but I felt like picking a fight. The more I listened to Blaine, the more I understood that people might want to scratch his beemer with a key. For starters.

"I suspect that he likes it that every side has a grudge against him by now," Jeff said. "Maybe that turns him on. Who knows?"

"How could anyone live such a lie?" I asked.

Jeff listened to Blaine for the rest of the ride while I tuned into my favorite fantasy: I was leading a secret GreenSWAT team that scuttles whaling ships, forcing their greedy and immoral crewmembers at gunpoint to jump into icy waters where they either drown or get diced into sushi by our specially trained orcas with GreenSWAT logos tattooed on their dorsal fins.

Jeff laughed at something, disturbing me.

I snorted with disgust and went back to my fantasy, where the Megan-like commando was giving me a tough assignment. I had to swim on a trained orca underneath a fish factory submarine which was harvesting the last known pod of humpback whales. "You're the only one I can trust with this," she said, touching my sleeve. "Promise me you'll come back alive." Her face was shining with admiration.

"Listen, Sam," Jeff said, startling me. "I know things have been a little tough lately between Elissa and me."

"Duh," I said.

"Don't *duh* me, pal!" he said quickly. Then he did one of his anger-control tricks, inhaling then exhaling quickly.

"El and I . . ." He sighed, then started again. "We're just in a bad phase now. Because of my job."

"You mean killing the deer?" I asked.

He pounded the steering wheel. "Don't start with that deer kill business. It's wildlife management! Gimme a break here. I'm trying to talk."

I watched the valiant raindrops falling on the windshield. They were immediately destroyed by the mechanical wipers. How pathetic and pointless their short lives were.

After a while, I said, "I guess things won't settle down until it's over."

"Over?" Jeff said. "History is all about nothing ever being over."

I glanced at his face. His eyes might have been filling with tears, though I hoped they were just reflecting light from the windshield. He was capable of tears, but most people would never know it, and that was the way he liked it. If he watched any movie that had a heroic pet dying (like *Old Yeller* or *The Yearling*), you could see tears trickling down his face.

I searched for something positive to say, something Elissa might come up with. "People get through things," I said.

"You're absolutely right," he said.

"I am?"

"People do get through things. So will we. But it'll take time to pull us back together, but eventually things will get back to normal."

I was supposed to say something, but the best I could do was nod.

W E DROVE BACK TO THE HOUSE. Elissa and Perry climbed into the truck. They were giggling about something, then shut up abruptly. It was obvious they had been talking about Jeff. I noticed he switched the radio from Michael Blaine to a real classical music channel.

At Green Valley, we got a fox of a waitperson with her face full of metal studs and hoops. Her arms were blue from tattoos. I avoided looking at her. She directed her scorn at Jeff, who deserved it for running his mouth off about how the font they used on the menu was difficult to read.

"What's a soyburger?" Perry asked. "Is that like a hamburger?"

"Yes," Elissa snapped. When she turned her attention back to the menu, I grabbed my throat as if I'd been poisoned. Perry and Jeff laughed while Elissa glared at me.

"You should know this, Sam," she said. "If everyone in the world ate soybeans, we could stop destroying the rainforest."

I watched Jeff's face for a color shift.

"To be fair," he said calmly, "a soybean does not have a complete set of amino acids."

"It has enough," Elissa said.

"I don't want to eat minnow acids," Perry said, grabbing his throat to copy me. He added a gagging sound.

"Stop that," Elissa said.

The jangling waitress eventually brought our food, and we began to eat in silence.

Elissa rubbed her forehead. "I'm sorry. I didn't want it to go this way. I have something to bring up. But I won't do it if everyone's going to be so crabby and sensitive."

"And babyish," I said, kicking Perry underneath the table.

"I'm not sensitive," Jeff said. "I'm just overworked. I mean with your car dying, then Patti having all this stuff for me to do. I could have worked on that place all night."

"I'm sorry we pulled you away," Elissa said. Her tone triggered my radar.

"What's that supposed to mean?" Jeff said.

"Oh, you love it," Elissa said. "Mr. He-man, Mr. Fix-it. Helping the *girls* struggle in their world without men."

"I don't even want to know where you're headed with that," Jeff said. He forked a square of soy sausage and chewed it as if he were eating dog poop. "What was it you want to bring up?" he asked.

Elissa put her hand on her heart and shut her eyes. "Okay. I'm changing my energy. Could we all just clear out the negative vibes?" She took in a deep breath and exhaled slowly.

I watched our waitress chuckle at us with another server, a thin male even more pierced and blue.

"Okay?" Elissa said. "Okay. Dive in, Elissa." She took a slow breath. "I'm going to be changing my religion."

Jeff nearly choked and reached for his water.

"What religion are we?" Perry said.

"Christian," Jeff said. "We're Christian."

"We *were* Christian," Elissa said, staring at Jeff. "Now I'm into Women's Spirituality. We do rituals in the woods. Not in manmade churches."

"That's not a religion," Jeff said.

"It is too," she said. "It's Wicca."

"Witcha!" Perry said.

"Not witcha," she said. "Wicca."

Jeff put his hand to his forehead. "Is this because we're fighting?" he said. He looked up and added, "Is this about the deer?"

"No, not just that," Elissa said. "But yes, some of that. That and other things. But it's not a reaction. I mean, it's not a *reactive* thing. It's part of me finding myself, knowing who I am. It's a good thing."

"How can you find yourself if you're not lost, Mom?" Perry asked.

"No, honey," she said. "I'm not lost. I'm . . ."

A stainless steel pitcher followed by a tattooed arm snaked in front of Elissa's face as she talked.

"Water?" the waitress said. I was sure she looked at me with understanding irony. *You poor thing*, she probably thought.

Elissa stared straight ahead for a few minutes as the waitress poured water very slowly into every glass, all of them untouched except Perry's. He stared at the tattoos as if one of them would lunge at him if he breathed.

"I want you all to know I see this as a positive thing," Elissa finally said. "Like financial planning. I thought you'd all be excited for me. It's like diversity. It's okay for us to differentiate from one another. It's a way of deepening our relationship with the world."

"But ruining your family in the process," Jeff said.

"That was the second thing I wanted to bring up," she said.

"Ruining the family?" Jeff said. "You got a positive spin on that too?"

"I want us to go see Dr. Rosen. Together. As a family."

"A shrink?" Jeff said. "Is he a Wiccan too?"

"Not at all. He's highly respected. He's written books. On lots of things, not just family therapy."

"Let me guess," Jeff said. "On the environment?"

"Yes," Elissa said, raising up her chin. "Bingo. I'll give you that one, mister."

Jeff released a huge sigh.

"He's not just your everyday therapist. He's a new kind of therapist."

"And what kind might that be?" Jeff said, staring at the ceiling.

"He's an eco-therapist," Elissa said with what one might call forced enthusiasm.

"An eco-therapist?" Jeff asked.

"I've heard of those," I said. Ms. S-T had told us about these along with eco-historians, eco-philosophers, and eco-economists, though that last one sounded weird now.

"And what does an eco-therapist do?" Jeff asked. "Psychoanalyze trees?"

"Most therapists, you see, look at the family as, well, just a family." She kicked in with a more genuine enthusiasm. "An eco-therapist uses the base assumption that the world, all worlds really, are full of stresses and imbalances. What we call problems. And what we call problems are often just coping mechanisms we've developed for living in an imperfect world."

"Like that guy we read when we were in college? The one who said schizophrenics are normal and the rest of us are nuts?" Jeff said.

Elissa frowned at him.

"What's a skitzo?" Perry asked.

"You," I said, glaring my eyes at him. "Be quiet." I was using a trick I heard you can use on dogs.

"How about a translation for the unenlightened," Jeff said.

"But you're an ecologist, Jeff, aren't you? I mean that's what your department is about, isn't it? Why would you be against—"

Jeff stopped her with a raised hand. "First of all, you're assuming I'm against this. I'm listening, that's all. I haven't said anything negative. Well, hardly anything. Secondly, ecology has a lot of meanings today. Ecologists, environmentalists, conservationists, everyone's using the word with a slightly different connotation. What kind of things does your shaman shake his stick at?"

"What's a shaman?" Perry said.

"A male witch," I said.

Elissa squeezed my arm to tell me that, though she appreciated my general support, I should shut up.

"Many of the women in my spirituality group go to Dr. Rosen," Elissa said. "For all kinds of reasons. Seasonal affective disorder. Depression. Bulimia. Menopause. They all say good things about him. Dr. Rosen shows them how they're reacting essentially to the crisis in the natural world, how pollution is affecting them, how their grief is a real reaction to the tragedy—"

"Elissa, Elissa," Jeff said, shaking his head slowly. Then he made the time-out sign. "Assuming the guy's legit, why would our family need to go see . . . this person?"

"The deer kill," Elissa said so loudly I looked around. The servers had heard—and I wanted to die. "We're all involved in the deer kill, like it or not. Not just because of your job, Jeff. The whole community's involved."

"It's not a deer kill," Jeff said quietly. "It's wildlife management."

"And we're killing each other." I said.

Nobody said anything for a few minutes.

That's when it came to me. I had to do more than a science project. And whatever it was, it would be big. It would probably be something neither of my parents would approve of.

"See?" Elissa said with an outstretched palm towards me. "We're falling apart. We need help." She picked up an orange pepper from my plate and began nibbling it. "What was your announcement?" she asked Jeff.

Jeff looked ill, a vampire near dawn. "Oh, nothing. It was nothing. Something about Ecoday."

"Ecoday?" Elissa said staring straight ahead. "What's . . ."

"They—I mean we—renamed Earth Day," I said, almost breathless.

"What's wrong with the old name?" Elissa asked.

"We're expanding it," I said, "into controversial territory." I managed to say this while looking straight at Jeff.

"I give up," Jeff said. "Doc Rosen, heal our family!" He said this like a Baptist preacher with his hands raised and his head bowed. When he looked up, we were all staring at him. "What?" he said.

"Is that the best you can do?" Elissa said.

"The very best," he said.

"Shit," she said quietly as she grabbed the bill. "What's the damage? Let's get the hell out of this place."

She paid the bill with a wad of bills she seemed to pull randomly out of her purse. We walked her out of Green Valley single file, like prisoners. In the car, Jeff turned on his talk radio station and, strangely, Elissa didn't challenge him. Normally such a move would ignite a dreaded family discussion, and we'd end up on the oldies station. Like Jeff's trained monkeys, we listened to more of Michael Blaine's ranting. I wondered how long his show was. Maybe he lived at the studio. We could find him that way.

Blaine said, "You know, people say I shouldn't hide behind anonymity, that it's a type of lie. Can you see them saying this to Bruce Wayne or Clark Kent?"

"So he's Superman now?" Elissa said. "That's a laugh."

"That doesn't make sense," I said. "Nobody would say that to Bruce Wayne or Clark Kent because they wouldn't know they were superheroes."

"Bingo," Elissa laughed. "Even my children see through Blaine's genius."

"Shh," Jeff said. "This is supposed to be funny."

"Oh, thanks for telling me," Elissa said as she turned and winked at me.

"People are mad about what I said yesterday," Blaine said. "Were you listening? I was brilliant. I said we need two sets of history books. One would assume all clever creative people were gay and or women, preferably 'of color,' as they say. The villains in this book would be the mean and nasty white Euro-Christian males. With an occasional Margaret Thatcher thrown in for diversity."

"That's so funny," Elissa said flatly.

"The other history book would be pretty much what we had when I was growing up. You know—Columbus discovers America, Christianity was a flowering of civilization, the colonists were simple farmers who found some more or less underutilized lands. That sort of thing. We could divide America up into two countries. You could move to whichever half told your story."

Kafka interrupted him with the weather and traffic. I pictured Dracula frowning at a satellite photo. Jeff turned down the radio. "So what's your eco-therapist like?" he asked. "Rosen, is it? Is he Jewish?"

Elissa laughed scornfully. "Ha! I knew you were hanging around Lenny too much. Jewish? What kind of—"

"Shoot me," Jeff said. "It's just the name. I wondered—"

"You won't like him, Jewish or whatever," Elissa said with aggressive cheerfulness. "Picture Jerry Garcia plus Carl Jung with an office in Marin County. Esalen meets Greenpeace, with a touch of Robert Frost. I think he fell out of an Outward Bound canoe trip some years ago and just stayed here."

"Why doesn't he just move back?" Jeff asked.

"Because we need him here. He's special here. In California, everyone's a therapist. They have drive-through therapy by now."

"Drive-through, huh?" I said. "Gimme a shake and two Prozac." Elissa glared at me. "Lots of kids are on that now," I said.

"Robert Frost, huh?" Jeff said. "I used to like some of his stuff. But I think they've outlawed rhyming poets by now."

"It was just an example to illustrate his folksy side," Elissa said.

"Jung's okay, except for his goofy ideas about UFOs," Jeff said.

"UFOs?" Perry said as if someone had put a quarter in him.

"He says we make them up. In our minds. As if!" I said scornfully. Suddenly I was on Jeff's side.

"Have you met him?" Jeff asked Elissa. "I mean, how do you know all this? Oh, wait—shh."

Blaine was back on, and Jeff turned it up.

"Show me a man or woman who does not have at least one active fantasy alter ego, and I'll show you someone who is dead to the world," Blaine said.

It was the first time Blaine had ever made any sense to me at all. I was thinking of GreenSWAT.

"What kind of degree does this Rosen have?" Jeff asked Elissa. "Don't tell me. A BA in socialist-ology or—no, no—American studies." Jeff laughed, but it didn't sound genuine.

"You're sounding more like Lenny every day, Jeff. But you're wrong again. He has a Ph.D. A couple, I think. In ecology, psychology . . ." She put a finger to her lip. "And I think comparative literature? He's a doctor several times over."

"I'll have to tell him I read *Ulysses* in college," Jeff said.

"The CliffsNotes, don't you mean?" Elissa said, looking out the window.

"I got the essence of it," Jeff said and he grew quiet.

Blaine said, "I'll tell you why I keep my identity secret. Because there are people who want to kill me. Yes, good 'ol Lutherans or whatever you people are here. Why? Because I joke about your sacred beliefs and because you can't figure me out. So some people figure I'm against them. Can't do that today. Gotta be clear. Gotta be on one side or the other. You see? Separate countries is quite an elegant solution.

"Here's a twist. Right in the center, we make the nation of I Don't Care. Right there in the plains states they want to rename Buffalo Commons, where nobody wants to live anymore. We'll live in teepees and laugh at our neighbors. Throw buffalo chips at them."

He kicked in a sound of canned laughter; the kind they use in sitcoms to make you feel guilty for not thinking the show's funny. Jeff turned it down.

"What are buffalo chips?" Perry asked. "Are they good?"

"Yummy," I said. "Salted buffalo poop."

Perry screamed in fake distress.

"Sam!" Elissa said. "Knock that off!"

"'Doctor' doesn't mean what it used to," Jeff said in an angrier tone. "Everyone's going around calling themselves 'Doctor' nowadays because they wrote a paper claiming Abraham Lincoln was gay."

"Patti's gay," Perry said. Then he started rhyming, exhibiting some of the behavior our parents worry about. "Gay way may say tay . . ."

"Where does he get that?" Jeff said. "Anyway, Patti's bisexual, if you must know."

"And you're the expert?" Elissa said.

"They might as well get it right. Hell, they practice putting condoms on bananas in third grade," Jeff said.

"And they test us on it," I said.

Elissa turned around and did her glare thing on me.

"Since when did Patti start calling herself a bisexual?" Elissa asked.

"I don't know," Jeff said. "She just is, that's all."

Elissa made an unhappy noise deep down in her throat, possibly unclogging a chakra.

CHAPTER FIVE

AS ECODAY APPROACHED, THE ECO-BUZZ at school grew louder. Mr. Katami and Ms. S-T flapped their jaws incessantly about how changing the name of the day could go national, how that would make us trendsetters, and nobody said the word but we all were thinking the same thing: how it would make us famous. They scheduled an Ecoday pep rally. Oddly, I looked forward to it.

Megan told us that public relations was a revolutionary tool, which was why she remained on the official Ecoday committee with Ms. S-T and the Kat. But she was upset that "Admin," as she called them, were focusing on trivia. It would be up to the Council of Nations, she said, to use the Ecoday to publicize the deer slaughter scheduled for Halloween. For all her complaining, she did get to make this statement on our closed-circuit TV: "The committee is a place where leading student activists work closely with the most progressive teachers."

The Ecoday pep rally was an assembly in a hot gym on an unusually hot March day unofficially sponsored by global warming. Metal army surplus fans rotated symbolically, not strong enough to nudge the heavy air. A V-tech fiddled with the ancient sound system until it screeched and whistled, making our ears hurt. Our ragtag radical cell—the infamous Council of Nations—sat close enough together to exchange private messages and insider jokes. We were giddy sitting on what we considered an edge. Ecoday would be our day.

Katami walked up the stairs to the stage, waving halfheartedly like he was a busy celebrity. Ms. S-T and the other teachers were already onstage, sitting in folding chairs and chatting with each other. Ms. S-T kept her legs crossed like a model. She did have unusually good legs for someone of Joni Mitchell's generation. The Kat began by saying something about making Ecoday a "celebratory carnival with a serious commitment to learning." He said the day would revolve around ecologically themed noncompetitive games and student theater presentations outside, weather permitting.

"Of course," he added, "what would an Ecoday be without a science fair? We're hoping we have a lot of really exciting entries. Science can work for a better world, despite what you may believe."

Megan sat upright on the end of her chair. Call me psychic, but I knew he was going to mention her by name. Her face gleamed with an inner light while pretending it was no big deal. *She has a future in politics*, I thought sadly. I was mainly sad because I assumed she'd be going there without me. I'd be in GreenSWAT, on the high seas.

"And we can thank Megan Lindstrom for the idea of bringing in local speakers to address us about important environmental issues," the Kat said. "Furthermore, we have located some participants among the parents of young people attending this school. Using the experts in our own backyard—that's what I call thinking globally and acting locally."

"That's the part that was my idea," Megan said quietly.

"I'd like to see your dad up there," Ryan said to me. "That would be a hoot."

From the look on Megan's face, I felt like I'd just eaten a rancid corndog at the State Fair. "Jeff's not speaking, is he?" I asked Megan, hoping there was no quaver in my voice.

"He's on the list of possibilities," Megan said. "But lots of people are on the list, even my parents. They have a great slideshow on the destruction of the Guatemalan rainforest."

"But this is supposed to be about local issues," Holly said. "Hello? The deer?" She made antlers with her hands on her head.

"I'm just saying they're on the list," Megan said. But I was certain she knew Jeff would be speaking.

"You're screwed, man," Ryan laughed. "Royally screwed."

I went into shock. Every word the Kat said seemed to confirm my suspicions that Jeff was on the agenda. Katami warned us that we wouldn't agree with everything we heard, but he expected us to be respectful listeners. He talked about other Ecoday events that would be going on around the city. The Unitarian Church was hosting an event called Peace between the Species. I'd been to that place before; it was completely white bread, without anything Jesusy around, no bloody crucifixes, no saints crushing snakes with their feet. They just had a bulletin board where members wrote their goals for improving the planet beside their photos, a sort of personals board for do-gooders. The goals were white bread too. Better recycling programs, working with the homeless, praying for whirled peas. Katami said we could get extra credit if we attended these events.

"Credit?" Holly said. "What is he talking about, credit?" She was right; there was no such thing as "credit" at our school.

Katami went on explaining the same things in different ways while I saw a grim vision of my future. I would live in total humiliation due to the simple fact that my dad, who I saw at that moment as a sort of killer clown, went before the school and ruined my life. Desperate, I conjured my best GreenSWAT fantasy, the one of the secret mission to scuttle whaling ships. In this version, I force the evil crew members to jump into icy waters. Too bad for them that the great white sharks they trained to kill eco-activists aren't that choosey.

After assembly we filed into the cafeteria for lunch. Megan told us to eat quickly so the Council would have time to meet. This was easy for me, as I had lost my appetite in the assembly. I could have eaten something like Gummi Bears, but of course they don't serve anything that tasty.

The Council convened on a set of beat-up benches left over from an ancient playground the school didn't have money to remove. They just told us to avoid that area. Regular kids never sit here because you can get splinters in your butt. Or worse. But we didn't mind, being tough commandos.

Despite my mood, the day was warm and sunny, the kind of day when kids are supposed to play radios outside and throw Frisbees. I hate Frisbees. Minnesotans generally take advantage of days like this as the weather here usually jumps from slush to suffocating heat. Urban myth has it that our state is in a unique position to benefit from global warming, but the Council doesn't go along with this. The Council resisted the cheerful weather, especially when we had work to do.

"I can't believe Katami," Megan said while pacing in front of us. "He's putting all this emphasis on changing the name of the day." Pacing was habitual with her when in "commander" mode. "Big deal," she said. "As if saying the magic word ecology makes everything better."

She was wearing overalls and a varsity jacket from a non-existent sports team. I wondered how safe the earth needed to be before she and I could relax enough to mess around.

"I said to him, 'Excuse me? Aren't we humans the problem?' Can you believe that? Making the animals take all the blame?" She rolled her eyes. "Katami wanted to make the theme 'the deer problem.'"

"Right on!" Holly said. "What did they say?"

"They said we mustn't get too radical because this was a public school. And worse . . ." She grimaced dramatically. "They put Mary Langsford on the committee."

Megan hated Mary Langsford, who was the student rep for the Animal Friends League. Megan said the AFL were mostly people upset about kittens being put to sleep at the Humane Society. In other words, they were interested in fluff.

"Cut to the chase, honey," Ryan said.

"Don't call me 'honey,' asshole," Megan shot back.

"Don't call me 'asshole,' bitch," Ryan said. He leaned toward her and wiggled his hands. "Woo, me big scared. Megan mad."

"How would you like it if I called you a dick, dick?"

"Go on, Megan, call him what he is—a big, fat penis," Holly said, and she broke into solo laughter. That's when I first suspected she and Ryan were doing more than flirting in class. I felt instantly jealous—another surprise.

Holly adjusted the black hat that protected her from the sun's UV poisons. She was in what she called her "late-post-Goth phase," admitting most kids had moved on to hip-hop and other rapidly morphing mini-trends. She wore a heavy brown cape clasped with a grinning demon pin, the brim of her witchy black hat shielding her pale face. From a distance, she could have passed for a Ukrainian grandmother.

"Get to the point, Meg," Holly said.

"Everything's so tame," Megan said. "We should be protesting. We should be blocking roads, climbing buildings . . ." She cleared her throat. "On the Web," she said, "kids all over America—hell, all over the world—are standing up and shouting and saying they're not going to take it anymore. People are doing things. Like spiking redwoods and putting sand in bulldozers' gas tanks. We're moving towards war. We're going after the bad guys—the evil scientists, the animal torturers, the land developers, the lumberjacks—"

"And the hunters?" Holly said.

"Yeah," she said, looking at me. "We gotta do something about them," she said. "Something big. Something dangerous. Illegal. Something that will get into the news."

"Right on, sister!" Ryan said. You could never tell his sarcasm from his enthusiasm. "Let's firebomb, burn suburban houses, free animals!" He raised his arms and pushed his chest muscles way out, looking at Holly while he did it. "The Council of Nations rules!"

I shifted uncomfortably. My cardboard deer project no longer seemed all that exciting.

"Tell her about your performance thing," Holly prompted like a wife. "Your deer die-in thing."

"That's no big deal," Ryan said with false humility. "Your basic street theater anarchist performance thing."

"But it'll be radical," Holly said.

Ryan warmed. "Yeah, I've got people willing to put their bodies on the line. It'll be a major deer die-in. We got costumes, antlers, the whole bit."

"Bodies on the line," Holly mouthed slowly, looking at Ryan. "When we found the costumes, I almost lost it. They were so geeky. I couldn't believe kids our age would ever wear something like this."

"Maybe it was a Christmas parody," I suggested.

"You're too nice," Ryan said to me. "You don't know about political action."

"Like that guy who dressed up like a squirrel and ran through Home Depot squirting people with cow urine?" I said. "Now that was a body on the line."

"I hope these costumes are better than your last action," Megan said. "Your fish costumes looked like earthworms. Nobody got it."

"They're better," Ryan said. "Way better. We're only using parts we found. We're customizing them at the Little Creatures of the Forest workshop."

"Wow," Megan said. "Really? They're like legendary."

The Little Creatures were a street theater group that had been active in Minnesota since the Beatles broke up.

"Well, not officially. Yet," Ryan said. "But we're getting unofficial help." He still had his chest puffed out as he talked. I noticed Megan looking at it as if she were hypnotized but didn't want to be.

"Way, way cool," Holly said, eyes riveted on Ryan's pecs.

"*Way way cool,*" Megan mimicked.

"Did someone ring for an asshole?" Holly said.

They stood up and faced one another like female baboons.

I didn't understand it totally, but they seemed locked into some hormonal surge mating competition thing. I had a shrinking feeling as I saw Ryan's chin featured on my GreenSWAT movie poster.

"Chick fight!" Ryan said, and he raised his fists.

Megan moved into Holly's space, but Holly stood her ground. They stared at each other for a while then started giggling hysterically. Worse, they began whispering.

"They're comparing our penises," Ryan said. "Or deciding to be lesbians."

Neither were things to joke about, I thought. Then Megan and Holly began hugging.

"Time's up," I said.

"What about the big secret project?" Ryan whispered. "Tell them about the deer condoms!" He started laughing like someone had told a joke.

"What?" Megan said. "Your project's against the deer kill, right?"

It was my turn to stand up and do the baboon thing. "Like I wouldn't be against it?" I said. "What are you saying? That I want to kill the deer?"

"It's his dad's fault," Holly said. "He can't help it; it's in his family."

"Thanks to Megan," I said, "my dad's speaking on Ecoday. It'll ruin me forever. I'm screwed. Royally screwed. Can you deny it?"

"Royally screwed, man," Ryan nodded.

"Shut up, Ryan," Holly said.

"I thought it would help," Megan said softly. "I mean, the kids will see through his arguments. They'll see that he's completely different to you . . ."

"You just got to prove yourself," Ryan said. "We all do. This is war. You'd probably be on the opposite side from your father if it came to war. We know that. We'll show the other kids how radical you are. The Council's what matters. We can do anything!"

"*I* can do anything," Holly said.

"I can do anything too," I said.

"Well, you know *I* can," Megan said.

The first bell rang. We began walking toward the prison.

"What about that project, Sam?" Megan asked. "How's it coming?"

"I'm building it at Patti's place so Jeff won't see."

"Patti's cool," Megan said dreamily. "Lesbians are excellent."

"Yeah, I wanna be one," Ryan said. We'd heard all of his jokes before, but this one always seemed self-evident. He ran ahead to catch up with Holly, which left Megan and me walking like a couple.

When the second bell rang, we were late, but I didn't care. We were all connected and purposeful again—our secret radical cell full of plans and enthusiasm. Best of all, I was walking with our general, Megan, as if she were really my girlfriend.

CHAPTER SIX

W E WERE HAVING BREAKFAST ON Ecoday morning, and as usual at the kitchen table, Perry and I elbowed for reading space. He was reading Garfield's *Lasagna Halloween*—the same book he read over and over. I was reading *Storm Nebula*, a book I tended to read when I was worried. At any moment I expected Patti to knock at the door with my deer project loaded in her van. I hadn't figured out how to explain why she would show up for no reason and offer to drive me to school. Also, Jeff was definitely speaking at the assembly. I felt as if I were eating my last meal, which unfortunately was sugar-free and pesticide-free granola with rice milk, Megan's favorite. I was eating it to see if she and I might be able to live together, which might even happen later that day if I were banished from my home.

"Good morning, everyone," Elissa said. She was dressed in a white-and-blue business suit, the kind she tried hard not to stain. "Happy Ecoday!" she said. Then she whispered to me, "How are you getting your you-know-what to school?"

"Patti's taking me—and it," I whispered back, glancing sideways like a spy.

"Uh-oh," she said. "I bet you expected me to explain all this. Is that it? You haven't told Jeff yet?"

"What do you guys think?" Jeff said as he stomped in. He was dressed in full DNR uniform—shiny buttons, epaulets, meaningless militaristic pins and awards all over the place. He even carried that flat-brimmed hat which, technically, he wasn't even supposed to have.

"I thought you might wear normal clothes," I said. I shot a narrow-eyed glare at Elissa to let her know that her lack of involvement in my urgent problems was not going unnoticed.

"Why?" he said. "I'm proud of my uniform."

I still felt sorry for him. He was so out of it. How could he imagine I would want to see him walk into my school looking like a South American dictator?

40

"Lookin' real sharp," Elissa said. "But comb your beard a bit, I think I see popcorn fragments. Put on your hat, and try making another grand entrance."

"Really?" he said, eyes brighter. He disappeared into the other room.

"So?" I said, resuming my urgent whisper. "What are we going to do?"

"We, Sam? We? You're the one that didn't plan for this. I've got a meeting downtown at nine. A big one. I can't wait for this to go down, honey. If we'd figured this out in advance, I could have dropped you off at Patti's." She looked at her watch. "I'm sure she's on her way over already. Look, just tell Jeff. He's going to find out anyway, isn't he?"

"Hand me that bread knife," I said. "I'll kill myself slowly."

"Me too!" Perry sang cheerfully.

"Don't try to cheer me up," I told him.

"Don't start with that suicide stuff," Elissa said. "I told you, I don't allow that. You want me to tell him, is that it?"

The doorbell rang. Perry opened his eyes wider, then ran to get it like a cocker spaniel—and rammed a shoulder into Jeff's crotch just as Jeff was entering the kitchen with a goofy smile on his face.

"Jesus Christ!" Jeff said, crumpling.

"Someone's at the door," Elissa said. "Sorry, honey."

I heard talking and footsteps. Perry walked in dragging Patti by the hand.

Patti touched Jeff on the back as he struggled to stand upright. "What happened to you?"

"Don't ask," he croaked like a frog. He tried to clear his throat. "What brings—"

"Patti," Elissa said. "What a surprise!" She moved rapidly toward her and they collided in a hug.

Patti leaned over and hugged Jeff too—a clumsy, quick one as Jeff was using the doorjamb to climb upright. She looked him over while Elissa busied herself pouring water into an ancient Mr. Coffee machine.

"Wow," Patti said, looking Jeff up and down. "Let me guess. The Canadians are surrendering?"

"Worse," Jeff said. "I'm speaking at the high school."

"Indoctrinating the youth of America?" she said. "So young, so innocent."

"Nothing you and your Prop19 people wouldn't stoop to," he said.

"Save it for your speech, big guy." Patti fingered the medals on his chest. "I must say there is something about a man in uniform—"

"That makes you want to shoot him?" Elissa said.

I could tell there was something she didn't like about Patti being in our kitchen.

"So?" Jeff said.

"Oh," Patti said. "Why am I here? I'm taking Sam to school. Didn't he . . ."

Jeff looked at Elissa, scanning her for information.

She shrugged. "Sam?" she said.

"Okay. I made a science project. I wanted to make it all by myself so I made it at the Hole," I said very quickly.

"The Whole Child," Patti corrected.

"You hid it?" Jeff said. "From me?"

He stepped backwards and leaned against the sink, touching his chest. The room seemed very small and crowded. "Because," he said, "it's something I wouldn't like. Is that it?"

Elissa watched me with a blank yet hostile smile.

"Uh," I said. "I thought it would be good, uh, for the little daycare kids to see me building . . ."

Patti shook her head, and her earrings chimed. "Sam," she said. This meant I should be honest.

"I just wanted to do it all by myself."

Jeff came to the table and sat at Perry's place. He leaned forward, propping his chin with his forearm. I noticed how small the table was, how we almost never sat together anymore.

"We used to do all your projects together," he said.

I looked at the cover of my book: a rescue in deep space, female general in tight khaki . . .

Elissa brought Jeff a cup of coffee then poured another for Patti. I resented her being so busy. What could I do—clean up?

Patti whispered, "Decaf?" and Elissa nodded.

"Maybe he's just growing up," Elissa said, touching Jeff on the shoulder.

"Tell the truth, Sam," Jeff said. "You hid your project because you knew I would disagree with it." He rubbed his forehead hard, shaking his head from side to side as he rubbed. "God," he said quietly.

"I'm sure he didn't mean . . ." Patti began, but Elissa spoke up.

"It's okay, Patti. Let it be."

Patti took a quick sip of her coffee.

"So what's it about?" Jeff said, eyes still aimed at the table.

"Science," I said. "Holly's friends turned me onto this university research on deer reproduction. I downloaded charts and stuff and pasted them up. Maybe you'll like it. It's all scientific."

"Experimental Station #47? I've heard of them." He snorted with disgust. "Wild, costly fantasies. But, yeah, I guess it's science. Don't know that much about it." His fingers traced tiny spirals on the vinyl tablecloth.

Then he sipped his coffee, which I took as a good sign. But when he looked up at me, I could see the edges of his eyes were a little red. I turned away as quickly as I could.

"I have to do what I think is right," he said. "That's all. I try to accept that you guys are against me on this, but I can't help feeling hurt about you doing your science project behind my back and everyone knowing about it."

Elissa brought the coffeepot over and refilled his cup. She placed her hand lightly on his shoulder.

"It'll all be over soon," she said. "Then we can get back to normal."

"Whatever normal is," I said.

"Maybe we should go to that eco-shrink," Jeff said. He stood up abruptly, put on a fake smile and his hat. "I gotta go. See you over at school, Sam. You can show me your project there."

And just like that, he left. I heard his heavy bootsteps on the wooden floor, a pause, then the door closing just a tad softer than a slam.

CHAPTER SEVEN

THE FAMILIAR NASAL VOICE ON THE RADIO in Patti's van said, "Ecoday? Have you folks heard about this? Big eco news for the eco-minded. Some local school has changed the name of Earth Day to Ecoday. This earth-shaking innovation started right here in Liberalopolis."

"You're listening to this?" I asked Patti. "That's Michael Blaine."

"Oh, he's okay," she said. "Contrarians like to piss everyone off. You never can figure out where they're coming from. But they're refreshing. Sometimes funny. Not as often as they think, but sometimes."

"But, he's . . ."

"Shh," she said. "I want to hear this."

"No one asked me my opinion," Blaine said. "But since all you soulless commuters are tuned into me whether you like me or hate me—hate is really more interesting—I'll tell you what I think we should do on this newly renamed Ecoday."

"This should be good," Patti said, turning it up.

Blaine said, "I think all of you, the whole pop-u-la-sh-un, ought to strip yourselves naked, walk into your nearest so-called park, wilderness, recreational area—any place with more than fifteen trees—and spend the night on a vision quest. Pray to whatever deities you can concoct in your desiccated little civilized hearts. Ask your god for forgiveness for what it is we have done here, making this desert of the soul we call civilization. Huh? Isn't that right, Yeti?"

He got an enthusiastic response in a barking language.

"His cohost, Yeti," Patti said.

"What happened to Kafka?" I said.

"So, you've listened before," she said. "There's a whole gang of different ones."

Yeti stopped barking, and they cut to a commercial for a hair-loss vitamin newly discovered by scientists but available now by mail order. I wondered why everything was "only $19.95 a month" now.

I was learning more than I wanted to know about Blaine, but the image of the entire city getting naked was fun. I had to remind myself that AM talk radio was enemy territory.

"He's crazy," I said.

"Yeah," Patti laughed. "My people want his head on a sharp stick."

I assumed she meant lesbians, but I was no longer sure she belonged to that tribe. "I can't believe they asked Jeff to speak," I said, half to myself. "I can't believe Megan let this happen."

"Maybe she thought she was forcing you to confront your demons," Patti said.

"I think she's testing me," I said. "She invited Jeff to test my loyalty, to see how dedicated I am."

"If you die of embarrassment, you were a good guy."

"Yeah, but a recently deceased good guy."

"Sam, I wish it was that easy to tell the good guys from the bad guys. It isn't, you know. It's possible someone in the administration thought Jeff would do a good job."

Blaine returned, talking about how people should only eat what they could catch and kill with their own hands on these naked Ecoday outings in the parks.

"Say a prayer to your god or your shrunken secular caricature of god before you eat that sparrow, squirrel, hell—earthworm," he said. "I don't care. But eat it raw, as god intended."

The van's digital clock said nine o'clock. I was late, but I didn't care. I wished we could drive to Montana.

Kafka was back: "Dramatic as always, Mr. Blaine, but vull of ze cow puckies— how you say? Ze cow poopies?"

"Today is a good day to die!" Blaine shouted in the background. Native American chanting and drumming swelled up, and then another commercial cut in.

———————————————————————————————

BEING LATE ON ECODAY WAS NO BIG DEAL. Most kids were treating it as if it were a school party day—the halls buzzing with the excitement of breaking rules. As I carried my project to the cafeteria, students walked past dressed in all sorts of costumes. There was a lot of laughing and holding hands, punches and running, typical generic teen giddiness. Students feigned innocence as they walked backwards toward known places where one could light up a joint. I passed a line of card tables set up near the door.

Mary Langsford sat at the first table. Her sign read: "Join the Animal Freedom League."

"Sam O'Brien," she said, cocking her head and laughing. "Want to sign up?"

Mary wore a powder-blue sweater buttoned at the neck, but my eye was attracted by the leaping whale broach pinned to her left breast. She had matching whale barrettes holding back her blond hair. Megan said she dressed like the good girls in 1950ish movies like *Grease*.

"I'm too radical," I said.

She pouted. "You can be in more than one group. I've heard all about your little group that meets at recess. So-o-o radical."

I made a face, but I had stopped and pushed her brochures around. I held my project high like a waiter with a tray.

"You know, Sam, you can do more working within the system than just being negative."

"Who's being negative?" I said, bringing my creation to eye level. "See, I made a science project. I'm participating." I noticed the cardboard background was starting to separate from the base.

She lowered her voice. "I heard you guys want to be little eco-terrorists. You'll end up in jail, just like that Unabomber guy."

"I don't know what you're talking about, Mary," I said. "I gotta go."

"Megan's a bad influence on you," she said, wagging her finger.

"Thanks, Mom," I answered.

I picked up my nametag and number from the self-serve science fair table. Other students, mostly geeks, wandered around looking for their assigned places, but there was no real system. My number had three digits, but all the tables were marked with four digits. This was your typical admin screw-up, so I claimed a table, ripping off the four digit sign and tossing it underneath.

My project looked pretty sad. Some of the toy deer had fallen off the base in transit; charts were peeling off the poster board. I silently blamed the Hole for forcing me to use cheap tape from their children's art supplies. They didn't even have a glue "gun," for obvious reasons.

Then I heard Megan's voice: "Sam, is this it? It looks . . ." She hesitated a moment too long, "wonderful." Her eyes scanned my written material. "How did it go with your dad?" She continued to read. "I mean, when you showed him?"

"He hasn't seen it yet," I said. "I made it at Patti's." That sounded so pathetic, I added, "But we talked about it."

"'Extrapolation of Deer Populations in Wirth Reserve and Alternate Scenarios for Insuring Ecological Balance,'" Megan read. "Very scientific sounding, but . . ." She frowned. "Where did you end up getting your data?"

"Most of it was right at the university site Holly turned me on to. It was pretty much all there. I just downloaded, cut and pasted. Voilà. Instant genius."

Holly and Ryan glided up out of nowhere, arm in arm. Holly wore her black in a new way. A lacey bra peeped out the top of her low-cut dress, accentuating her breasts. I tried not to stare as she leaned over to read the fine print on my project.

Ryan noticed and shoved me over with his hip. He wore a Grateful Dead T-shirt that looked so old it had to have been his dad's. Ryan was proud his dad's stuff was real, not the remakes flooding the neohippy boutiques. His jeans clung to his underwear by some static magic. A Day-Glo orange hunting vest and wraparound sunglasses completed his look.

"Whoa, dude, you did that?" he said. He tried to high-five me, but I fumbled the return slap. I was still focused on Megan's face, which told me something was wrong.

"Sam?" Holly said. "Uh, I think I've got some bad news for you." She was still hunched over.

"What?" I said, annoyed.

"My sister? The one works at that deer experiment at the U?"

"Yeah? The one who gave you the website?"

"She changed her mind. About what they're doing there. Now she says it's 'a goddam concentration camp for deer.' I kid you not. I'm so, so sorry. I should have told you. I never thought . . ."

I was too upset to speak for a while. Then I said, "What does she know? This is science. Maybe they didn't give her a raise or something. Maybe she's pissed at the university. It doesn't mean—"

Megan touched my arm. "I wish you hadn't kept it so secret."

"I wanted to surprise . . ." I said. "I don't get it. What?" I was still defending, but I knew I had already lost the battle, the war, everything.

"I just found this out," Holly said. "Honest. It's not like I go around thinking 'How does everything I hear affect Sam O'Brien?'"

"I'm sorry, Sam," Megan said. "I didn't know what you were doing."

"This can't be," I protested with a shrinking voice. "Their website was so cool, so . . ." I spaced into silence, then started up again. "They're working on deer contraceptives . . . It's an alternative . . . They have all this data . . ." I sounded like a criminal defending himself.

I stared at the project, picturing how Elissa and Patti had hovered over me, telling me how good it was, how clever I was, how much my friends would like it.

"It's . . ." I began again, but I had completely run out of air.

I half-expected Ryan to joke about deer condoms, but he tried to help. "Maybe, like, the university is evil. They just put an evil spell on you or something."

Megan said, "I'm sorry to tell you this, Sam, but it's pretty well known the place is evil. I never said much back when Holly was so proud of her sister. It didn't matter then. But I've read about it since. They have all kinds of animals there, not just deer. It's very high security, so you know they must be doing some really evil shit."

"How was he supposed to know that?" Ryan said.

"You guys should read more," Megan said. "I mean more than science fiction and comic books."

"Fake greens are everywhere. They're like space clones, the fucking liars," Holly said angrily. "Every fucking corporation is trying to make themselves look eco-cool these days."

"Yeah," Ryan said. "Like we're such idiots. It's all over the TV. Green forest destruction. Green non-recyclable packaging. Green nuclear waste, for Chrissake."

"It's actually worse at Experimental Station #47," Megan said. "I heard they're experimenting with the deer's reproductive organs."

"Oh, god," I moaned, and I covered my face.

"Think about it," Holly said. "Being caged up and forced to test contraceptives?"

"Depends on what the females look like," Ryan said. "I wouldn't turn down Bambi's mom."

Holly giggled and shoved him, saying, "Men are such assholes."

Megan cut off the playfulness with a growl, "It's not funny. Fake Green is so . . ." She growled again, a rare tactic she used when she couldn't find words.

"It's not your fault, Sam," Holly said. "It's everyone's fault. We're all to blame."

"Yeah, but I'm the one who's going to look stupid," I said. "I was dumb enough to make a project promoting their side."

I looked at my project with disgust. It was a monstrosity, created by an idiot who was force-fed media crap. This idiot proudly promoted Experimental Deer Station #47. His charts, conclusions, everything clearly relied on the university data. He even credited the neo-Nazis in his text.

Megan touched my arm. "Don't worry, Sam. People around here aren't as well informed as we are. Just let it go."

"Yeah, only geeks do projects anyway," Ryan said. "No offense. I mean, they don't even have a contest anymore."

"Ecoday's already ruined for me," I said. I knew the university professors weren't really neo-Nazis, but at the moment I wanted to kill them. I was imploding into a black hole of hatred. The world was pressing on my chest, and I wanted to push back. I wanted revenge.

"Yeah, and it's getting worse, dude," Ryan said. "Here comes your dad."

"Oh-my-god," Holly giggled, putting her hand to her mouth. "That uniform! Oh-my-god!"

I saw the uniform first, the shiny medals, the ridiculous Mounty hat. Jeff was skirting the edge of the auditorium like a security guard. I hunkered down, the Council following me.

"What are we going to do?" Holly whispered.

"Throw some water on him and maybe he'll melt," Ryan said. "Sorry, no. Pull the fire alarm?"

"Don't be a child," Megan said.

Holly peeked up like a prairie dog. "Oh-my-god," she said. "He's coming this way."

"Ditch," Ryan said, and he and Holly took off, crouching while running down the aisle. Megan and I stood up.

"Sam," Jeff called, waving to me. He should have been in the Guinness Book of World Records for the Most Clueless Person in the Universe.

"Dad," I said through a squeak. I cleared my throat and said, "Jeff." Megan pushed me toward him, away from my project.

"Hello, Megan. Got a minute to show me your project, Sam? I want to see what you kids are up to."

"Excuse me, but I've got a few official duties to attend to," Megan said. "I'm on the committee . . ."

"Yeah, yeah," I said a little rudely. "Go on."

Like a prisoner leading cops to the evidence, I walked Jeff straight to my Extrapolation of Deer Populations in Wirth Reserve and Alternate Scenarios for Insuring Ecological Balance. He leaned over and looked at it.

"This is great, Sam. God, you sacrificed your little soldiers? This must mean a lot to you. I like what you did with this."

I saw through his fake niceness.

"Why did you think you had to hide this from me? I mean, it's inconclusive data and all as nobody takes those guys seriously over there. Nobody. Though I'm sure they mean well. The real problem with contraception is cost—"

"It's crap," I said.

"O-K," he said slowly. His hands made the give-it-to-me motion. "What's that about?"

"It's all wrong. It's bullshit. I just found out that place is another front for Fake Greens. They can make anything look good. That experimental station is a concentration camp for deer, any way you cut it."

"And the great expert who informed you of this is?" he said. "Let me guess. She's under twenty."

Megan, Ryan, and Holly suddenly surrounded us: the cavalry had arrived.

As a chorus, they said, "Hello, Officer O'Brien."

Jeff smiled at me. "The experts return?"

Ryan blurted, "We need Sam, sir."

"For the performance, sir," Holly said.

Jeff stepped back and waved his open palms. "He's not my prisoner."

They grabbed my hands and began pulling me.

"A concentration camp for deer?" Jeff said. "You kids really believe that?"

"Come on, Sam-I-am," Ryan said. "We gotta have more bodies for the Die-In."

Jeff laughed. "The Die-In? What's a—"

"Good morning, Mr. O'Brien." Mr. Katami had snuck up on us. My friends stopped pulling, and I wanted to see what would happen.

"I hear you're sponsoring a Die-In," Jeff said, hitting the side of his head with an open palm. "I'm so out of it. We used to have Love-Ins and Be-Ins. Now I know I'm getting old."

"We like to give the students room to express themselves," Katami said. "We get to see what they're thinking about, worrying about. We can see into their world when they use their own language. Like rap music shows us inner-city life. It's a small contribution to diversity."

"Like rap music," Jeff said, nodding.

Katami looked tired. "I don't condone the lyrics of—"

"But they all think the same way," Jeff said. "How does that constitute diversity? And more interestingly, how does that happen? Doesn't diversity of thought count for anything?"

Mr. Katami sighed. "We try, Mr. O'Brien, we try. But we don't control their content." Then he brightened. "That's why we invited you to talk."

"Ah, the sacrifice," Jeff said.

The Council exchanged looks on this one.

Mr. Katami moved closer to Jeff, taking his elbow as if Jeff were a disturbed student. "Mr. O'Brien, I'll show you where we're setting up your talk."

"Sure," Jeff said. "But can I watch the Die-In? Especially if my son and his friends . . ."

As the Kat lead him away, a distance opened between Jeff and me. When Jeff looked at me over his shoulder, I had a strange sensation he was on a boat, drifting away from my dock.

"I like your dad," Holly said. "I mean, wearing that the uniform takes guts."

"Shut up, Holly," Ryan said.

Megan put her arm over my shoulder. "You'll see," she said. "It'll all come together."

"We'll all come together?" Ryan said to make it dirty, and Holly pushed him and laughed.

"I hope your costume will cover my face," I said to Ryan.

"Mostly. But what doesn't will be covered up with brown face paint. Nobody will recognize you. C'mon, this will be great. I need the bodies."

We followed Ryan out the back door.

"I need the oblivion," I said.

CHAPTER EIGHT

I n the prop room, I lost myself for a moment in the giddiness. Ryan dressed like a hunter in red plaid and a blaze-orange vest. When the deer actors got into costume, they began bumping into each other. Someone started a series of jokes like this: If a deer has sex in the forest . . . It went downhill from there, as most of the jokes reminded me of my project.

Despite the papier-mâché antlers wobbling on my head and the brown cloth itching my skin, I liked being hidden. The world looked different from inside Ryan's crude deer costume. I remembered being a child and how hiding in a box or under a blanket divided the world into inside and outside.

At the sound of a gong, our deer herd moved toward the bright sunlight. I avoided looking at the crowd, fearing I'd see Jeff. I was sure he'd recognize my eyes.

We gamboled about as per instructions. Ryan had shown the gambol—a spastic jumpy thing not unlike punk dancing. Ryan primed us to listen for three rapid gongs signaling the shift from gamboling to dying. The gongs were supposed to represent bullets. He told us to space out the dying, but when we heard the three gongs, we became a chaotic mass of leaping, bumping, falling, dying deer. Worse, most of us giggled, even me.

Ryan hissed at us from somewhere, but that only made it funnier. Laughter ripped through the herd and the crowd as we died. Ryan gonged and gonged, louder and louder as if trying to cover it up.

I gamboled a while, not sure I was ready to die. When I chose my fatal gong, I thought it would look cool if I started spinning as I fell. Instead, the spinning made me nauseous and I had difficulty breathing. Something that felt like a Doc Marten went into the crack of my butt. Ryan had said there wouldn't be a specific signal for the end of the piece. That was his gimmick. We were supposed to lie there, a dead deer sculpture, for as long as we could stand it.

I liked lying dead. I wondered if I could stay there all day.

Stupid voices started saying mocking things like, "Are they really dead?" Others said, "How long are they going to stay that way?" Or "Is that Justin? Justin?"

I could sense the dead deer getting up one by one. Their conversations trailed off as they walked toward the school. I stayed still for a long time until a foot nudged me.

"Excellent," Megan said. "You won."

"I thought I'd stay here all day," I said. "My personal monument to death."

"So they'd talk about you after you're gone," she said. "Typical."

"I'd become a myth."

"Don't push it," she said. "C'mon, you gotta show up for your dad's talk. You got to show you're not afraid of him."

I took off my papier-mâché antlers and cloth mask. She laughed.

"You have black smudge all over your face. Let's go clean up."

In moments, Megan and I found ourselves alone in the prop room. I was staring into a tiny, greasy mirror, feeling sorry for myself as she began wiping the black makeup off my face. Her touch was soft and tingly.

"Can't we stay in here for a few hours?" I said. "Guard the costumes or something?"

"If you don't show up, it'll be worse for all of us. Kids will think you're scared."

"I am scared."

"Trust me on this," she said, touching my hand. She rubbed my face with a fresh baby wipe. I closed my eyes, and the smell took me back to a warm, safe time.

"Thanks," I said.

"It won't come off until you shower."

"Wanna join me? We could sneak into the boys' locker room no problem. No one would be in there."

"Sam!" Megan said. She pretended to be shocked with her mouth wide open. "You never say anything like that to me. I believe you're trying to talk dirty."

"How dirty do I have to get for it to work?" I asked.

She laughed and slapped me on the arm, but there was something making me uncomfortable. It was as if, underneath, she was saying I didn't know how to talk dirty. Was she implying she hung with people who were better at it? It got me thinking about who that might be and why I couldn't talk dirty. It wasn't a good time for this kind of speculation.

"Let's talk about that some other time," she said. "Council work is out there, Sam."

THE AUDITORIUM WAS AS PACKED AND STUFFY as I was filled with dread. There were chairs set up on the gym floor, but Holly and Ryan had saved us choice seats on the bleachers. A small table on stage held a pitcher of water and three glasses. I recognized the rickety old easel that snapped itself shut like a mousetrap at the oddest moments. The Kat was monkeying with our ancient mike, the kind 1940 gangster molls sang into.

Finally, Katami began talking. I pretended not to pay attention while joking around with Ryan, but one ear was trained to hear key words signifying Jeff's introduction. Then I heard it. The Kat said, "You may not like everything Officer O'Brien has to say, but I expect to see no disorderly conduct," and he smiled that thing he called a smile and looked around. "Without any further ado . . ."

Ryan chanted quietly, "Ado, ado, ado."

Holly whispered, "What *is* ado?"

"May I present Officer Jeffery O'Brien of the Department of Natural Resources." The Kat started clapping and stepped back. No one joined him in the clapping.

Jeff strode on stage in all his Boy Scout glory. No, he looked more like a wiry, enthusiastic monkey impersonating a Boy Scout. The audience went deadly quiet as even the whispering died. The Kat clapped for a moment or two longer. A few teachers, then a few brown-nose students, joined in, but it was pathetic.

"Thank you, Mr. Katami," Jeff said. "Do you like the uniform?" He twirled around. Holly laughed, but quickly put her hand to her mouth, and Megan stared at Jeff with her piercing Unitarian eyes.

"How many think we've got a deer problem in our city?" Jeff asked from stage.

At first no hands went up. Megan snorted with satisfaction. Then a few tentative hands rose.

"Who are those jerks?" Megan said.

"Not many of you," Jeff said. "I understand that. I know some of you who don't even want me to say 'deer problem.' Call it what you will, but we've got an overpopulation of these wonderful creatures right here."

"I'm sure he thinks they're wonderful creatures," Holly said.

"You know I'm talking about the Wirth Reserve," Jeff said.

An electric buzz zipped through the crowd.

"You know what ecology is, right? Where do we get our idea of what a balanced ecosystem might be?"

I was surprised he was this good a speaker. I don't know what I'd expected, but it hadn't been this.

Some guy I didn't know raised his hand. "It's what America was before white people came and messed it up?"

Laughter. Jeff laughed too, but I knew it was his fake laugh.

"Why not go back ten thousand years earlier, when half of our continent was covered in ice and animals had an equal shot at having a Neolithic hunter for dinner? Or go back further than that, back when dinosaurs considered our rat-like ancestors merely skimpy appetizers?"

People seemed to be paying attention. I didn't know what to make of that.

"You could go back to the earth as a bubbling ball of volcanic activity, when the most advanced life was a single-celled animal swimming about in green slime."

"Where the hell is he going with this?" Holly whispered at me.

"Like I know?" I said irritably. I'd heard it before, but it wouldn't help to mention that.

"When I say 'future,' what do you see?" Jeff said. "Most of you see it in terms of Mad Max or Blade Runner-style post-nuclear catastrophes. Am I right? There aren't many images of the good guys making a sustainable Garden of Eden out of this mess, huh?" Jeff paused in order to swallow and take a breath.

"He's pretty into science fiction," Holly said.

"There is a family resemblance," Megan said.

"Let's say—for argument's sake," Jeff said, "for fun—that you, the good guys, win. Picture that. Sustainable vegan agriculture, everyone walking around wearing cotton, carrying non-toxic beverages in mugs fired in the community kiln. Very California."

Someone yelled out, "Surf's up, dude!" People laughed.

"You got it—surfing in the newly cleaned-up ocean. You solved racial problems by blending everyone into mocha. You've solved energy problems with renewable solar, thermal and wind power. You're a spiritually advanced society. What happens next?"

"Darth Vader shows up!" a jock guy yelled.

"Good," Jeff said pointing to him. "But let's say it's not old Darth wheezing in his helmet. This is a public school, so . . ." He flashed a smile at Katami. "So let's call him, or her if you like, Nature. Specifically the Dark Side of Nature. She could hit your ecologically balanced world at any moment with many kinds of nasty surprises."

Megan furrowed her brow.

"Just when you got the animals re-educated to love one another, the predators safely switched over to soyburgers, let's say a volcanic explosion filters out the sun for a couple of years. Did you know that happened before? When Krakatoa erupted in 535 A.D.? How about a meteor? You've all seen the movies. Scientists believe a meteor the size of Manhattan probably wiped out the dinosaurs. Some say we're due for another."

Someone stood up near the front. I recognized Mary Langsford's pale-blue sweater. "We're all concerned about the deer, Officer O'Brien," she said as if impersonating a kindergarten teacher. "Everyone wants to hear about the deer situation. Why do you insist on killing the friendly deer in the Wirth? Can't we live in peace with animals?"

"Whoa, it's the Mary Langsford Show," Ryan whispered. "The powderpuff's got guts, even if she's totally out of it."

"It's stupidity," Megan said, her face was stony with anger. "She's gonna ruin everything, I just know it." She turned to Ryan. "We need anger." I watched the two of them exchange a silent communication I didn't understand.

"It's too early," Ryan said as he slid off the end of the bleacher. I slouched down as he yelled, "Why do you have to kill a bunch of tame deer? That's what we want to know." Ryan sat back down, a fierce look on his face.

"Thanks for your input," Jeff said with a smirk. He walked away from the mike, nodding. The mike picked up his quiet repetition, "Okay, okay," like a street person talking to himself.

I thought about melting into the floor like the evil android from the future in *Terminator II*. I doubled over, staring at the gum under the seats and the stains in the floor no cleaner could touch. I took a breath and allowed my eyes to return to the world, scanning like a periscope.

"I know this game," Jeff said. "I've even played this game. In college, way back in ancient times. Tell you what. I'll give up my script if you give up yours. Let's just forget the planned presentation. Let's get real." He wadded up his notes and sent a crumpled white ball on a slow, dramatic arc into the audience.

All student eyes turned to the Kat. I'm sure they were thinking what I was thinking: No throwing paper in the auditorium, but all the Kat did was squirm.

Jeff walked back to the mike and grabbed it firmly. "You want to talk about death? Let's talk about death."

There was a new vibration in his voice. Maybe he was too close to the mike. The ancient sound system broke into a high-pitched whistle then crackled dangerously. He backed off and smiled at the thing, tapped it, then started in again.

"Kids are fascinated with death—right? Everyone's always telling you that you shouldn't be, but nobody says why. People call it morbid, unhealthy. They wring their hands and say, 'Why can't you be interested in bright cheerful things?' You know what? They're wrong."

Someone yelled, "Go Death!" Someone else yelled, "Right on!"

"This is good," Holly said. Ryan elbowed her while Megan reached for my hand. Was she reaching in pity for me, or comfort for her. I hoped it was a random wave of horniness.

"You can't talk about ecology without talking about death," Jeff said. "Life and death are two sides of the same coin. Things die so other things can live. Things eat other things. Cute things eat cute things, which makes it all that much harder to decide who's right and wrong. Your cute kitty brings you a beautiful dead sparrow. The word balance sounds nice and tidy, but underneath that word is a world of fierce living and desperate dying. Ugly eats cute, but also cute eats cute."

I looked around and was amazed to see that this death angle was working. The place had quieted down; people stared at the stage as if they were being hypnotized.

"Your dad's weird," Holly whispered to me. "But I kind of like the death stuff. People don't talk about death at school unless someone offs himself or gets shot on a playground in Texas."

I listened while giving her my "Jesus Christ!" look of disgust.

Megan and Ryan exchanged that look again. Again, Ryan shook his head. I knew I could have pursued it, but they were leaving me out of something, and for the moment that was okay.

"I'm not saying things haven't changed," Jeff said. "Your world looks and sounds more violent than mine ever was. You play *Quake III* on your computer in the morning, blowing away bad guys in a spray of blood before breakfast, then refuse to dissect a frog in biology class because it's too cruel. You dance to rap lyrics about rape and torture, then eat vegan because it's the obviously compassionate thing to do. The TV news home delivers killings, disasters, mutilations, war, genocide, not to mention bus accidents in Pakistan—878 feared dead."

He paused to breathe, and everyone was so quiet I could hear both his inhale and his exhale.

"Every day there's a new threat to your food, water and air. Every day some new danger pops up—terrorists, Frankenstein food, political kidnappings, sexual slavery. All this plays against the same background noise my generation grew up with— weapons of mass destruction, nuclear and now biological. Let's not forget your famines, earthquakes, fires. What about plagues? AIDS, malaria, the return of TB. What about smallpox? Does all this have an effect on you? You bet it does. You are all affected. Big time."

He stopped and took a drink of water. I could see his hand shake as he swallowed.

"So," Mary Langsford shouted. I had to admire her persistence. "So, because there's so many evil things in the world we should accept animal murder?" She sat down right away. People around her patted her shoulders.

"You want the truth, right?" Jeff said, ignoring her. "Civilization is a fragile thing. Chaos, real or imagined, is ready to swallow us up at any moment. It might be the chaos of a kid walking into his school and blowing away his classmates. It might be the chaos of a genetically modified gene going Frankenstein and suddenly we're extras in *The Day of the Triffids*. Chaos rules!"

Ryan whispered to me, "What's a triffid?"

"It's from an old science-fiction movie," I answered as if I were on a quiz show. "They're plants from outer space that walk around and eat people."

"Cool," Ryan said. "Killer Plants." He air-Uzied them with double index fingers.

"I don't like this," Megan said. "He sounds too . . ." She blinked. "Too believable, for lack of a better word. It's dangerous. Ryan, when are you going to do that . . ." She looked at me, but went on anyway. "That thing? This is obviously bullshit, but I'm afraid people are starting to think Sam's dad makes sense."

"What thing?" I asked.

"Don't protect your dad," she said, pulling her hand from me as if I'd burned it.

"I hate the fucker too," I said a bit whiningly.

Megan said, "Then do something!"

"Killing animals is murder!" Ryan shouted, hands cupped over his mouth for volume.

Jeff leaned closer to the mike and responded in a low voice, "We're all killers. Every person in this room is a killer."

Mumbling and shouting broke out around the room. Some of it was shock, some excitement, some urgent denial.

"Every breath you take," Jeff said. He began talking faster and louder. "Every step you make—yeah, like the song—you kill something. Microorganisms, whatever, but living things. Did you know the average person consumes about twenty animals a year—cows, pigs, and chickens? Somebody's got to kill them. You don't. But you do eat them. How many of you have eaten a Big Mac or a Whopper or a Chicken McNugget in the last week? A baloney sandwich? Tuna?"

He began swaggering around the stage.

"He's vulnerable here," Megan said. She waved her arm back and forth like a giant windshield wiper.

"A question?" Jeff said calmly. "Ah, someone actually raising her hand."

Megan stood up. "Mr. O'Brien?" she said. "What you're saying about meat eaters, some of us believe that meat eating is part of the problem, a big part. We're vegan. We don't wear leather, either. We're out to put an end to all this . . . cruelty." She looked around for cheers, but nothing happened. I thought she deserved something, but I couldn't move.

Jeff opened his mouth as widely as he could. He pointed to a tooth with his thumb and index finger. "Can you tell me what these are, Megan?" he said. "These teeth? I'll tell you. They're called incisors. They're carnivorous teeth. Your cows and horses, your herbivores—they don't have incisors. Nature made us this way. Meat was the diet that made us human."

"That's just history. Tofu and soybeans give us all the protein we need." She looked around again for support but received nothing but silence. I hated those silent people, but I was one of them.

"Megan, you can't change what you are because you've watched a few Disney films. Your body evolved as a predator's body. Have you ever wondered why humans can run marathons? What other animals can run marathons? Predators who run down prey, that's who. Like us."

Megan knees bent slowly, lowering herself to the edge of her chair.

"What about that big brain of yours that thinks up brand-new words like 'vegan'? How did we evolve such a huge brain that can think such lofty thoughts? The human brain is the most energy-consumptive organ on this planet, and it has to be fed. It grew and evolved on meat, my dear. How did your ancestors make it through the Ice Age? Meat and skins. You owe your entire existence to meat. Doesn't that give you pause?"

"That's speciesism," Megan said, popping back up and enunciating the word clearly. "Humans aren't the center of the world. Who speaks for the animals? Are they better off that we have this big brain that figures out how to kill them?"

"Yeah, who's speaking for the deer?" Mary Langsford yelled. "We love the deer. Doesn't love count for something?"

Megan rolled her eyes at me and sighed deeply. "Goddam her," she whispered.

"You love the deer?" Jeff said, pointing at Mary. "And who has appointed you spokesman—excuse me, spokesperson—for the deer? Just what are you doing for the deer exactly, besides saving them? Have you ever witnessed a starving deer? I've seen hundreds of deer starve—bucks, does, and cute little Bambi fawns. Despite our best efforts to feed them, I've seen entire herds die. Have you ever smelled rotting deer flesh in a spring field bursting with flowers? I have. Have you ever really saved anything, young lady? Ever?"

"We could feed them," Mary said, barely audibly. "Or move them. Anything besides kill them."

Someone shouted, "Republicans are deer killers!"

"It's not that easy, pal," Jeff shouted right back. "Besides, what does that have to do with anything? I vote for whoever happens to give more money to the DNR and, given we're a state agency, that generally is your good old Democrats." He sighed and rubbed his forehead like he was removing stage makeup. "Believe it or not, I love nature. Just like you. And just like you, I'm doing my best to save this goddamned earth."

Megan nudged me to look at Holly. Holly was staring at Jeff with her mouth wide open, definitely in a trance.

"Ryan," Megan whispered. "Are you going to do that thing or not? It's now or never."

Ryan slipped out of this seat and lowered himself off the end of the bleachers. I admired his stealthy ninja-style movements.

"What's he doing?" I asked Holly.

She shrugged. "Organizing some theater thing."

I knew Ryan and Megan had been cooking something up without me. That hurt, but at the same time I couldn't have been too useful. At that moment I was grateful to be out of it. The crucial question was: Did this elevate Ryan's status in Megan's eyes?

Jeff walked stiffly away from the mike, paced around the stage, then walked back. He spoke softly and seriously: "People, I got news for you. Life isn't simple. I wish it was, I truly do, but it just isn't."

I wasn't listening anymore. I was thinking about Ryan. Why hadn't Ryan invited me to help? Didn't he trust me? Why were he and Megan keeping this secret from me? Were they going to hurt Jeff?

Movement from the side of the room caught my eye. Ryan's people were gathering near the end of the bleachers, dressed again in full deer costumes. They crouched, keeping their antlers low. I felt a sharp pain of betrayal. Wasn't I supposed to be part of this?

"That's the reason we're here today, isn't it?" Jeff said. It sounded as if he were winding down his speech. "Ecology isn't simple. Ecosystems are like people. They are very, very, complicated."

Ryan yelled from the back of the room, "Save the deer!"—and a boom box under the bleachers kicked in with a pulsing rock beat. I recognized EarthDeath's song *Let the End Come*.

"Here we go," Megan said.

Ryan's costumed herd ran toward the stage leaping and shouting, "Save the deer! Save the animals!"

The Kat rose up from his seat. Moving his arms in jerky, puppet-like motions, he said, "Oh, no. Oh, no." Other teachers rushed up toward the front of the auditorium, Ms. S-T, Mr. Johnson, even George the janitor.

"I can't stay here," Megan said.

"But you said," I said.

"You stay," she said. "I just can't." She lowered herself off the end of the bleachers as nimbly as Ryan. I wanted desperately to join the deer people, but I remained frozen to my seat. Next to me Holly laughed and pointed as if she were at a circus.

In seconds, Megan was beside Ryan, motioning kids in the audience to join them. Jeff smiled down at them, his arms folded across his chest. The deer people gamboled around. Students cheered from their seats, but few joined the performers.

Soon the teachers had surrounded Ryan's little group. With outstretched arms, they penned the performers as they might real animals.

Megan's clear voice rose high above the others, chanting and shouting Earth-Death's chorus: "Destroy the destroyers! Kill the killers! Wash the world clean again!"

The Kat was barking orders from the stage. I watched Jeff gather up the charts and graphs he'd never used. It was all over as the teen animals were herded into the halls. As the herd passed raising fists and peace signs, the bleachers emptied as we all headed back to our homerooms. It was slow going, and I looked back at stage. I felt some relief that everyone was gone.

But just as the crowd turned the corner of the hallway, I saw Jeff. I ducked so he couldn't see me. What was he doing here? I couldn't believe it, but some kids had surrounded him as if he were one of those inspirational sports speakers who had done something famous once. They asked him questions, not in angry or confrontational tones either, just plain questions.

Jeff seemed to be answering a question about Gaia, the Earth Goddess. I knew he wasn't into this as I had heard him argue with Elissa, but he sounded respectful. Kids were laughing, but not in a mean way, in a way like someone had told a joke. I couldn't believe it, but they seemed to like Jeff, to enjoy him. The absolute worst part was that they weren't just geeks and nerds. There were all kinds of kids there—jocks, hip-hoppers, preps, every subspecies of teen.

I hated them all. I hated Ryan for doing his thing, Megan for betraying me, and Holly for laughing in the bleachers. Most of all I hated The Kat for inviting Jeff.

I hated Jeff most of all. How could he have done this to me?

The rest of the day was a blur, but the Kat's scolding us over our closed-circuit video system was memorable. He called Ryan's performance a protest, which made Ryan jump up and silently cheer. Ms. S-T sort of smiled at him when she told him to sit down. Soon the Ecoday workshops and teach-ins kicked in as planned. I wandered around trying to avoid being recognized. Before the day was over, Ryan's protest became more dangerous and dramatic in the retellings. I heard kids say they were going to trash the school. Worse, I heard other kids repeating stuff Jeff said, but not sarcastically.

"You want to talk about death?" kids quoted Jeff. "Let's talk about death." As if it were a line from a popular movie.

I wanted the day to be over. I wanted to get to my room and play Game Boy under my blankets, or watch hours of my taped *Strange But True* shows. I avoided humanity until the last bell rang and the buses had left, and then I went back into the cafeteria to pick up my science project. I hadn't made any arrangements to have anyone pick me up.

I waited till everyone was gone. George the janitor, who smelled funny but was the wisest man in the school, was stacking the empty tables where the science projects had been. I saw my project on the floor against the wall. It looked sad.

"I wondered if someone was coming for that one. Is that your work, son?" I nodded. "It looks like you put a lot of work into it," he said. "How are you getting that thing home?"

"I'm not taking it home," I said. "It's over." I picked it up and looked around for a large enough garbage can. Only George's portable dumpster on wheels was big enough. "I'm tossing it."

"You're tossing it?" he said. "All that hard work? Aren't you proud of it? Show your parents!"

"No," I said. "It's all wrong, a mistake. The Nazis . . ." A catch in my voice warned me to stop.

"Nazis?" he said. "The Germans?"

"No," I said. "The scientists. They're all lying to us." I lifted the thing and dropped it into his dumpster.

He shook his head as I crushed the project down. "Are you sure you're—"

I got out of there fast. Outside, I was alone with my personal misery and defeat, and as I walked home it was Elissa's voice that bubbled out of my depression and inspired me. She'd tried to teach me what she called inner guidance techniques, and I heard her voice say, "There's a message in everything, even in hard things. What's the first word that comes to you?"

I knew the word instantly. It was "revenge."

Her inner guidance follow-up would have been, "And how can you activate this word?"

I could activate it by sending it to those who most deserved it, the neo-Nazi scientists at Experimental Deer Station #47. They needed to be taught a lesson. They needed to pay for their crimes.

CHAPTER NINE

AS HOLLY GOT OUT OF THE CAR, I saw she was wearing her open-toed, sandal-like things with the mini-platforms. What was she thinking? Ever since she saw that miniseries about Patty Hearst getting kidnapped by the Symbionese Liberation Army—which I had to admit was a very cool name—Holly got more serious about being an animal activist. She did not, however, leave fashion behind.

As soon as she hit the muddy hill with those shoes, she wobbled as if she were on stilts. She fell backward, right on the little Goth cape she insisted on wearing.

"Oh-my-god," she shouted, as if we should all laugh.

"Get up and shut up," I said, sounding tougher than the usual me.

I wasn't the leader. Nobody was supposed to be. But firm, serious, Megan remained our spiritual leader if for no other reason than she was the only one who had read all the important magazines from our mentors: Animal Liberation Front (ALF), People for the Ethical Treatment of Animals (PETA), and EarthFirst!

According to our plan, the mud should have been too cold and stiff to hold footprints, but we trudged up the slope, leaving evidence of shoe sizes, if not name brands. I stopped and stared down at my Nikes, Ryan's Doc Martens, Holly's platform jokes, and Megan's sensible Timberlands.

"What's keeping you, man?" Ryan whispered over his shoulder.

"We're leaving tracks!" I said as I scrambled up the slope after the others.

"No looking back," Ryan said, which sounded good at the time.

We were in the process of liberating the inmates of the university's Experimental Station #47. The station was a one-story brown building on top of a small hill. A fence surrounded the complex just as you would expect at a concentration camp. The prisoners, of course, were deer.

As I reached the top of the hill, I saw our group in full silhouette. With a sinking sensation, I realized that it was more than the mud or Holly's shoes that we had failed to anticipate. Although we had waited for the darkness of a new moon and even watched the Weather Channel giddy with thoughts of crime, we had forgotten about the lights. Hundreds of them had been put up the previous spring in an effort to prevent a national rape epidemic from settling on the campus, and now they bathed us in a science-fictional glow. Anyone looking up the hill could have spotted us easily.

"There's the hole," Holly said, pointing to a crude pile of boards at the base of the otherwise impressive-looking fence.

Holly's sister, the one who delivered deer pellets to the station, had told Holly about the hole. A coyote, she'd thought, had tried to dig into the deer compound, and graduate student slave laborers had done a crude repair job.

I walked up to the boards and kicked one off easily.

"Classic carpentry," Ryan said.

Another kick and the whole thing collapsed. We stood there looking at the hole like a bunch of idiots. Probably we were all afraid to enter.

A gaggle of deer, mostly does, but at least one buck with an impressive rack, stood there looking at us through the fence. They snorted and sniffed as if they had allergies. I wondered if they were angry that we'd roused them from their cud-chewing sleep. How would they know it was for their own good?

I imagined asking Jeff someday if deer even chewed cud, then banished the thought. Jeff was the last person I wanted to think about.

"They want food," Ryan said.

Of course, I thought. *These are tame deer, used to people.* That thought led to another less helpful thought: Why were we freeing tame deer?

"Move, everyone," Megan said like a female action figure mysteriously born to Unitarian parents. "Remember our rehearsals?" she said. "Let's get this job done and get out of here."

With her black ski cap pulled low over her frowning face, she didn't look anything like the female action figures I'd grown up loving. Where was the tight-fitting Lycra jumpsuit of the Planeteers or the huge mane of Xena when she was ready to kill?

Ryan dived through the hole first. This awakened me from my longing for Xena, and I ducked down and crawled. The jagged metal fence tore my light windbreaker and dug into my back. *DNA traces,* I thought.

The deer stepped back a few feet but not far enough for my comfort. Their scent was half-sweet, half-foul, like sweet-and-sour pork left overnight.

Three of us got through and faced the quiet herd. As Holly wriggled halfway through, the big buck stomped his feet and snorted. We froze.

"Nice deer," Holly said, looking up at him from ground level. Her videocam bag, the one I'd told her not to bring, was stuck in the fence's wire.

"He's not a freaking dog," Ryan whispered, in a tone used in wildlife documentaries. "He's protecting his harem."

Holly managed to join us, breathing heavily. I heard the crinkle of a candy wrapper, and she threw something at the buck, and it hit him in the chest—and he snorted.

"What the hell are you doing?" I said.

Instead of charging us, the buck lowered his head and nuzzled something on the ground. Then he licked it.

"Granola bar," Holly said. "They're full of oats, you know."

"Move," Megan said.

Ryan ran toward the door of the building. In less than a minute, I heard glass smashing.

"I'm in," he said.

The sound of the glass had stunned me. I looked for Megan as if to check with her. How far had we agreed to go? Instead I called up a slideshow of animal atrocities that Megan had shown us: scientists spraying stinging poison in bunnies' eyes, scientists poking hot electrodes in exposed monkeys' brains. The images convinced me that we were the good guys. We were defending the earth.

When I caught up to Megan, she was spray-painting a Day-Glo "W" on the station's brown walls. We'd talked about slogans and logos. Our symbol had to be mysterious but at the same time something any idiot could figure out. We settled on a "W" in a circle as our sign. It stood for Wirth, of course—the place where the DNR would soon slaughter deer unless we could stop them.

Holly picked up a rake and began smashing windows. "How does that feel?" she asked one of them. "Do you want more of that?"

I ran toward the dark doorway that had swallowed up Ryan. More smashing sounds came from inside. I flicked on my flashlight and saw Ryan running around the room knocking things over like a lunatic. Destruction can be exciting if it's for a good cause. When would I ever get to do something like this in normal life? I felt camaraderie with freedom fighters all over the world. I jumped into our music video with full permission to destroy.

I kicked over computers and pushed piles of papers off desks. I poured out any liquid I could find—from old coffee from Styrofoam cups to Frankenstein beakers of goo that, for my Nikes' sake, I hoped wasn't acid. I knocked books out of bookcases, using the sweeping arm gestures bad guys use in movies when they're searching for microchips.

Megan and Holly joined us. In minutes the main room was trashed, and as we moved into the inner offices, a weird thought hit me. Elissa was always saying we kids should have more fun. I thought she should see us now.

Megan whispered, "Over here."

I followed her voice and saw a virtual prison of furry victims just like in Megan's photos. Rats, mice, guinea pigs and rabbits stared at us from death row.

"Free the animals!" Holly screamed.

We began opening cages and trying to shoo out the captives, but they were too far gone. Like little Patty Hearsts in little closets, they didn't want to move. We had to start dumping them. It felt mean, but I figured one day they would feel some rudimentary form of gratitude.

Ryan and I developed a system. I knocked over anything on top of the cages, then threw open the doors; he forcibly liberated the creatures. I saw him grab rabbits by the ears, two in each hand and toss them onto the floor.

Then we were smashing things again. Smashing was hard work. My arms felt as if we'd been smashing for hours.

"What about the deer?" Holly asked.

I hit the side of my head. "There's gotta be a gate," I said.

I ran out and found a sliding gate big enough to let vehicles in. It was mounted with a black box that looked computer-operated. I rushed back inside to be the hero and figure out the code.

I saw a strange light flickering over the cages. Holly's voice said, "And so the brave warriors freed the prisoners . . ." She was talking to her videocam.

Megan had overruled my objection to the documentation idea. Holly convinced her that we might need the footage for a documentary on our origins. As the light flickered over my face, I tried to look swarthy and just.

"Hel-lo?" Megan said. "The gate's control mechanism?"

"I found it," Ryan said.

I flashed my light at him. He stood in front of a complex console full of buttons holding a socket wrench as if it were a tomahawk. Obviously, he was not the right guy for the job. Before I could reach him, his non-techie paws pushed random buttons, then began beating the console with his wrench.

"Goddammit, Ryan," I said. "Move aside."

Then I saw something happening in the deeryard. Lights were flashing. In panic I saw the campus police, backed up by the St. Paul police, backed up by a shoot-first antiterrorist SWAT unit of the National Guard, then realized that the strobing lights were perched along the top of the large gate, which was rolling open.

"I did it," I said. Ryan, off smashing something, didn't notice I was hogging credit.

Holly, Megan, and I stared at the deer. They just stood there, maybe waiting for the feed truck. Or maybe they weren't ready for the unknown.

We walked outside. We looked at the deer, and the deer looked back at us.

"This isn't what I'd call working," Megan said.

"Can we let them stay if they want to?" Holly asked.

"No way," Ryan said, rushing at them. "Shoo," he said flapping his arms.

The buck looked at us scornfully, even dangerously for a moment. Then he took off through the open gate with the half-dozen does behind him. The four of us applauded as flashes of white disappeared down the hill.

"At least their tails still work," Holly said.

"They're free," Megan said. "Our first official action." She sounded slightly dazed.

"Yeah, but free to go where?" Holly asked.

She had a point. The area had lots of parks and trees, but they were interrupted by benches lit by anti-rape lights. The path to freedom would be no slam-dunk.

"Whose side are you on anyway?" I hissed at Holly. "Let's get the hell outta here," I said, and I pulled Megan's arm gently.

The fence lights continued to flash. A horde of rodents was meandering around the yard. The rats and mice were mostly white. The rabbits were white, brown and calico, as were the guinea pigs. The brown rabbits, who probably had the least degenerate DNA, took off through the open gate. Most of them nibbled deer pellets from overturned feeding bowls. I was too tired to be mad at them.

I said, "Back to the vehicle!" with military conviction, and everyone took off.

We headed down the hill and across the field to Ryan's brother's truck. I tried to smear some of our tracks as I left, but it was hopeless. Then were all back in the truck, hyperventilating Ryan's brother ancient pot fumes.

Ryan got us back to the highway in silence. Just as we began to relax and breathe normally, I saw them, the deer. Something was wrong. They had miscalculated. Instead of following the thin strip of trees that would have led to a forested suburb, that granola-eating buck had led his harem onto the freeway. And this wasn't just any freeway; it was a big, hairy one, the main route connecting Minneapolis and St Paul.

"Oh-my-god," Holly said.

"Jesus Christ," Ryan said.

We watched helplessly as the deer, one by one, leapt easily over the short barrier fence and moved out onto the asphalt. Headlights lit them up from both sides.

A semi-trailer coming at us from the left, met the buck in mid-leap. He flew onto the chrome engine encasement, rolling on his back just long enough to look like a hunting trophy before he disappeared over the side. The truck jack-knifed across the highway, knocking vehicles in front of it off the road and Ryan veered with a sharp right onto the grassy shoulder. We drove along slowly at a sharp angle to the road.

"We're going to flip over," Megan yelled. She sounded nearly hysterical, far from her usual self.

Ryan slowed more as the previous summer's weeds clogged his wheels.

The cars on the freeway kept moving ahead. A Land Cruiser slammed head-on into two does. They went down, one of them caught in the vehicle's right wheelcase and dragged twenty feet, leaving a red band of blood on the asphalt. The other, stunned, ran up the embankment toward us. Her tongue hung out and her head wobbled back and forth as if her spine had turned to rubber. She practically shoved her snout into our windshield, which made the girls scream. White foam flecked with blood frothed from her mouth, spotting her white chest fur with dots of red.

I felt sick.

"We have to do something!" Holly screamed. "This is our—"

"Don't you say it!" Ryan shouted.

I looked at Megan. Her face was completely wet with tears. Her mouth opened and closed as if she wanted to talk, but nothing came out.

"We can't help them," I said, mainly to Ryan. "Just get us the hell out of here."

Ryan drove, but I couldn't stop myself looking back. I couldn't see any deer moving, only what might have been pools of blood and carcasses.

Beyond a public relations disaster for our "W" with the circle around it, I pictured other horrible things. There was reform school, where I would learn to be a career criminal. Perhaps there would be foster care, or, worst of all, endless family therapy sessions.

I tried not to imagine humans screaming in the cars and trucks we left at the site, but I heard screaming anyway. It took me a while to realize it was coming from our car, from us. I put my hands over my ears and tried to calm myself with this thought: Just deer died, only deer. But the thought made no sense, and it certainly gave me no peace.

CHAPTER TEN

AT DINNER JEFF SAID, "Obviously they were kids. The intruders were so incompetent they couldn't be dangerous." He said it while staring at me, studying my reaction.

I just shrugged and said, "Violence like that seems pointless."

But Elissa sniffed something. It didn't help that the next few nights I woke up more than once all sweaty and screaming after having nightmares about the deer on the highway. In my dreams, the buck survived and was hunting me down with the intention of impaling me on his antlers. Elissa tried to comfort me, then got suspicious when I wouldn't tell her what the nightmares were about.

Then there was that mysterious phone call from Ms. S-T, who normally never called. Afterwards, Elissa asked me all about Megan and did we have "a little political group or something?" She looked sideways at me when I shrugged and went all teenage on her.

After that, she again started bringing up the eco-therapist. She hounded Jeff about how our family needed help. When Jeff asked for evidence, she'd cry and say that he was no longer the man she'd married. Sometimes she'd cry a long time.

One night, I drifted off to sleep listening to them yelling. They covered a lot of ground. Starting with my nightmares and supported by something Ms. S-T said about my choice in reading, they moved on to the way Perry talked in rhymes. Often they ended up at the deer kill by way of Elissa's "new religion." There was even a strange fight about Jeff fixing too many things at the Hole when things around our house were in a shambles.

The following morning, Elissa announced that they had agreed to take us to see the eco-shrink, Dr. Hermes Rosen. Jeff said nothing, just nodded.

I HOPED JEFF AND ELISSA WOULD BE FIGHTING the morning of our first scheduled visit, to take the pressure off me. They weren't, which was weird. They laughed and even touched a bit at breakfast. I knew Ryan would say that meant they had sex last night, but that's just too gross to think about.

Rosen's office was in what middle-aged women call a cute part of town. Everywhere you looked were coffee shops, bread stores, educational toy stores—the kind without anything good—and gift shops up the wazoo. I will probably never know who receives these gifts and, more importantly, why.

Rosen's building looked as if it were made out of mud. Elissa called it adobe, but Jeff said it was just stucco. Anyway, it was a perfect office for Rosen because it looked like it had been clicked and dragged over from California.

A woman at the reception desk was not much older than me. This was not good. She had several earrings on each ear, a standard nose ring, and a sweet tattoo of an egret on her forearm. The office was hot and humid, full of droopy tropical plants and wicker furniture.

"We're here to see Dr. Rosen," Jeff told her as if she were challenged.

"The O'Brien-Johnsons," Jeff said. When she didn't respond right away, he added, "Are here."

"Britt," the young woman said, flashing me a look that made me want to sit down and cross my legs.

"Excuse me?" Jeff said. "You're . . . British? Is that what you're saying?"

"That's her name, honey," Elissa said as she slipped her arm through Jeff's.

"Oh," Jeff said. "As in, 'My name is Britt, I'll be your receptionist today'?"

Britt laughed. It didn't seem fair that Jeff could make her laugh.

"You're right here on Dr. Rosen's schedule," Britt said. "With the hyphen and everything."

"And is he right where he should be?" Jeff asked.

"He's just finishing up his meditation."

"Ah," Jeff said, staring in the direction of her egret.

"Would you like some herbal tea or something?" she asked.

"I'd love some," Elissa said. She put out her hand to shake. "I'm Elissa."

Britt's thin white arm, covered with Indian bracelets, uncoiled toward Elissa and reminded me of a show I'd seen on snakes.

"I'm the mother and the Mrs.," Elissa said, smiling foolishly. "But I go by Elissa, even with my kids. It's just something we believe in."

"Uh," Britt said slowly with her eyelids half open. "That's, uh . . . very modern."

I cringed, desperately wanting to give Britt the impression I had just shown up for laughs. How could I signal her that it was just fine with me if she made fun of my parents?

"Any chance I could get some coffee?" Jeff said.

"Don't make coffee anymore," Britt said. "I mean since Java Jake's opened across the street from Starbucks."

Jeff said, "Could you be a sweetheart and run over—"

"Jeff!" Elissa said. "She doesn't know you're kidding!" Turning to Britt, she said, "He's kidding. He's like that."

"She knew he was kidding," I said, and Britt smiled at me.

Jeff sat down in a wicker chair, which squeaked as he shifted around. Elissa sat on a wicker love seat at the far end of the room. She had to duck to avoid the fronds of a large plant. Perry got on his knees and crawled behind one of the trees.

Wanting to show Britt I was hardly a member of my family, I sauntered up to her desk. She continued studying a Chinese anatomy book that showed human organs as half-inflated, poorly positioned balloons. I popped a hard candy in my mouth from a dish on her desk. Silently, I gagged.

She smiled without looking up. "Godawful things, aren't they? Ginseng really sucks."

I looked for a place to spit out the candy.

"You must be Sam," she said, still not looking at me. "I heard about your group."

"Our . . . group?" I choked more seriously, then uncoolly spit the lozenge into my hand. "What group?"

"The secret one," she said. "At Lindbergh? The one with Ryan? That cute radical guy?"

"Oh, *that* guy," I said. "Yeah, he's my bud." I leaned closer and winked. "There is no secret society. Let's just keep this our little secret."

She gave me the thumbs-up and a wink, then got up and opened the door to Rosen's office. She was rail thin but muscular. "Why don't you all wait in his office?" she said. "Oh, your tea," she said to Elissa. "I forgot. I'll get it." She giggled.

"We wouldn't want to disturb his meditation," Elissa said.

"Oh, he doesn't do that in his office. He meditates in the rock room." That giggle again. "His rock zoo, I call it. Whatever."

If I lived with her for years, I wondered, would I grow to love that giggle or would it ultimately destroy us?

Rosen's inner sanctum was another bright room filled with plants. Obviously, he wanted to be in California. Everything was beige and nubby, made from pale fabrics with lots of texture. There was a salt-water aquarium with Day-Glo fish nosing the glass. Uninspired piano music came from invisible speakers, and I smelled cinnamon and lemon, like cookies made with furniture polish.

Perry made a beeline toward the sound of a leaky faucet and discovered the miniature stream on the floor by the windows. Water cascaded over round black stones poorly concealing the black plastic streambed.

I wandered around touching everything, thinking how strange it was to allow people in your office when you weren't there. The walls were covered with framed posters. One showed a climber on a rugged peak holding up his arms for the photographer, who must have been in a helicopter. The caption read, "You thought you could never go there, but here you are." Another showed a guy walking on a deserted beach. It read, "There is a place like this. It's called your dreams."

Rosen's desk wasn't much, just a low table with a round Zen meditation cushion behind it. Five years earlier Elissa had brought one of those home from a class she'd been taking. She'd sat on it while she watched a video about Japanese monasteries, then thrown it in with the other pillows.

There was also a beat-up leather book on the desk. It looked like it could contain spells and pictures of demons. A fountain pen the size of a cigar sat on top of the strange book. There was one photograph on the desk, a winter scene with a mountain in the background, centered by a tiny naked figure in a half-frozen stream. An invisible penis was hidden in black fur. I hoped it wasn't Rosen, but somehow I knew it was.

A hidden door opened and the short bearded man in the photograph walked out. The room he was leaving looked like a geologist's closet—shelves lined with rock specimens. He shut the door quickly. "Hermes Rosen," he said, mainly to Jeff.

Rosen was bald on top. He wore the hair on the side of his head long and curly, tucking behind his ears in a way no hair person would approve of. He had a full beard, and everything hairy was salt-and-pepper. At least he didn't have a ponytail. He was short, but did look strong.

He stared at us for a minute, then started making hand movements as if pulling various scents toward his nose. After an excruciating thirty seconds of this, he said, "Forgive my little rituals. I'm just taking in your energy."

"A smelling ritual?" Jeff said. Elissa nudged him, but Rosen smiled.

"You might say that."

"I've heard so much about you," Elissa said. "All my friends say—"

He silenced her with a wave. "Don't make me blush. It doesn't go with my color scheme." He seemed rude but continued to smile. I pictured him standing in that river naked. Had Britt taken the photo? Had *she* been naked?

"Sit, everyone," he said.

Perry sat in front of the fish tank. Elissa slid next to him, beaming her fake smile. Jeff and I took the two nubby white chairs facing each other. Rosen lowered himself slowly onto the Zen cushion. He opened his warlock notebook to a blank page and uncapped his expensive pen.

"How many eco-psychologists does it take to screw in a light bulb?" he said, looking at me.

I felt like a beetle on a pin.

"Are we starting?" Jeff said.

"Someone just answer," Elissa sighed.

"Okay," Rosen said. "None. Because we really don't exist."

"That's not funny," Perry said.

"Dr. Rosen's trying to teach us something," Elissa said.

"Could you call me Hermes?" Rosen said. "Or just Rosen. And you can forget the doctor thing." He turned to Perry. "It wasn't very funny, was it?"

"No," Perry said.

"Glad we cleared that up," Rosen said. "You see? This is going to be easy."

"Jeff," Rosen said in a slightly deeper and more formal voice. "Would it surprise you to hear that I am a hunter?" He tugged at his beard.

Jeff's head snapped backwards fast, almost hitting a poster of a guy surfing.

Perry slid off the couch and crawled over toward the waterfall contraption. Rosen saw him but pretended not to.

"A hunter?" Jeff said, pulling on his own beard hair. "Frankly? Yes. Yes, it does. I have to admit, I am surprised."

"Yes, sir," Rosen said. "Still a novice—always want to be, though. But, once a year, I make the trek to Northern Michigan. Petoskey area. Ring a bell?"

"I don't know about a bell," Jeff said, "but I hear the hunting's pretty good up there. Or used to be."

"*For Whom the Bell Tolls?*" Rosen said.

"I know that. Don't tell me," Elissa said. She wiggled.

"Hemingway," Rosen said a bit impatiently.

"Yes!" Elissa said, snapping her fingers.

"In my day, he was required reading in high school," Rosen said. "Not anymore. Tossed aside along with Mark Twain. What are you gonna do?"

Jeff studied Rosen as if Rosen were basically strange.

"Yes, Petoskey, Michigan," Rosen continued. "That's where the Hemingway family had its wilderness retreat. It was much wilder in the early part of the century, of course. You're right, Jeff. We have to work hard to find huntable land up there now."

I watched Perry rearranging the stones in the fake stream.

"A hunter," Jeff said, cocking his head to the side and smiling. "This isn't some kind of bond-with-the-client trick, is it?"

"Oh, no," Rosen said. "It's for real. Every year something different. One year it's game birds—pheasant and quail. Another year—whitetails, though I've only done that a few times. We eat everything we shoot. That's the whole point. The exercise keeps me honest the rest of the year so I can have my occasional steak without guilt. I've even hunted raccoons and squirrels, but they don't taste so good."

"People eat rats on television," Perry said.

"Stir fried or tartar?" Rosen laughed.

"You hunt raccoons?" Elissa said. She held her heart with flared fingers.

Rosen shrugged. "It's important not to be predictable." He winked at Jeff, but Jeff didn't smile. "Elissa?" he said. "Are you still with us?"

She had moved far back on the sofa, still holding her heart. Her head leaned against the aquarium and the fish clearly wanted to eat her.

"Raccoons?" Jeff chuckled. "I'll be."

"Look," Rosen said. "I'm not here to play one side against the other. I'm here for the whole family. Okay, quick lecture. The family as an ecosystem. Ecosystems have tensions, dynamic equilibrium, even when not particularly stressed. Family tensions arise from the clash of genetics and culture, throw in gender, sibling issues, and the quickening pace of cultural change for good measure. On top of that, there's the unique emotional, psychological and spiritual make-up of each individual, things you can't easily explain by nature or nurture."

"Isn't this a bit, well, political?" Jeff said.

"Bear with me, I'm closing," he said. "Have you ever heard of Hegel, Sam?"

He caught me drifting off into my fantasies. It felt as if I were in school. "Are they a group?" I said. "If they're rap, I wouldn't know them."

Rosen roared, "Best answer that I ever got!"

He raised one hand and looked at it.

"Thesis," he said. Then he raised the other. "Antithesis." He slapped them together suddenly. "Synthesis!"

"Synthesizer-based Euro-trance," I said hopefully.

He laughed again, but I didn't know if that was a good thing.

"You are lucky kids, Sam and Perry," he said. "Perry? Hello? Excuse me, Perry, could you please put those stones back where you found them . . ."

Perry froze with a wet stone in each hand.

"Oh my goodness," Elissa said, lurching to her hands and knees. She crawled over to Perry to help with the stones.

"You boys are lucky children. You stand at the synthesis of a new culture. From the diverse opinions expressed by your mother and father, you are in a unique position to understand the world in an entirely fresh way. That, Sam, is the music of Hegel."

"Uh-huh," I said. "I guess."

"Your mother is the Thesis. Forgive me, Elissa, if this sounds patriarchal. Your father is the Antithesis. And you boys . . ." he slapped the air again, "can make a synthesis of their understanding of the world. That's lucky."

Elissa was saying "But" as she hauled Perry back to the couch.

A smile bloomed on Rosen's face. Practiced, I figured.

"I know, I know," he said. "There's a dark side to everything. We'll get to that, but let's slow down, shall we?" He looked us over with a raised eyebrow. "So, who's our deformed frog?"

"Frog?" Jeff said, battle-ready.

"I know this one," Elissa said, actually raising her hand. "The frogs up north? The ones they've been discovering with no legs or extra legs? All sorts of deformities."

"But what?" Jeff said.

"Mutant frogs," I said excitedly, because we were on *Strange But True* territory, my territory.

"Exactly," Rosen said. "They found frogs with three eyes, like you said, Elissa. All kinds of things. At first they thought they had a frog problem; then maybe it was a water pollution problem. Possibly something related to the ozone layer."

"Global warming," I said intelligently. I held back my other, wilder and probably more true theories.

"Good, Sam. So they figured it might be traceable to human behavior. Not a frog problem per se, but a human problem."

"Excuse me, Doc," Jeff said. "This is my—"

"I prefer Rosen, or Hermes," Rosen said.

"Excuse me, Mr. Rosen," Jeff said, "but I know about that story. DNR guys worked on that. It was never clear what did that to the frogs. We worked on that until the funding dried up. It could also have been disease, a virus, perhaps stress from overpopulation due to loss of predators, sun spot activity, or . . ."

"Thank you, Jeff," Rosen said with faint but detectable sarcasm. "You fell for my trap. My point is that you can call a problem many names, but it's hard to find the cause. In many cases what's happening might not even be bad, but an attempt on nature's part to react and adapt."

"But those poor frogs," Elissa said. "I'm sure it was the chemicals—"

"Elissa," Rosen said. "I'm not so literally interested in those frogs. I'm trying to build a metaphor here. Obviously, I'm not that good at it."

"Listen, Rosen," Jeff said, "don't assume just because I'm a DNR man, I can't understand metaphor. I understand where you're going with this mutant frog thing. It's all the father's fault. Right? It's always the father with you guys."

Hermes Rosen sat there looking at Jeff for a long time.

"Wrong, sir," he said quietly. "I surprised you once; I might even surprise you twice. I wasn't going there. Nope, nope, nope. A family systems therapist might go there, yes. But not me. I'm a late-millennium phenomenon, under the wire. Let's face it, therapy's been around for over a hundred years, and the world's worse for it."

Elissa opened her mouth as if she were going to say something, but then took a deep in-breath instead. Perry slid off the couch, looking for trouble.

"I know enough about you, Jeff, to know you're not an easily categorizable fellow," Rosen said.

Before Jeff could say anything, Perry had spilled Rosen's All Natural AquaFish Salt Water Aquarium Food with Soy Emulsifiers all over the floor.

"Oh, I'm so, so, sorry!" Elissa said, and she lunged once again to her knees, grabbed Perry by the back of his shirt, and yanked him away from the disaster. She began raking the flakes into a pile with her fingers.

"That's terrible," I said as if I cared.

"Just leave it," Rosen said with a sigh.

My mind wandered to Britt. Britt would clean it up. I pictured her bending over the fish flakes. From there it was a small leap to Rosen locking her in that rock closet to make her his sex slave. Then I'd find out, and I'd contact my GreenSWAT team from a miniature cell phone implanted in—

"I think it's time we tried something different," Rosen said. "Something fun, another game. Shall we?"

Had we already played a game? I wondered.

Rosen stood and went to rock closet. He brought a rock about the size of a human head cut in half. At first he held it against his chest, dull side out, it's surface like dried lava, as dull and pitted as the surface of the moon.

"I won't go into a big description of where this rock came from," Rosen said. "This is not a magical rock, though it is a crystal. And even though one could go into a whole story about rocks, specifically this kind of rock, I won't. At least not now."

He took a breath, and I held mine.

"Let's just say this rock, as a piece of the earth—bear with me here, Jeff—is full of what you might call history. To a geologist, it has a unique story. To me, it's an object of beauty. Did you boys know that the ancient Samurai—you know Samurai, right?"

Perry leaped off the couch, pretending to attack me with a sword. "Yee-ahhh!"

"Yee-ahhh," Rosen said. "All that ninja stuff you kids are swimming in? It comes from the Samurai. Did they throw knives or practice swordplay when the big tough Samurai visited each other? No. They sat and drank tea. They admired an object of beauty the host set out. It could be a piece of sculpture, a cup, a bonsai. Or a rock.

"These big tough Samurai would talk about the object, comment on its beauty. Sometimes they would make up a spontaneous poem about it and recite it to each other. I know there's got to be at least one person in this room thinking this is sissy stuff."

Jeff and I exchanged guilty glances.

"But this is about seeing," Rosen said. "Seeing the world as it really is. We're going to take a minute to let the world talk to you. Through this rock!"

He turned the rock to face us for the first time. Its insides looked like a miniature crystal cathedral, one half of a cosmic space egg that gave birth to a crystalline superhero. Its edges were swirls of gray and white lava. Toward its center, the swirls gradually turned into clear crystals, like ice or diamonds. The closer to the center, the more purple the crystals became.

"It's beautiful," Elissa said.

Even Jeff leaned forward, cocking his head.

"Amethyst, isn't it?" Elissa asked.

Rosen nodded. "And here's the game I like to play with this particular amethyst," Rosen said. He knelt down and placed the rock on his low table. "We might call it the Samurai game. I want you to know I don't consider this magic. I'm not a big woo-woo guy."

"Woo, woo?" Elissa said stiffly. Patti called Janine's women's spirituality group "woo-woo"—meant as a put-down. "New Age, crystals, healing energies, all that?" Rosen said. "No offense, I hope."

Elissa nodded, but I could tell he'd lost status with her.

"We're going to pretend this is a talking rock," Rosen said. "You are going to close your eyes. We'll take turns. The rock will face you. All you have to do is listen to what the rock has to say. Then, you'll share."

"So it won't be confused with woo-wooing," Jeff said.

Rosen rolled his eyes. "Give me a break here, Jeff. I'm going to tell a story, okay? Everyone up for this?" He barely stopped to get an answer. "Okay, everyone close your eyes."

Rosen fingered a remote control hidden under his low table to pipe in the same sedated piano music we'd heard in the lobby. It reminded my of the stuff Elissa played in the sun porch when she did yoga. It would knock her out sound asleep, even when she was in some twisted position.

"I want each of you to take a long look at this rock. Study it. Try not to let your eyes wander to other parts of the room or to other people. When you are ready, close your eyes. Give yourselves a minute to settle into this. You do this too, Perry. It'll be fun."

Perry gave him a look.

"Everyone got your eyes closed?" Rosen asked. "Good. Now slow down your breathing. Way down. I want each of you to listen to the rock. Hold the rock in your imagination."

He inhaled loudly through his nose, held the breath, then exhaled loudly. He sounded congested.

"Now," he said in a much louder voice. "The rock will speak to you. Remember, this is a game. Okay? Ask the rock, 'What message do you have for me?'"

I shut my eyes. I saw deer-like things coming at me I didn't want to see, like the things in my nightmares. Woo-woo things. I opened my eyes, rubbed them, shut them again. The things were still there, visions of horror I wasn't going to share with anyone in that room.

I wanted to stop the game. I could ask stupid questions like I did in school to kill time or entertain the class. Was the message inside me or the rock? If I just saw pictures, was that still a message? How did I know these images belonged to me? Maybe they were gamma rays loaded with data from the Discovery Channel.

I shut my eyes again just to see if I could get away from it. Maybe the channel had changed. The answer was no. The visions, the nightmares, were all over me, running through me. Uncontrollably.

I was on the freeway with the deer herd. I was in Ryan's Die-In costume, but the others were real deer. We were all running, blinded by the headlights. We searched for an opening, a path to the forest. I watched my tribe fall one by one, and they sensed I wasn't one of them. I was just a human spy, a scientist studying their reactions to crisis and death. The big buck knew it. He approached me and pulled off my cloth mask with his teeth. He forced me toward an oncoming truck with his sharp antlers.

I opened my eyes. Rosen peeked at his watch, then closed his eyes again. "Take another minute to finish up," he said.

After what had to be five minutes, he said, "Okay. Open your eyes."

I was shaking and sweating but, miraculously, no one noticed. I was a controlled nuclear test in a granite silo. All I could think of was how important it was that Britt not see me so rattled.

"Oh, I feel so refreshed," Elissa said.

"I'm hungry," Perry said.

"Almost done, folks. Just one more thing," Rosen said. "I'll turn the rock. As it turns to you, you can tell us what you saw or heard. Okay?"

Nobody said anything. I was concentrating on looking relaxed. My breathing was more or less normal.

"Perry?" Rosen said. "Why don't you go first? What did you hear, son?"

"The rock told me to give back the Game Boy games I took from Sam."

"My games?" I said. "The ones I thought I lost?"

Rosen's waving hand cut me off before I launched into a display of outrage. "Hold it, Sam," he said. "Just make a mental note that there's something you want to talk to Perry about later."

Perry said, "Rocky said—"

"Rocky?" I said "*Rocky?*"

"I named him Rocky. The rock."

"Let it be," Elissa said.

"Well," Perry said, after shooting me a victorious pout, "Rocky showed me the time Sam put Mr. Hairy—"

"That's his ratty old teddy bear," I said helpfully. Elissa stabbed me with her eyes.

"He put Mr. Hairy on the top of the bookcase in our room where I couldn't reach. Sam said Mr. Hairy wanted to commit suicide because he got assigned to me by the demons who rule the world of toys. Mr. Hairy stopped liking Sam after this and he doesn't even like being in the same room as him. Plus," he said, sticking out his lip at me, "I didn't *hide* his games. I was helping him. Mom—I mean Elissa—says he's addicted to them. I was just helping—"

"What crap!" I said.

I couldn't believe we were paying someone money to hear this. The good news was that it worked me out of the nightmare place I was in. Anger can be healing, as Elissa would say.

"Thank you for being honest, Perry. I'm sure you and your brother can talk about this afterwards." Rosen missed the raised fist I shook in Perry's direction. "Elissa?" he said.

Elissa wiggled like a hen sitting on eggs. She straightened out her denim skirt and looked around nervously.

"I saw . . ." She glanced from Jeff to Perry, then back at Rosen. "I'm not sure I should say."

"It's okay. Trust your family."

"Well, I was walking in the forest, you know, the Wirth?" She looked at Jeff, then down at her hands. "I came upon a scene. It was a crucifixion, like in a Catholic church? But it wasn't Jesus on the cross."

"Who was on it?" Rosen said.

"A deer. A huge deer with giant horns."

"Antlers," Jeff corrected icily.

Rosen motioned him to be quiet.

"He had the body of a person, human-like, with arms and legs sort of. Like half-deer, half-human."

"Like the chupacabra in Mexico," I said. "That's a half-goat and—" Rosen shushed me.

"Yes, the big buck was crucified," Elissa said. "Like Christ."

"That's it?" Rosen said. He seemed excited. I could tell he wanted us to get messages like this from the rock. "Did the deer say anything?"

"He said, 'Do what you have to do.'"

"But did he tell you what that was?"

"She thinks she's psychic," Jeff said. "Like her witch friends. They're all psychics."

"They're Wiccans," Elissa said. "Jeff's angry because I'm joining a women's spirituality group."

"Ah, that's interesting," Rosen said.

"I thought you'd think so," Elissa said. "We're reading a book by that local shamanic guy, Stewart Spiranga. Have you heard of him?"

"Oh, yes," Rosen said. "Interesting guy. They kicked him out of the university for being a bit too radical. That was a feat. It's not easy to get kicked out of there."

"I think it was his stand on human sacrifice that teed them off," Jeff said.

"He doesn't advocate human sacrifice," Elissa snapped. "He merely thinks that our judgment of cultures that—"

Rosen made a "T" with his hands. "Time out," he said. "We're not going to be able to resolve this one today," he said. "You two could come back. As a couple if you'd like. We could have it out."

"This part of your marketing pitch?" Jeff said.

"Listen, pal," Rosen flushed red and angry. "If you were sinking in quicksand, you'd make wisecracks at the people with the rope. They could change their minds, you know."

We all sat there in shocked silence.

Rosen chuckled, "Let it go, Jeff. Let's move on." He turned the rock to face Jeff. "Your turn, big guy. Show us what you got."

Jeff looked embarrassed. I almost felt sorry for him. Perry and I looked to Elissa, but she didn't say anything. Surprisingly, Jeff talked.

"At first," he said. "Nothing. Nada. I said to myself, 'This is nonsense. This is Elissa's territory.'"

"That's good," Rosen said. "What then?"

"After a while, I heard a small voice. Then it got louder and deeper. It was an old man talking."

"Here we go," Elissa said, rolling her eyes. "I get a crucified deer, but you get God."

"Be fair," Rosen said quietly.

Jeff ignored them and went on. "The voice said to me, 'You are carrying an important message.'" He stopped and looked embarrassed again.

"That's great!" Rosen clapped his hands. "Did he tell you what message you carry, Jeff?"

"The voice said, 'You are meat.'"

I laughed; I couldn't help it. Elissa did too, but tried to stuff her hand into her mouth.

"Hey, guys," Rosen said. "A little respect here." I thought he was close to losing it too.

"Okay, okay," Jeff said. "That's what I heard. So what?"

"Is there more?" Rosen said.

Jeff shook his head.

"Got an interpretation?" Rosen asked.

"I didn't get to interpret mine," Elissa said.

Rosen glared at her.

"I don't know," Jeff said. "It's like I told the kids at Sam's school."

"Don't remind me," I groaned.

This time *I* got the glare. Elissa and I were starting to have fun.

"I told the kids that meat-eating is what made us human. It's true, you know."

We all looked at him. We were burger-eaters, waiting for more.

"God gave man this garden to use and care for, to shepherd, to husband if you will," he said.

"I hear Lenny talking," Elissa sang in a teasing voice.

"So what?" Jeff snapped. "If you can have a spiritual awakening, so can I!" He crossed his arms defiantly. "God gave us this earth to serve and protect," he said. "Like it used to say on police cars before they changed it to 'How's your self-esteem today?'"

"Oh, pul-eeze," Elissa said.

Rosen stood up and walked toward the door. I thought he was going to leave, but he stopped and squatted into a martial arts stance. He did a few very fast karate moves, a sequence I knew from Ryan was called a *kata*. He was good but looked funny. I'd never seen a short out-of-shape person try to do karate before. Apparently satisfied with what I knew to be only a partial *kata*, he walked back calmly and sat down.

"Just had to dissipate some negative energy there," he said. "Good work, every-one. Thank you all. And thank you, Rocky. You got a new name." He laughed. "As they say, first you are a rock, then you aren't a rock, and then you're Rocky."

"Donovan," Elissa said. "A Donovan song?"

"Ten points," I said.

"What did Rocky tell you, Sam?" Perry said. I was hoping he'd forgotten me. Just as I was formulating a killer response, involving Mr. Hairy's suicidal impulses, Rosen said, "I'm afraid we've run out of time, Sam. I'm sorry. I guess you'll have to tell me another time."

"Another time?" Jeff said. "But Sam's why we came. I mean, his teachers are wor-ried about him. We're worried about him. He's been having these nightmares . . ."

"I have a sense it's private?" Rosen asked me with a raised eyebrow.

I nodded enthusiastically.

"Sam, would you like to come back and talk to me, alone, sometime?"

I frowned. A trick.

"Jeez," Jeff said. "Talk about time management—"

"No one gets out of quicksand in one session," Rosen said. "Could I have a word with Sam? Alone. One minute, I promise."

Jeff looked lost. Elissa pushed him toward the door and took over. "Of course, Doctor, I mean, Rosen—oh, for god's sake, whatever. Yes, of course. We'll be out here in the lobby, Sam. Waiting."

Rosen ushered them out and shut the door.

"Sam, I know something upset you when you looked at the rock. Rocky. I didn't want to put you on the spot, especially with the, ah, tension in here. What's happening to you is complicated. You're on the verge of becoming a man. Some traditions say in order to do this, you need to be initiated."

"You mean like in a fraternity or something? Like swallowing goldfish?" To me becoming a man meant many things, but mainly having sex. I thought of Britt first, then Megan. I felt guilty Megan was second.

He smiled. "Don't we starve in the midst of plenty? No. I don't mean goldfish. Or girls, if that's what you're thinking. It's something I'd like to talk to you about in private. If you have the guts that is."

"Guts for therapy? This is a trick, right?"

"I'm a busy man," he said. "Why would I bother? Think about it. I'll leave you with this. Traditional cultures, cultures with initiation, all say your father cannot initiate you. Nor your mother either. And neither can your therapist."

"But an eco-therapist can?" I said. I was still suspicious, looking for his angle. Maybe I'd just watched too many commercials in my life.

He smiled. "A person may appear in your life. Perhaps it's a person already in your life. It could be a man or a woman. Even an animal, if you're lucky. This person would be your spiritual guide. Watch for it."

"This isn't woo-woo?" I said.

"Woo-woo or not," he said. "Watch for something to happen. Help may arrive soon."

"I'll keep my eyes open," I said.

"Oh," he said. "And don't get yourself killed while you're trying to figure it out. Let's focus on the cages we're in, okay?" He motioned toward his heart.

I opened my mouth, but he shut the door on me. My heart was beating, but I wasn't thinking straight. By mentioning the word "cages," was he signaling that he knew my Council had something to do with the deer release? Or was it some Zen saying or folksong lyric by Donovan?

When I turned, I saw Britt giving me the thumbs-up. *Help may arrive soon*, I thought.

CHAPTER ELEVEN

MEGAN LIVED IN A NEIGHBORHOOD OF LAWYERS AND CEOS. Technically her neighborhood was urban, but its inhabitants enjoyed all the comforts of suburbia. The lake near her house was featured in every poster or brochure falsely promoting Minneapolis as a tundra-free zone. Friendly modern skyscrapers rose over the trees, the joggers, dog walkers, and yuppies run-walking around the lake like butlers in nerd training. In these pictures, it was always spring, every tree and flower in bloom.

Oddly, it was on just such a stereotypical spring day that I biked to Megan's house for the mysterious meeting. I laughed to myself at the people out enjoying the sun. Beautiful people networked all around me, just like in those posters. Little did they know a subversive had just ridden past.

Megan's house was huge, with the fake "Gone with the Wind" columns. I wandered into the backyard with my bike looking for something to lock it to, but saw nothing but flowers jumping at me from every direction.

I found Megan and her parents staring at me from a glassed-in section. They looked like owlets in a nest, instinctively frozen at the approach of danger. The mother cradled a huge coffee mug with both hands. It made her head look small and doll-like. The father looked at me over reading glasses as if I were a slug approaching his garden. They both had nearly white hair like the alien children in *Village of the Damned*.

I felt myself shrinking under their gaze. Finally, Megan waved at me as she cranked open a window.

"Hey, Sam, you're . . ."

I'm what? I thought. *The gawky teen from the wrong side of the tracks?*

"Early," she finally said.

I pretended to look at my nonexistent watch, following that with a half-assed gawky shrug.

"Go around front," she yelled through cupped hands. "I'll zap the garage door. You can leave your bike in there."

Everyone knew this swanky neighborhood suffered from lousy thieves. They'd steal garbage cans, shrubs, concrete animals on porches.

I followed the humming sound to the rising robotic door. I stared at the two matching white mini-vans, classier versions than Elissa's white one.

"What's with the clones?" I said.

"A bit anal, isn't it?" she said. "Forgive them, they're Swedish. They have this super-practical blood. They think everything out carefully. You see, the vans are interchangeable. They think they're challenging the idea of individual car ownership." She shrugged. "I mean, it's original."

"Scary," I said.

She pulled me toward her and licked my ear. "I'll protect you," she whispered.

We held hands as we walked up to the front door, and I forgave her everything, including the flowers. My expectations ticked upward.

I let go of her hand quickly when I saw her parents' serious white faces gazing at me from the front porch. Up close, they looked even more like a brother and sister. They even wore matching white pants and yellow golf shirts.

"Hello, there, Sam-I-am," the father said with what you might call gusto. "We sure are supportive of what you young people are doing."

"You are?" I said trying not to sound suspicious.

As we moved into the foyer, the father moved in on me, violating my personal space. He observed me with pale husky eyes and even laid a hand on my shoulder. Without thinking, I probably looked as if I were going to bite it, and he removed it quickly.

The mother, with the same steely blue eyes, said, "You kids give me hope for the next generation. For a while there, it looked like social justice was in danger of dying out." They both laughed as if someone had said something funny.

Megan looked sheepish. She knew how weird they were.

"Mother's right," the father said, flashing a politician's smile before snapping back to a serious expression. "But we don't want any of that—what do they call it? That monkeywrenching! Eh, son?"

I did what a real spy would do if confronted by such a challenge: met it head-on. "You mean those kids who freed the deer?" I said.

Both parents moved in closer. "Why do you think it was kids?" the father asked.

Unlike a real spy I backed up, bumped into a tasteful table, and sent a glass horse crashing to the floor.

"Oh shit," I said, diving for the pieces.

The old Swedish fart was faster than me. He dipped like a seagull, snatched up the horse's torso and held it close to his chest while hunkering down a second time. We picked up pieces as if we were in competition. We grabbed a horse leg at the same time, but I pulled it away.

The mother said, "Don't worry, Sam, it's just a thing." But when I looked up, she was glaring at me. I considered crawling through their legs and making my escape through the front door. Megan could make up a story about abuse flashbacks or something.

"They're clean breaks," the father said optimistically. "I'm Dirty Harry with a glue gun. Make my day!" He pointed his index finger at me, and the mother laughed.

"Don't you have to be somewhere?" Megan asked them. "At church?"

"Oh, I wish we could stay," the mother giggled. "I would love to meet your special guest. I've heard so much about him . . ." She put her hand over her mouth. "Whoops."

"I'll tell you all about it," Megan said.

I wondered how much Megan had told her parents. First the Sam-I-am thing, then the monkeywrenching comment, now the mystery guest. I didn't like it.

"Don't get wild," the mother said without meaning it.

"Not these kids," the father said. "They're all business, business, business. Aren't you? You kids gotta save the world. No one else is doing it."

"Daddy, you understand me," Megan said, laying her head on the father's shoulder.

A bit much, I thought.

"By the way, Sam, Megan tells us you don't go to church," the mother said. "You ought to come and check out our programs for young people sometime."

"My mom's a Wiccan," I said. "Nature is her church." This caught them off guard. They looked at each other with frozen smiles.

"It's an eco-feminist women's spirituality thing," Megan added. "Sam's mom is really cool."

"You probably think we're old fuddy-duddies living here in Kenwood," the father said. "But don't be mistaken. We're activists. Like you guys."

"We do all kinds of things," the mother said. "We don't just sit around and—"

"Pray!" they said together.

"We're selling organic vegetables to stop landmines," the father said.

"Tell them about the other thing," the mother said. Her finger pecked the father's shoulder like a hungry parrot. "Tell them about the victim thing!"

"Oh, yeah," said the father. "We're bringing landmine victims here. To the Twin Cities. From all over the world. Fitting them with prosthetics."

"Prophylactics?" I said deliberately.

The father reddened and pronounced the word for me. "Pros-thet-ics," he said, over-enunciating each syllable. "Artificial limbs? Minneapolis has been in the prosthetics business since the grain mills started whacking off workers' limbs left and right." He made chopping gestures.

"Father," the mother said. "They don't want to hear about the family business. We sold that business a long time ago, dear. He still loves to talk about it, though. You kids get on with your meeting. I'm sure you'll have lots to talk about."

"Saving the world takes a lot of elbow grease, right, Sam?" The father winked at me. "No time for foolishness."

"You bet," I said. "We're not like normal kids with all their sex, drugs, and rock and roll." I gave them a big grin.

"Sam-I-am!" Megan laughed while she punched me hard on the arm. "Always the comedian." She glared at me, but her parents laughed as if I were Johnny Carson's ghost.

I opened my mouth to say more, but Megan stepped on my toe.

The mother blew Megan a kiss as she pulled the father through the front door way.

"Jesus, what were you doing?" Megan said. "Trying to get them to distrust you?"

"Sorry about the horse," I said. "They made me nervous."

"They like you. So far. Don't blow it. Let's go down to the rec room. Holly and Ryan should be here any minute."

"Rec room?" I said. My cynical side had been held back for too long.

"You got a problem with that?"

"And how come they know about the mystery guest?"

"I had to tell," she said. "You'll see."

The day took a downtick as I imagined some old Unitarian geezer telling us about sit-ins in the seventies. I followed Megan down the carpeted stairway to the rec room, which looked like a set from *The Brady Bunch Go to Sweden*.

"So this is a rec room," I said, more cynically than I felt.

A jumbo screen TV sat in front of a sectional sofa, its wall-mounted speakers placed strategically around the room. A recent model Macintosh sat on a little desk in the corner with a screensaver fading in and out on pictures of vanishing wildlife. I recognized the slimy salamander that stopped a dam project somewhere.

Someone had arranged three black snack bowls neatly on a low black table. The shiny Asian-style table reminded me of Rosen's desk. One bowl brimmed with whole cashews. Another had trail mix. The third had two kinds of cheese chunks, some of them stabbed with toothpicks. Little black cocktail napkins fanned out next to the bowls.

"Mother," Megan shrugged. "What can I do? I'm stuck with her."

"It's cool, Megan," I said. "Really."

"Oh, right," she said. "I'm sure you're thinking, 'How can they call themselves progressives while they live like this?'"

"I'm sure you put the room to good use," I said. "Showing sex education movies to landmine victims."

"Hel-lo?" she said.

"On how to use prophylactics," I said.

She burst out laughing, and watching turned me on.

The doorbell rang, and she charged up the stairs soundlessly, taking several at a time. The sign of a leader, I'd read somewhere.

I examined a peanut during my taste-tests of the snacks. It was Megan who told me how commercially farmed peanuts are nearly toxic with pesticides and preservatives. I popped it into my mouth assuming this one was organic. It was also unroasted and unsalted. Un-everything. I spit it into a black napkin and looked for a place to toss it.

Holly and Ryan came slowly down the stairs, touching. They had a whispering thing going on that made them appear more couple-ish than ever. Holly looked tired though.

Ryan cased the place like a burglar. I looked at his square jock face and rumpled good looks with my usual mixture of envy and resentment. He even had a lock of blue-black hair curving casually onto his forehead like Elvis.

Megan called down that she was bringing drinks.

I held a bowl out to them. "Care for some Corn Chex surprise?"

Holly recoiled and turned to Ryan. "See?" she said.

"Nice electronics," Ryan said. He walked over to the big TV and picked up two remotes, one in each hand. "Bam! Bam!" He shot the screen and it snapped on to the Discovery Channel. Elephants in crisis. He shut it off.

Holly sat on the couch and began petting her own forehead.

"You okay?" I asked.

"Bad aura day," Ryan answered for her.

"Shut up," she snapped. "You don't know the first thing about auras." She pet her brain again. "Why are we here, anyway? This place is so pre-SLA Patty. It gives me the creeps."

"Lighten up," I said. "They use it to entertain amputees."

Megan appeared holding a tray of drinks. She paused in the middle of the stairs. The girls stared at each other for a moment. Whatever went on between them was off my radar.

"What's with the Patty Hearst thing anyway?" I asked Holly. "Can't you find someone more current to obsess about?"

Holly turned her acidic gaze on me. "Maybe I should pretend I'm a world-famous eco-terrorist? With—what is it—GreenSWAT?"

I looked for Megan, wanting to hurt her for revealing what she alone had known. She was conveniently offloading sodas from a black tray.

"So what if Megan's parents are rich?" Ryan said. "Isn't that diversity?"

"Doesn't apply," Holly said.

"What the hell are you talking about?" Megan said coldly.

"Look at this place. Isn't that teak?" Holly said. "Hundreds of refugees could live here."

"You wouldn't know teak if . . ." Ryan said. He frowned, unable to complete the thought.

"It infected you with ebola," I said for him.

"Better close your mouths before your brains drops out," Megan said. "None of you has the slightest idea what you're talking about."

"Duh, I'm just a dumb jock who wants to be a famous actor . . ." Holly said, mimicking Ryan.

"Shut up, Holly!" Ryan shouted.

"Abuse! Abuse!" Holly squealed.

"Dammit, Holly! Shut up!" Megan said. She was losing it. A single tear from her right eye wandered down her cheek.

"Yeah, shut up," I said. "Everybody."

"So what if I have problems?" Megan said, and I wondered if she meant the rec room problem.

"I'm sorry," Holly said. "I'm just queen bitch today." She pressed her palms to the side of her head. "Maybe I'm jealous," she said. "My house is so Kmart. Drunken Kmart with drunken Kmart furniture. Drunken Kmart dinners." She erupted into body-wracking spasms of tears. Suddenly she and Megan were full-contact hugging. I wondered what breasts would feel like pressing against each other.

"Have a healing Corn Chex," Ryan said to Holly, holding one up with his fingers.

Holly took it with her long brown fingernails, then began to giggle. "I actually like Corn Chex," she said.

Over their hugging heads, a pair of legs in camouflage pants and black army boots was creeping down the stairs. A terrorist had entered Megan's house.

CHAPTER TWELVE

MY EYES WENT WIDE, NOT YOUR MOST IMPRESSIVE GreenSWAT-trained reaction. Megan followed my gaze and broke off her hug with Holly. "Stewart!" she said. "Why didn't you didn't ring the bell?"

The adult she called Stewart walked among us. He was an aging boomer, roughly Jeff and Elissa's age, only scruffier and wilder looking. He had a rounded Scandinavian face dominated by a bulging forehead bordering on Star Trekkian. His straggly reddish hair was gathered into an unfashionably long ponytail, a soul patch of red whiskers sprouting just below his lower lip. His outfit looked consignment shop paramilitary. He walked over to the TV.

"Cool," he said. "I practice my traditional stalking skills whenever I get a chance. Spent a week in the forest with Tom Brown to learn that. I call it shamanic activism. That's a new synthesis I've trademarked."

"Beyond cool," Holly said flatly.

Stewart shot her a look, then moved to the snack bowls. I smelled garlic, cigarettes, and boot polish as he passed me.

"I'm talking about real stalking here," he said, "not following celebrities. Stalkers have to be unpredictable. Why, you ask? Because nature is unpredictable. Wiggly, snaky." He did a curvy thing with his hand before it dived into the cashews. "The Japanese call that gyo."

"You're Stewart Spiranga?" Ryan said with barely suppressed celebrity worship.

"Oh-my-god," Megan said. Her hand shot to her mouth like that of a ditz. "I'm sorry. Introductions. Yes. This is Stewart Spiranga. The Stewart Spiranga, the famous activist."

"I don't value fame," Stewart said.

"Unlike us mortals," Holly said.

"I admit it was a little weird getting off my motorcycle out front," he said. "I'm a little out of place in this neighborhood."

"Che Guevara visits the White House," I said without looking at Megan, and Stewart laughed. One point for me.

Megan forced us to sit in front of Stewart on her sectional sofa as if we were going to watch a birthday party magician. Holly and Ryan snuggled together looking anything but radical. Megan sat upright, uncomfortably alert.

Then Stewart reached into the pocket of his baggy combat pants. He drew out a closed fist, crouched down, and opened his hand. A white disc about the size of four stacked poker chips sat in his palm. I guessed electronic, something you'd find hanging in a plastic bag at RadioShack.

He wiggled his eyebrows as he pulled another handful of the things from his pocket and tossed them onto the table. We stared at them stupidly.

"The body of Christ?" Holly said.

I noticed how Stewart had already learned to ignore her.

"Technology," he said. "It can work for you!" he said in a mock radio announcer voice. "These, my friends, are mess-with-a-hunter buttons. Trademarked." He laughed.

"I hope they're not explosives," Holly said. "I couldn't . . ."

"They're not bombs," Megan said. I sensed she already knew all about them. She wore this fake reporter frown she'd use in class when she held back for the sake of dumb kids.

Stewart explained they were component parts of a stick-on doorbell system. Digging into another pocket, he came out with a remote control. He aimed the device at the pile of buttons. They began to dance and shriek like a litter of high-pitched car alarms.

Holly held her hands over her ears and shouted, "Make them stop!"

Stewart aimed the remote, pressed, and the buttons stopped. "You can't buy them this obnoxiously loud," he winked. "I had my electronics experts modify them."

"You want us to do something with these?" Megan said carefully.

"I get it," I said. "You sneak up on a sleeping deer and attach a buzzer to each one. Then you zap them awake on the big hunt day. Easy."

"Not that far off," Stewart said. "You're the guy with the DNR dad, right?"

I flushed with shame. Megan touched my arm.

"But he's very against all that," she said.

"Cool," Stewart said. "We'll come back to that."

I wasn't sure I liked that, but I now carried a hint of specialness.

"No offense, but you guys lack leadership and direction. Disorganization ends up in fiascoes like what happened with those deer at the university. I mean, whoever might have done that . . ." He tisked. "Amateur shit. Amateurs make us look bad. I'm sure you guys wouldn't do anything that stupid."

He knows! I thought.

I looked at Megan to see if she looked guilty, but she stared straight ahead. Stewart got up and began pacing.

"Let's just say whoever did that was lucky they didn't get caught, okay? Rumor has it the cops are still looking for the so-called criminals."

"Why do you keep bringing up that deer action?" Ryan said, glaring at Megan.

"Just a random example," he said, obviously lying. "Let's move on. Let's focus on messing with the DNR."

He looked at Holly and frowned. I followed his gaze. Holly had curled into a fetal position.

In a tiny voice, she said, "Those poor deer. So awful. All the blood . . . their faces!"

"Holly," I said. "Get it together." I flashed Ryan a do-something look.

"Oh-my-god, oh-my-god, oh-my-god," Holly said, covering her face with her hands. "All I can see is blood!"

Ryan turned to Stewart and said, "She really loves deer. She taped the TV coverage and watched it over and over. No one could stop her."

Stewart grinned, "Sensitive is good. Just not here."

Megan put her hand on Holly's shoulder. Holly whimpered and jerked as if she had a serious nervous disorder.

"You gotta have backbone for this kind of work," Stewart said.

"She's got all kinds of backbone," Ryan said to Stewart. Speaking sweetly to Holly he said, "C'mon, Hol, snap out of it. You're freaking everyone out."

I drifted back to that scene on the highway and remembered the doe looking in through the windshield.

"Sam?" Megan said. "You too?"

I shook my head.

Ryan rocked Holly like a new parent. "I think we can go on now," he said.

"People aren't doing enough," Stewart said. "Not nearly enough. No one around here is ready to die for this thing."

"Die?" Megan said.

"I could see myself dying," Ryan said, nodding with his chin sticking out. "But I'd want people to know why I died."

"Like the SLA," Holly said weakly.

Stewart pulled a chair from the computer table. Facing it away from us, he sat on it backwards.

"People say we're too civilized to die for what we believe in. Mindless soldiers can die for what the bosses say we believe in. The ancients believed that, to keep the world running right, people had to give real sacrifices to the gods. Sometimes a life. Your own, maybe. Or maybe your child's."

"We're against that sort of thing," Megan said. "Aren't we?" She fidgeted uncomfortably.

"The gods get their sacrifices from us whether we like it or not," Stewart said. "We just call it violent crime, or terrorism, or war. Call it whatever you like, but the gods still get their sacrifices."

"I didn't expect this to be so . . ." Megan said.

"Woo-woo?" Holly said from Ryan's lap.

"Let me ask you a question," Stewart said. "Do you know why primitive people made animal and human sacrifices to the gods?"

"We don't call them primitive anymore," Megan said. "Our teacher, Ms. S-T. She says——"

"Cut the PC crap, Megan," Stewart said. "I'm way past that. You won't hear what I have to say from any of your politically correct teachers."

Megan rolled her eyes and sighed. The sigh wiggled through her entire upper torso.

"I'll tell you why I can call them primitives," Stewart said. "Because I am one." He puffed out his chest and pointed his thumb at his left pec. "We primitives believe that the gods want blood." He sighed. "Too much for you guys? Did any of you see that issue of *National Geographic*, the one where they found the frozen kids up in the Andes Mountains? I know you saw it."

I shrugged.

"Now that was a little hard on your multicultural crowd, explaining how it was okay to sacrifice children to the weather gods," he said. "Okay then but not now. Right? You want to know a secret?"

"Sure," I said.

"Some cultures are smarter than others. The trick is knowing which is which. That's not as easy as it sounds. Now take your human sacrifice, for example. It has a much longer history than any other form of worship. You call what the Unitarians do in their church worship? You think the gods care about social justice in Nicaragua?"

"Of course they do," Megan said quickly. She looked up at the ceiling a moment and added, "Which gods are we talking about exactly?"

"Bingo," Stewart said. "Not only which gods, but the right gods."

"How can a god be right or wrong?" Holly said.

"The devil's wrong, stupid," Ryan said to her.

"Let's not go there right away, Ryan," Stewart said. "Let's say the right gods are the ones that are truly effective up there, like good lobbyists." He laughed, but none of us got it. "And even if we knew who the right gods were. What would they eat? Prayers? Oh, Lord, won't you buy me a Mercedes Benz?" He laughed. "Are we feeding them what they want?"

"I really don't get this," I said. "Why do we have to feed gods anyway? I mean— they're gods. Can't they just eat whatever they want? Or not eat? Why do they have to eat at all?"

"I'm not sure why we're even talking about gods," Megan said. "What does this have to do with deer?"

"Bottom line? No bullshit?" Stewart said. "You remember the Rolling Stones?"

"Geezer rock," Ryan said. "Made some good songs, shoulda retired twenty years ago?"

"Yeah, right. One of their good songs was *Sympathy for the Devil*. Remember that?"

"I hope this isn't going toward Devil worship," Megan said.

"No, not there," Stewart said. "Just the facts, ma'am. But think about it. Who is whispering in the Tutsi's ear that he should go kill his neighbor the Hutu? Who's convincing some suburban kid with a videogame for a cerebellum that he ought to break into Uncle Buck's gun cabinet and blow away his classmates? It's all the same thing. Hungry gods. They're doing the whispering."

"You're talking about Satan," Ryan said as if he were going to do something about it.

"Oh, grow up," Holly said.

Stewart shook his head wildly, his wispy hair floating. "That's not my scene. Let's cut to the chase. We got ourselves an out-of-balance world precisely because we're trying to think our way out of it, trying to manage it, make everyone go home happy. Life as a non-competitive sport. Ha! Anyone notice this isn't working? Now, let's take our situation here at Wirth."

"Finally," Holly said.

"Some people say the Wirth's got too many deer. Other people say the problem is too many hunters. Another bunch of do-gooders think they can outlaw death, starting with these here precious bambis. Let me tell you something—they're all wrong."

"What do you mean outlaw death?" Megan said.

Stewart slipped into a falsetto voice. "Retrain those nasty carnivores in the wild to eat soybean mush." Dropping back to his regular voice, he said, "The gods won't stand for that shit. I kid you not. That's why, before this thing is over, there's going to be some deaths. There has to be."

The Council exchanged looks.

"Did you ever wonder why hunters are such a clumsy lot, shooting themselves accidentally or shooting their kids or the neighbor's cow? It's those hungry gods again. Call 'em the gods of ecology, if it that makes you feel better. Whatever they are, they seek balance. The circle of life, like in *The Lion King*?"

I laughed, and he nodded at me and smiled.

"Human blood must be shed along with the animal blood. We eat animals, slaughter millions of them every year. Humans have to die too. Indians knew this."

"We don't call them that," Megan began before she bit her lip.

"So we're back where we started," Ryan said, "dying for a good cause. You call it human sacrifice to make a point. I can dig that."

Something was bugging me. I snapped my fingers. "Michael Blaine," I said. "He said something like that. You sound like him. My dad says Blaine just tries to piss everyone off. To make them think." I pointed at him. "You're Michael Blaine!"

Stewart laughed a laugh that looked real.

"I've been called worse things," he said. "Blaine has his uses. But Jesus, Sam, he's just a comedian. I'm serious here. I'm not here for my health. Or my ego."

"Yeah," Megan said. "Michael Blaine? Sam, why are you listening to him?" She turned to Stewart. "My parents are going to be back soon. I don't want them hearing us talking about human sacrifice. These things." She picked up a handful of the white disks, then put them down quickly. "What exactly do you want us to with these?"

"You'd get grounded good for human sacrifice," Holly said.

"Yeah," Ryan said, "a whole week without Corn Chex surprise!" They howled meanly.

"Children!" Megan said.

"Oh, ouch," Holly said.

"You *are* acting like children," Stewart said. "Knock it off. The action is a piece of cake. Before the hunt, one of you guys sneaks into the Wirth and places some of these babies . . ." He picked up a white disk and held it up to his eye like a patch. "At sites likely to spook the deer into a major stampede. When the rednecks are out there in their blaze orange, we blast the buzzers, freak the deer. We'd like them to run right out of the park so we can get it all on video. Or maybe live television."

He smiled like an evil clown and aimed his remote at the buttons. They shrieked to life, hopping around the table. Holly screamed and covered her ears.

"Jesus Christ!" Ryan yelled.

Stewart shut off the beepers with his remote.

"Jesus," Ryan said. "Then what was all that human sacrifice talk? What was that all about?"

Stewart shrugged. "I just wanted to give you the big picture. We're hoping that some of those nutso hunters shoot each other. Of course, it could be dangerous for the person that sets up the buzzers. Some of our people could get hurt."

"Won't the gunshots chase the deer out of the park?" Megan asked.

"They're limiting the hunt to bow hunters," Stewart said. "None of you know this? Sam, you should know this."

"Bow hunters?" I said. "I dunno. Maybe Jeff's hiding stuff from me about the hunt."

"That wouldn't be good," Stewart said, and I wanted to ask him why, but I didn't.

"Why can't you set the buzzers out? Why do you need kids like us?" Holly asked.

"It's a range issue, isn't it?" Ryan said. "You need to activate the buzzers from inside the park. And since they don't have timers, someone near the hunters has to activate the buzzers."

"Impressive," Stewart said.

"For him, it's miraculous," Holly said. But it was teasing, and they tickled each other.

"Check this out." Stewart stood up and stretched one arm straight while pulling the other one back. Clearly he was shooting an arrow.

Holly said, "Robin Hood?"

"I'm a bow hunter," he said. He looked disappointed as he sat back down. "You guys don't get it, do you?"

"How many syllables?" Holly said.

"Our people will be infiltrating the hunters," Stewart said. "We can trigger the buttons, but the buttons have to be placed the night before. Chances are the DNR pigs will be expecting adults to do the monkeywrenching. We have to concentrate on acting like hunters. We need someone they wouldn't suspect. Someone small. Some without a record. Someone who might be able to move freely around the pig camp."

He looked directly at me, but I looked down immediately. My heart pounded.

"Someone who could get into the core group of the hunters. Someone who can slip into the forest without being noticed."

Ryan said. "Cool. You need a James Bond type, an infiltrator. I can do that, no problem." He shook his head hard. "Who am I infiltrating?"

"The power core, which in this case is an interesting cult. They call themselves the Hunters of Men. Can you believe that name? They're Christian bow hunters, a fundamentalist Masonic lodge sort of thing full of DNR guys, cops, firemen. Rumor has it they'll have the inside track on the permits."

"Hunters of Men?" Ryan said. "Sounds like a bunch of losers. Maybe you'd be a better choice than me, Sam."

It was a decent joke, but I wasn't in the mood.

Holly giggled and slapped him. "Let's kick this idiot out, Megan," she said.

Stewart's face moved close to me. I could smell his garlic and natural toothpaste breath.

"I was thinking of someone," he said, "close to the DNR. Someone who could learn a lot by being on the inside."

"How inside is inside?" I asked.

"Deep inside. I want someone to infiltrate the Hunters of Men."

"That's got to be you, Sam," Megan said, surprising me. She'd known Stewart would go here all along.

"Tham-I-amth's tho thweet," Ryan lisped, and he made kissy smooches at me.

Stewart snapped at him, "Cut that shit, asshole."

"Whoa," Holly laughed, covering her mouth.

"Me?" I asked. "Why me? Everyone knows how I feel. Everyone knows I'm against my dad."

"Do they, Sam?" Megan said. "I mean, really?"

I felt desperate but told myself not to look it.

"What about my mom—Elissa? She'll never believe I changed overnight. She knows how . . ." I stumbled, "smart I am."

"You could pull it off," Megan said. "I mean it would be hard and everything, but you said yourself that your parents are so distracted they're hardly noticing you. I mean, you told me what Rosen told your mom about initiation and all that. You could go over to Jeff's side and pretend it was about becoming a man and all that crap. You're set up perfectly for that."

"Especially when they don't care about you," Ryan added, back in his helpful mode.

Megan was right. I could do it. But why? Wasn't my life complicated enough? What would I get out of it?

Megan came closer to me, touching me on the arm. My skin tingled under her fingers. "It's got to be you, Sam," she said. "You're strong enough, brave enough, smart enough . . ."

"Cute enough," Ryan added, and Holly hit him with a pillow.

"Can you help me with Elissa?" I asked Megan.

"Sam, fooling your parents is not as hard as you think," Stewart said. "Just don't spring in on them all at once. Practice disagreeing with your mom by siding with your dad. Do it gradually. Be irritating. Be unpredictable. Be a teenager. You can do that."

"I could help," Megan said excitedly. "If I treated you like a jerk."

"So what would be different?" Holly asked.

"You'll be like a GreenSWAT agent, but for real," Megan said. "In your own house."

"GreenSWAT?" Stewart asked. "Am I missing something?"

"Nothing," I said quickly. "Just a private joke."

"Not a thing," Holly said. "Believe me."

"We could go to the Little Creatures Workshop," Megan said. "Sam's mom is practically running things over there these days, she and her posse of witches. I mean Wiccans."

"Those peacenik puppeteers?" Stewart said. "A big waste of time except when they do get the press to come out."

"Isn't she always bugging you to go there, Sam?" Megan said. "I'll go with you. We'll argue in front of her. We could have a big fight. I could call you names."

"You could rip off your shirt and whip him," Ryan said. He stood up miming the scene.

"I thought I told you to shut up," Stewart said.

Ryan crumbled. I'd never seen anyone put Ryan down so effectively. Maybe I could learn things from Stewart after all. Maybe, in some weird way, my mentor had just appeared.

Megan and Stewart exchanged a look. They'd had this all figured out. Megan was the key. I felt a flush of anger, but it was quickly replaced with an image of Megan and me kissing passionately.

"I'll do it," I said.

"Then it's settled," Stewart said way too quickly for my taste. He started gathering up his buzzers. "Make it so."

We all heard bumping around sounds upstairs.

"My parents," Megan said, her little kid hand over her mouth.

"Hello down there!" Megan's father sang out. "Is everything all right?"

"Just great," Megan sang. "We're just finishing up. They're dying to meet you," she said to Stewart. "They've read your book. I'm sure that's why they came back early."

"I thought we were trying to keep this low profile," Ryan said, but everyone ignored him.

Megan's parents waltzed down the stairs as if we were having a cocktail party. "Yoo hoo?" the mother said. They introduced themselves to Stewart with utmost awe.

"I told our minister you were coming to our house, and he was very excited," the mother gushed. "He wants me to ask if you'll come speak to our congregation?"

Before Stewart could answer, the father jumped in. "I want to hear about your leaving the university. Too progressive for those old geezers, huh?" He was all buddy-buddy in tone.

"They don't like us action folks much," Stewart said with a bit of a fake country accent he hadn't used with us.

"How true, how true," the father said. He clapped Stewart on the back. "Can't wait around for academics to save the world. Not like when we were in school. We closed down—"

"I'm sure Mr. Spiranga knows all about the sixties," the mother laughed.

"The kids need history," the father said.

The adults drifted upstairs, talking about a speaking engagement at the Unitarian Society. Ryan and Holly went back to cuddling on the couch. It was an opportunity to slip away, but I wanted to do it with style. I wanted Megan to notice, run after me and say something sweet like she wished her parents would go on a long vacation.

Instead, she drifted upstairs—to be with them.

CHAPTER THIRTEEN

THE DNR HATCHED A PLAN TO GET ALL THE VARIOUS deer kill factions to talk to each other, though it sounded more like putting them into a hot school gym so they could yell at each other.

They chose Lindbergh High, which was not entirely a coincidence. Katami, disappointed that inventing Ecoday hadn't landed him on the cover of *Progressive Principals*, had come to Jeff with the offer. What this meant for me was sitting through Katami's closed-circuit transmissions on how our schools might "facilitate healing forums for communities in crisis." Facilitating another shot at publicity is what he meant.

Then Megan began to get email instructions from Stewart. She read them to the Council excitedly. Unfortunately, Stewart nixed our cool ideas for disrupting the DNR's meeting. Without going into detail, let's just say they involved rats, cockroaches, and lots of ketchup. Stewart said we should concentrate on his original plan, which he called "Operation Green Bond."

I thought about pretending to be on Jeff's side so I could infiltrate the Christian underground. I was certain I could pull it off. It wasn't like anyone was tracking me too closely at home. Jeff stayed overtime at work planning the big meeting with Lenny and his DNR gangsters. Elissa was also out all the time, either with her Wiccans or her computer clients (often they were the same). Now her volunteer work with the Little Creatures of the Forest Puppet Theater was ballooning into a second career or third career, depending on how one counted.

Perry and I bonded around lying to them, saying with straight faces how we "thought" the other parent said they'd be home early. It was better than divorce; no one had custody.

Perry and I enjoyed being latchkey children. We ate microwave pizzas and popcorn for dinner every night, watched as much TV as we wanted, played *Corridor of Blood,* (an M-rated video game for extreme, realistic violence we borrowed from Ryan's older brother). We splattered bad guys' brains in narrow virtual tunnels until we fell sleep without brushing our teeth.

Megan hatched a plan to visit Elissa at the puppet theater and stage a fight with me. It was supposed to be part of my conversion to bad thinking. I was a bit uncomfortable with how excited Megan got about it.

———

THE DAY WE BIKED TO THE LITTLE CREATURES WORKSHOP, Megan showed up at my house in a Lycra racing outfit and the aerodynamic insectoid helmet of a serious biker. She even had racing goggles. I almost didn't recognize her.

"What are you doing, Megan?" I said.

"Biking?"

"Your outfit?" I added.

"What about it?" She took off her helmet and shook her hair in a way I'd seen only on TV. "Remember, we're working undercover," she said.

"How does your outfit relate to arguing in front of Elissa? That's what we're going to do, right?"

"It'll help me be a little meaner than my ordinary self," she said. "I've been thinking about how we could do it. You start criticizing the Little Creatures, and I defend them. Call them sexist, homophobic and racist."

"Racist?" I said.

"Elissa can't handle all those at once," she said. "Nobody can. It's a PR trick." She winked. "I'll play the good guy to Elissa, the mean bitch to you. Be prepared. I'll have to call you names. I think I might enjoy being a bitch."

"You usually do," I said. Recently she'd liked it when I called her this.

"Fucking A," she said, tossing her hair like that shampoo model.

I concluded this mixing sex and danger was Megan's way of getting serious about Operation Green Bond. She was being a Bond girl if I was being a Bond guy. The good news was this meant eventually we'd have sex, like at the end of every Bond film.

"You're wearing that?" she said, frowning.

I looked down at the same baggy blue jeans I'd worn all week. My ratty Earth-Death T-shirt was from a special almost-clean pile. Latchkeys don't do much laundry.

"And what's with the backpack?" she added.

I didn't want to say it contained essentials such as my latest science-fiction novel.

"Tools for survival," I said. "I'm on assignment here. You're not the only one undercover."

"The question remains," she teased. "Whose covers are you under?" This was the Lycra talking, I was sure of it.

Ryan had told me that when women ovulate, their hormones make them more receptive to sex. He had said when a woman suddenly teases you or flirts with you in a new way, she might be ovulating. Ovulating meant horny, and he'd said guys have to pass information like this on to each other like they do in tribes. You won't find it written down, he said, and to check it out, I searched my mother's sex library, skimming *Our Bodies, Our Selves* and *The Joy of Sex*. I'd found interesting drawings of women looking between their legs with a mirror, but nothing that said teasing meant a woman wanted sex.

So now I looked at Megan with my version of a knowing, worldly smirk. I concealed the fact that having sex with anyone other than myself seemed more remote than starring in my own GreenSWAT movie.

"Perhaps," I said slowly, "you'd like to come back to my place? After our little adventure, I mean. Perhaps shower off some of that gorgeous sweat and snack on, say, microwave pizza and popcorn?"

"That doesn't sound like you, Sam-I-am. I thought you didn't like green eggs and ham."

It was an old joke. She slouched toward her new mountain bike with a model's walk, knowing I was watching. Then she giggled, hopped on her fancy bike and took off.

Over her shoulder she yelled, "Maybe you could eat them with a fox in a box!"

I tore after her on my beater bike.

"Yes. I would eat green eggs and ham," I yelled. "I would eat them, you fox!"

We laughed and raced like normal kids.

My house was down-market from Megan's: this wasn't news. She would know this, I assume, even though I've never had her over and probably never would. What I noticed as we rode through my neighborhood were the vehicles. There were rusting Ford Explorers, black Chevy Blazers with boat hitches and oversized tires, and endless beaten-up minivans, most plastered with bumper stickers advocating some way the person reading them ought to change.

As we rode east toward the center of the city, we went further down-market: pre-airbag Caprices with side mirrors held on with duct tape, Gremlins and Hyundais of indeterminate year, heirloom Chrysler LeBaron monsters.

I felt intensely alive riding with Megan. I was surging with dizzying alertness, like the time I lost track of how many espressos I pounded down at Starbucks and explained the whole Narnia series to someone who didn't care.

We rode past Latino groceries, African-American hair braiding salons, and bars with names like Yukon Territory. The streets began to have real pedestrians on them, not just joggers or people rushing off to have manicures. Somali women with covered faces walked in little groups, carrying bags from Jerry's Food World. Two cops had a small group of black kids against the wall and were frisking them. By Minnesota standards, we were in Harlem.

We spied our destination, a converted porno theater The Little Creatures had taken over. It still had the old name on the marquee, "The Classic." We locked our bikes to a mess of metal that was either a bad sculpture or a bike rack hit by a truck. I tried hard to look streetwise and relaxed but at the same time checkout the young African Americans hanging around us.

"They're looking at your bike," I whispered to Megan.

"Don't be racist," she said. "Maybe you're hanging around your dad too much."

The theater smelled bad. I wondered if there were some smells you can never renovate out of a porno theater. There was mildew, roach killer, old paint, and probably other smells no one likes to think about. I smelled a whiff of sage too. Elissa used to sage our house every time she and Jeff had a big fight, though she hadn't bothered to do it in a long time.

The deserted lobby looked like Mexico before the Spanish destroyed it, the walls covered with murals of hefty Aztecy-looking goddesses. The goddesses could have been sisters with their straight black hair and hawk noses, though each had a different skin color—brown, red, yellow. Human and animal skeletons danced in the background, happy, it seemed, to be dead.

"This is really something," Megan whispered. "It reminds me of the Day of Dead stuff I saw in Guadalajara."

"Cool," I said. "That's exactly what I thought. Mexico."

She nudged me with her elbow and whispered, "Practice disagreeing with me."

"Mexico?" I said loudly. "Are you kidding? It looks a lot more like . . ." I drew a blank, then flashed on a picture I saw once in art class. "Tahiti."

"Tahiti?" she laughed harshly. "That's so dumb!" She forced a stagey laugh.

I didn't know if I was going to like this.

"Sam! Over here," Elissa's voice rang from one of several dark doorways leading deeper inside.

She burst out of one of them and attempted to hug me. I dodged it expertly, almost tripping her.

Regaining her balance, she studied Megan's tight outfit. "Megan, you look . . . different. Good different, I mean."

"Hello, Mrs. O'Brien," Megan said.

"Call me Elissa."

"Do I look good different too?" I said.

Elissa's face fell. "Aren't those the same—"

"Yeah," I said, rubbing my shirt. "They are. It's my look."

"The murals are so wonderful," Megan said. "I was just saying how this reminded me of Day of the Dead."

"You've been there, right?" Elissa said. "Sam told me you showed slides to the class. Last winter, right?"

Elissa suddenly looked sad and sighed. "I've always thought we'd all go someday. Take the whole family. Well, someday I'll go. Maybe alone."

"What's the connection with Day of the Dead anyway?" I said, trying to change the subject.

"The Little Creatures?" Elissa said, and she went into a mini-trance, then snapped out of it. "Oh, they look at the dark side of life, but in a celebratory way. Like their politics. They attack many kinds of evils, like capitalism or HMOs or genetically altered food, but they do it in a fun way. Very un-American to be playful with one's criticism, don't you think?"

"Cool," I said like a teenage idiot.

Megan elbowed me, reminding me to be antagonistic.

"I mean," I said. "It's cool in a hippie sort of way, isn't it? Like you have fun with all this stuff and think you're changing things when you're really just having fun."

Both of them looked at me as if I'd spoken in tongues.

Elissa's smile went brittle. "Well," she shrugged, "we old hippies still run the place, for better or for worse."

"She's right, Sam," Megan said. "We owe so much to the hippies, really. Even though . . ." She stopped and scratched her head. "Things have gotten a lot worse."

"Let's change the subject," Elissa said. She began speaking with drama, like you do when you read to a child. "Inside, you'll find some secret preparations taking place. Some of those old, ineffectual hippies are planning a major protest."

"What are you protesting?" I said.

"That bogus community meeting the DNR is planning. We're gonna bust it up." She pointed to her breasts with two thumbs and made a tough-guy chin.

"Jeff's meeting?" I said, not faking my outrage.

"I don't care whose meeting it is. It's bogus, stacked against the deer, stacked against justice. We can't allow this charade."

"But," I said, "they're working so hard. They're trying to invite . . ."

"Who? Oh, his little friend Patti and that Prop19 group? All they care about is urban planning. People, not deer!" It sounded bad put that way. "And the Audubon Society? Give me a break."

She studied me for what seemed like a minute.

"Something's wrong with you," she said. "You're spending too much time with Jeff! Look at what's happening to your thinking!"

"Yeah, you jerk," Megan said. "I told him that. What the hell's wrong with you?"

Elissa and I both looked at Megan.

"Well, you're still my son, and I have a right to influence you. You better not speak a word of this to Jeff, though. I'm warning you, Sam. If you ever want to play another videogame in your life, that is!"

She turned her back on us and began walking away.

"Come on. Maybe you'll get into the spirit of it when you see the workshop."

Megan whispered to me. "Good work, Sam. You really looked like you were defending your dad."

"Thanks," I said in my Bondian way.

Something bothered me—a lot. I wasn't acting. At least, not consciously. Perhaps, I told myself, I was method acting.

We followed Elissa into the main theater, a dark, cool room with an empty stage and rows of scrappy chairs. Graffitied Greek statues stood at either side of the stage. The guy statue wore a tunic and tested the air with his finger. The lady balanced a vase on her head. You could see where the graffiti showed through like scars under makeup.

Elissa's tour was geared for fellow conspirators. Apparently I was forgiven for my lapse into Jeff-loyalty.

Behind the stage there was a passageway, very Batcave-ish. The crude doorways were just holes in the wall. Elissa turned and said apologetically, "They're gonna clean these up one of these days. But they've only had this connecting space for three years."

"Whoa," I said, and I stopped dead, gaping at the huge space opening in front of us.

It could have been a medieval army camped around many fires, all the bodies busy with some task. Fluorescent ceiling lights glowed like UFOs. Clip-on lamps lit up the small working groups.

We walked down a cluttered path to one of the work areas and smelled fresh paint, sawdust, and traces of marijuana. College age kids with Rasta hair placed strips of wet newspaper on chicken wire frames. They wore paint smocks that looked like recycled canvases of abstract art. Other groups painted papier-mâché masks of animals and odd beings. Women putting together costumes and flags were bent over a line of whirring sewing machines. Mythic beasts were taking shape all over the room.

Perry bounded up to me, all smiles in his dirty paint smock. He tried to hug me; but I dodged.

"Hey," I said, "don't get paint on me."

"Sam, I'm going to be a deer!" he said.

"They're letting little kids be in the protest?" I asked Elissa. "Isn't that dangerous?"

"Dangerous?" she said. "A DNR meeting? You got to be kidding. Everyone's going to be asleep. We'll be like a halftime show."

"But you're not on the schedule," I said. "What if there's a riot?"

"Sam," she sighed, "the Creatures have been doing stuff like this since the sixties. Give them a little credit, huh? People know this is theater. They'll respect that."

Perry took me by the hand and showed me the mask he was painting. It had a vaguely deerlike snout but was blue with yellow dots. All around us adults and children were painting similar heads in similarly realistic color schemes.

"There was a reason I wanted to show you guys what we were doing," Elissa said with a guilty smile. "I don't know what you're planning in that little group of yours I'm not supposed to know about . . ." She looked at us for a reaction, got nothing. She shrugged. "Why don't you guys join us? We can always use more actors. Sam? I understand you had practice with dying deer?"

I panicked, thinking she was referring to the deer on the highway.

"You mean on Ecoday?" Megan said. "Sam was marvelous." She flashed me a look, reminding me of our mission to be irritating. "Wait—Sam didn't actually perform that day."

I started to deny any involvement, then caught myself. "I don't know," I said. "Ruining Jeff's meeting? Endangering children? And what about all the people who come to listen? You're just going to wreck it. Mr. Katami says we should be facilitating healing forums for communities in crisis!"

Megan laughed. "Since when are you listening to Mr. Katami? I can't believe you said that. Just yesterday, you said that was all a . . ." she looked at Elissa, "bunch of crap. What's gotten into you, Sam? You think this so-called healing forum will help the deer?"

A woman wearing a Honeywell Heavy Chem III gas mask ran toward us carrying a small dry-erase board to her chest. In the dark cavern, Janine fit right in for a change. She whipped out a marker and wrote. "We got problem!"

"What's wrong?" Elissa said loudly. "An accident? An auto accident? Oh my god!"

Janine shook her head angrily. She wrote, "Patti coming here. MAD!"

"Mad?" Elissa said, instantly switching to mad from horrified. "About what?"

"Who's that?" Megan whispered to me. She nodded at Janine.

"Patti's girlfriend," I said. "You know, the lesbians who own the Hole? Patti's the super-activist one, Janine's the woo-wooer."

"Oh, *those* lesbians," Megan said, nodding. "Cool." She frowned. "But what's with the gas mask?"

"E-I," I said, liking how it rolled off my tongue.

Megan cocked her head. "Environmental Illness," she said, switching to encyclopedic mode. "Allergic to synthetics, pesticides and . . ."

"Yeah," I said.

Janine was agitated beyond writing now. She dropped her board and started jumping up and down like an old-fashioned punk dancer. She was pointing at Patti, who charged down the aisle toward us, went right up to Elissa, took her by the elbow, and walked her a few yards away from us. Janine stopped jumping and crossed her arms. She breathed heavily.

I strained to hear, but they were just out of earshot. Then their volumes began rising. I heard Elissa's familiar mocking tone, the one she used on Jeff so effectively. Elissa was in fact saying something about Jeff. I heard his name.

Megan whispered, "Should we leave?"

I gave her the *are-you-kidding?* look.

"I can't believe you're taking Jeff's side on this," Elissa was saying. "This hurts, Patti. You're killing our friendship along with those deer. And to think you were practically my best friend."

"We studied it from all sides, Elissa, believe me," Patti said. "I wanted to tell you personally. It's the best thing. You don't have to agree with me, but that's what we decided. All of us, the whole committee."

"Who are you kidding? You *are* that committee. This will hurt. They'll use this as proof of division in the community. I thought that's what Prop19 was all about. So-called community!"

"Don't take this so personally. There's room to disagree here. And yes, we are working on community. And we've got reasons to go along with the DNR on this. That doesn't mean we buy everything they say. But look at your own position. What's it based on? Nostalgia? Sentimentalism?"

Janine made a growling sound and began jumping again. So they were fighting too. She wrote on her board, "Kill Bambi = Sentiment?"

Patti yelled over to her, "Yeah! Exactly!"

"You're supporting the deer kill?" Elissa said. "Siding with the DNR? I can't believe my ears."

Elissa held her heart and looked around for support. This was no longer a private conversation. Other people in the room were gathering around us as the argument grew louder.

"Did they offer to support your precious Prop19? That's it, isn't it? You cut a backroom deal."

"Oh, grow up, Elissa," Patti said. "You know better than that. It was a tough call if you cut out all the Bambi crap. I have to announce it at the community meeting, but I wanted you to know first." She shot an angry look at Janine. "Before we had a press leak."

"I know what you did," Elissa said. "A backroom deal with Jeff! You two have fun working it out?"

Patti looked at Elissa as if Elissa were nuts. "Get a life."

"I'm trying to hold onto the one I have, thank you very much!"

"What are you talking about?" Patti asked. She lowered her voice and tried to say something just to Elissa, but it was too late. Elissa had an audience.

"You know very well what I mean," Elissa said. "You and Jeff!"

Megan looked at me bewildered. "What *are* they talking about?"

I remembered Jeff and Patti flirting and how strange I felt about it. Lesbians should have made Jeff uncomfortable given his recent swing to the right. But Patti didn't. In fact, he now seemed to find excuses to "fix things" at the Hole even more than he used to.

"I have no idea," I told Megan.

"In case you haven't noticed," Patti said. "I'm a dyke, Elissa."

"Then why don't you act like one?" Elissa shouted.

The group of mask painters around us was getting noisier, talking, and arguing among themselves, pushing up against us from behind. Janine was next to me trying to write something. Her motions were spastic, her writing practically scribbles.

Patti walked and stepped up on a small platform. Suddenly she was much taller than the rest of us.

"Look, you guys," she said. "Things are complicated. What you heard is true. The Prop19 group is pulling out of the Wirth coalition."

The crowd made mumbling noises.

"We looked at the facts and the wider issues of communal sustainability. I know it's not pretty, but if you take out the sentimentality, look at the watershed issues, the destruction of the forest . . ."

"Traitor!" someone yelled.

Patti ignored him. "It's a bigger issue. This emphasis on the deer ignores the urban realities."

"Save the deer!" another male voice boomed from somewhere in the crowd.

"All life is sacred!" said a pleading woman's voice.

"Save the deer!" a new voice shouted.

Patti looked more energized than frightened by the confrontation. She looked fierce, her crescent-shaped earrings swinging like tiny scythes.

"Listen, people," she said. "I'm not here to rain on your parade. I think it's great that you express your opinions. That's community as far as I'm concerned. Protest all you want. Mix it up. So what? They can deal with it. But just don't make the mistake that everyone who disagrees with you is evil!" She pointed at them dramatically.

"Evil, evil, evil," some smartass chanted.

Janine was hopping around again.

The smart-mouth chanted, "Evil, evil!"

Others chimed in: "Save the deer!"

"Fucking dyke!" someone shouted.

"Who the hell said that?" Patti yelled as she pushed into the crowd. For a moment it seemed like a rock club, Patti diving into the mosh pit.

Janine was grabbing at her mask with shaking hands. She didn't look good. Instinctively, I grabbed her by the arm and shoved my way through the crowd. Given the way Janine clutched my arm, I knew I was doing the right thing. There were actually fewer people than I imagined, but I pushed a few of them anyway.

I headed back through the various rooms with their distinctive smells, flashbacking on a Greek myth Elissa used to read to us, Perseus and the Minotaur. When I saw the giant Aztec women lounging on the walls of the lobby, I knew I was home free.

Janine and I stepped outside into the bright sunshine. She pulled off her mask and took big gasps of air like astronauts in bad science-fiction movies who shout, "It's air! I can breathe!" But to her, air could be liquid cyanide.

"You okay?" I asked.

Janine continued to take deep breaths while digging her claw grip into my forearm. "Thanks." Inhale, exhale. "Sam." Inhale, exhale. "I-am." A weak smile.

"Well, the air isn't great out here, either," she said gasping. "With the street traffic and buses and all." She paused for a breath. "But it's breathable, that's more than I can say for that place. Something was clogging up my mask. I don't know. That's not supposed to happen. Maybe it was a psychic attack of some kind."

"Maybe you just had to get out of there," I said. "Your mask was taking care of you."

My eyes wandered to the bike rack thing.

"Shit!" I said.

My bike was still locked to the battered sculpture, but Megan's was gone. "Someone stole Megan's bike!"

"That's so sad," Janine said.

"Sad?" I said, feeling pure shame. My crappy bike didn't even interest thieves. I imagined kids laughing at it while they rode away on Megan's.

The theater doors burst open and bodies spilled out—Patti, Megan, Elissa, Perry, and a bunch of people in smocks. At first I thought everyone was laughing. Perhaps they were, like the thieves, laughing at my bike.

I was wrong. Some were laughing, but not a friendly kind of laughter. I caught words: Patti, Prop19, deer kill, ridiculous, betrayed.

Megan came up to me with her hands on her hips. "Where did you go?"

"He saved me," Janine leaned on my arm and stroked my hand.

"What happened?" Megan said.

"Something with her mask," I said. "But I have to tell you something." I nodded toward the bike rack sculpture. "Your bike's gone."

"Oh, great!" she said. She ran over to the twisted metal sculpture and kicked it. "Why didn't they take yours?"

"Look at it," I said.

"Oh," she said more quietly.

Elissa came over to us. I talked fast, explaining Janine, her mask, the bike that was stolen, and, most importantly, the bike that was not stolen.

"At least you still have one," she said, missing my point completely.

Patti and Janine leaned against their turquoise minivan. They talked intensely, gesturing wildly. Patti reached out and began stroking Janine's hair. They hugged.

Patti walked over and said, "Thanks for helping Janine, Sam. I wasn't exactly in a position to." She looked around at Elissa, Megan and me. "I guess we're all on different sides at the moment, but I hope it won't affect our friendships."

I let her hug me, a special treat for her for having had such a hard time. She smelled like organic hand cream, lemon, and wheat germ. For a panicky moment, I felt like crying. I guess those endless afternoons at the Hole meant something to me, even though I'd always said I hated the place. Patti and Janine were family to me. I didn't want anyone to hurt them, even the people on my side.

Patti said, "Wait a second, Sam. I've got a book for you. I'll get it."

As Patti ran back to her van, I found Elissa and Megan both glaring at me. Neither looked happy. Maybe I was doing something right. Megan and Elissa were supposed to be together. Me and Jeff—and now Patti—were together.

Patti opened her van's sliding door and rummaged through a straw basket. A tall thin woman in a blue dress with stars all over it came up to Elissa.

"Multi-user server?" she said, smiling and pointing to herself. "Remember the clueless one?"

They hugged and began discussing computer networks.

"Meg," I whispered. "We aren't really fighting, are we? I'm supposed to be helping the other side."

"Sure, Sam," she said irritably. "Can't you tell I'm acting too?"

"Not really," I said.

"Here it is," Patti said as she returned, breathing heavily. She handed me a book. "A friend lent it to me, so I want it back."

I wasn't prepared for this tattered book with an old-fashioned drawing of a Plains Indian on the cover: *The Sacred Rites of the Lakota Sioux*. I studied it, puzzled. It looked like something from an antique Boy Scout troop.

Megan grabbed it out of my hands and paged through it.

"Don't be too rough with it," Patti said. "It's old."

"I bet it calls them redskins in here," Megan said, furiously turning pages. She turned back to the inside cover. "Aha," she said. "Copyright 1939! I knew it."

Patti took the book gently out of her hands and handed it back to me. "Excuse me, but I don't think history began in 1975."

"I know that," Megan said. "But most of it was written by white males. Racists. Why are you giving this to Sam?"

Patti said, "Girl, why don't you go explain to those African-Americans why deer they'll never see ought to be the top priority in their lives."

Elissa came up behind Megan and put her hand on her shoulder. "Megan. Sam. Don't fight. This is upsetting and confusing for all of us. We'll process it on the way home. And don't try arguing with Patti. She's too good. This has been a long time coming. She doesn't value the spiritual side of all this. The souls of animals are just as—"

"Stuff the woo-woo crap, Elissa," Patti said. "I think this Wiccan thing is really softening your brain."

Elissa saw the book in my hands. "What is that? Propaganda?"

"Some kind of racist thing," Megan said.

"Oh, that's good," Patti said. "All books are propaganda. Elissa, you know I'm not a big Native American rah-rah person, but our committee spent lots of time studying their traditions. I learned a lot. It had an impact on our decision."

"Native Americans lived in harmony with nature, everyone knows that," Megan said. "If this book says anything different, it's a lie. I know a lot about Native Americans. In school we studied—"

"Listen, Pocahontas," Patti said. "What's wrong with you activists—as you call yourselves—is you've got no appreciation of history. All you animal rights people and New Agers just ransack Native American culture, taking all the feel-good shit. What's the expression? 'Take what you like and leave the rest?' You hang your little dream catchers in your cars, burn sage, and pray to the four directions, but you toss aside anything that doesn't fit in."

Elissa said, "Like what?"

"Ecological damage that native cultures perpetrated on the environment. Or the constant tribal warfare even before the white men came."

"She's ranting, kids," Elissa said. "It means nothing. Let's go."

Forcing myself to stay in Operation Green Bond, I said, "Wait, at least we can let her finish."

Elissa showed her teeth at me.

"And what about women's rights?" Patti said. "You just ignore women's problems in Native American culture because it suits you. Widows had a rough time of it. And female babies went into the stewpot during famines, I kid you not."

"You can't compare . . ." Elissa said.

"What about hunting?" Patti said. "Paleo-Indians put one heck of a lot of Pleistocene mammals on the extinction list."

"Says who?" Elissa said. "I never—"

"What about ceremonial cannibalism? Or the ritual murder of children to appease the weather gods?"

"That wasn't the Native Americans," Elissa said. "That was cave people. You're sounding like that Stewart Spiranga, talking about human sacrifice. It makes me ill."

Megan and I shared our first conspiratorial look in a long time. Why was everyone bringing up stuff like this? It was spooky.

"Thanks a lot, Elissa," Patti said. "Low blow on the Spiranga thing."

"What about speciesism?" Megan said.

"Speciesism, girl, is just sentimental crap," Patti said. "You're avoiding history. You're avoiding anything that challenges your precious, simplistic Disney view of good and evil."

We all looked at Patti in horror. Talk about low blows. Being called of "Disneyish" was the worst.

Janine, with her mask on, walked over and held up her dry erase board. It read, "No Listening!" She nodded vigorously while pointing at each of us individually.

Patti laughed at her board. "Welcome to history, people. Listen, it's been fun, but I gotta go."

She disappeared behind her van and reappeared getting into the driver's seat. Janine mumbled unintelligibly, but moved to the van and got in. She rolled down her window. Patti leaned over her, gesturing for me to come closer.

"Sam!" she called.

"Don't go, Sam, she'll only pollute your mind more," Megan said, gripping my arm.

I pulled away and ran toward the van.

"Be careful with that Stewart," Patti said. "I know you kids are talking to him. He might be a little crazy. Tell me you'll be careful."

"I don't know what you're talking about," I said.

"Just be careful," she said with a sigh.

"Just because he's on our side doesn't mean he's crazy," Megan said directly into my ear.

"You don't know what you're getting into," Patti said, more to Megan than me. "Just check it out. Be careful, all of you. I mean it. No bullshit."

CHAPTER FOURTEEN

I SHOVED *THE SACRED RITES OF THE LAKOTA SIOUX* into my backpack and headed toward Uptown, where the remnants of punk culture survived shoulder to shoulder with the Gap latte world and newer variations of hiphoppity cool. Its best feature was that it had plenty of coffee shops, including my favorite, The Angry Cup.

I don't really like coffee, but there were times when the only legal drug for people my age was called for, times just like this, when I needed to stew in my own brilliance and watch my angry coffee thoughts race by until I was exhausted. This would take a while, but I had the time.

I got a triple espresso and opened the *Sacred Rites of the Lakota Sioux* to a drawing, a boy in a loincloth standing in a forest at night. The trees looked threatening, like in a Grimm's fairy tale illustration. The boy held up a long pipe as its smoke formed the bodies of a bison, a wolf, a bear, and an eagle. Something to do with Boy Scouts, I assumed.

I turned to the copyright page that had upset Megan and found something she had apparently missed. The owner had written his name in a fancy script, "Please return this book to H. Rosen."

I closed the book quickly and asked my angry coffee buzz the meaning of Patti being connected to Rosen. I didn't get more than my initial impression that something dark and conspiratorial was at work. I sat a moment, looked around for something else to read, found nothing, then reopened the book. I read the whole thing in one sitting.

I should say I'm a fast reader when I want to be, especially when I'm angry and have had only sugar cookies for dinner.

The book was better than a lot of science-fiction books. Better still because it was true, more or less. By the time I looked up from it, dark clouds were gathering on the horizon for a serious summer storm.

I did not head home. I knew I'd find Elissa and Jeff arguing, or, at best, Perry alone wolfing popcorn and playing *Corridor of Blood.* I needed a secret clubhouse or special spot to go to. I thought about Elissa the night she came home and ended up in the room over the garage. No, I wouldn't go to that garage. I decided to go to the Wirth.

THE LONG RIDE GAVE ME TIME TO BROOD and freak myself out about the storm. I had images from *The Wizard of Oz*—me as Dorothy getting swept up in a suspiciously gentle tornado, which landed me in my GreenSWAT future.

I took the road that runs along Minnehaha Creek. One side was forested park, the other expensive houses. I could hardly stand looking at the lighted squares signifying human habitation and its grim domestic scenes. The dark trees were much more comforting.

I got angrier. I made up a rap lyric and sung it over and over. *Screw them all. Screw them all. Get a stick and beat them all.*

By the time I got to the park entrance, I felt as if my evil twin or someone had driven me here against my will. A sign said bikes weren't allowed on the trails. I'd been in the Wirth at night before, mountain biking with friends a million years ago. We broke all kinds of regulations and felt tough. We pretended to be at war with hikers. Kids' stuff by today's GreenBond standards, but the gentle hiker folk could surprise you and chase you with sticks like Neanderthals if they caught you on their trails.

The parking lot was empty—but handicap accessible. The porta-potty still lurked reassuringly in the bushes where I remembered it. Another sign said the park closed at sunset.

I had to admit fear was beating out anger. I thought of Elissa wandering out here alone. I was concerned with my beater bike and how it would handle these trails already damp with dew. If I were Elissa, I'd send positive messages to my trusty pony. She would tell me to be "one with my bike," repeating her favorite phrase: "Fear is the mind killer."

And thinking these things did help. I got past the signs, the porta-potty, and the worries about my tires. Riding up the path, I suddenly felt great, barely angry anymore. I changed "*Screw them all*" to "*Go, just go. Ride, just ride.*"

And I rode excellently. I was a sneakers commercial. *Go, just go.* Just do it. The wind kicked up and whipped through the trees. It was corny, but I'll admit I talked to my bike. I told it that it was my friend. I talked to the moon, which was almost full. It said it was my friend too. Even the pine branches slapping me in the face were my friends. Things were going my way; I would be all right.

I rode and rode, hardly noticing where I was going. I thought I knew this park well, but it was a big place, miles and miles, really. Jeff always said it was a miracle for a park of this size to be so close to a second-tier city. I rode until my muscles ached.

My joy didn't last forever. The evil twin part of my mind started playing that old Talking Heads song about psycho killers: *"Psycho-killer, qu'est que c'est? You better run, run, run, run awa-a-ay!"*

Once it got into my mind, I couldn't get rid of it. I was running deep, deep, deeper into the hands of the psycho killers.

I tried to think of an antidote. That was the first time I thought about Rosen's Lakota book. It said the Sioux warriors would greet the day with, "Today is a good day to die!"

Then fear and fatigue opened a door to the dark side. I made deals with myself. I said I'd rest at the top of the tallest hill in the park. How far could that be? It was hard going. Finally, I had to walk my bike up the last few yards.

Branches swayed and reached at me. Psycho killer fears gave way to your classic ghost fears, zombie fears, and fears of wild animals escaped from the zoo. Even Blaine's weird story about released mountain lions came back to me. Would his listeners be inspired to do what he said? Or would they know it had been a joke?

From there, it was a short distance downhill, emotionally speaking. I ended up feeling stalked by the chupacabra, the vampire-goat-zombie-killer-thing from Mexico that hitched a ride across the border in truck of illegal aliens, murdering them all. The puzzled police couldn't figure out the bloody mess. Sam O'Brien's body was never found.

I moved on to witches, perhaps the scariest because I knew they were real. What if I came upon a coven of middle-aged Wiccans dancing naked around a fire? What if my mother was there?

I made it to the top of the hill and sat on a huge rock, which was still warm from the day. I added thirsty on top of everything else. I thought about my dad, how he always says you should never go into a forest without at least a water bottle. "People die first from thirst," he'd say. "Remember that. First rhymes with thirst."

I lay down on top of the smooth boulder and hugged it for warmth, pressed my cheek against it, and closed my eyes. I pretended that the rock was Megan and kissed it. "Megan," I said, "this is the perfect place to do it. Our secret spot." I even thought about humping the rock.

That's when I heard the first rustle. It sounded very close. The sound came a second time, and my heartbeat kicked in harder. I sensed somebody or some *thing* large was moving into the clearing.

"Who's there?" I said like people do in stupid movies.

Eets only me, senor, El Chupacabra.

I tried the Marine approach, ordering myself to relax. "Sam-I-am," I said to myself, "knock off these ridiculous childish fears, you pussy. Who do you think you are? Perry? Jesus H. Christ!"

The rustle came again. I waited to face my death.

Instead, it began to rain. Friendly little pit-a-pats, pit-a-pats all over the place like that awful chorus in "Bambi." I looked up and fat raindrops hit my face. Maybe this was the thing I sensed, just the rain starting. I was sensitive, attuned to nature.

Then I saw it. Something was there. My heart kicked into a faster beat, and I couldn't inhale. My muscles went limp. I couldn't have run to my bike if I wanted to.

It was a deer, the huge buck. He stepped out of the forest and into the clearing. I'd seen racks like his on a cover of Jeff's *Outdoor Life* with bylines reading, "Where to get the big ones."

The deer walked closer to me. I had flashbacks to the university and wondered if he knew about that. He was much larger than the university buck. I opened and closed my eyes a few times. If he were a hallucination, he would disappear. Then he snorted and stamped the ground, his breath came out as a white cloud. He was Big Buck—no doubt about it.

Possibly he knew I was responsible for the death of his kin on the highway. He was sent here on a mythical mission of revenge. He was going to kill me. I wondered how long it would take him to charge and how it would feel to be impaled.

I thought of Rosen's book. Could it be possible that this was the moment they talked about, when the young man meets his spirit guide and gets his new name? In the book, not only did the Indian boys fast and pray, but they stood in loincloths for days with their arms outstretched. All I'd done was ride my bike and skip dinner except for sugar cookies. No way was I an initiate. I was just a hungry, cold, thirsty and tired American kid on a trail he shouldn't be on.

Big Buck raised his head as if he had heard my thoughts. His ears moved around like radar scanners. I pictured him dead, on the cover of one of Jeff's magazines, held up by a smiling man in an orange vest. The thought should have filled me with guilt, but it didn't.

Big Buck was looking at me. Was he trying to communicate? What? Could he want to be on the cover of that magazine?

I decided I was hysterical in a quiet way. My science-fictional caffeinated mind was getting the better of me. Something else was happening. What did the book say? The Lakota said, that to become a man, a boy must go into the forest, alone. His power animal will come to him—and choose him, like Big Buck was choosing me. Maybe Big Buck was in fact my power animal. Maybe he understood how human society had degenerated beyond the Lakota's worst nightmares and I was the best he could get.

But his tribe had degenerated too. They were practically pets now, giant squirrels. Maybe Big Buck understood that I was the closest thing he was going to get to a guy on a vision quest. Maybe he understood it was Sam O'Brien or nothing.

He exhaled a cloudy breath and jumped back from me, his whole body moving in a quick jerk. Then, as suddenly as he appeared, he reared up like a horse, turned, and leapt into the brush. He was gone.

Instantly, I missed him. I sat there, hardly breathing, watching the hard rain all around me. I might have been crying. Tears mixed with the rain on my face, and I tasted salt. The rain was coming down faster and harder. Part of me was saying, *"What a baby you are!"*

But I couldn't help it. I picked up my bike and walked it down the hill, looking in the bushes every now and again to see if he was watching me.

* * *

Yellow shafts of light beamed from my house as I approached. I thought of using this energy-wasting scene as an attack point. Go on the offensive right away. But once inside the door, not only the offensive strategy, but my whole strange night faded away.

Both of my parents sat on the couch. I braced for a confrontation, a barrage of questions, anger, embarrassing expressions of worry.

But no, they remained calmly reading. Was it a trap? Had they planned this? My stomach noticed the remains of snacks near them, an empty bag of Doritos and a Diet Coke on Elissa's end table. Jeff's side had a jar of honey-roasted peanuts (only half-finished, I could see) and a couple of alcohol-free beer bottles.

"Do you know you have every light in the house on?" I asked.

"Excuse me?" Jeff said. He turned theatrically to Elissa. "Did you hear someone enter the room? Someone we've been worrying about and waiting for?"

"Sorry I'm late," I said. "I had . . ."

They stared at me.

"Business." I salivated, edging toward the peanuts.

"Business," Jeff said. I assumed he was trying to stay calm, but he wasn't that good at it. "Which business would that be, Sam?"

"This isn't how we said this would go," Elissa said to Jeff. She came over and hugged me. "I'm glad you're safe. What happened? Where were you?"

"We give you a lot of freedom to come and go," Jeff said, also getting up and coming over. "But this is taking advantage."

"I, uh, had a lot to think about," I said.

"It's past midnight," Elissa said. "I called Ryan's. I even called Megan's parents, thinking you might have gone over there."

"You called Megan's?" I said.

I pictured the husky-eyed Unitarians realizing I not only broke crystal horses but wandered at night like a homeless person. *"I know he's a nice boy, Megan, but really . . ."*

"I also called Holly's parents," Elissa said. "They didn't seem to know who you were though. They worry me."

I went for the couch, grabbing the peanut jar on my way.

"Don't sit on the couch!" Jeff yelled. More gently, he added, "You're soaking. I'll get a towel."

He pulled a straight-backed dining room chair over for me to sit on. He got a beach towel from the linen closet and threw it over my shoulders. I managed to stuff a handful of peanuts into my mouth. My head was a jumble. Why hadn't I thought about what to say to them?

"You're muddy too," Jeff said. He took off my boots in an oddly sweet gesture. That instantly turned into a search for evidence: "This isn't dirt from the road. Where were you?"

"I took a walk." Breathe, I reminded myself. "In the Wirth."

"When it was closed?" Jeff said. He stood up and paced, still holding my muddy boot.

"I know it was wrong," I said. "Is there anything else to eat? I'm starving."

"Didn't you get any dinner?" Elissa said. "I knew it."

I finished off the nuts and went for Elissa's Dorito bag. I shook some orange crumbs into my hand. Elissa headed off for the kitchen.

"Sam," Jeff said, staring at the orange flakes now all over the carpet.

"Any lemonade left?" I yelled at Elissa.

"Excuse me?" Jeff said. "I don't think we're done talking about your behavior here, young man."

"Sam, honey," Elissa sang from the kitchen. "Come in here and help me get you a proper snack. Then we'll talk. We'll be out in a second, Jeff."

"He needs help to get a snack?" Jeff said. "Our great big night traveler needs help getting lemonade?"

As soon as the kitchen door closed behind me, Elissa moved in, her face ripe with conspiracy. "What really happened?" she said.

"Elissa, I saw him."

"Who?"

"Big Buck. In the Wirth. I saw him. He talked to me. Sort of."

Elissa took a few steps backwards, holding her hand against the small purple flowers on her flannel nightgown. She closed her eyes as if she were going to faint, but I knew she was only "having feelings."

"You *talked* to him?" she said. Then she frowned. "Was Ryan's brother with you?" she asked.

"No. No drugs. None at all. You know I don't do drugs. I just heard him—in my mind. I mean his mouth didn't move like animals in Disney movies. It was a mental thing, mostly."

"Oh, Sam, I'm so happy for you," she said quietly, her eyes filling with tears. "Well, what did he say? Can you tell me?"

"I'm not sure you're going to like what he said." I wasn't sure I knew what I was going to say he said.

"Why not? What did he say?"

"He said he had to die. For his people."

"Really?" she said, and her mouth opened. She didn't seem angry. I thought she would be. I continued improvising my story.

"Yes," I said. "He said as the prince of the forest he had to die. Like a sacrifice. To save his tribe."

"This is so, so weird," she said. "It's just the vision I had with the rock. In Rosen's office. You remember. The tarot card of the hanged man, only it was a deer?" She looked out the kitchen window into the dark night. "I think I know what this means."

"Oh?"

"The king must die," she said. "It's an old Celtic thing. Well, many cultures have something like it. To insure a good harvest or whatever, the king must die for his people. Sometimes it's the real king, sometimes a special king. Christ, you know, was just a variation on this . . ."

Something was wrong. She was too happy about all of this. I wasn't supposed to be in here bonding with her around magical animals. My new GreenBond identity demanded that I piss her off. I was blowing all the progress I'd made that afternoon at the Little Creatures.

"But," I said, "what I think he was saying was that it was okay for the hunters to shoot him. Maybe it would be, like, okay for the king to have his head mounted on the wall. That would be the sacrifice."

Her faced narrowed in anger. "Goddammit," she said, pointing a finger at me. "That really pisses me off, Sam. I thought you were being serious. Don't mess with me like this."

Jeff called out from the other room. "What's taking so long in there?"

"One second," Elissa sang back cheerfully. "We're out of lemonade. I'm making some fresh . . ." She took the pitcher out of the refrigerator, poured it down the drain, and got a can from the freezer in a smooth motion.

"But you said the gods want a sacrifice," I said.

"Hold it. Hold it one second. I never said that. It was that Stewart Spiranga who said that. Is that where you're getting this?"

"No. How could I?" I said. "I just thought maybe the deer weren't so . . ." I could hardly say it, "upset about the hunt. Maybe they understand that."

"It's Jeff," she said. She made the lemonade while she talked. "You've been spending way too much time with him. I sensed it. I've been away too much lately. This has to stop. Tell me where you're getting these ideas, Sam. Is it Jeff?" She raised a wooden spoon as if it were a weapon.

"It's the book. The book Rosen gave me."

"When did Rosen give you a book?"

"Well, Patti actually gave it me. But it was from Rosen."

"That book Patti gave you at the Little Creatures? Aha! So she's behind this. Oh, great. So it was propaganda. Now she's trying to convert my son."

"What book?" Jeff said as he pushed his way into the kitchen. "What's this about a book? I heard Rosen's name, Patti's name, something about a book. I thought we were going to discuss this stuff together."

"Your little friend Patti gave our son some kind of book," Elissa said. "He claims it's Rosen's, which I can't believe. I think Patti's working on him to turn traitor. There, now you're up to date. Happy?"

"Sam?" Jeff said. "What is she talking about? What book?"

"A book on the Lakota Sioux initiation," I said. "It's an old book. Just on Indians."

"So what's the big deal?" Jeff said. "How could a book—"

"Megan said it was racist or something," Elissa said.

"She doesn't know anything about it. She just assumed that from the date it was printed," I said.

"Where is this book?" Elissa demanded. "I want to see it. Jeff, maybe it's one of those Hunters of Men things."

"El, I have no knowledge of this book. Let him talk, for Chrissake."

"It was interesting," I said. "All about hunting and vision quests and, well, different ways the Indians had of connecting with animals."

They both looked at me. I was definitely on stage. I didn't know what to say next now that I had both of them in rapt attention.

"That's why I went into the forest. I was confused. I felt, in the forest, that if I contacted nature . . ."

"The forest is a good thing," Jeff said. Elissa nodded, and I remembered: the goodness of forests was one of the few things they both still agreed on.

"It's what one does in the forest we disagree about," Elissa said as if reading my mind.

"And when I saw the deer," I said.

"What deer?" Jeff said.

"A deer that talked to him. Tell him that, Sam. Tell him like you told me," Elissa said, mocking me.

"Well," I said with a little laugh. "I knew it didn't really talk to me. I was just admiring it and wondering what it might be thinking about. You know, having the biggest rack in the forest? It was huge."

"How many points?" Jeff said.

"I can't believe this," Elissa said. "You're measuring a coffin here. That's not how you told me, Sam."

"I'm doing the best I can," I pleaded.

"El," Jeff said. "The boy is tired and hungry. I'm sure he knew the deer didn't talk."

"Like it talked to his crazy mother?" she said. "Oh, I get it. I know what you're doing, Sam. You tell one story to me, and a different story to Jeff. Patronize your wacky mother, tell her the king of the deer told you he has to die for his herd . . ."

I caught Jeff's eye and shrugged as if we both knew what was really happening. His expression told me we had to stay calm to keep Elissa from getting too upset.

"This isn't our agreement, Jeff," Elissa said. "About respecting each other's positions. Hell-o?"

"Respecting positions, huh?" he said. "Taking the boy to your workshop without telling me was . . ."

And then they were off, one in a gray uniform, one in blue, shooting popguns at each other. I grabbed the pitcher of lemonade and a box of oatmeal bars that Elissa had insisted were sweet enough to call dessert. I went back into the living room, ate a week's worth of the bland things, and waited. I threw a random tape into the VCR from my *Strange But True* collection, partly to muffle the voices coming from the kitchen. I wondered if their yelling would wake Perry, barely noticing how immune to it all I was becoming.

The tape was about lycanthropy. Werewolves, that is. The earliest documented werewolves said that changing into wolves was a voluntary act.

I found myself repeating the word "voluntary" over and over. A guy in Germany claimed Satan gave him a magic belt that turned him into a wolf so he could run around in the woods and chase women. Werewolves wanted to be wolves, not like the disinformation from Hollywood where their bite was a victimy thing. True werewolves sought out the power of the wolves.

This gave me hope. If guys could change into wolves because they wanted to, surely I could succeed at convincing Jeff and Elissa I'd changed into a hunter wannabe.

Elissa came out first, looking tired and red-eyed. She shot me a disgusted look. "Happy with yourself?" she said. "Great. Werewolves, too. Just great."

"What?" I said with my hands out.

"You know what," she said. "This is a fine plan, Sam, but you can't fool me. I'll be totally pissed if you get yourself killed with this nonsense."

Then she started to cry. She could always make herself cry by bringing up one of one of our deaths, even Jeff's. She put her fist in her mouth as Jeff came slowly out of the kitchen.

"I'm not going to interfere here," Elissa said. "But I do have one demand. Of both of you. And I'm pretty firm about it."

Jeff and I looked at each other, already co-conspirators.

"What?" he said.

"Sam has to go to Rosen to talk about all this. I mean, the book and all. I'm sure Rosen can put it into perspective. I want Sam to go alone. I'll step out of it, if that's what you want, but I want him to talk to someone I trust. Besides, if it was Rosen's book that—"

"Fine," I said. "I'll go."

They both looked at me, surprised.

"I'll go," I repeated.

It would have been impossible for me to want to go to Rosen. Forced to go was perfect, but I didn't find the idea totally repulsive. I'd talked to him in my mind while I'd read his book. I wanted to tell him about Big Buck and wondered what he'd say.

"Okay," she said. "I'll call tomorrow and make an appointment. Deal?"

"Deal," I said.

Jeff nodded. Elissa turned and went upstairs, her fist back in her mouth.

"So what's really going on?" Jeff said when we were alone.

"I don't know," I said—always a good place for a teenager to start, especially if you're about to lie. "It was just an idea. Maybe that deer was trying to tell me it was okay for the hunt to go on. That it's part of nature and all that. So, I'm thinking maybe I should hear, well, the other side. Your side. Sort of."

"Sam," Jeff said with hungry eyes. "Don't jerk me around."

"It's true," I said. "I, uh, want to learn more about the other side." I swallowed hard. "The hunters' side."

"So you can infiltrate us?" Jeff laughed. "Then run back and tell your friends how crazy we are?"

I wanted to say, "Yes, exactly," and be done with the whole thing, but I didn't.

"No, no, it's not that," I said. "I'm changing. Maybe, I mean. I don't know. What about the Indians? That book says they prayed to animals for permission to kill them. Is that true? Why did the animals allow themselves to be killed?"

Jeff shook his head, wearing a little smile I didn't trust. "I don't know, Sam," he said. "This is all a little much for me tonight. Your mother wants you to go to this eco-shrink, so go. After you've gone, we'll talk." He started up the stairs, then turned back. "It's okay to change your mind. You're young still. This is the time to try things out." He frowned. "Only don't get into trouble, okay?"

"I won't."

That night, I had a strange dream. Big Buck, with a crown on his head; and dressed in Day-Glo orange, was hunting me. "We need a sacrifice, Sam-I-am," he said, calling out to me. I was hiding, terrified. His voice sounded like Stewart's. "You do love the deer, right?" he said. "Prove it, then. Die for us. You can be the king for a day." He laughed.

I woke up so scared I found Perry's Mr. Hairy and held him. This freaked me out. I decided I needed someone to explain what might be happening to me. Rosen would have to do.

I would have to leave out a few things, like that we were the ones who had released those deer. And that we'd been talking to Spiranga. And that I woke up terrified and held a dirty old teddy bear in the middle of the night.

CHAPTER FIFTEEN

BRITT WAS OFF THE DAY I CAME. A little card with a smiley face on it announced she was at acupuncture class. I lurked around her desk looking for personal items, wondering what it would be like to hook up with a healer type. You'd be healthier, provided you could stand the part where she makes you swallow goat liver extract.

Rosen popped his head into the room and caught me. "You can come in now, Sam. I'm ready for you."

I flopped on his couch like I did at home. "Can I do it this way?" I said.

"I'm not a psychoanalyst," he said. He sat upright at his little desk. His fancy pen sat on the leather-bound book.

"Is that what they call the ones who listen to your dreams?" I said.

He shrugged. "You can tell your dreams to anybody you want. Why, did you bring one?"

"Uh—uh—uh," I said, wagging my finger at him. "You can't trick me into talking that easily."

"I don't waste time trying to trick people. Why don't you tell me why you're here? Something happen?"

"My mother wanted me to come." I stared at a poster that said, 'You Know What You Need.'

"She said something about a book."

"A book?" I said, trying to act innocent. "Oh, *that* book. The one you gave Patti to give to me. The book on the Lakota Sioux."

"So that's who had my book!" he said, getting up from his desk and running to his bookshelf. "You say you got it from Patti? Where does she get off lending my books to people?" He seemed genuinely pissed. I'd planned a major offensive here but now felt a bit intimidated.

"I thought you told her to give it to me," I said. "That it was all a plot."

"What possibly for?" he said, sitting back down.

"I thought you were conspiring. With Patti and Jeff? To help them get me on their side. About the hunt, I mean." Each sentence was painful to get out as he stared at me with a stern expression.

Then he burst out laughing. "You actually think professionals go around spending uncompensated time trying to trick young boys into changing their politics? Too much TV, my friend."

"I thought maybe the DNR was paying you," I said, feeling ridiculous.

He laughed again as he shook his head. His laugh was really starting to irritate me.

"I've had that book many years," he said. "I got it when I was a Boy Scout. It means a lot to me. I want you to take care of it. And I want it back."

"You were a Boy Scout?"

I was totally freaked I was talking to a Boy Scout. Scouts were the low, bottom feeders in the river of cool, lower than carp.

"Were you one of those that hung on and on and became . . . what did they call them?"

"Eagle Scouts," he said. "Yes. The ultimate nerd, an Eagle Scout."

"Maybe you shouldn't tell your customers that," I said.

"Clients," he corrected me. "And thanks for the free marketing advice. But, hell, I could care less. I'm proud of being a scout."

It was my turn to chuckle and shake my head. Seeing Rosen as an Eagle Scout put things in perspective. And to think I had come there for wisdom. I glanced at the clock, picturing myself sauntering out, meeting Britt just as she got to the office, breathless from acupuncture class, just in time for her morning coffee break. I smelled blueberry muffins and, in my mind, fingered her egret tattoo.

Rosen leaned across his low table toward me. "Now that you've changed, you'll understand why I was an Eagle Scout."

"Uh, sure," I said, completely lost. I was imagining uncool little Hermes, the chubby kid who ate lunch alone in the school cafeteria reading about Indians. Cool kids—me among them, cool but vaguely sympathetic—mocked him.

"Why did your parents name you Hermes?" I said.

"You mean why did they draw attention to my uncoolness?" he said. "Like *A Boy Named Sue*?"

"I never heard that."

"Johnny Cash. The absent father names the boy 'Sue' so the kid'll grow up tough enough to survive. Well, I'll tell you. I hated that name—Hermes. Can you believe they named me that?"

"Elissa said you probably named yourself Hermes. Like her friends who change their names to Rainbow or Starhawk."

"God, no," he said. "I begged my parents to change my name to . . ." He raised his eyebrows. "Ready? Dave Johnson. Can you believe it? A Jewish professor of literature marries an Episcopalian Classics professor, and their son wants to be called Dave Johnson. The Rosen part came from my dad, a Jewish family name that slipped out of their fingers on Ellis Island."

"Ellis where?"

"Forget it. The Hermes part came from my mom. Like it would make me study the classics or something. Why am I telling you all this?"

"Wasn't Hermes the same as Mercury? The guy with the wings on his helmet and feet?" I said.

"Yes. Impressive."

"Elissa," I said by way of explanation. "She tried to show me how comic books steal from myths. The old Flash character was based on Hermes, I think."

"Unfortunately winged feet didn't come with the name," he said.

"With a name like that," I said. "You must know a lot about the gods."

"What do you want to know?"

"Why do gods demand blood sacrifices?"

"Who says they do?" he said. "Does that have anything to do with why you're here?"

I shrugged. "Just curious. Why do they?"

"Depends," he said, "on which gods you're talking about, who is asking the question, and from what space they're asking. Gods have their own ecologies, you might say. There are many levels of talking about them."

"Like?"

"There's the literal level where they're all up there fighting for title of King of the Universe. There's another view that the gods are outer projections of our psyches. Externalizing them helps us understand who we are."

"Those kind aren't real then."

"Real enough. You're dealing with the unknown either way. People are pretty lost, in general. We're always looking for maps anywhere we can find them. Sometimes religions hand us a map; sometimes they come in dreams and we have to figure them out."

"Why did you mention dreams?" I asked suspiciously. Had I told Elissa about my dream? I couldn't remember.

"That's just one way the unconscious accesses us. Like the rock exercise I did with your family. By the way, you never told me what you saw."

"Oh, nothing much," I said. Like I was about to tell him and get carted off to a juvey jail to get raped. "Just nightmares, the usual stuff."

"Nightmares, huh?" he said, and he gave me that stare again.

"I did have a dream." I swear I hadn't planned to say that.

"And?"

I froze. My mouth opened but nothing came out.

"It's probably nothing," he said. "Just the usual stuff, nightmares and all that."

"Oh, yeah? Usual?"

I knew it was a trick but didn't care so I told him everything. About Big Buck walking like a human, dressed in blaze orange, hunting me. I told him about how Big Buck put a crown on my head and wanted to sacrifice me. I left out that he spoke in Stewart Spiranga's voice. That was top secret Council business.

"Big Buck said I could be the king," I said. I took a breath and said the next part quickly. "And I could prove I loved the deer by dying for them. What do you think, Doc?"

"I think you're a very lucky young man."

"How's that?"

"Does the expression 'rites of passage' mean anything to you?" he asked.

"Ms. S-T's talks about it," I said. "We study all kinds of multicultural crap with her. We studied rites of passage—Bar Mitzvahs and fraternity hazing and how they beat up gay soldiers. We even studied female circumcision. She showed some gory pictures that made me ill. Our class wrote the U.N. about it."

He shuddered. "It's a start, I guess."

"So my dream is a rite of passage? I'm, like, a man now?"

"To grow up, we have to move from the world of King Baby—the arrogant pursuit of self-interest—to the world of adulthood. I'd say you're in an initiation process. Not one you sought out, but one that sought you out. That's what I meant by lucky."

"I understand. I'm lucky I've got friends who can haze me into adulthood."

"Hazing isn't initiation," he said more sternly. "That's an extension of the adolescent need to find a tribe. Recruiting peers is a lot different than getting the guidance of older men. Or spirits."

"How do you know who's supposed to be your guide?"

"Let me tell you a story," he said. When I rolled my eyes, he added, "It's not longer than a commercial."

He took a deep breath while he closed his eyes. He opened them.

"In tribal societies," he said, "the guide or guides sometimes kidnapped the initiate and took him away to live with the men. The mothers played along, pretending they were upset that their sons were stolen. But they knew the boys needed this to grow up. The shamans prepared the boy for the experience of transition. Indian societies sent him into the forest on a vision quest. It was difficult and involved physical stresses. On his quest, he would find his connection to a power animal and get a new name. Sometimes it happened in a dream; sometimes it was hard to separate dream from reality. Through his vision, he learned which clan to join, the one associated with his power animal. Eagle, bear, whatever."

"That's a nice story and all, but I don't see—"

"Find yourself in the story, Sam. Where are you in it? Do you know who's on your side? Have you been kidnapped yet? Has your shaman appeared? Have you had your vision, or are you preparing for it? How will you know your spirit guide when he shows up?"

I thought about it, but it was confusing. Who was kidnapping me—Stewart or Jeff? Megan? That would be nice. But I was only pretending to be kidnapped by Jeff and his pals, so did that count? Stewart could be my initiation guide. He was asking me to do something difficult. Did that mean Big Buck was my power animal?

"It's hard," I said.

"It's supposed to be," he said.

I nodded. "How will I know?"

"There ought to be a guide appearing soon," Rosen said. "He or she—it could be a she—will be in some way a surprise. At first you might think of him as someone who is messing with you, taking you away from home perhaps. There will be an element of surprise and an element of discomfort. That might be the kidnapping. And a door to your new world."

"But what if," I started cautiously. I wanted to be sure not to show him my cards. "What if there are more than one possible guide and they are sort of competing for you, trying to recruit you? Let's say they all make you uncomfortable."

"Like you're being torn apart?" he said. "From what I see, you have Jeff on one side, Elissa on the other, maybe your friends on another side. They're all pulling on you."

"Maybe they'll pull me apart."

"Like your sacrificed god? Is that your fear? Listen, the only death here is the death of your childhood, Sam. And in a sense, that is a sacrifice. The death of childhood is a sad thing to the child you were."

"It's like you said. Everyone wants me to be on their team, to see things the way they see it. Even my friends, Megan, Ryan, even Holly. Everyone's pressing in on me with their views, wanting me to do things. I'm getting confused. I mean, sometimes it seems that all people care about is that other people agree with them. They don't really care about right and wrong. They don't really care about the deer or the so-called health of the park. Everyone just wants to win."

"That can be dangerous," he said. "You could pick the wrong one."

"There is a wrong one? You mean like in *Star Wars*—the dark side and the light side?"

"Yes, it's possible to make the wrong decision," he said.

"What would happen then?" I asked.

He shrugged. "Tragedy, death and destruction. Lost lives, ruined careers, bitter years."

"Oh, that's all. What a relief," I said. "How will I know who to follow?"

"The still small voice inside you. You have to listen to it. That's what we were practicing with the rock."

He took a sip of tea and made a face.

"You kids don't listen very well," he said. "You're swimming in the space junk zone, your heads filled of videos, movies, songs, games, trivia. Thousands of years of cultural garbage shot out into space and all you can do is grab at it as you float by."

I caught him glancing at his watch, and I nearly panicked. I had to say something dramatic.

"Maybe I'm going crazy," I said.

"Did you know," he said, "that Indians said that the people who go crazy are the shamans who have not accepted their power?"

I shrugged. Elissa had told me a lot of crap about shamans over the years, but it hadn't made much of an impression.

"Shamanism is," he said, "the ability to move between worlds. And, I should add, coming back in one piece. Which is not as easy as it sounds. Here you are. Everyone is grabbing at you, saying, 'Come into my world.'"

"Yeah," I said slowly.

Then all of the energy went out of me. I went limp. I felt as though I wouldn't be able to move from the room without a nap. I certainly couldn't face Britt, sharpening her fingernails out there, reading books on Chinese herbs.

"Sam, we're out," he said.

"I know. I know. We're out of goddam time!" I nearly shouted, holding my head, which started to throb.

"We can't remake the world in one hour, Sam," he said gently.

I pulled the crumpled check out of my pocket and threw it on the table. "I feel half-out," I said.

"Half-out," he said.

"I watched a friend's cat give birth once," I said. "The cat started running around when the first kitten started coming out. The kitten's legs and tail stuck out of her mom's butt like she was growing a mutation. The cat ran up to me, like I could do something to help her. My friend thought it was a big joke, but I was practically crying. I hardly knew the cat. I yelled at him to do something to help the kitten."

"Did he help?"

"No, but he stopped laughing."

"And the kitten?"

"The half-out kitten died."

"I'm sorry," he said.

I couldn't help myself. I started crying for that half-out kitten. God, how embarrassing, I thought. I had to stop. What about Britt?

"I need an assignment," I said, gripping the couch hard. That stopped my tears. "Or I swear you'll never get me out of here."

"That's a new one," he laughed. "Usually they can't wait to get out of here. Okay, an assignment. Your assignment, Sam, is to listen to everyone. Visit all the worlds. Listen to what they have to say. If it helps, think of yourself as a journalist or an infiltrator."

"A spy?" I perked up. Was everything suddenly going to make sense?

"A spy is good. Spy on all the worlds. Take them in. Don't argue. Listen, but don't give yourself to anything. I guarantee that after a while, it will be clear who your guide is and what it is you have to do."

"Where do I start?"

"You'll know where. People will say, 'Why don't you join me over here?' and you'll go places you would never go to before. Some of these places will be good places, and some will be bad. Don't tell people you're just visiting."

"If I get caught?" I said. "I mean, for spying."

"You'll think of something. You've got a smart mouth. And, by the way, I'm not your guide."

"I hadn't thought—"

"Well, I'm not. I might be a shaman, but I'm not your initiator. You'll find him. Or her. Whatever. Now if you're in here one more minute, I'm calling in Britt to help me tear you off that couch."

I was out of there in less than a minute—with what I wanted. Rosen had said it was okay to be GreenBond, to do what I had to do. With my secret identity confirmed, my coolness surged. I was it.

Incognito.

I breezed past Britt oozing coolness. She looked up from her textbook and smiled. I knew she could sense my cool, smell it. Women are like that. They know.

"Arrivederci," I said. I didn't even know I knew that word.

CHAPTER SIXTEEN

THE COUNCIL OF NATIONS SAT ON A CURB in the school parking lot. Ryan had brought cigars to celebrate my last night before going underground. He and I puffed bravely on them when no adults were looking. Holly leaned her head on Ryan's shoulder while batting away the smoke. She had offset her sickly white skin with lipstick the color of mud and a Goth frock of black lace. Deep-set zombie eye makeup completed the look, such as it was.

Megan sat down next to me, close but not touching. "This is stupid," she said, blowing away secondhand smoke. "What are you little boys proving by smoking?"

"It's a Native American thing," I said. "We're reclaiming their sacred weed from Big Tobacco."

Ryan thought this was funny and went into a coughing fit. I got the idea partially from reading Rosen's book, which was full of Indians leaving little packets of tobacco as offerings.

We watched people get out of SUVs and minivans and head toward the school auditorium. You could tell which side they were on. Hardcore hunters wore camo. I would like to say they were all fat, but they weren't.

Some hunters came with look-alike wives and scowling farmy kids, all of them in camo. Others in their tribe wore denim overalls and lumberjack flannel even though it was a hot summer night. They all gave us dirty looks as they walked by. Maybe it was the cigars.

"Boy, I feel sorry for you," Ryan nodded toward a group of vested guys walking by. "Those are the people you're supposed to infiltrate?"

He was pointing out hunters wearing goofy green vests, the kind that would go well with lederhosen. Ryan discovered this was the uniform of the elite crack bow hunter unit, the Hunters of Men.

It was a shocking thought. Here I sat with my friends, laughing at the people I expected to take me in as one of their own. It frightened me that I'd soon be rubbing shoulders with them. I pictured myself trying to laugh at their racist jokes while improvising an explanation of how Jesus came into my heart and told me it was time to kill animals. The whole idea was absurd.

I puffed some sacred smoke at the sky.

"Hey, what's with those orange squares?" Megan said. All the hunters, vested and non-vested, had Day-Glo orange squares pinned to the fronts of their hunting caps. The squares were logo-free and flapped as they walked.

"Mark of the beast," Ryan said. "Six six six."

I rubbed out my cigar because it was nauseating me. Megan turned to me with a smile, as if I'd done it for her. She laid her hand briefly on mine. Before I could lay my hand on top hers, she pulled it back.

What you might call "our people" were also streaming by. They included basic golf-shirted liberals; New Agers in wrinkled all-cotton clothes and Guatemalan vests; and a tough-looking lesbian contingent with buzz cuts and tiny glasses who looked like they could beat the shit out of an equal number of fat hunters. Punkers with old-fashioned Mohawks bobbed along with other misfits, many of them in full dress leather, pierced and tattooed.

The hairdos reminded me of Rosen's book. It kept creeping into my GreenSWAT fantasies. I imagined myself doing a vision quest in the woods, contacting a powerful spirit animal, and accepting unusual quasi-superpowers for use in the war on the animals.

Then a family walked by, and I swore they looked Native American. I wasn't sure, but I took it as a sign. I imagined myself sitting with them and asking them how to do a vision quest between the boring DNR speeches.

Holly got up with a sigh. "I'm going in," she said. "I'll save us some seats."

"Near the aisle," Ryan yelled after her.

"What's wrong with her?" Megan asked Ryan, and I noticed how we'd all accepted they were a couple.

"Women's stuff," Ryan said. "I don't know."

I heard a familiar laugh and looked up to see Elissa in the distance. She was hanging with her Wiccan group, a bunch of distinctly odd-sized women. Not just big ones who made Elissa look trim, but some very tall and others almost what they would call "height-challenged." They looked like they were waiting for something.

I had an odd feeling watching Elissa that this was a side of her I didn't know. She looked fun and outgoing, laughing and talking in ways I'd never seen at home. Her arms moved like a stand-up comedian when she talked. She moved around from one person to the next, touching, laughing, gesturing.

135

"There's Elissa, Sam," Megan said. "Go say hello."

"Or maybe goodbye," Ryan said.

I hadn't thought of it that way, but he was right. Since that night was my coming out as pro-hunter, my relationship with Elissa would never be the same. Even later, if I explained why I had to do it, she might not believe me. It was a risk I had to take.

"Heads up," Ryan said. "They're he-e-ere!"

The sun was nearly gone, but I could see the familiar murals on an old school bus. It parked in a far corner of the parking lot. There was enough light to see the paintings of half-naked Aztec goddesses with animals crawling all over them. The Little Creatures of the Forest had arrived. Elissa's gaggle of oddly sized Wiccans walked toward the bus waving.

People in costumes poured out of the bus. Some wore the same type of baggy costumes Ryan's group had used on Ecoday. They carried papier-mâché deer heads painted all kinds of weird ways. They moved quickly, almost militarily.

"Isn't that Perry?" Megan said. "He's so cute!"

It was Perry. I recognized the deer head with blue and yellow spots he was carrying, and something about seeing him bummed me. Then I pictured Jeff, over-caffeinated, organizing his charts and note cards, wrestling with the collapsing easel, optimistically joking with Lenny, completely ignorant of the forces gathering in the parking lot ready to destroy his so-called community meeting.

"During the Civil War," I said, "you had to kill your brother or mother if they were on the other side."

"I know where you're coming from," Ryan said. "This is America."

"I'm not sure that's exactly how it worked," Megan said with a little superior laugh.

"We're talking about family civil war," Ryan said. "My theory. If either parent mentions civil war—any kind of civil war, historical, whatever—that means the marriage is over. I know about this, Megan. I've made a study of it."

"Study of it? You?" Megan laughed. "Show me the statistics."

"I'm talking from personal experience, thank you very much, Miss Smartass," Ryan said. "It happened to my family and we're fucking Catholic. We don't even believe in divorce."

"When you try to help people, Ryan," Megan said, "you usually make them feel worse."

I'd wanted someone to say this to Ryan for a long time.

"Hey, a pound of preparation is worth its weight in gold," he said. He blew smoke at us and stood. I noticed the crowds heading toward the auditorium had thinned to a trickle.

Megan took my hand in both of hers. My head filled with images from nature shows on hormones and mating rituals.

"I know what you're thinking now, Sam," she said.

How could she? I was picturing geese mating for life.

"It must be hard . . ." As she bit her lip. "One parent on each side." She tried to smile. "Just don't go there. Our plan is solid, solid as a rock. And your mission, or whatever, won't make it any worse or better for your family. I mean, they're pretty much fucked up as it is."

"Man, I could take your class on how to make people feel good," Ryan laughed.

Megan waved him away angrily. "Think of it as . . ." She paused, thinking. "Something you're doing for . . ."

For my love, I thought.

"For the earth. Yes, the whole earth and all the animals in it," she said, clapping like a child.

All the screwing animals, I thought. *All the animals screwing.*

"You'll always have the Council," she concluded with something like a smile, which was actually just squishing her mouth toward her chin. "I think we should move inside," she said. "I hope Holly got it together to save us some seats. She didn't look good, did she?"

"Too much poetry," Ryan said as we headed inside.

The auditorium was at least twenty degrees hotter than outside. Katami ran back and forth between two World War II surplus fans, positioning them toward the audience. The hunters sat together on the left side of the room; our people sat on the right.

We found Holly sitting on the left side, dangerously near enemy territory. Ryan laid into her for being on the left. Megan defended her by pointing out that it helped my mission. Then the two girls sat next to each other and fell to whispering.

I looked at the audience and spotted the Native American family sitting with the hunters. I felt sorry for them, assuming they had made a mistake. A guy from a local news station wrestled with his shoulder cam near the front of the stage. A sharp-featured woman with a stair-stepper body pranced around him like a restless horse.

Janine sat in the front row with her Honeywell Industrial strapped on, adding her touch of science fiction. I wondered if Janine and Patti were having a lesbian version of a civil war. I assumed they would be rational, respectful creatures that listened to each other and took turns responding.

I followed Janine's gaze and found Patti on stage. Some other people wandered around the stage props, consisting of two card tables, a bunch of folding chairs, and that evil trick easel loaded with Jeff's posters.

I almost didn't recognize Patti though. She wore a black party dress and looked surprisingly sexy. She sat at a card table with her legs crossed, sucking on a pen. I found myself staring at the pen, watching her tongue flick out and lick the end. Her hair was longer than she'd worn it for years, weirdly similar to Megan's.

Jeff walked on to the stage, chatting with Lenny. Their dorky uniforms reminded me of the day he spoke at our school and I'd wanted to crawl under my chair. Lenny was pure linebacker, much bigger than Jeff. With their matching beards and Lenny's sash across his torso like an Albanian dictator, they looked like a comedy team, Lenny the big pompous one, Jeff the skinny wisecracking buddy.

"God, they look like a couple of pansies up there, don't they?" Ryan said.

"Jesus, Ryan," I said, surprising myself. "That's my dad up there."

"I'm trying to help you, man," he said. "Distance."

Megan whispered to Ryan. "You're an idiot, Ryan."

"Whoa," Ryan said, vibrating his outstretched hand at her. He turned to me and whispered, "Toughen up. I mean, I hate to say it, but how do you know they're not gay? Gay dudes love to dress up in Nazi costumes and military shit. Everyone knows that."

"Well, I didn't know you were such an expert," I said.

"You calling me gay?" Ryan said.

"You answering?" I said.

This was a routine we used to do for fun, but neither of us was laughing at this moment.

"Cut it out," Megan hissed.

We shut up for a minute. I knew what I'd have to say to end it.

"Okay. So they do look like a couple of Boy Scouts."

"'You da man!" Ryan said. He tried to high-five me, but I missed his hand.

"You too, now!" Megan said as if I were a child. "Do you have to copy everything he does?"

She was right. I sacrificed a lot to laugh with Ryan. Laughing with Ryan felt as close as I could get to being like him—simple and handsome, without psychological complication, being liked by everyone no matter what stupid things you said.

"You've got to learn how to distance better," Ryan continued in low whisper. "Otherwise, it's too hard. It's like anything else. Like in football when you have to smash a guy in the face. Distance. Or in basketball when you trip someone when the ref's not looking. Distance. It's a life skill you have to practice. Let me show you."

He looked around the room, then nodded at a fat hunter a few rows in front of us. "That guy," he said. "Try him."

"Try him what?" I asked.

"Distancing him. It's like hating, just not as personal." He scowled. We both knew I was dragging my feet, but I wasn't sure why.

"Here, I'll show you," he said. "You concentrate on him, study him, come up with all the reasons you hate him and hate his lifestyle. Fantasize—you're good at that. Fill in all the details till you're ready to rip his throat out. It's easy. I do it all the time. Give it a try."

I began to concentrate on the fat hunter, using my considerable powers of imagination. I followed Ryan's instructions. Concentrate, study, morph details into a hate profile. I was surprised how easy it was.

"Hey," I said, "I'm good at this."

"Hello, everyone," Katami's over-amplified voice began. He cleared his phlegmy voice, then said again, even louder, "Hello, everyone." He tapped the antique microphone, sending thumping drumbeats and a piercing whistle through the sound system. "Hello? Can you hear me in the back?"

There were more students in the audience than I realized: "Yes, Mr. Katami."

"Okay, then," The Kat smiled his big Japanese-American smile.

He blabbed about nothing for a few minutes, waiting for the stair-stepper lady to switch on the camera, but she was waiting for something else.

Katami changed his tone to a scold. "I expect students in the audience to act like ladies and gentlemen, or you will be shown the door by our volunteer ushers." His hands floated up like the pope blessing a crowd. He nodded to Mr. Sandstone, our gym teacher on his right, and Mr. Hegelian, aka Mr. Science, who waved nervously at the crowd from Katami's left.

"Scary," Ryan laughed. "Heavy duty security." He lowered his voice. "When the action starts, Sam, stay away from Sandstone. Stoner can be an animal. Go toward Hegelian, he's the pushover."

"When is the action going to start?" I said. Something was wrong. Why didn't I know?

"Just wait," he winked, patting something in his cargo pocket. "Something not on the program."

And with that, Katami turned the mike over to Jeff.

CHAPTER SEVENTEEN

JEFF BEGAN INTRODUCING THE OTHER PANELISTS on stage, not a very tough-looking group. There was an old lady representing the Friends of Wirth—a birding society—who looked as if she'd retired from teaching in 1942 and still wore the same dress. A guy wearing a golf shirt represented the local Sierra Club chapter. He wouldn't shake my world. A young woman dressed in a Bulgarian peasant skirt hailed from the Wirth Protection Society, a group the Council once had hopes for. Then there was Patti, the head of the Prop19 Task Force of the NeoUrban League.

Prop19 didn't have that much to do with the deer kill. It was supposed to be proposal to limit growth in the metropolitan area, pure and simple.

Jeff introduced Patti. He worded his introduction carefully as if people didn't know Patti was a turncoat. Ryan said we should have brought pies to throw at her. I played along but winced at the thought.

Patti walked up to the mike looking sleek. Someone whistled and she smiled. An adult voice yelled, "Prop19 sucks!"

Jeff grimaced as if he'd bitten into a lemon. He took back the mike. "People!" was all he said.

Boos and hisses began rising from the hunters' side. From the good side, a middle-aged guy in a Hawaiian shirt stood up and yelled back, "Let her talk, for Chrissake!"

People around Hawaiian Shirt started cheering, "*Prop19! Prop19! It will make the city green!*"

"Believe me," Patti said, "I know Prop19 is controversial. But I'm not here to try to convince you all the goods things it can do for all of us."

Groans and laughter from the hunters.

"What I have to say might be even a little more controversial," she said.

The rustling and mumbling calmed down.

"As you may know, the Metropolitan Council, who originally drafted Prop19 but turned the campaign over to the citizen-run NeoUrban Committee, of which I am president . . ."

"This ain't controversial, this is bureaucracy!" someone yelled from the crowd.

"After reviewing the whole situation at the Wirth," Patti said, "the Met Council and the NeoUrban Committee—"

Catcalls and boos. She held up her hand.

"Here it comes," Megan said.

"Have decided to support the DNR in a limited, one-time only, herd reduction program via a lottery hunt." Patti stopped, looked up, and waited.

The room got completely quiet. No coughing, laughing—nothing. The Stair-Stepper news lady pulled her cameraman over, and they started shooting.

Then the hunters broke into cheers that sent charges of fear through my body. A weird flapping sound accompanied their voices as if a flock of birds had entered the room. I looked around thinking maybe the Creatures had released doves. Then I saw how the hunters were rapidly nodding their heads, making their Day-Glo flaps flop up and down.

"Oh-my-god," Holly said. "They're flapping!"

"That's very good," Megan said with a finger across her lips. "Really quite clever."

"I'll make a note of it," Ryan said.

"That turncoat bitch," Holly said. "I never thought she would really do this to us."

An ounce of sympathy for Patti leaked out of me, but I squashed it. I didn't need any more confusion.

"This is pathetic," Ryan said. "We never should have allowed her to get up there. The Creatures should be here by now. What are they waiting for?"

I had the oddest feeling. Jeff had infiltrated Patti's mind, and Elissa was now screwing up by not releasing the guerilla performers.

Patti went on, over the noise. "I am authorized to lend whatever support our organizations can offer to educate the public . . ." Her voice broke and she paused for a breath.

Wild shouts continued from the Orange Flappers, who began getting out of their chairs. They jumped and waved their hats. Some raised their arms straight above their heads in victory.

Patti was still talking. She blathered on about her committee's concern about the water quality for the urban poor and her committee's desire to keep the Wirth reserve a functional ecosystem.

Megan listened, adding little retorts. "Oh, I'm sure," and, "Oh, really?" and "Whoa, where did that come from?"

"Wilderness is over," Patti concluded. "We have a responsibility to manage the whole planet now, like it or not."

"She's getting weird now," Holly said.

Patti ended abruptly. Jeff calmed the crowd enough to give each of the other speakers a few minutes. They were all, as planned, against the hunt. I found their statements weak and predictable, lacking the drama of Patti's announcement.

Then bustling sounds came from the back of the room. I turned and saw the Creatures grouping near the open doors. They carried primitive-looking instruments—drums, horns, noisemakers of all kinds. They were organizing into lines.

"Finally," Ryan said.

Jeff opened the floor to questions as Katami dragged another 1940s mike into position near the front of the audience. He adjusted its height and blew it to screeching life.

A tall mean-looking hunter walked up to the floor mike. He had a dark black beard and the deep eye sockets of a killer.

"Excuse me, gentlemen," he said. "And ladies." His baritone voice echoed through the room. "How come you DNR fellas ain't got the courage and courtesy to comment on what a lot of us are wondering about?"

Jeff said, "And what would that be, sir?"

"There's a rumor circulating that the harvestin' will be limited to bow hunters. Rifle hunters have been eliminated. And none of you had the guts to mention this to us."

"There will be press release," Jeff started, but he stopped and turned. Lenny had come up from behind and covered his mike. They exchanged a few intense but unheard sentences.

"Can't decide which lie to tell us, huh?" the big guy said. The hunters laughed.

Jeff stepped back, frowning. Lenny moved forward and answered Black Beard: "We didn't mention it because this forum is not addressing the technical aspects of the hunt, many of which have not been worked out. But I can confirm that we have not ruled out the use of firearms, but we're studying the issue given the proximity of the reserve to human habitation and the likelihood that there will be protesters picketing the cull."

Black Beard jumped in. "Ha! It's true, guys, after all our support. You screwed us!"

Many of the hunters reacted by standing up and jeering, raising their fists, breaking out in little chants. I noticed the ones who were not standing. Many of them wore the goofy green vests of the Hunters of Men—the Christian bow hunters, of course.

"Listen," Lenny said. "This is what's going to happen, though it's not official yet. The first wave is reserved for bow hunters. There will be a limited number of permits available to rifle hunters for a second wave."

Someone from the other side yelled, "Sounds like an invasion force!"

Black Beard quieted his faction with a fluttering palm motion. "One more question," he said. "We also happen to know, Lenny, that you yourself are a member in good standing with the bow hunting organization the Hunters of Men. Am I right?"

"The hunt will be fair," Lenny said. "Permit numbers will be balanced between bow and rifle people, if that's what you want to know. And to answer your second question, yes, I am a member of the Hunters of Men, and proud of it. But this has no bearing on . . ."

The standing hunters didn't listen to the rest. They started to get out of their seats and spill into the aisles. Heated discussions broke out between the standing hunters and the seated vest-wearers. Mr. Sandstone moved toward them cautiously with his hands outstretched. His mouth moved, but it was too noisy now to hear any individual.

The Audubon representative, the thin old lady in the ancient blue dress, stepped up to the mike. "May I please speak?" she yelled. "May our side ask a question?"

The hunters ignored her.

"Okay, guys," Ryan said with a glance to the back of the room. "It's chaos time. Sam, can you postpone your conversion thing? We need you here. I expect you to do your part. When you hear the signal, show me what you can do."

"What are you talking about? What signal?" Megan said to Ryan. "Something's happening that I don't know about, right? You're doing something dangerous."

"This is war," Ryan said. "I'm not messing around with that GreenBond fantasy crap. We have to act now. Sam, prove you're with us by taking out your fat friend there." He nodded at the fat hunter and slipped out of his seat.

"Who is he, Ryan?" Megan said. "I don't like this."

I watched Ryan make his way to the front of the auditorium.

"Wait," I said, but he was gone.

Was he pulling out the Council? Of Operation GreenBond? Suddenly I felt childish and foolish. He was off, acting on his own, like an adult. As usual, I couldn't tell whether I admired him, was pissed at him, or worried about him.

More strange sounds arose from the back of the room, clanging bells, beating drums, human voices, and primitive horns.

The room became a circus. People in deer costumes of all sizes ran down all the aisles with noisemakers. Musicians dressed as raccoons, squirrels, and rabbits beat percussion instruments or blew on recorders as they followed the first wave of deer. There were children with tambourines among them. The costumes, the puppets, and the music had transformed the tension in the room into joy.

"Welcome Little Creatures of the Forest!" Ryan's voice yelled triumphantly through the commandeered floor mike.

A huge puppet entered the room on the hunter's side, rising to its full height of twenty feet. Its head bobbed on a central stick as performers controlled its arms with smaller poles attached to the hands. I knew the Creatures called this puppet Mother Nature, but I never understood why since she looked like an Eastern European peasant with a confused expression on her face. A second puppet appeared behind her, a tall white skeleton painted on black fabric. Its hands reached for Mother Nature in a threatening gesture. A third puppet, Paul Bunyan, moved slowly down another aisle waving a huge papier-mâché gun over the crowd.

A chorus began chanting from an invisible location, I suspected from a portable CD player. It sounded like cats whining and moaning in unison, only not as angry.

Gunshots broke out, rapid-fire like a machinegun. It came from the area where I last saw Ryan.

"I gotta go help Ryan," I said.

Megan grabbed my arm with a claw-like grip. "You don't think? Ryan?"

I remembered him patting his pocket, but I couldn't go that far. "No way," I said. "Why would he?"

Megan and I stared at the auditorium. It had become one of those scenes you see on TV—the screaming panicky crowd scene. Everyone stood up, screamed, and clogged the aisles in desperate escape. Stock footage, but different when you're in it.

The Creatures's music didn't stop as the gunfire broke out again. I couldn't tell who was shooting whom. The people in deer costumes responded to the gunshots in a very strange way. They held their hearts and stumbled around like we did on Ecoday. Was it possible they were adding real horror and death into their show?

That's when I got it. I had been in this piece. It was the same one we did on Ecoday. It had the same costumes and the same faults. The gunshots broke out again in little bursts. They weren't nearly as loud as real gunshots.

"Firecrackers," I said.

"What?" Megan said. "You're right. How incredibly stupid."

"Ryan," we said together.

Megan leaned over to Holly, who had curled into an embryonic ball. She whispered, "It's just Ryan, Hol, setting off firecrackers. People will get that." When she came back up she said, "I hope."

I watched Fat Hunter wiggling on his chair, laughing. The hunters seemed to know the gun noises were firecrackers and think it was funny. I focused all my anger on Fat Hunter as he stood on his folding chair, teetering, yelling, and laughing. He was wadding up programs and throwing them. Other hunters were doing the same thing, throwing wads at the dancing Creatures.

Lenny was at the stage mike. "Everyone calm down," he said in a soothing but commanding voice. "There is no firearm discharging. I repeat. There is no firearm discharging. The noise you heard was firecrackers." He took a breath and tried again, "Everyone calm down."

People continued to scream and rush the exits. I needed to do something. Ryan wanted me to prove something, to show I was involved. "Go ahead," I heard him say in my head. "Show me what side you're on."

My knees were shaking as I went for the aisle.

Megan grabbed my shirt. "Where the hell are you going, Sam?"

"I gotta do something," I said. "I got to be part of this."

"You can't go out there," she whispered. "What about GreenBond? Your conversion? You can't afford—"

"I haven't changed yet. My people need me."

"What people?" she said.

"Elissa and Perry are out there," I said. "I have to help them. They might be trampled to death."

This startled her into silence. I pulled away before she could find a reason for me to stay put. By this time, my knees were quaking so badly I either had to move or sit.

I headed toward Fat Hunter. Just as I reached him, he turned and gave me an inspiring sneer. My whole meditation on hating him surged into random access memory, energizing me. My hands sank into his love handle as if it was made of foam rubber. He fell like a fat pink domino against the row of guys next to him, who were also standing on their chairs. It was pure Keystone Kops, only scarier.

I ran into the crowd to hide. I glanced at the stage. Despite Lenny's calm harangue, the representatives of the anti-hunt groups lay prone on the stage, covering their heads their hands. No Patti. No Jeff. No Ryan.

Though I didn't know what to do, the secret high of warfare was surging through me. I hadn't felt this alive since we'd freed the deer. The Creatures had given up their performance and were looking for a way out. In all of the confusion this was impossible, so they ended up blocking the exit doors. Fights and shouting matches were breaking out. On the right aisle, panicking suburbanites and costumed freaks mixed with the Creatures, everyone pushing like a soccer panic in Bolivia. Bodies packed in around me, pushing, whining, cursing, and yelling.

"Why is this happening?"

"Was that gunfire?"

"No, stupid, it was firecrackers!"

"This isn't right."

"This is dangerous."

"Let me through. There's a child here!"

I turned and saw Perry's yellow-and-blue spotted deer head. I yanked it off and found Perry's tearstained face looking up at me.

"What are you doing?" a person still in a deer mask asked me.

"Sam-I-am," Perry said through his tears.

"It's okay," I said. "He's my brother, I'll take care of him." I grabbed his hand, grateful to have a mission.

"C'mon," I said kindly.

I began shoving my way through the crowd toward the exit doors. I felt oddly heroic and hoped Megan was watching. A group of hunters blocked my way, their leader the fat hunter. He pointed at me and they made their way toward me by shoving Creatures left and right. He looked bigger and more dangerous now. He grabbed a Creature in a pink doe mask by the shoulders and knocked off her mask.

"I have to help that girl," I told a guy in a golf shirt. "Hold my brother's hand for a second, will you?"

"Your brother?" he said.

"I'll be right back," I said.

I plowed directly toward Fat Hunter through the chairs, making my own aisle.

"It's you, you little shit!" he said and he grabbed me. I smelled Dr. Pepper and Cheetos as we struggled.

"Hold it, fella," a voice said behind me. "Fun's over." It was an even larger guy in a green suede vest. His Hunters of Men logo was clearly visible at eye level: a bow and arrow intertwined with a cross.

"This guy attacked me!" Fat Hunter said, his face tomato red.

"It's over," the Hunter of Men said. He reached out and did something like the Vulcan touch to the guy, who let go of me.

I looked around. People in those green suede vests were all over the place, calming people, both hunters and Creatures alike. I found Perry and took his hand back, thanking the golf-shirted man.

Slowly, the Hunters of Men were making a difference. They put their hands on Creatures's shoulders and stopped them from playing their instruments. They whispered to hunters and pointed them toward the door. I watched several of them surround Black Beard, who, fists up, was yelling something, then dropped his hands and turned toward the exit like everyone else.

The great horde flowed toward the doors and out into the parking lot. The giant puppets had made it out the door. Hunters walked beside Creatures, Hunters of Men beside punkers, generic white people beside black lesbians. Everyone seemed zombied out, but in a good way. It was strange and a little magical.

CHAPTER EIGHTEEN

I DECIDED IT HAD TO HAPPEN IN THE BASEMENT, in Jeff's cave, a place I usually avoided. Since he was still working overtime a lot and when home was often crouched over a newsletter layout on our computer, I had to stay ready to jump when the opportunity arose.

It happened on a Saturday morning. Jeff and I were alone in the house. Elissa had taken Perry with her to the Little Creatures Workshop, as was their routine.

I heard the clomping of Jeff's work boots on the wooden stairs to the basement. It was time to make my move. I gave him a minute to settle in. I had this weird idea to bring him a treat. I searched the fridge and shoved a non-alcoholic beer deep in my combat pocket. Then I walked silently down the stairs.

Jeff looked up, startled. He sat on the basement floor, his hunting guy goods all around him—camo outfits, bullet belts, game pouches, orange vests, all the accoutrements of a deer-hunting trip. It couldn't have been more perfect.

"What'cha doin'?" I said.

"What?" he said. "Is something wrong?" He moved as if to rise.

"Don't get up," I said. "I just wanted to talk to you."

"I'll come up," he said.

It was a bit pathetic the way he stood, as if blocking his hunting stuff from my critical vision.

"No, no," I said. "I came down here on purpose."

"Why? To make fun of my murder gear?" he said. "What's your new angle?"

"A peace offering," I said, handing him the beer. Then I deliberately sat down cross-legged amidst all his murder gear. "It just feels right to be here."

"A beer?" he said with a smile. "At 10:00 a.m.?"

"It's non-alcoholic."

"I know that, Sam. But?" He sat down facing me, also cross-legged and snapped open the can. "Okay," he said with an untrusting smile. "Okay."

"I never come down here anymore," I said, looking around.

"Sam," he sighed. "A peace offering for what? Did you do something?"

"No, nothing like that," I said. "I just want to talk to you. Ever since the community meeting. I just couldn't ever find the right time or place."

"What do you want to talk about?"

"That meeting?" I pushed pain into my face. "It was hard for me. Confusing."

"In what way . . . confusing?" he said. Was he even the slightest bit interested in my bait?

"Well, there I was sitting with my friends, who, as you know, are against—"

"I know, I know." He took a sip of the beer.

"And some of the stuff you and Lenny were saying? And Patti too." I checked out his reaction to her name. Nothing. "Started to, well, hit me differently."

"Anything in particular?" he said.

I shrugged. "Oh, lots of stuff. All of it, really. It started to make a new picture. And then when those Little Creatures interrupted—"

"Those little monsters," he said, clenching his fist. "I couldn't believe Elissa brought Perry into that."

"Well, yeah. Me too. When they messed up the meeting and all. I, well, didn't like it. And then I saw those guys? The guys in the vests?"

"The Hunters of Men? What about them?"

"They were the real peacemakers there. Not the Creatures. They . . . surprised me. It got me thinking."

"Well, the Hunters of Men are a little far out, even for me," Jeff said. "Lenny's been trying to get me to go to a meeting, but, to be honest, I've never been."

"Maybe it was that book about Indians," I said, talking with renewed energy. "I've been thinking a lot about Indians lately and, well . . . I mean they were very spiritual people and everyone, both sides, seem to think they had this great ecological relationship with the earth."

Jeff's face told me he wasn't hooked yet. I needed to make it more personal, more about him.

"Like you said, Jeff, and Rosen says, the Indians were hunters. Respectful hunters. Thinking about them has made it all come together for me." I took a chance. "Like a big vision thing."

"Jeez, Sam," he said. "I thought I would never hear words like this from you."

I froze to force back a smile.

"That meeting was such a fiasco," he said. "But if this one good thing came out of it—your vision, as you call it—well, then it was worth all the effort. All the pain."

He leaned over and tousled my hair like they do in movies.

"I've missed you," he said.

We both knew that was too much, too fast. He pulled back.

"I mean missed talking like this," he said. "Without having to defend ourselves all the time. That's what I meant."

"I've missed you too . . ." I said, "Dad." I looked for a reaction, at the same time watching myself. I didn't feel as if I were acting.

He looked down, rubbing his beard vigorously. It was a good sign that he hadn't corrected me on the 'Dad' thing.

"When I was in high school, I read books also," he said. "Books changed me too."

"From what to what?"

"Am I all that different?" he said dreamily.

Dreamy was not good.

"Elissa says you changed," I said.

"So, you discuss this with her?" he said. I heard civil war canons.

"I thought it was only fair to hear your side of the story," I said. "I mean, my vision was to get your side now. I'm interested. I think I'm ready to hear it. I'm . . . more mature now. More open."

"I guess it serves me right, huh?" he said. "I probably seem a bit unbalanced to both of you, huh?"

"She never says unbalanced. Not exactly."

He stopped and looked at me. "God," he said, "sometimes it's like we're already divorced but living together." Then he looked at me nervously. "Sorry, that didn't come out right. It's just hearing what Elissa says is wrong with me reminds me of divorced people. How they're always hearing from the kids what they other parent says about them. That's all I meant."

"So you are getting divorced," I asked.

He took far too long to answer. "I don't know, to be honest. This deer thing . . ." he sighed. "is bringing out our differences in a way that makes it seem . . ." He stared at a Day-Glo orange vest.

"Seem possible?" I said.

"Yes, possible. To be honest. Not what I want, but possible."

"But I want to know . . ." I said. "There's something I never understood about you and Elissa."

"Shoot." He said and he smiled. "So to speak."

"You and Elissa were hippies together, right? You say she's still a hippie. You're not. How did all this happen?"

"It's no secret we were hippies together. There's photographic evidence all over the house. Hell, I even have the same beard." He made a "V" with his fingers. "Peace and love, brother. What makes you think I'm not still a hippie?"

"I've seen the pictures. You and Elissa, together, protesting the war. In your long hair and bell-bottoms, the whole outfit. What happened? Where did your new phase come from?"

He lay back on the ground on all the camo clothes. He took a deep breath and exhaled slowly. "You mean all this?" He gestured toward at the wooden shelves filled with camping, hunting, fishing gear.

"Why did I change from peace-and-love to a gun-toting murdering slob?"

"That's not," I began, then shifted tactics. "Yeah, why?"

"Phase one, the idolizing child, turned into phase two, the rebel, in college. Like everyone else, I got reasons for rejecting Dad's world. Some came from books, some from girls, some from profs. My reasons weren't all that different from yours. You might say they were the ancestors of yours. 'We can live in peace and harmony on the planet if everyone agreed to eat soybeans.' That sort of thing."

He took a swig of his beer, then looked at it as if he had picked up the wrong can.

"One thing I got from my dad was anger," he said. "When the Vietnam War was on, I channeled all that fierceness into being a war protester. In a way, being a protester was similar to being a soldier. Everyone around me was so sure the war was wrong there was really no discussing it. The only people who wanted war were old guys in Washington, the geeky engineering students and these R.O.T.C. guys on campus we used to call Nazis."

"And Elissa was there with you?"

"She was there, yes. Totally paranoid that we were all going to be rounded up and shot, but there. She egged me on. She said I looked sexy in a bandanna. She told me how important it was to resist the war machine, even though I was the one who ended up cutting classes to go to the marches. She managed to stay in school and get her degree." He made a face.

"Like Megan," I said, not meaning to.

"Yeah?"

"No, never mind. Go on. What happened next?"

"The war ended. We left the college womb and tried to settle down into the socialist utopian communal thing, working at the local co-op in exchange for wholesale prices, avoiding cars so we wouldn't pollute the planet, generally staying righteous, staying above it all. We even worked at hating Target shoppers, can you believe it?"

Remembering hating Fat Hunter at the community meeting made me squirm, but I pushed on.

"You sounded, uh," I said. "Cool."

"Yeah, once I was," he laughed. "We thought we were very cool. But Elissa got pregnant—with you, Sam-I-am. Being dirt poor was suddenly not so much fun. Riding your bike to the co-op in the snow, stuffing your backpack with organic tuna you can't afford but your wife says she has to have for the protein wasn't exactly my idea of sustainability. Nor was falling over with this backpack-and-bike setup, spilling said tuna in the snow."

"Is this your biking-miles-in-the-snow story?" I said.

"That bad, huh?" he laughed. "It's true, but the geezers always say that, right? There were other things that stopped being so much fun. I got tired of the people. Crabby Marxists scolding that you didn't deserve your twenty-percent discount this month because you didn't work enough the previous month. Endless community meetings to fight a high rise that goes in anyway and wipes out a sub-standard Peoples' Daycare in a decrepit church. Endless hours spent arguing tactics among ourselves while the bulldozers went about their work. We were losing. I felt like we were all losers."

"Your music was pretty good."

"Great," he smiled. "So were the murals on the pyramids. So what? One day I cut my hair and Elissa cried."

"Moving to phase three now, are we?"

"Early phase three, yeah. It was a gradual thing. I was always a little uncomfortable in the hippie identity. Like you, I could blame it partly on the Native Americans. I read everything I could get my hands on. I think I was trying to figure out where we went wrong. I read Margaret Mead, Malinowski, Whorf, Levi-Strauss."

"Were they activists?" I didn't even know the author's name on the book Rosen gave me.

"More like thinkivists," he said.

I felt exhaustion crawling up my legs, paralyzing me as it went. I pictured it as a virus spreading from a bug bite on my big toe.

"One day it was just gone for me," he said. "I started shopping at the SuperValu. I made peace with Target. I avoided the co-op. Elissa began to crave steak. It started during her pregnancy. Pretty soon we were like wolves, growling over the half-cooked flesh. So it was all sort of your fault, Sam."

"Gross," I said.

"I got a job at a publishing house and Elissa cried some more about us selling out. We got married to shake down our relatives for kitchen gear. We had you, and we both cried. Partly it was joyful crying, but I think we cried because the world hadn't changed like we hoped it would. We thought we were the vanguard of a new life for the world, something organic and natural, close to Mother Earth, sustainable. Any of this sound familiar?"

Spookily, it did. "Not exactly," I said.

He just smiled; he knew I was lying.

"So that's how the hippie world died for you. What then? Is this still phase three now?"

"Okay," he drained the last of his beer. "It's been a while since I tried to explain this to anyone." He sat up again and gave me that look in the eye. "Phase two was, you might say, in its death throes, but phase three really didn't kick in until sometime after Grampa died."

Grampa had died when I was five, younger than Perry was now. My memories of Grampa were vague, unreal. I saw myself in the memories on a screen, as if I were in a movie and watching the movie at the same time.

"Right after Grampa died," Jeff said, "I went into a sort of shock. I guess Elissa was in shock too, or she would never have put up with me. I dragged out Dad's hunting stuff and put it up all over the house." He chuckled. "By the time she snapped out of it, we were living in a hunting lodge."

Real or not, this was what I remembered: stuffed trophy bass, photos of Grampa on various hunts, antlers, deer hooves made into bookends, tusks, shooting contest plaques, a stuffed fox family. Despite what I thought of dead animals, the memories felt warm and fuzzy.

"Elissa made you get rid of them," I said. There had been "funny" stories about this. "That must have been a big fight."

"We don't fight, Sam. We discuss." He paused and smiled. "Yeah, it was one of the first big ones."

"After the fight and putting away the stuff, you wanted to be like Grampa? So you changed? Phase three?"

"I mythologized my dad instantly, forgot all his meanness. Yes, he was mean, what they call a mean drunk. I hate to tell you this, Sam, but your grampa was a mean drunk. But I worked at the myth. I made him into my own personal Teddy Roosevelt. I would look at his stuff and think about him and miss him even though I was missing a person he never was."

"Like in *Blade Runner*," I said.

"Huh?" he said. "Oh, the fake memory thing. I get it. Funny. Anyway I met Lenny about that time. He worked at the publishing house, in sales. He was a very 'up' guy in a hip suit. He was impressed with Grampa's stuff, even though he was from a hunting family from Wisconsin. Deep rural roots and all. I fed him stories about how great Grampa was, trying to one-up his stories. Which was difficult because his people were hunters generations deep. Sometimes I made stuff up."

"But you didn't have to," I said.

"No, but I did anyway. Lenny wanted to get out of sales, get a real job, closer to the earth, he said. He was studying to become a DNR officer on the side. To my mind, this was a bizarre blue-collarish move, but his family was all for it. We became friends. We shot guns. We shot bows. We fished. We drank. Eventually, all the shooting and friendship and hunt club camaraderie won me over. But going to AA together, that's what really did it. You wouldn't believe what we went through. Crying together, all kinds of shit."

Jeff and Lenny crying together was too much even for my advanced imagination.

Jeff studied my reaction. When I kept silent, he went on. "It felt good, hanging with the guys. Much better than the squabbling Marxists Elissa brought over to our house to discuss the morality and the dangers of breast-feeding on this toxin-soaked planet."

"In other words, she didn't change," I said.

"Being a mom changes you big time. But in a different way. My stuff freaked her out, but she loved me, I guess. We had a baby. She knew she couldn't stop it, so she started saying things like 'It's a guy thing.' Or 'It's a dick thing'—if you want to know what she really said."

I could picture Elissa saying this, but I hadn't particularly wanted to hear the dick part. "So Lenny pulled you into the DNR?" That exhausting imaginary virus had moved up to my diaphragm. I couldn't take much more of this.

"Yeah," he said. "End of story. Except for one thing. A secret."

"Secret?"

"I should have used the word 'private,'" he said. "But 'secret' is okay. You know that everyone has secrets, right? You understand that secrets, privacy, whatever, are part of life, right? What you're asking for is one of my secrets. Do you understand the seriousness of that?"

"Yes," I said.

I wondered if I should back out. Was I about to hear something such as Jeff really killed his father and now he had to kill me for asking about it?

"You're not from Venus or anything?" I asked.

"It's nothing all that dramatic. Let's just say it's not something I talk about a lot."

"Oh," I nodded. I desperately wanted to appear casual. I glanced at his face, and he had a weird little smile.

"If I don't tell you now, you're gonna think it's some big scary thing, like I murdered someone."

"I promise I won't go to the cops," I said in all seriousness.

"This isn't TV, Sam. This is life."

"Okay." He inhaled loudly. "I'm not really an outdoorsman."

"What are you talking about?" I said. "You're doing outdoorsy stuff all the time. You're in the DNR. You're not a fake!" This mattered to me. I wanted him to be a real outdoorsman. What else was he if not that?

"I didn't say fake," he snapped. "Just not as gung-ho as most the of the guys around me. They're maniacs."

"But you teach—"

"I know a lot. I read. I've done most of it, enough to get by. Fly fishing, elk hunting, skeet shooting, varmint hunting. But the truth? You want the truth, right?"

"Do I?" I said.

He shrugged. "The truth is I'm a wannabe. To most of these guys, this stuff is second nature. They learned it from the men in their families. Like Lenny. It's in their genes. That sounds sweet, learning it from your family, but it's almost never cozy— the learning. It's hard learning in hard families. Sometimes the only tenderness these guys saw from their fathers and brothers and uncles was how they patted their old hunting dogs or gently gutted a fat goose they worked so hard to get. That's tenderness, manly tenderness."

"Jesus," I said.

"These guys have a nose for who's got it and who learned it from books, and they never forgive you for not going through what they went through to get it. They can smell book-learning a mile away. They hate it, and therefore, they hate me. God forbid I should teach them anything. They love it when I screw up and call something the wrong name, a book name."

"But you know so much. You speak, you lecture, you—"

"They put me where I could do the least damage, plus what I was trained to do. Publications. PR. I can't help it, but I'm good at it. They put me in a desk job on top of everything else!" He stood up, his face red.

I wanted very much to be in bed, curled up, my mind in a science-fictional world. I could see his hands shaking. He sat back down and put his head in his hands. What if he cried? He reached out and put his hand on my shoulder.

"I'm sorry for laying all this on you, Sam. Maybe it's more than you need to know. Maybe I just wanted to talk. I'm not sure you were the right audience for this, but I'm just sorry."

He looked close to crying again, so, my exhaustion shot, I said. "I've got secrets too."

He leaned over me awkwardly. I smelled neutered hops on his breath. He moved next to me, way too close.

"Why don't you tell me your secrets, Sam? I mean, if you want to. Tell me the worst ones, the ones you don't want to tell anyone." He stroked my forehead. His hand felt cold but oddly good. I closed my eyes, partly out of embarrassment. "God, you're forehead's hot," he said. "You might have a fever."

I grabbed his sleeve before he could jump up and get the digital thermometer and all that. He stayed and went back to petting my forehead. Something like lava was bubbling near my surface.

"What's it like for you inside there?" he said softly. "I hardly know you anymore, Sam. It's like the world—the shit of the world—has gotten in the way of us. God, I hate politics."

"It's more than politics," I said. I wanted to be tough and dramatic, like Megan. I didn't care about my undercover mission anymore. I was losing it. I wanted to say stuff that would send him away.

"It's ecology," I said. "It's the earth. The whole earth's been between us."

He stayed and petted me, and I kept my eyes closed.

"Tell me," he said, "what it's like having this big responsibility of saving the earth?"

He could have said that as a put-down, but he didn't. I felt as if I were being hypnotized, going into a trance. Everything was reversing. He was infiltrating me. I couldn't fight it, so I didn't.

"The earth is dying," I said louder. I opened my eyes and moved my head away from his hand.

"Tell me more," he said.

"I can't tell you if you don't know," I kind of yelled. It felt like yelling, but I don't think I actually was.

"What can't you tell me?" he whispered.

"Everything's ruined!" I said.

"Like?"

"Like the ozone hole over Antarctica."

"And?" he said.

"All the species going extinct. Thousands every day."

"More," he said.

"Chickens get their beaks clipped off so they won't peck each other to death. Rich ladies make people trap foxes who gnaw off their own legs to escape. Pesticides in food give people cancer and no one cares. AIDS in Africa—thousands are dying every day and no one cares. Mad cow disease infects most of the world and no one cares. The rainforest is getting destroyed, thousands of acres every day. The whole world wants to be like us and eat at McDonald's, and you can't stop them and convince them what they have is better. Nobody gets it, all over the world, nobody cares."

I had to keep talking now. I feared silence. I feared being done. I tried not to think I was messing up my plan.

"No one cares about the mountains of trash we're making or the nuclear waste that's going to be poisonous for thousands of years. No one cares about global warming. Oh, they have their conferences in New York, but when New York's underwater they'll just move their conferences to Omaha while people starve and die all over the world . . ."

"More," he said gently.

I had to search for more, so I sat there a second with what I suspect was a dumb look on my face. It only took me a minute to think of more and let it rip. Frankenstein foods. Pollution of space. Corporate conspiracies to crush sustainable agriculture. Oil spills. Oil running out. Deformed frogs right here in Minnesota. It kept coming, the whole gruesome download. Until I was shaking.

That feeling that I said was tiredness turned into anger for a while, but then the tiredness returned, but it was something else, something quivering, something scared. And then it happened. My dad reached one arm behind me and one arm in front of me and he hugged me. I put my head on his shoulder and inhaled his scent. I hadn't smelled him this way in years. I smelled leather and smoke and some kind of herbal aftershave or shampoo, and his body odor, strong but not too foul, a smell I associated with lost childhood, with falling asleep on his lap.

CHAPTER NINETEEN

LENNY OPENED A LOCKED CHEST BOLTED to the floor of his truck. He pulled out two rifle cases, slung one over each shoulder, then handed a small metallic suitcase to Jeff.

"Sam, get the bows out of my car," Jeff said.

I took two plastic bow cases imprinted with tree-and-leaf patterns, and we headed toward a cheap sign: "Hal's Gun and Archery Range."

Entering the Range felt like penetrating enemy territory. Everywhere I looked, I saw scenarios of dead animals in gruesomely realistic poses. Dead raccoons, dead pheasants, dead ducks, dead quail, dead walleyes, dead muskies, dead large-mouth bass, dead small-mouth bass. And, of course, dead deer.

Jeff and Lenny walked up to the counter and began talking to a fat Paul Bunyan in a plaid shirt and overalls. He had a bushy gray-and-black beard swept to either side like I've seen on those famous turbaned soldiers from India. He eyed me suspiciously from over Jeff and Lenny's shoulders. I grabbed a pamphlet from a kiosk, something about training bird dogs.

When I looked back, they were all bobbing their heads and chatting. I stuffed the book in the rack, took a deep breath, and walked over. I leaned on the counter, close to Jeff.

"This young fella with you gentlemen?" the Bunyan said, giving me the eye.

"Shore is," Lenny said with a wink.

"I just wasn't sure," the Bunyan said. "We get young people coming in here pretending they're undercover agents. You know, doing the big expose for the local youth rag. They sneak around looking for Nazi paraphernalia and secret stashes of handheld nukes. We just have to watch for it is all."

"That ain't me," I said. "No, sir. I wanna kill me some stuff."

"No need to go over the top, son," Jeff said.

The Bunyan's face finally cracked into a smile full of teeth pointing in all directions. "*Aww-right!*" he said. "Virgin, huh? Good for you, boy. Never too late to start killin' stuff." They turned their attention back to buying bullets. "What are you gentlemen shooting today?" the Bunyan asked.

"I brought along my nine millimeter—just for fun—and a couple of rifles, thirty-ought-six," Lenny said. "Then we're going to head over to the archery range."

"Showin' the boy the whole arsenal, huh?" the guy said.

"Boy's going on his first deer hunt this fall," Lenny said.

"Then you came to the right place," the Bunyan said. "I hear you can do some easy bow hunting over at that Wirth Reserve." He fluffed his beard with the back of his hand. "If you're lucky enough to get a permit, that is. The deer there are pretty tame, but what the hell, they gotta go." Then he leaned in closer and said, "Some folks don't like shooting tame deer. Say it ain't sportin'."

Jeff and Lenny looked at each other. "We know all about that," Jeff said irritably.

"We're DNR officers," Lenny said quietly.

"DNR, huh?" the counter man said too loudly. "Lemme ask you this. How come the DNR ain't lettin' rifles hunt the Wirth? They kill a lot cleaner and faster than your average arrow kill. We figure you could do more to get the humane kill message out. Cut down on some of that anti-gun PR. That's what we figure." His face and body shifted into a posture of aggression. He fluffed his beard to the right, then the left.

"Listen, buddy," Lenny said, addressing the man behind the counter. "We're not here on DNR business," His tone was level, neither a whisper nor a shout. "Unless you want us to make it an official visit. We could look around, make sure everything's up to code. All your mounts taken fairly in season. That sort of thing."

The guy's face twitched as he tried to suppress a snarl. Lenny headed us toward another crude sign duct-taped to the wall "Gun Range This Away." We followed arrows made of duct tape down a stairway, through a vending area with a couple of tables, ending up at another counter with another Bunyan.

"Another counter?" I said.

"You gotta get your ear protectors and paper targets here, Sam," Lenny said.

Lenny seemed to know this geezerly clerk though, and they chatted easily. The guy, whose skin looked like beefy jerky, spoke in short raspy sentences, punctuating each statement with a deep rumbling cough. A full ashtray sat on the counter, a smoking butt balanced on the lip.

"Human or animal?" Beef Jerky asked.

"Huh?" I said.

"The man's just asking us to pick targets," Lenny said.

"The shape you'll shoot at," Jeff said. He was losing patience with me. "There are human shapes and deer shapes to pick from."

"Human," I told Beef Jerky.

"Give us a couple of deer targets," Jeff said, tossing a scornful look at me.

"Give us some of each," Lenny said, touching my shoulder with his hand. "Just for fun."

The man handed us the targets along with three sets of old-fashioned headphones and some big, geeky glasses.

Jeff put his stuff on quickly and shouldered a rifle case. He left me at the counter with Lenny.

"What's wrong with him?" I asked.

Lenny shrugged. "He needs a little time to get used to the new Sam-I-am."

"Sam-I-was," I said softly. Lenny raised his eyebrows for an explanation, but I shook my head. He showed me how to put on the gear. I copied everything he did; then we walked toward the glass doors that lead to the shooting gallery.

Going through those doors felt important. I pushed through the first, then the second set of heavy glass doors, imagining it was a science-fiction portal.

Jeff was already positioned in a shooting stall. I watched him attach a deer target to a clothesline contraption and send it fluttering out onto the range. There was something calculating about him, something a bit scary, as he dropped bullets into slots practically without looking. He propped his elbows up on the barrier. *Blam, blam, blam. Blam, blam.*

I moved behind him to see how he'd done. As he reeled in the paper target, I could see a neat pattern at the center of the deer's chest.

"Good shooting," I said.

He ignored me, and I instinctively looked at Lenny. He cupped his hands over his mouth to pantomime shouting.

I tapped Jeff on the shoulder and yelled, "Good shooting!" He smiled a little cowboy smile, though I still felt as if I were bothering him.

Lenny guided me to another stall. He slapped his case on the ledge and opened the two snaps simultaneously. A shiny pistol lay there like a vampire in a red velvet coffin.

"Wanna try it?" Lenny said. "Pick it up. Aim it toward the range."

The gun was heavier than I expected. As I held it in my hand, a powerful feeling raced up my arm and into my brain. My whole body turned into one big hard-on, which naturally made me think of Megan.

Lenny stared at me with an eager expression and the nodding head of a drug pusher. "Nice?" he said. "It's a Sig Sauer P239 nine millimeter. Full-size power in a personal-size handgun."

"You sound like a commercial," I said, clicking my neck sideways to get rid of Megan's imaginary insults.

"Maybe I am," he said, wiggling his eyebrows.

Close enough to get a whiff of his Cheerio and garlic scent, he showed me how to load the pistol. He loaded a human target on the clothesline contraption and reeled it away, then handed the pistol to me. He positioned me to shoot, manipulating my limbs.

"Arm outstretched. Support the gun with your left hand. Yeah, that's it. Feet apart. Watch for the recoil. Good. Now line the bead up with the V on the scope."

I nodded.

"When you're ready, go ahead and squeeze the trigger," he said.

I wiggled around a bit, feeling the placement of my arms and legs so I could remember it for next time. As I aimed, a wave of fear came over me, making my hand tremble. Did it bother me I was using a human target, or was I just choking?

Lenny touched me on the shoulder. "Think of a criminal threatening your family," he said.

I tried imaginary villains. Darth Vader, Venom, Magneto, Sauron. Nothing worked.

"I can't do it," I said, relaxing my stance.

"Think video game," he said. That had been Ryan's advice too.

I squeezed the trigger before getting into proper position—and the reverberation disoriented me and my elbow buckled—and the recoil knocked the gun into my cheekbone painfully.

I stepped back, touching my cheek. No blood. The pistol dangled from my arm.

"You okay?" Lenny asked. I nodded as I rubbed my cheek. I looked to see if Jeff had seen me screw up, but he was firing away.

"Try again," Lenny said, repositioning my hands.

This time the gun didn't hit my face. Half a dozen shots later, I was hitting the target more or less where I wanted. That surge hit me again, mostly as a tingling in my balls. Lenny switched me to a rifle with a deer target.

The rifle felt very different from the handgun, more respectable. There was a completely different set of associations. Besides hunting, there was the military thing where they hand rifles to kids to protect our country. Then there were those kids who broke into their weird uncle's gun cabinet in order to use rifles to pick off schoolmates.

I followed Lenny's instructions and shot for a while. I lost track of time. Lenny eventually tapped me on the shoulder and motioned for me to follow him back out the glass door portal. Jeff was walking ahead of us. We passed Beef Jerky smoking and nodding while trying to suppress his little cough eruptions.

Lenny picked a wobbly round table in the vending area with molded chairs as light as Styrofoam. Jeff pushed buttons for cream and sugar in an ancient coffee machine, then swore as he spilled some on his hand trying to manipulate the cup out of the opening. I got a Mountain Dew. Lenny got a Dr. Pepper.

Lenny spread my targets out on the table. "Nice shooting, Sam," he said, raising his eyebrows and looking at Jeff.

Jeff nodded. "Good," he said.

Lenny and I exchanged looks.

"Okay, pal, what's bothering you?" Lenny asked. "I mean, unless it's something you don't want to talk about in front of Sam. I've had about enough of this, thank you very much."

Jeff looked up, shocked. Then he sort of crumbled and stared into his cup.

"Sam knows all about it," Jeff said. "It's Elissa. She's been talking about moving out. She says it's just until the hunt's over. I thought it was just talk, but when she heard I was bringing Sam here, she went ballistic on me. I'm worried. Can't get it out of my mind. I'm not sure I'm doing the right thing here. Being in the DNR seems to be tearing my family apart."

"We could pray," Lenny began, but he stopped dead with a stare from Jeff. "Or not," he added.

"I bet you never thought you'd get me here," I said, trying to change the subject.

"Sam, I'd pretty much given up on you. I felt like your mother had gotten hold of you and she wouldn't let go."

This made me, the undercover me, feel crappy. "When the tribal elders came for me, she hid me in the hut and wouldn't let them take me," I said intelligently.

"What the hell are you talking about?" Jeff said.

"I know what he's talking about," Lenny said. "Initiation. The old tribal way— kidnapping the boys. Am I right, Sammy?"

"Oh, from Rosen's book," Jeff said, nodding. "The men kidnapping you and taking you into the forest and all that."

"That eco-scam shrink Rosen?" Lenny said suspiciously. "What kind of book did he give you, Sam?"

"He's not a shrink," Jeff said. At the same time he and I both said, "He's an eco-therapist"—and then we laughed.

"I won't ask what the hell that is," Lenny said.

"Don't," Jeff said. "It's not as bad as it sounds. The guy's a hunter."

"Catch and release?" Lenny said.

"Catch and eat," I said, showing my incisors. "His book's on the Lakota Sioux—their coming of age rituals mostly. Vision quests and all that."

"I can handle that," Lenny said. "Not exactly your Christian position, but I can handle it. Some of your tribal peoples, including some American Indians, were moving toward a monotheistic view. They just needed a little push."

"You mean after they cooked up some Jesuits, lost a few dozen wars, got decimated by syphilis," Jeff said.

"Don't turn history into an art form, my friend." Lenny clucked his tongue and shook his head. "But still, in my view, the Sioux were okay. Wankantanka ain't exactly Our Savior, but at least he sat in judgment."

"I didn't know you were so open-minded," Jeff said.

"Speaking of open-mindedness," Lenny said. "Since you gentlemen are so interested in initiation and all."

"Uh-oh," Jeff said.

"Hear me out," Lenny said to Jeff. "You know I've been after you forever to come to a Hunters of Men meeting."

"Yeah?" Jeff said. "You're offering me cash now?"

"Well, sir," Lenny said. "Sam and I had a few minutes to talk the other day, and, well, Sam's willing to give it a try. Aren't you, Sam?"

I nodded, fearing my voice would give away my fear.

"So you two had this all planned?" Jeff said. "Go, if you want to go. Who's stopping you?"

I hadn't anticipated this. I looked to Lenny for rescue.

"No can do," he said. "Minors need an adult companion. Lawyers run the world, you know. Milk cartons? 'Have you seen this child?'"

"What's in it for me?" Jeff asked.

"I'd take over teaching Sam archery and getting him ready for the hunt. As members, the two of you would have a better chance to hunt the Wirth . . ."

"I can't hunt the Wirth," Jeff said. "Are you kidding me? I'd be fired the next day."

"What about Sam? Think of him. He wants to show his friends that he's willing to let go of some of this deep ecology shit that's infecting this country. Are you ready to help him put an end to it?"

A growling noise came from Jeff.

"I think we should let Sam decide," Lenny said. "The Hunters of Men might know what you're going through, Sam. We call it running the rapids. You're moving fast, changing fast, not sure who your friends are or who your enemies are. Sound familiar?"

It did. It sounded like Hermes Rosen. In any case, I'd already said yes on account of my assignment.

"What do you say, Sam?" Lenny said. "Can you handle a muscular Christianity that challenges you to be all you can be?" His hand was back on my neck, kind of massaging it, which spooked me in a different way than thinking he was going to wring it.

"Sure," I said. "I'm up for it. I can handle it. You with me, Jeff?"

Jeff grumbled. "Okay, but I want a fur hat and I ain't jumpin' into no baptismal pool."

CHAPTER TWENTY

I T WAS OUR FIRST REAL COUNCIL MEETING SINCE STEWART had descended into
Megan's basement months ago. We went to our old spot like migrating birds,
but everything had changed. The summer lawn guy had stopped cutting the area,
and wild grasses and nasty weeds nearly covered the beat-up old benches, making them
look even more like ruins. Holly said it looked like someone had buried a body there.

Megan paced as usual while the rest of us found seats on the decaying benches.
Megan was dressing older, less field commando, more commando on holiday in Rome.
I liked it, but it also scared me a little. I wondered if her Unitarian parents were getting
through to her. "*Think of your future,*" they probably said to her. "*You don't want to
hang around those losers forever.*"

Megan wanted us *all* to check in about what we had done or were doing—or
planned to do—to get back on task about stopping the hunt. I proudly told them
about the Hunters of Men meeting, bragging that I had passed all Lenny's archery
tests. I studied Megan's eyes for admiration, but saw only irritation.

"No way," Ryan laughed. "You're really going to a Hunters of Men meeting? Are
you gonna wear a cute little green vest? Way to go, man!" He scratched occult symbols
in the dirt with a long stick while he talked. "I have to hand it to you, Sam. You did
better than I would have."

This was not like him, too complimentary. Something was up with that.

"I feel disconnected from whatever plan we're supposed to be doing," Megan said.
"For all we know, Stewart's forgotten about us. I can't believe we haven't seen or heard
from him since that meeting."

"We have," Holly said, looking smug. "I've been emailing him."

The three of us stared at her.

"Networking isn't your thing," I said.

"Who says? What, Megan gets to do everything? It wasn't so hard to find his address. I just emailed him. I told him what we've been doing. I told him about your archery thing, Sam. Everything."

"God, Holly," Megan said. "What is this, a secret relationship?"

She shrugged. "Somebody had to do it. It just turned out to be me. So what? He thinks I'm smart. I even emailed him some of my poetry. He says it's like Emily Dickinson, only darker and more up to date. He said I should be our go-between. 'A poetess is a natural shaman.' That's what he called me."

"I can't believe this," Ryan said.

"He told me other things too. Things you might want to know about."

"Like what?" Megan challenged.

"He told me it was the Hunters of Men who beat people up at the community meeting. They're dangerous, Sam."

"That wasn't them," I said. "That wasn't the Hunters of Men. Those were other hunters. The H.O.M.s were trying to calm people down."

"Sam?" Megan said. "They're getting to you already. Pretending you're a trained secret agent doesn't make you immune to professional brainwashing."

"It's not your fault, guy," Ryan said. "They mess with minds for a living."

"You forget," I said, trying to show confidence. "I live," I paused for dramatic effect, "completely undercover now, in an active civil war zone. The people around me are constantly trying to get inside my head and manipulate me to be on their side. You underestimate me, my friends."

"You're talking weird," Ryan said. "You're probably one of them already. Like in the *Body Snatchers*? It can happen in your sleep, dude."

"Do something hunterish, Sam," Holly clapped, and she laughed like a child.

I stood up slowly, pretending to load an arrow in a bow. "I'm gonna kill me somethin'," I said. I crouched and stalked toward Megan. "I'm a gonna git me a coonskin cap so people think I'm some critter in the forest."

"You don't have to do this," Megan said.

"What? Am I offending you?"

"I mean the whole thing, the whole undercover thing," she said. "It's obviously affecting you."

"Then I'm gonna shoot me one of them Bambis, maybe the king of them Bambis," I said. "Shoot 'im right through the goddam heart, I am, I am. That's why they call me Sam-I-am."

Holly screamed and held her ears.

"She's cracking up," Ryan said.

"Ryan's right about one thing," Megan said. "Stewart is kinda weird. I mean, I like Aztecs as much as the next person, but he freaks me out with that human sacrifice crap. I'm not sure I trust him."

"That doesn't matter now," Holly said. "We told him we'd do it. We can't just back out now. What would happen to the movement if we just did what nice people asked us to do? We have to trust someone. We have to just do it."

"Why are we only talking about me?" I asked. "What are you guys doing?"

Megan placed her fists on her hips. "Like you're the only one working."

"Our fearless leader—defying death as a student intern," Holly said.

"Don't start," Megan warned her.

"What a dangerous job," Holly said. "Little Miss Junior Reporter."

"I can't believe you said that," Megan said, her mouth unhinging like a reptile. "That's so ignorant. Nothing happens in this world without PR anymore. Ask anyone. And it's not a cushy job, for your information. I'm doing it to get skills for the movement. Why don't you try something difficult, little Miss Feel Sorry For Yourself?"

"Cushy, cushy, cushy," Holly sang.

"What about you, Ryan?" I said, tired of the same old catfight.

"Besides football?" Holly said, switching targets.

Ryan ignored her. "Coach says real commitment is putting your best self on the line, and that's what I'm doing."

"That assumes you can find yourself," Holly said. "Cut the sports bullshit, will you, Ryan? It's just supposed to be a cover."

"I'm working with the Creatures," Ryan said. "They're planning a big event, bigger than what they did at the community meeting. A big protest march and rally on the night before the hunt. With speakers, music, the whole big." He turned to Holly. "I bet you didn't know your precious Stewart Spiranga was speaking."

"We don't discuss mundane crap like that," Holly said.

"We should all do what we need to do. What we have to do." Ryan spoke with unusual sincerity: "You have to do what's right for you. Be your own master." He looked at us with Michael Jordan earnestness, puffing out his chest.

Holly practically spit at him, "Spare us the fucking football philosophy."

Ryan snapped, "Just because I'm being a positive person, you can't stand it."

"Oh, you're so positive," Holly shouted. "You think you can screw everyone else over!"

"What's that supposed to mean?" Ryan said.

"You know," she said. She pointed to her stomach.

Megan and I looked at each other in horror.

"What?" Ryan insisted.

"You got me pregnant," Holly said. "Mr. Fucking Positive."

Now Ryan showed horror on his face. "Oh, fucking Christ!" he said. "I knew it! I knew it was something like this!" He held both hands to his head. He kept repeating, "Oh shit, oh shit, oh shit."

"Are you sure, Holly?" Megan said. "This isn't one of your little games, is it?"

"I don't joke about life and death," she said. Then she started to cry, and I started to believe her.

"Does anyone else know?" Megan said, and I marveled at her ability to instantly ask an intelligent question.

Holly sputtered, "Just Stewart."

"Stewart?" Ryan said, standing. "What the hell is that? He knows before me? Maybe it's his, if you're such email buddy-buddies!"

"Right," Holly said, suddenly her sober acidic self. "I downloaded his sperm."

"God!" Ryan said, walking around with clenched fists to his ears. He scared me so much I moved away from him.

"Stewart thinks I should have an abortion," Holly said.

"What are you talking—Stewart?" His eyes went wide. "It just doesn't feel like I'm involved here."

"Screw you!" Holly said. "Fetus is yours all right, Ryan. There's no one else."

"Fetus?" I said. "Fetus—as in a name? Fetus? You named it *Fetus*?"

"Stewart said I should claim a woman's right to abortion," Holly said. "In traditional societies, women always chose who lived and who died. Women always had the final say on whether to have a baby, and they still should today."

"This isn't Ms. S-T's class," Megan said quietly. "We're talking real life here."

"So now I can't have my own ideas either?" Holly said. "You're the only one who can have ideas?"

"Whoa," Ryan said. "You *cry* when you see roadkill. Now you want to kill your— Fetus? You named this thing you have your ideas about killing? Are you completely nuts?"

"You talk about Sam being brainwashed," Holly said. "Ryan, you don't even believe in Catholicism, but you say what they taught you to say. They programmed you. Permanently. You're damaged. You can't think for yourself."

I had to admit Holly was in a weird place, crying one minute, shooting intelligent acid the next.

"Remember those dead deer on the highway?" Ryan said.

Holly started to cry again, this time more like a little kid. "That's not fair," she said.

"You think you can handle a dead baby then?" Ryan said.

"For god's sake, Ryan, it's not the same thing," Megan said. "And you don't have to keep bringing up the deer to torture her."

"Stewart probably thinks abortion is a sacrifice to some pagan god," Ryan said.

Holly screamed as she lunged toward Ryan, knocking him off his stump. They rolled around for a few minutes wrestling. Megan and I watched for a few minutes, then separated them.

Ryan found his stick again and tapped it with renewed energy. Megan paced. The first warning bell rang. We had five minutes to figure out the world.

I watched two beetles attached to each other. The bottom one carried both of them through the sand. Fighting or having sex, I couldn't tell which.

"What I want to know is . . ." I said, and I stood, "do you, Megan, support me, Sam-I-am? Personally, as a person?" It sounded garbled, but more or less was what I wanted to say.

"And take whoever-he-is for your lawfully wedded whatchamacallit?" Ryan said.

"Shut up," I snapped at him. I turned back to Megan. "I mean not just as a part of the Council of Nations or because we committed to Stewart or because you believe in what we're doing. Do you support me personally—as a person?"

Megan approached me and shut her eyes. She opened her eyes and took my hands, sending a surge of blood to my groin. It was the first time in a very long time she'd done anything remotely seductive.

"Of course, I do, Sam," she said. "But this spy thing—I'm not sure I like it. I'm proud of you for doing it and all. It's brave, but I worry about you. It's really dangerous what you're doing, in all kinds of ways."

"I can handle it," I said. I wanted to make a joke, but looking into Megan's eyes felt too good.

"What about me?" Holly said. "What am I supposed to do? Save the earth by overpopulating it or by aborting Fetus?"

This shut everyone up big time.

Megan sat beside Holly. "I've been thinking, Hol. My parents might agree to take the baby if you want to have it. I mean, they take in people from El Salvador all the time. We have the space."

"Oh, right, Patty Hearst," she said. "We'll all just move in like the Symbionese Liberation Army and breed the next generation of revolutionaries."

"You know," Ryan said to Holly, "you're a cold bitch sometimes."

"But," Megan said, "if you choose to terminate—"

"Don't even go there," Ryan said.

"Why not?" Megan said. "Does your pope even care about overcrowding the earth? I don't think so."

"Just don't start," Ryan said. "I'm sensitive about that."

"I didn't think you had any other sensitive parts," Holly said.

"Split, Ryan, if you don't want to hear reality," Megan said. She turned back to Holly. "If you choose to, well, exercise your choice . . ."

"She means kill Fetus," Ryan said.

"Ryan!" Holly screamed.

"Stop it," Megan said. "Just stop it!"

After too long of a silence, Megan went on: "Holly, you have an important job. I mean, while you're figuring out . . . the other thing. You can continue to be our go-between with Stewart. Go back and update him. Tell him we're still with him."

Holly saluted, then wiped tears away.

"Okay, then," Megan said. "Holly talks to Stewart. Sam infiltrates the Christian crazies. Ryan works with the Creatures. I stay with my media work."

Amazingly, she had done it, succeeded in making it sound like we were a revolutionary cell again, all working toward a common goal.

The last bell rang. Holly got up abruptly and began walking toward the school. Maybe it was my imagination, but I thought I detected a slight waddle. Ryan ran ahead and joined her. Holly said something to him, probably mean. We watched him sprint past her toward the school.

THE COUNCIL AVOIDED EACH OTHER AFTER THAT MEETING for a couple of weeks. I think we all pretended to be undercover as an excuse for not talking. Except Holly.

She wanted to talk, which was all the more reason to avoid her. When I saw her lurking around with dark circles under her eyes, I'd worry about her for a second but make sure she didn't see me.

I went into serious science-fiction mode. My books comforted me with their predictable stories of misunderstood individuals confronting evil empires. I was rereading *The Luna Chronicles* for the thirteenth time. The hero manages to have sex with a foxy guerilla commando leader (a near-human alien) before she gets infected and vows to destroy him. I pictured the commando leader as Megan, proving once again that a sex life is easier to imagine than have.

One afternoon, Holly found me in the geek corner of the cafeteria, my new place to hide. It bothered me how well I fit in, huddling over the remains of my greasy lunch listening to the geeks prattle on about computer games, rip-off upgrades, and illicit downloads of one thing or another.

"Sam, what's going on?" Holly said. She sat down next to me, breathing heavily.

I gave her a quick once-over. She looked puffy but not overtly pregnant. The Goth thing made her look ill, but then again that was the point. She wore one clunky piece of jewelry, a lump of turquoise on a silver chain.

"Turquoise," I said, nodding toward her grown-up cleavage.

"It's supposed to help you make decisions," she said. "I'm getting zero help from you guys."

My eyes wandered to my open book, and I started reading involuntarily.

"Hel-lo, Sam? Where did you go?" Suddenly angry, she added, "What's with you people? Everyone's doing that."

"Doing what?"

"Disappearing, evaporating. Poof. Megan's turned into Lois Lane. Ryan's spends all his time flexing in the mirror as if football is some kind of fashion runway. He won't even return my emails. Some radical cell we are. When Patty was—"

"Don't start with the Patty Hearst thing," I said. "We're modern teenagers. We mature more slowly."

"That's what I thought too," she said. "But flaky has consequences." She sighed and looked around. "Who are these people? Can I have one of your fries?"

"No," I said. "You gonna have it? The baby, I mean."

She shrugged. "Megan thinks I should. She got her parents to agree to take care of it. At least she says they agreed." She rolled her eyes. "We could all be one big sit-com."

"You gonna do it?"

"And raise him Unitarian?" she said. "Are you kidding?" She opened her eyes wide and pushed her face close to me. "Those eyes. I don't know if I could do that to Fetey. Maybe he should stay up there in the angelic zone."

"*Fetey* now? And *him*?" I said. "You're scaring me now, Holly. Calling it Fetus was creepy enough, but Fetey? If you name it, you won't be able to . . ."

"To kill it? We kill lots of things with names," she said quickly. "Pets, prisoners on death row, criminals, 4-H pigs, old people."

"See? The turquoise is working," I said. "You're getting clearer."

"I'm nearing the end of my first trimester, Sam. If I'm gonna dump Fetey, it's soon or never." Her face did look different now, still swollen and sad, but oddly sweet. I let her eat some of my fries.

"I talked to Stewart again," she said. She wiggled around on the bench uncomfortably. "It's so weird over there."

"You went to his house?"

"Home office," she said. "He said women must be the ones who decide what to do with . . ."

"Their feteys?" I said.

She deepened her voice: "He said, 'Women's freedom to choose is an important right to protect. No government has the right to interfere with the business of the gods.'" She gobbled two cold, twisted fries.

"Are you craving, like, pickles and ice cream?"

She waved me away. "I don't want to talk about that. Let's talk about something else. I want to hear more about this magical deer encounter you had. Like, a deer talked to you?"

I lowered my head and looked around suspiciously. "How did you find out about that? I haven't told anyone."

"Janine told me." She made a gas mask pantomime.

"Janine? Where?"

"At Planned Parenthood. She's a part-time counselor there. She's the one who gave me the turquoise. She said Native Americans use it to reduce mental confusion." She giggled. "That's why they put it in all their jewelry for white people. Isn't that great?"

"Janine told you?" I said. "She must have heard it from Elissa." I imagined a chain of women whispering my secrets, all of them giggling.

"Don't worry," she said. "She thinks it's cool. She thinks you're special." She patted my arm. "She doesn't believe this so-called conversion."

"That's bad, remember?" I moaned. "I can't believe people are talking about me. What about Stewart? Does he say anything about me?"

"I hate to tell you this, but," she grimaced, "he knows about your deer vision too."

I slapped my forehead with my palm. "Stewart knows? Who told him? Janine?"

"No I did. I'm sorry, I didn't know it was such a secret. I thought it was cool."

A cold wind rushed through me. I felt suddenly very alone. I was back in the forest on that night with Big Buck staring down at me. His animatronic mouth moved. "You must kill me," he said. "For the good of all." I shivered.

"What's wrong?" Holly said. She was licking her fingers like a cat cleaning itself.

"There are parts of that I don't understand. Parts I didn't want anyone to know. Confusing parts. Stewart might think I'm flaky and pull the assignment. All this work practicing my bow at the range would be for nothing."

"Sam," she said, "you ought to be talking to someone about this. What about that Rosen guy?"

"I can't. Jeff says he's Elissa's guy. I'm supposed to be over that now."

"What about Stewart?"

"You forget—I'm undercover. I'm going to the goddam Hunters of Men meeting on Sunday morning. People could be following me even as we speak. Watching me. Some Hunter kids might go to this school."

She looked around quickly, then gave me a puzzled look. "I doubt it." She switched to a southern accent: "They don't let no hillbillies in this here school." In her normal voice, she continued, "Now you're scaring me. Maybe you should wear this turquoise for a while."

"No, thanks," I said.

"Why don't you talk to me then?" she said.

I couldn't think of any reason not to. She already knew most of the story.

"If you really want to know, I'll tell you," I asked.

We went outside and walked back and forth along the perimeter fence like neurotic zoo animals. I blabbed out the whole Big Buck story to her, including details I was surprised I even remembered. I felt lighter as I talked. I wondered if this was what people meant by intimacy, this lightness. It wasn't so bad. The story, however, did sound seriously crazy in the light of day.

"Big Buck said you should kill him?" she asked. She had her natural mocking expression in her voice, but I felt she was trying to be sincere. "Sam, you didn't get into any of Ryan's brother's stash that night or anything, did you?"

"I wasn't on anything. I swear."

"So this mystical creature, this creature from another world, this angel, this god, told you to kill it because there were too many of his kind?" She spoke in a dreamy way, as if reciting poetry.

"Well, I wouldn't call him a god," I said.

"Maybe your buck god was speaking to me too," she said in a small faraway voice. "To all of us. There's more people than there are deer, you know." She looked at me, and I didn't like what I saw. Her face was morphing. There was a new craziness creeping into her eyes.

"Listen, Holly. Don't get spooky on me. You know there's no connection between this and your . . . thing. Okay, Fetey. If that's where you're going . . . well, just don't. These things are just happening at the same time. That's all. They're not connected. Deer are deer. People are people. Don't mix apples with pears."

"I suppose you've never heard of synchronicity?" she said. "This has synchronicity written all over it."

"Of course I've heard of synchronicity," I said. Like many unusual concepts, I had a vague memory of Elissa saying it was important.

"Just so we're on the same page, to me it means things that go on at the same time are connected even if they don't look like it to dead white men," she said. "A butterfly flapping its wings in Brazil or somewhere can start a hurricane in Africa. That's science. Freud or someone discovered it, and then these white male scientists tried to cover it up. You're not the only one who reads. I'm learning all about this, Mr. Smartie. I'm reading astrology. I signed up for a class at the Free U."

She reached into her huge purse and held up a book with a tattered paper jacket, *The Cycles of the Moon and How to Live with Them*.

I wasn't sure what I wanted to say. *Strange But True* covered astrology. Planetary cycles did make people crazy. All kinds of crap happened on the full moon—murders, pregnancies, UFO sightings.

"Everything is connected," she went on. "Rock musicians are even singing about it now. Truth is really coming out of the closet. You just might want to update yourself." She shook her book at me, then stuffed it back into her bag. "Maybe Big Buck was trying to tell you something but you can't interpret it yourself. You should talk to someone, preferably someone not white and not male."

"I'm talking to you," I said. "And it's not going so well."

"Oh, you know what I'm saying. Don't be stupid."

You tell people your secrets, I thought, *and they call you stupid. Is this intimacy too*, I wondered? I decided I didn't care for it.

"Don't hitch a ride on my story," I said. "It's not about you. It's mine. It's about me. Things are just what they are sometimes, Hol. This has nothing to do with you. It's like you're sucking my story out of me and injecting it into yourself."

"I'm really a vampire," she said, doing a surprisingly good impression of the undead, complete with snarling mouth and clawed hand raised against the sun.

"That explains the outfit," I said. "Every time I think about this deer thing, it seems weirder. Maybe it didn't happen at all." I felt a prickling sensation in my throat and something tickling the corners of my eyes.

We were once again up against the edge of the fenced-in yard, the edge of the known universe, as we used to call it in happier times. Holly began to walk down the little hill back toward the parking lot. I caught her arm as she slipped.

"I'm not vampiring your vision," she said. "I have plenty of access to the other worlds. I don't need yours. You'll see."

CHAPTER TWENTY-ONE

THE HUNTERS OF MEN HELD THEIR WEEKLY MEETINGS in the basement of an Evangelical Free Church of Something or Other in a nameless blue-collar suburb of Minneapolis. I had heard about giant Christian churches with health clubs and travel agencies, but this wasn't one. This building looked more like an accounting office.

Jeff and I met Lenny in the parking lot. Jeff had been silent on the drive over, so even seeing Lenny was a relief.

"Gentlemen!" Lenny shouted, flying at us and threatening a group hug. Jeff and I were both good dodgers, and a little smile passed between us.

"You won't regret coming," Lenny said.

"Where's my fur hat?" Jeff said.

"Do we get vests like yours?" I asked.

"You earn that vest, boy," Lenny said. He slapped us on our backs then directed us toward the building with a hand on my neck.

We funneled down a stairwell behind a bunch of standard-issue Bunyans, all in their green vests. I eyed the few other teenagers suspiciously, but they ignored me. As the line slowed, I craned my neck to see why. A grizzly-sized man talked to each person before they passed through an inner door. The man had a black beard that outlined his round, reddish face, a camo cap on his mane of salt-and-pepper hair.

He laughed with each person as (I imagined) he asked them what they had killed recently. He ended with a hug and a belly laugh, one per customer.

When we got to him, he grabbed Lenny in a backslapping bear hug, which I found painfully embarrassing. Jeff, as hug-o-phobic as I was, put his arm over my shoulder.

"Jeff," Lenny said, "this is Big Pete. He's Chief Hunter this year. A sort of master of ceremonies."

Jeff shot out a stiff hand, which Pete took in both of his. Pete looked silently into Jeff's eyes for a few seconds, way too long for my comfort.

"I welcome you," he said finally. "Bring us your grief."

"And this is Sam," Jeff said, thrusting me toward Big Pete. "My son."

"A new recruit?" Big Pete said. "Fantastic! We need the kids!"

He grabbed my face between his dry, calloused hands. I thought he was going to kiss me.

"Welcome, Sam. You are a very lucky young man."

We entered the inner chamber of the basement. If you paid me to say something positive about the room, I'd say it was clean. No dust bunnies were visible to the naked eye. The air, however, was something else. Male-generated carbon dioxide merging with toxic methane gas (from burps and farts) crowded out any free radical oxygen molecules. Christian rock played on the sound system.

An usher walked us toward the front, to a special row where they apparently kept new guys under observation. Lenny kept stopping to talk to people, and I had a chance to look around with my jaw clenched.

I was sure my nervousness would get me spotted and bounced. I tried to calm myself by remembering who I was and what I was doing. The name was Bond, Green Bond, on a mission to save the earth, starting with innocent deer.

What did the various Bonds do when they entered the inner sanctum of an enemy? Keep busy noticing things. I noticed green vests, jeans, truck rally T-shirts, sports jerseys, and dress flannel. And caps, lots of caps.

Just as my Bond mind began working, I saw Fat Hunter, the guy from the community meeting. I forced myself to study the man carefully. Was this the guy? I wasn't one hundred percent sure.

Big Chief Pete appeared on the little stage. He held both arms straight up, each hand making a "V." Everyone stood, and the room quieted instantly.

"Hail, fellow Hunters of Men!" Pete bellowed.

"Hail, Chief Pete!" the crowd bellowed back.

"We have some newcomers here tonight, thanks to Brother Lenny," he said. "Stand up, Sam and Jeff O'Brien! Let's give them a hunter's welcome."

The room erupted into a loud growling, "Grrrr."

I stood and felt Jeff grab my shirt and pull me down to my seat. Everyone else was already sitting. People seemed to be laughing at me. Big Pete had made a joke at my expense.

"But seriously," he said. "Glad to have new blood." Then he addressed the group. "Gentlemen, let's start with our hunter's prayer."

Almost everyone bowed their heads.

"Let us pray," Pete said. "We pray for strength to preach the gospel of Jesus through the example of our stewardship of God's great wilderness. We try to bring the faithless back to God as we bring the game to the table, devoting ourselves to the church of field and forest, where salvation is as elusive as the game we hunt. Praise to the Great Hunter, Jesus Christ!"

"Praise to the Great Hunter, Jesus Christ!" the men said in a unified voice.

Shuffling and noise broke, but Peter quieted the room again.

"For the sake of the newcomers, I'll introduce this next section of the meeting. Needless to say, you must already have been sworn to secrecy from Brother Lenny that anything you see or hear in this room stays here." He seemed to be looking straight at me. "Or we'll come after you," he added.

Everyone laughed, except me and Jeff.

"The next section of our meeting is put aside for testimonies of kills, particularly allowing for the part we keep hidden from others, and sometimes from ourselves. The grief of killing we show only to each other." He looked at me again. "Unlike some of our critics out in the world, we don't think grief is a reason to give animals the vote." Laughter from the audience startled me. "But we honor our grief nonetheless. Do I have a witness?"

Immediately a young man, maybe twenty, rose from the back of the room. "Chief Pete, I wish to speak." He wasn't a bad-looking kid, as farm kids go. In fact, he reminded me vaguely of Ryan.

"Tell us of your grief," Pete said.

"I got my first deer," the young man said in a quavering voice.

I expected the guys to break out and cheer, but they turned to him in an attentive silence. What shocked me more was that the guy started crying. Then he told a brief story of the stalk and the shot. He told of taking the kill shot photo with his uncle, then tying the deer up to gut it.

"When I cut it open," he sobbed. "I just started crying. His eyes were so beautiful and big, looking at me. I couldn't get over the fact that minutes before he was this wonderful creature running free and now he was—because of me—dead. Dead!"

It moved me a little to see a guy my age cry, though the "Dead!" thing was a bit much.

Then the men said, "Dead, dead, dead." It was some kind of chant, or signal that this speaker was done. It spooked me. Pete called on another guy. This one was an old farmer. He talked about killing his oldest pig and making bacon out of him. It was his special pig, a pet he'd kept after his kids left home. He too sniffled a little. He didn't end with the "Dead!" thing—he just sat down.

Pete called on others. We heard stories about other hunting kills, other farm animals being slaughtered or pets put to sleep. Usually there was something special about the animal, but not always. Some guys told stories that sounded like very ordinary hunting stories except that they cried at the end for the quail, the coyote, or the mass of prairie dogs. One guy cried about a large muskie.

It was fascinating and scary at the same time. I wanted to nudge Jeff and ask him if this was what AA meetings were like, but his face looked weird, twisted in sorrow, quivering, on the edge of crying maybe.

Startled, I stared straight ahead. This was getting serious. Pete still seemed to be looking at me, but I wasn't sure. Maybe it was some technique like they used in old paintings that made his eyes seem to stay on me. Just as I was losing my sense of reality, Jeff stood up.

I wanted to grab his shirtsleeve and pull him down. But it was too late. He was already saying, "I killed a dog." Tears already ran down his face. "I kicked it to death," he said. "When I was drunk. A long time ago." He covered his eyes with his hand and Lenny touched him on the arm. "I was drunk. It was one of the things that got me sober, kicking that damn barking thing to death."

Another shock: he was talking about my dog, Corky! Corky had disappeared when I'd been about five, and we hadn't spent all that much time looking for him.

My body spasmed in a way it never had before.

"I want to apologize to my son here, Sam, for what I did. I'm sorry, Sam. And I want to apologize to Corky for doing that to him. I'm sorry, Sam. I'm sorry, Corky."

Jeff was sobbing now, even making little sounds. I was frozen. It was like I wasn't there. I remembered Corky and hated Jeff for killing him.

Lenny stood up and put an arm around Jeff, gently pulling him into his seat. Pete's eyes still bore into me. I felt fragile, as if I would crack if anyone touched me. I fought off images of Corky alive. Corky dead. Corky being kicked by a drunk Jeff.

"Thank you, Brother Jeff, for being willing, on your first visit, to tell us that. May we all feel the grief of being weak creatures of the flesh."

"Dead, dead, dead," the men intoned solemnly.

"I pray to the Great Hunter to forgive us our sins," Pete sang. "Forgive us our trespasses as we forgive those who trespass against us. And now, gentlemen, the Bucket o' Blood."

Bucket o' Blood? I thought.

"For the sake of our visitors, a little introduction," Pete said. "I am sure you know, as Bible-reading Christians, the story of Christ's Last Supper, as well as the fact that it was based on the Jewish Shabbat. We borrowed from a couple of traditions, in all humility, to make out little ritual here that reminds us of who and what we are. The bucket, please."

Two guys came out. One carried a simple wooden stool, the other a very ordinary-looking metal bucket.

Pete held out what looked like a pincushion full of pins.

"The Lord said to the Israelites," he said, "when they were enslaved by the Egyptians, 'Mark your houses with the blood of a freshly killed lamb, that my angel will know to pass by your homes.' And the Jews killed the lamb . . ." He took a pin and stabbed his finger, squeezing a drop of blood into the bucket.

"I add my innocence to the lamb's blood," he said.

He reached into the bucket and pulled out his hand, two of his fingers covered in what I assumed was lamb's blood. He made a line below each of his eyes like war paint.

"And the angel of wrath," he said, "knew to pass by the houses of the Israelites so marked. And Jesus said, many years later, 'This is my body. This is my blood. Do this in memory of me.'"

Pete stepped away as a line formed. People walked up, took a pin, and stabbed their fingers as he had done. They walked away with bloody paint under their eyes.

"This is crazy," I said very softly. What I meant was I was feeling crazy. I wanted to do it, and I didn't know why. Maybe it was suddenly being flushed with horror of what Jeff had done to Corky. Maybe it was to show all these jerks that I could do what they did and I didn't have to be one of them.

I stood and waited for someone to pull me down, but instead Jeff stood up and joined me. As we moved out, Jeff found and squeezed my hand, letting go quickly before I could respond or ignore him.

I partly blamed Rosen's books, since my head was filled with Indian lore. Then I did it, the whole thing: stabbed my finger as Pete smiled at me, dripped my blood into the bucket, dipped my hand into the warm liquid, and made the brave marks on my face. One of the attendants handed me a gauze pad for my finger. I, cowboy, nodded thanks at him and went back to my seat, where I couldn't stop thinking about Corky.

CHAPTER TWENTY-TWO

THE COUNCIL WAS PRETTY MUCH OVER. I saw Holly and Ryan at school arguing and whispering in various corners. At school, it was weird with Megan also. Neither of us knew what to say about Holly or the Fetey situation. We tried once, and Megan ended up crying, so we stopped.

I'd convinced my dad that Megan was too radical for me, so she and I had to meet secretly at coffee shops. It had its romantic spy side. I looked forward to the meetings even though Megan mostly complained about sitting around with her parents.

Once, at the coffee shop, Megan looked around, then said, "Psst. Take a look at these."

She handed me a bunch of papers. Mostly they were just announcements by the Little Creatures of the Forest about anti-hunt protest events—marches, talks, parties of various kinds. There was also a form to send in to sign up for Tent City.

"What's this Tent City?" I said.

"Oh, we already changed the name. How do you like Free City? Free the deer? Huh?"

"So this is the overnight camp?" I asked.

"We had to. The hunters will be starting very early. If we waited for our people to get enough coffee in them to get over there, it would all be over." She smiled. "I'll have my own tent. You can come visit."

"I'll be there," I said. It seemed pretending to be spies was freeing us up to say things we otherwise would have had a hard time saying.

"Look," she said. "Your mom's in this one."

The Little Creature news release showed Elissa's picture. They described her as a "a local business owner, eco-feminist activist, and the newly elected Creatures spokeswoman."

"God, I feel like I hardly know her," I said.

"She's working hard," Megan said. "Of course, you know I think the Little Creatures are a bit dated, but they do bring out the bodies. And sometimes the TV cameras."

She began reading from another paper, "Nine Ways You Can Help Save the Animals," in a sexy whisper:

"Consider alternatives to leather when you buy shoes," I read. "Don't go to zoos or circuses with animals. Avoid products from companies using animals in experiments, even if it's just rodents. Eat cholesterol-free tofu products. Engage any hunter you know in a discussion of why they hunt."

She looked up at me. "So, why do you hunt?" she asked playfully.

"To balance nature," I said. "And to be honest about our place in the food chain."

She frowned. "You said that a little too convincingly. You're scaring me again, Sam."

I got defensive and fumbled around, going on about what a great man Stewart was. I exaggerated how excited I was to screw up the hunt.

"I don't know," she said. "We're counting on Stewart too much." She shook her head. "I mean, we should have a bunch of different plans all working together. What if his buzzers don't work?"

"Well, maybe someone will shoot me then, thinking I'm a deer."

She reached to touch my hand, almost spilling my coffee. "Don't even say that," she said.

"We have to enjoy the time we have," I said. "There are no guarantees in this world. We all have to do our part."

"Oh, that would be so awful," she said. She squeezed by hand harder. "You absolutely have to come to my tent. I just decided."

"Decided what?" I said, but my crotch knew what she meant.

She smiled, maybe blushed—I couldn't tell. "A surprise," she said. "For my eco-warrior man."

Like a portal to another world, I suddenly had a new fantasy to add to my GreenSWAT inventory. But this one was real, or might be real. In my mind it was called "Megan's Tent."

THAT NIGHT I SPENT A LONG TIME AT HAL'S, blasting away at one target after another. I wanted to get in as much practice as possible before the hunt. It was also a relief to do something where I got exactly the results I wanted.

I wasn't worried anyone would miss me. Elissa was ignoring me even more than usual. She hardly talked to me anymore. She'd write the times and locations of her meetings on our calendar and disappear with Perry for days, it seemed. Jeff was treating me more like an adult roommate, which had both good and bad sides.

As I biked up the driveway with my bow case strapped to my back, I noticed something was different: Elissa had parked her sky-blue minivan in the driveway. At this hour, it would normally be parked in the garage. A second minivan—older, burgundy, rusty—sat next to hers. It had to be one of Elissa's friends because anyone coming over for Jeff had a gas-guzzling SUV or pickup.

I was hit by a very strange idea for a prank. I took off my shirt and smeared my chest and face with dirt from the garden. I opened my bow case and nocked an arrow against the string. I cracked the door open and stepped in quietly using the hunter's stalk that Lenny had taught me.

The house was much messier than usual. It looked like someone had been searching for something and left the mess as they moved on. The idea of robbers came to me.

When I heard noises coming from my parents' bedroom, I began to believe in robbers, just enough to get my heart beating.

I walked silently into the darkness at the top of the stairs, my breathing shallow and fast. I stood outside my parents' bedroom door, listening to drawers open and close.

When the door began to open, I raised my bow. When someone definitely not Elissa barged out at me suddenly, my arrow released itself. A female figure screamed and crumpled to the ground.

Elissa appeared at the door and shouted, "Sam!" as she crouched over the person. "Have you gone completely insane?"

I couldn't bring myself to say anything.

"Are you hurt?" Elissa asked the woman.

A childish "No" came from the crying woman on the floor. I felt relief so intense I felt dizzy. Elissa sat beside the woman and pulled her onto her lap. The woman had her hands over her face, so I didn't know who she was. I crouched down to set my bow on the floor. I looked at the women stupidly.

The woman's cries sounded almost like laughter. She had a haircut like Patti's, but that didn't make sense. When she dropped her hands to cover her nose and mouth, I recognized her eyes.

"Janine?" I said. I looked around for her gas mask, assuming I'd knocked it off.

"Of course, it's Janine!" Elissa said angrily. "And you probably triggered an abuse flashback." She cooed at Janine, "Honey, take a big breath and hold it for as long as you can. You're just scared."

I got on my hands and knees and began searching for her mask.

"What the hell are you doing?" Elissa said.

"Looking for her gas mask!" I said, with as much attitude as I dared.

"She doesn't need it anymore. Where's your shirt? And why are you covered with dirt? What's happening here?

I cringed. What *was* I doing? The three of us breathed heavily for a couple of minutes and didn't speak. Janine closed her eyes while Elissa patted her head.

"Sam, I'm waiting for an explanation," Elissa said in a calm voice. Her eyes pierced me.

"I was just . . ."

"You're confirming my worst fears, Sam," Elissa said. "You're losing the ability to distinguish reality from fantasy." She turned her attention back to Janine. "Are you all right, honey?"

Janine sat up and wiped tears from her eyes.

"I knew this would happen," Elissa said. "Jeff doesn't know what forces he's unleashing here."

"Sam-I-am," Janine said, and she smiled a little.

"Janine," I said as if I were just learning English. "What happened to . . ."

"My mask?" she said. "I'm off it. Isn't that great?"

Elissa stood up and said, "I'm too angry to talk to you right now, Sam." She went back into the bedroom, crouched over the dresser, and began pulling on a stuck drawer. "Goddamn thing," she said.

Janine and I stared at each other. She touched the dirt on my face. "Practicing for Halloween?"

"Yeah," I said. "I'm gonna be Hiawatha."

She laughed. Elissa yelled from inside. "I'll Hiawatha you!"

"It's a miracle, Sam," Janine said. "I've had a healing."

She tilted her head to the side like a parrot, playfully touching my shoulder. Dirt came off on her fingers and she looked at them. "I got rebirthed. I got a fresh start."

"I heard of that," I said. "You pretend you're getting born again, roll around with blankets and pillows on the floor?"

"That's not how I explained it to you," Elissa yelled.

I remembered something about getting over the trauma of steel forceps grabbing your head and pulling you out of your mother. I kept my voice low: "Janine, what's going on here?"

She put a hand to her mouth. "Oh, Sam," she said. "No one's told you, have they?"

"Told me what?"

"Your mom," she said. "She's moving in with me. Until the hunt is over. I assumed you were coming along."

"Moving out?" I said. "Elissa?"

"It's all just temporary. Everything's just temporary, Sam. Patti moved out too. We all need some space. Come with us."

Then Janine explained how she and Patti had been arguing all the time and had talked it over and gotten this idea to take a sabbatical from each other. Then they talked to Elissa, who was arguing all the time with Jeff, and it all just came together, a good solution for everyone. Patti had moved in with another friend, but she still helped out at the Whole Child.

I stood up and walked into the bedroom. There were piles of clothes and junk everywhere. Elissa sat on the ground with her underwear drawer on her lap. It was full of frilly panties and bras.

"I never have any decent underwear," she said.

"Why are you doing this?" I said, sitting on the bed with an angry flop.

"Because it's best," she said. "I think we'll all be less angry with each other if we don't have to eat breakfast together the day this thing goes down."

"Ryan says stage three of divorce always starts with someone moving out on some excuse that it's going to save the marriage."

"Ryan the expert," she sighed.

"Everything he's said has come true," I said. This wasn't true, but it sounded good.

"Listen, Sam, I would have told you earlier, but you were never around."

"Never around?"

"Okay, *I* was never around," she said. "Whatever. This is damage control at this point. I know this isn't the best timing, but would you consider coming with us?"

"But I'm . . ."

She put up her hand. "Before you get all uppity and outraged, mister, I want you to hear what I have to say. I think after the behavior I just witnessed, I deserve a hearing."

She repositioned herself to face me.

"I don't know what you're up to with all this hunting, saying you're on Jeff's side, watching his movies, eating his meat diet, and leaving your friends behind, but I'm suspicious about it. Something's up with that, something fishy. Don't tell me you're not still seeing Megan."

I opened my mouth as I formed a defense, but said nothing, and she smiled at my confusion.

"At the coffee shop?" she said. "Don't deny it. I have my spies. I don't know what this is all about, and if I knew, I probably wouldn't like it. But I'm giving you a chance here to opt out of this thing you're caught in. Right here and now. Come with Perry and me. Jeff will understand. He's gotta know this isn't real. We have things you can do to be useful. The Coalition, I mean. Drop your play-acting, be with your friends, and still call yourself a radical. Join the Little Creatures protests. Let this whole thing go. Now I want you to think about this before you answer me."

Though words formed on the tip of my tongue, it wasn't easy to blast her back. Maybe it was because I'd nearly killed Janine, but Elissa's offer hit me hard. I'd been living a tense life with no one suspecting how hard that was. Megan was suspicious that I was really changing into a hunter. Ryan and Holly were off in their own world somewhere. Stewart was a distant ghost. I'd been alone with my Bond fantasy for a long time.

And Elissa kept hitting the button: "Listen, Sam, it's just for a week or so. You can be yourself with us, without all this game playing. This must be exhausting."

"What about Jeff?" I said.

"Jeff?" She shrugged. "He knows I'm leaving. He's busy with the hunt, in case you haven't noticed. You'd be helping him out, in a way. You know he works best alone. He can pretend he's at Lenny's hunting camp or something."

"What about after?" I said.

"After what?" she said. "You mean *after* after? I've scheduled us all to meet with Dr. Rosen the Monday after the event. I figured we can talk it through, get our feelings out, decide if we can put Humpty Dumpty back together."

"They couldn't," I said.

She frowned.

"Put Humpty Dumpty back together," I said.

"They didn't have crazy glue back then, Sam. Or hot glue guns. What do you want me to say?"

She shifted her attention to the picture my arrow had broken and picked it up. "I can't believe you hit this," she said. "It's like symbolic."

It was a photograph of Elissa and Jeff in full hippie regalia. Their smiling faces looked so young and innocent I couldn't look at them. She picked up my arrow and handed it to me, then began plucking glass shards out of the rug and dropping them onto the remaining shattered glass of the photograph.

"Sam, as you and I both know, deep down, you're still on the my side. We know this, don't we?" She looked at me with piercing eyes, but I didn't flinch. "You've got so many layers of pretending going on here, but this isn't one of your science-fiction fantasies. This is dangerous. You're asking too much of yourself. Someone's going to get hurt."

"Or maybe killed," Janine said from the open door.

"Janine, would you go check on Perry?" Elissa said. "He's playing his Game Boy in his room. Thanks."

"You mean *my* Game Boy in *my* room," I said.

"Listen to yourself. *Your* Game Boy? How old are you trying to be? Do you even know? Huh?" Janine disappeared and Elissa shook her head. "You never should have stopped seeing Rosen."

"Rosen?" I said. "It was all his idea." I didn't even know what I was saying was his idea, but I had to blame somebody for something.

"What was?"

"It's all in that book he gave me on the Lakota. Blame him, why don't you?"

"Sam, that was meant to be metaphorical. A story you'd relate to, something you could think about. You don't have to do it with real bows and arrows and forests and deer, for Chrissake."

"Then why don't you blame Big Buck too?" I said. "You said he was sending me a message."

"Now I *am* worried," she said. "You're delusional. Are you on drugs?"

"No, I'm perfectly sane," I said. I looked at myself in the dresser mirror. A half-naked savage covered with streaks of mud stared back at me.

"Why are you doing this?" she asked.

I took the offensive instead of answering.

"Why are you doing what *you're* doing? You don't even like animals that much. You hate mice and sparrows. Ants, mosquitoes. You're just doing this so they'll mention your name in newsletters and you'll get new clients."

"Is this the place in your movie where I slap your face?" she laughed. "Okay, I'll be straight with you, if you promise you won't go blabbing this around to everyone." She got up and shut the door. "Don't tell Janine. Promise?"

I nodded.

"The deer aren't all that important to me. No. Not really."

I copied Holly's shocked expression with a gaping mouth, but I'm not sure it worked with the mud on my face.

"My reasons for doing this are complicated," she said. "I'm a leader now. I've never really been a leader before. I've always known that I had the skills and intelligence, but organizations always scared me."

"So this is a career move?" I asked. "Something to put on your resume?"

"Nice try," she said. "People are depending on me, and I like that. I do care about the issues, sure. I don't want hunters tromping around with guns in my backyard. That's just not okay. The Wirth has become very important to my spiritual life since I've become a Wiccan."

"But you're kind of faking it, in a way," I said. I thought I'd found a ledge to break my fall. "And that's why you're accusing me of being a faker! Maybe you're just . . .'" I searched for the word she would use.

"Projecting?" she said. "Maybe. But look at it this way. I could, perhaps, with the help of the fascist courts, as you would probably say, force you to come with me. Instead I'm asking you politely, knowing you're going to turn me down. Why do you think that is?"

"Because you don't care?" I said.

She made the game show buzzer sound to indicate my answer was wrong.

"Listen," she said. "I've lived with Jeff a long time. Now, I didn't have a father like his, so I don't know all he's working out there. My parents wouldn't even trap a mouse in a live trap. Well, not until they moved to Florida, but that's another story. And I'm not immune to Jeff's logic—he's a smart man. I know better informed people could make mincemeat of his arguments, but sometimes . . ."

She trailed off, making a face as if she'd bitten into something foul.

"I didn't expect you to come with me," she said. "And I don't particularly approve of all the bonding you and Jeff are doing around shooting. Why does it always have to be shooting with you men?"

She picked up my arrow and handed it to me.

"Obviously," she said. "It's not my agenda, but all in all, I think what's happening with you and your father is beyond this particular issue. I'm getting out of the way. You do what you have to do."

"Like in the book," I said quietly.

"What book?"

"The one Rosen gave me. It says during initiation a boy has to leave his mother and go with the men."

She shrugged. "I don't know about that. I mean I respect Native Americans as much as the next person, but from a woman's perspective? The Lakota Sioux are hardly my ideal society. They were a pretty testosteroney group. But, sure, fine. Initiation. Go with the men if that's what you have to do."

She was quiet for a while. We both stared at the image of us in the dresser mirror. It reminded me of one of those not-so-funny movies about a savage boy lost in the jungle returning to live in New York.

There was a soft rapping on the door.

"Everyone okay in there?" Janine said tentatively. "Perry wants to come in."

"Tell him we're just finishing up," Elissa answered. "One more thing, Sam. You know, Perry was hoping I could get you to come."

"Perry's going with you?" I said.

"Of course," she said. "What would he do here? Be a weapons caddy?"

I'd always said that if a UFO abducted Perry, my life would be that much better, but Elissa taking him away felt different. Of course, he would go. He'd been mommy's trained monkey all summer.

"Make sure he takes Mr. Hairy," I said.

"That old bear?" Elissa said. "Sammy, that's so sweet." She moved to hug me, but I moved back like a wild animal.

"I just want to give you a hug. Is that so terrible?"

The rapping on the door got louder.

"*Mo-om?*" Perry's voice had an edge of false hysteria in it. "Can I come in? Now?"

Elissa whispered, "I think we're done. Don't you, Sam?"

Tired of talking, I nodded. Elissa opened the door and Perry fell onto the floor.

"What are you talking about?" he demanded. "Secrets?"

His face was red and streaked. He'd been crying. Elissa took him in her arms, lying back on the bed.

"You'll have your own secrets someday, Perry. You won't want everyone to know them, will you?"

"I don't want to be like Sam," he said.

The front door slammed. Jeff and Lenny's laughing voices came up from the stairs.

"I still can't believe it," Lenny said, his big voice carrying up the stairs easily. "Can you believe at the last minute those mucky mucks caved to the rifle lobby?"

"They caved in to pressure," Jeff said. "Someone got to the governor. I'm sure they used some kind of perverted diversity argument."

We all looked at each other as if we'd been caught doing something illegal.

"Hello?" Jeff called. "We been robbed here or what?"

Janine looked at Elissa. Perry looked at Elissa. Elissa looked at me. I laughed.

"Hello," Elissa sang back. "Just us robbers up here. Don't mind us."

Jeff and Lenny's conversation faded in and out. They were coming in and out of the front door, probably unloading stuff.

"Someone threatened a discrimination suit I'll bet," Lenny said as his voice returned. "All that whining that we were excluding rifle hunters, muzzle loaders . . ."

"I smell a conspiracy," Jeff said. "Someone pretending to be on our side is trying to mess this up."

Their voices faded away again.

"You said they wouldn't be here," Janine whispered.

"I guess I was wrong," Elissa said. "I'd better go down and face them." She raised her eyebrows at me. "Last chance."

The men's voices returned.

"That's good," Lenny said. "I hadn't thought of that. Like those kids in Seattle who got duck hunting licenses and went out there with shotguns to scare off the ducks."

"Yeah," Jeff laughed. "I heard about that. Didn't one of them get hurt? Can you imagine? They wore their platform shoes and sneakers into the mud."

"Must have scared the ducks pretty good," Lenny said, and they both laughed.

The mention of platform shoes in mud brought back a painful memory of Holly's shoes at Experimental Station #47. I couldn't sit there any longer. I had to do something.

I ran out to the railing and called, "Hello?"

"Hey, Sam!" Jeff said. "We were just talking about you. Why are you—"

"Whoa," Lenny said. "He's one step ahead of you. He's already dressed like Tarzan."

"What were you talking about?" I said.

"How would you like to camp out in the Wirth and live like Indians for a couple of months?" Jeff said. "The three of us could take care of this deer problem."

"Hi, Jeff," Elissa said, walking out.

"What's up, hon?" Jeff said. His face dropped the smile. He knew what was up.

"Well, I warned you," she said. "It's time. I'm taking Perry and spending a few nights at Janine's."

She and he looked at each other. I held my breath and exchanged a look with Perry.

"I understand," he said. "Sam, you're staying, right?"

"Of course." I made the snorting noise for ridiculous questions. I left Elissa, Janine, and Perry and went down the stairs. They all went back into the master bedroom and shut the door.

"What's all this stuff?" I said. "Are we having a garage sale?"

Orderly piles of camping stuff were everywhere—tarps, tents, flashlights, camo outfits, orange vests, hats, boots. All over the dining room table were piles of paper—maps, stacks of forms and a two-gallon ziploc bag filled with deer tags.

For dead deer, I thought.

"Gear," Jeff said. "Guy stuff. What we'll need for the weekend. I'm glad you're here, Sam. You can help get your gear sorted out."

"My gear?" I said, sounding like an idiot.

"What you'll need for the hunt," he said. "You can't go out there like that, as much as I'd like to. We're sorting through it tonight."

Reality crashed in on me. Perry and Elissa were leaving. I would be alone with these guys, maybe for the rest of my life.

"You should try on some of these clothes," Jeff said. "I assumed you'd wear my old camo outfit and my old orange vest. I set them out for you. It's what I wore on my first hunt." He picked a pile of leaf-fabric clothes off the floor and stared at it.

The idea of wearing a real deer hunter's costume hadn't occurred to me. It made me realize how little I'd thought out what was really going to happen. All I remembered was Megan saying that if I wore camo, I couldn't come to her camp.

"Can't I just wear jeans?" I said.

Jeff rolled his eyes at Lenny as if they'd talked about this.

"Sam," Jeff said. He tried to lock onto my squirrely gaze. "Would you play football without a helmet? Soccer without—"

"A jockstrap?" Lenny added, chuckling.

"Thank you, Lenny," Jeff said. "I think I can handle this. Here, you'll need this too. It's human odor suppressant. You know you need that, right?" He handed me a pump spray of Scent Killer.

"Made from deer urine," Lenny said, and watched for my reaction. "You spray it all over yourself. Girls love it."

"Cool," I said. "I'll wear it to school."

They gave me a dumb job—to make the piles neater. Jeff kept glancing up the stairs. We were all waiting for Elissa and her entourage to make the grand exit.

The bedroom door opened and the three of them, including Perry hugging Mr. Hairy and stabbing me with his eyes, walked down the stairs. They each carried some kind of duffel or small suitcase.

"Hello, Janine," Jeff said. "Congratulations on being mask-free."

She smiled and looked down. "Thanks, Jeff," she said in a small voice. "Sorry about . . ."

Elissa and Jeff stared at each other as Janine took Perry outside.

"You got the number," Elissa said, "if you need it."

"Yup," Jeff said in a distant cowboy dialect.

"Well," she sighed. I could tell she wanted more of a scene. "Good luck." She held out her hand, and they shook hands. I'd never seen them shake hands. It did not feel good.

"Bye, Sam," Elissa said. She gave me a hug I didn't even fight. Then she turned and moved quickly out the door.

Lenny disappeared down the basement mumbling something about duffel bags.

"Sam," Jeff said. "About Elissa and me." He looked around, for Lenny, I guessed. "I don't want to not say anything. But I don't know what to say."

"You don't have to say anything," I said. "This is just hard. For everybody."

He breathed a sigh of relief: meaningful talk was over.

"I am a little nervous for you," Jeff said. "Excited too. But I wish I could be out there with you when you get your first kill."

Lenny reappeared dragging some duffels. He handed one to me, and I began to pack some of the gear they told me was mine. Jeff and Lenny went back to talking and laughing.

I stole upstairs and found Jeff's stash of condoms in the drawer next to their bed. I stuffed a couple of them into my fake-leather toiletry kit. I was thinking about becoming a man, planning my trip to the Megan's tent.

CHAPTER TWENTY-THREE

I TRIED TO FIND SOMETHING TO WEAR THAT MIGHT WORK in both camps. The weather was typical October, hot days and cool nights, which made my choices harder. I felt like a double-agent looking in his closet, complaining, "*I have nothing to wear!*" I ended up in army surplus pants and a camo T-shirt I used to wear as a gag. I threw a blue jean jacket in my pack along with a canteen and some granola bars.

"Sure you're gonna be okay in the old 'one-man'?" Jeff said as soon as we were out of the driveway.

He was referring to the mildewy one-person tent I had insisted on bringing for myself. He'd wanted to "bunk" together as he called it, but I'd insisted on being as independent as possible.

"I'll be fine. I think it will be more challenging for me to be in my own tent."

"Ah," he said, "for the initiation." He laughed.

I knew this was a test to see if I'd laugh at New Agey stuff like his buddies did. "I'm not into that anymore," I said, managing a smile. "That's way over."

"I hear Rosen's going to be hanging around," he said.

"On whose side?"

He shrugged. "Both, I guess. He volunteered to be a hunt marshal."

"A what?"

Jeff explained that the DNR and the Coalitions (meaning the Coalitions Against the Hunt) agreed to have hunt marshals patrolling the border between the two camps. Their job was to keep the crazies and pranksters from sabotaging each other. He said it was complicated by the fact that the bow hunters and the rifle hunters were not being particularly friendly to each other.

"Why would anyone from our camp want to go over to Free City?" I asked, reversing the test.

"We're not honoring them by using their name," Jeff said angrily. "What are they free of? We're the ones who believe in freedom."

"Maybe they were thinking about the deer," I shrugged. "Like free to run wild or something."

His stared at me. I replayed my words, wondering if I'd accidentally defended the enemy.

"The difference is that we admit we're predators," Jeff began. "They think they can change everything with slogans and marches. Making demands." He laughed. "Reminds me of college."

"That must be hard," I said.

"Not particularly. This must be harder for you." He reached his hand over and touched my shoulder. "You have a lot of friends over there."

"Well, I figure I'm setting a good example. I mean, if they don't want to be my friends just because I disagree with them, then . . ." I didn't know what would follow *then*.

"America was built on that sort of independence," Jeff said. "I'm glad you're finally showing some backbone with that crowd."

"I got more backbone that I can stand at the moment," I said. It came out sounding more like irritation than I'd wanted it to, but we were pulling up to a checkpoint.

"Mr. O'Brien," the DNR security man said, touching a finger to the brim of his hat. "We have a special parking area for you over there. That your son?"

"My boy," Jeff said with a big smile. "Got him a buck tag too."

"That's terrific, sir. We need all the young hunters we can get. My kid's protesting."

"Sorry to hear that," Jeff said. "My wife and youngest are probably over there too."

The guard shook his head. "Strength and honor, sir."

Jeff nodded and we drove off.

"Strength and honor?" I said.

"That's what the Roman legionnaires used to say before battle," Jeff explained without looking over.

The main DNR tent seemed to attract a bunch of unusually tall guys. Either that or I was feeling small. In the old days, I would have defended myself by theorizing about height and the killer instinct, but I was too nervous. They all had some urgent business to discuss with Jeff or Lenny. Despite the underlings trying to shoo them away, they stood around like movie extras, all wearing the same mix 'n' match costume components—blaze-orange vests, camo this and camo that, logos of hunting groups plastered everywhere. The patches had names that sounded like they were buddy-buddy with the animals they killed: *Ducks Unlimited, Pheasants Forever, The Wildlife Federation,* the *Minnesota Deer Hunters Association.*

My thoughts kept drifting to Megan alone in her tent. I was eager to set up and disappear. I paced around awkwardly until Jeff noticed me and came over.

"You're going to be okay here tonight?" he said. He looked worried. "You know I'm going to be very busy, probably late into the night."

"Oh, sure," I said. "I knew that. I brought some books and some homework."

The homework was a slip—too obviously a lie. But I had brought Rosen's Lakota book, which I could claim was homework if I were challenged.

"That's great, Sam," he said. "I think all your discipline at the range is paying off." He looked over at some hunters giving a young officer a hard time.

"There's work to do around here. Pitch in where you can."

The guy in a lower-caste uniform ran up to us and pulled Jeff away with urgent whispers.

"This fellow will show you where to put the tents up. Can you manage both of them?"

"No problemo," I said.

"Great," Jeff said over his shoulder as he walked away. "Check in with me before you turn in."

"Yes, sir," I said, giving him a little salute.

Setting up was hard, but I figured I had at least an hour to kill before the sundown. When I crawled into that smelly little tent, I liked it immediately. It held back the world. Maybe I wouldn't come out at all. Maybe I could sleep through the whole night and into the next day. Then it would all be over.

I read a bit of the Lakota book, ate some trail mix, and sipped from my canteen. But mostly I thought about Megan. Finally, it was time. My plan was to sneak over to Free City and spend a few hours among decent, moral people, especially Megan. Later, I would change into my camo, slip back here, check in with Jeff if necessary, then sneak into the park to begin my sabotage mission.

But first I had to be seen around the hunters' camp by people other than Jeff— just in case. I wandered around the camp for a while looking bored and purposeless. I even volunteered to stir a vat of pork and beans cooking over a fire. When I figured enough people had seen me, I went back to my tent, took off my camo T-shirt, and stuffed it into my backpack with the rest of my camo hunting outfit.

It was definitely time to move out.

You couldn't get into Free City by just walking through the front door. I planned for a sideways move, though it couldn't be through the forest. The DNR had fenced off the park's border with orange construction mesh. Since Jeff had alerted me to the marshals, I planned to use a little Lakota stealth to avoid them. Apparently not many people wanted to sneak from one camp to another—for obvious reasons. Getting caught would be ugly.

I had to sneak out of the hunters' camp and make a huge loop. But it worked. As I entered the Coalition territory, my true home, I relaxed. I enjoyed seeing strangely dressed people, so different from the grays and browns and camo of the hunters. People wore bell ankle bracelets and colorful peasant-wear. Others wore animal costumes identifying them as Little Creatures of the Forest. Because it was Halloween, there were people in costumes: vampires, ghosts, even a fairy princess.

I smelled marijuana, Indian spices, incense, bread baking in a fire pit. A tarot card reader worked by candlelight under a large tree. Any kind of music you'd want was playing somewhere in the camp. I heard rap, hip-hop, industrial, geezer rock. People played guitars and those funny bongos from India. People sang—I recognized witch chants that Elissa sang in the shower sometimes. I heard a Joni Mitchell song and wondered if I'd stumble across Ms. S-T and Katami making love in a tent. I was full of peace and love. Why had Jeff stopped being a hippie?

I looked for my friends, but no one looked vaguely high school age. They looked like what the establishment newspapers call "professional activists from outside the area." Eventually, I found Megan sitting by herself near a bonfire. From a distance she looked young and lost. She was using a staple gun to attach posters to wooden sticks. The posters said, "Wrong, Wrong, Wrong" in bold red.

As I approached, I saw that she was dressed in her favorite Israeli commando outfit. That was my name for it anyway. I liked the look; even her unwashed hair looked sexy.

"Megan!"

"Sam?" She spoke as if she were on drugs, which couldn't have been true.

"Are you okay?" I asked.

She snapped out of it, jumped up, and hugged me. "Sam!" she said. "Oh, Sam, I'm so glad to see you."

This was not typical Megan behavior, but I liked it.

"Where is everyone?" I asked.

"What everyone?" she said. "The Council is so over. What a joke. We haven't been a functioning cell for months. Maybe we never were."

"What about Holly?"

Megan sat down and continued stapling, using her thighs as a workbench. I sat beside her.

"Don't do it that way," I said. "The staple could go through and hurt you."

"You sound like Jeff," she said.

We sat in silence for a while until she sighed. "Holly had her abortion," she said without looking up.

I felt a surprising wave of nausea. How many times had I heard it was a woman's right to choose this? All over the city there were billboards with cute babies saying things like, "My mommy wanted to kill me."

"What's wrong with you now?" Megan said.

"I ate a hot dog for lunch."

"A hot dog?" she said. "Today of all days?"

"I'm undercover. You have to do things."

She paused a moment, then said, "It's okay she did this, you know."

"I know, I know," I said quietly, rubbing my temples. "Who was with her?"

"How should I know?" She spoke angrily, but wouldn't look me in the eyes. "She and Ryan were hanging out."

"Ryan?" I said. "He was so weird about it before. I can't see him changing all that fast and being, like, supportive."

"She should be with women now," she said.

I gave her a wide-eyed glare.

"It's not like I haven't tried, Sam. She's been rejecting me ever since school started. She says I'm too . . ."

"Too what?"

"Masculine. Isn't that mean?"

"Maybe she meant it as a compliment."

"Oh, right," she said. "Don't start with that. You know how I feel about war and violence."

"She's not here, is she?"

"No, but I saw Ryan. He looks wild, like he did that night at the community meeting."

"He's probably planning something dumb, like those firecrackers," I said.

She grabbed my forearm. I pulled her up and swept her up in my arms like a World War II movie hero. I didn't realize how much I wanted this sign of her attraction and need. I held her for a few minutes until we got embarrassed.

"What's supposed to happen next here?" I said. "I heard something about Stewart speaking here tonight."

"He spoke earlier today on campus, so I don't know."

"What do you mean you don't know? I got business with this dude." At that moment, I felt as if he were my drug connect. "The buzzers?" I said.

"There was trouble."

"What kind?"

"Protesters."

"The hunters," I said.

"No. Worse. I wish it were just the damn hunters. That would have been easier. No, Sam, these were people in wheelchairs. It was awful."

"Wheelchairs? Were they at the right event?"

"Unfortunately, yes. It's probably some right-wing plot to discredit Stewart. People, journalists, have garbled his message. They say he's into mercy killing and human sacrifice. They carried signs like 'Ask us before you kill us.' Isn't that horrible?"

"Elissa said he's into sacrificing to the gods," I said.

"That's not it at all," she said. "You know Stewart. He loves controversy. It's part of his method to shock us into thinking. My dad explained it all to me. All he's saying is what's most important in life is how much happiness a creature is able to have. A happiness quotient or something. My dad says the protesters have blown it way out of proportion."

"So he's speaking prophylactically," I said.

She giggled. "I suppose it doesn't help that every time he tries to explain why the Aztecs sacrificed children, it sounds like he thinks that's a good thing." She shrugged. "I was never all that into him. It was you guys . . ."

"And your parents," I said.

"Oh, now you're attacking my parents? Jesus, Sam, I'm worried about you. Is it Jeff? Lenny? I knew they were getting to you. They're so manipulative."

"And Unitarians aren't."

Megan stood, took a few steps away from me, and stumbled.

"I'm really tired, Sam. I haven't been sleeping well. There's so much to do. When I lie down, I worry about the deer. I worry about everything. The world, everything that's wrong. There's so much to worry about."

I took her arm, steadying her like a boyfriend.

"Let's take a walk," I said. "Do you really need to be out here? Are you organizing anything right this minute?"

"The signs," she said vaguely, gesturing at the pile.

"Someone else can do it," I said.

"But it's my dad's staple gun," she said.

"Grab it," I said. "I'm taking you to your tent. You should lie down. Where is it?"

She pointed the way. When I turned my eyes away from the bonfire, it was hard to see, but I think she was smiling at me.

I switched on my little pocket flashlight. We passed a field of tents, neither of us speaking. The mist was coming up, and I could barely make out where the tents ended and the fields began. I knew it was a mirage, but the tents seemed to go on forever, like a vast army of reinforcements come to support Big Buck's herd.

"Hey," Megan said. "Listen."

"It sounds like a powwow. Let's go take a look."

"No. You should go to your tent and lie down. You're tired. You just said so."

"I've always wanted to go to a powwow," she said, rubbing my arm. "Ten minutes, Sam. Then we can go back to my tent."

CHAPTER TWENTY-FOUR

THE DRUMMING GOT LOUDER. It stopped and started up as if someone were talking in between. We found a sign tied to a tree with colorful yarn. It said: "Samhaim Dis a Way. Starts at 9."

"Samhaim?" Megan said. "What the hell's that?"

"It's the Wiccan name for Halloween," I said. "Elissa," I added to explain my knowledge.

"You still think we should check it out?"

I shrugged. "It's been going for over an hour. It's probably over."

"Well, if you insist," she said. "But we'll just stay a minute, okay?"

Women seemed difficult to communicate with sometimes, so I just nodded.

The path took a winding route through the forest, ending in a parking lot. Two shirtless drummers wearing papier-mâché masks studded with horns and teeth guarded the entrance. Behind them, a big crowd listened to a guy talking from a raised platform. His voice sounded familiar, though I couldn't place it. The whole area was lit up with a circle of mosquito torches, giving it that primitive, scary look of a cannibal feast.

The speaker paused, the crowd cheered happily, and the two guys wailed on their Congo drums.

"Can we go through?" Megan asked politely. One of the guys nodded and we walked through.

There were more costumes—Arab robes, African caftans, saris. There were also plenty of beads, feathers, and face paint in addition to the usual tattoos and body piercings. A guy in a Scottish kilt walked by, a furry white purse flopping at his crotch.

"Albino beaver," I whispered to Megan.

"Better be faux," she said.

"Or you'll do what?"

The drums continued, but a geezer couple straight out of Woodstock hopped to their own beat. They wore matching tie-dyed T-shirts, and his salt-and-pepper beard matched her perm.

"Look," Megan said, nodding toward a group of Native Americans in traditional dancing costumes with fur ankle bracelets. They shuffle-danced in a far corner. Their bells jingled rhythmically.

"Are they real?" I said.

Next to them, a guy wearing only a Sumo jock-diaper thing was doing Tai Chi.

Megan elbowed me in the ribs and pointed at the guy on the raised platform. It was Stewart dressed like an Aztec priest. Megan and I looked at each other. She giggled. I struggled not to show shock. Up to this point I'd been counting on Stewart as a serious guy, my adult mentor in eco-tactics. He wasn't supposed to be a complete wacko. Then I remembered.

"It's Halloween," I said.

Stewart quieted the crowd by raising his arms and flashing a double peace sign. People obeyed and shut up. He began talking, using a preacher-like voice I barely recognized as his.

"Okay, so here's the tough part," he was saying. "The Aztecs practiced human sacrifice. I won't deny that. Yes, they tore out the hearts of warriors, slaves, men, women, and, yes, children."

Megan clutched my arm. Suddenly we were back at the cannibal feast. I looked for an exit.

"Why did they do this?" he said. "Because they believed the gods feed on us, whether we like it or not. The Aztecs called it like it was. The earth is just a massive compost heap. The universe is a huge hungry mouth. We eat the earth, our children eat us, then earth eats them."

The crowd said, "Ho."

"Ho!" Stewart said.

Megan gave me a questioning look. "It's a Native American thing," I said, once again relying on information Elissa had fed me.

"You're so smart," she said, still holding my arm.

"And handsome and cool and—"

"Don't press your luck," she said.

"And the gods are planning something," Stewart said. "Right here in our own little park. But whose side are they on?"

"Our side!" the crowd yelled.

"I can't hear you!" he yelled back.

"Our side!" they yelled louder.

"That's better. These fool hunters aren't gonna get away with this. Are they?"

"No way!"

"Let me ask you a simple question, and you call out your answer. Do you want to save the earth?"

"Yes!" the crowd screamed.

"Is that it? Is that how little you care? Let me ask you again. Do you want to save the earth?"

"Yes!" they screamed much more loudly.

"That's better," he said. "Let me tell you people something. There are four billion plus people on this planet and a lot more coming down the pike. More greedy mouths to feed on earth's last forests, crowd out the last of the animals. Imagine this. Billions of hungry, sucking mouths and ultimately more people for the compost pile. Against this, we're nothing. We're not even enough to stop the wound from bleeding.

"The only possible difference we can make is if we are totally fearless, if we put ourselves totally on the line. We must be brave. We must call upon our brothers and sisters of the warrior nations who have come before us. You know what I'm talking about. People like the Aztecs, like the Lakota Sioux. We are the Divine Wind. The avenging hurricane. We join our Native American brothers and sisters slaughtered by the greedy whites. We join them in shouting, 'Today is a good day to die!'"

The crowd yelled back, "Today is a good day to die!"

"The hunters are the enemy—these white men who have convinced themselves they own everything—the whole world and all of us in it. They think they can do with it what they please—commit genocide, oppress women and minorities, drag gay people behind their trucks, tamper with DNA, and execute people for being black and poor. They can do anything they want. Do you think this pleases the gods?"

"No!"

"No, it does not please the gods. But you do. You people here please the gods because you are the new warriors of the new earth, and you know it!"

This got a big crowd reaction, complete with horns, whistles, and Ho's. Stewart quieted them down again and paced for a moment.

"Saving a few deer here in our little backyard skirmish—even assuming we are successful—in the big picture? It's nothing. But the gods are watching. You'll see. They'll give us a sign. It will be unmistakable."

A solid cheer rose.

Stewart put up his hand. "Not so fast," he said. "This isn't going to be that easy. I'm going to challenge you before this is over. This sign I'm talking about. It's a death sign. We have to give them back what they deal."

Confusion and murmuring replaced fading cheers.

"I don't mean we are going to hurt anyone. But we'll let them hurt each other, won't we? It's like Aikido. The energy you release turns back and defeats you. They will hurt themselves!"

The crowd cheered with almost the same enthusiasm as earlier.

"All over the world cultures are rejecting Euro-American hegemony. The newspapers call it spreading chaos, a resurgence of feudalism, warlordism, pointless tribal violence. They work for the bosses and they're trying to scare us. But don't listen, my friends. These people are on our side! They want their world back, and they're not afraid to die for it!"

The drummers started up.

Stewart shouted, "Crush the forces of globalization! Crush American ecocide of Mother Earth! Death to capitalist, blood-sucking pigs! Death to capitalism!"

Megan pumped her fist and yelled, "Death to capitalism!" The crowd broke into happy chaos.

Musicians of all skill levels joined the drummers. Stewart danced around on the stage, beating a tambourine. "Please stay around. There's more to come." He dropped into the darkness as a rave beat began pulsing. Suddenly we were in a nightclub. People danced.

CHAPTER TWENTY-FIVE

MY FLASHLIGHT BEAM LANDED ON A MOUNTAIN FACE logo on a tent. I knew it was Megan's because it was expensive and sky blue, her favorite color.

"Here it is," she said. "Not much, but I call it home." She squeezed my hand, which sent blood to my nether regions.

"It's nice," I said. "Expensive."

She pulled her hand away.

"I meant that in a good way. Jeff says you should spend money on good equipment, it's more efficient in the long run because—"

"Jeff again? Sam, listen to yourself."

She unzipped the flap and ducked inside. I followed her, blathering on, trying to regroup. We knelt down, and I flashed my spot of light around the interior. Three T-shirts and two pairs of jeans were neatly folded in the corner. A pink beanie baby octopus lay on the sleeping bag. Megan turned on an expensive gizmo that was basically a flashlight but transformed into a little lamp.

"An octopus?" I said. I picked it up by one tentacle.

"I get scared at night," she said, grabbing it away from me and pretending to love it.

"That octopus is one lucky guy." I was trying to sound Bondian. I let my knee touch hers for a moment.

"Now that we're here," she said, "at the hunt? The real hunt? It feels scarier than I expected. I mean your people have real weapons. And there's a lot of anger. On both sides." She shivered. "Maybe we shouldn't be here."

"You are my people, Megan," I said, touching her chin with my hand. I remembered how Holly always said Megan was really a chicken at heart. "Nothing bad's going to happen here," I said. "This is Minnesota. The ancestral home of nicey-nice."

"Minnesotans killed plenty of Native Americans—women and children too. Hello? Viking blood?"

"You don't mean the football team, I take it."

"Remember those protests in Seattle?" she said. "They started out just like this one. Friendlier, even. At least they were trying to talk to each other."

"I'm the one who should be scared. I'm the one doing the dangerous thing," I said.

"You're still going through with it? I wasn't sure. You haven't said much about it."

"Of course I'm going through with it," I said. I didn't even have to pretend I was shocked.

"But you don't even have Stewart's little gizmos."

"They'll show up."

"The hunters are just going to let you waltz in there and do this?" she asked.

"There are a few details I've kept to myself," I said. "For security purposes."

"What, now I'm a security risk?"

It hit me hard at that moment how much I hadn't told her. I hadn't told her about seeing Big Buck in the forest. I hadn't mentioned Rosen's initiation book since we'd fought about it ages ago. I hadn't mentioned how often I was going to Hal's Range to shoot. And I certainly hadn't mentioned that I enjoyed it a little.

"What's the big deal?" she shrugged. "You sneak in, set some buzzers around, and walk out. What's so hard? You'll be out of there before the shooting starts. If it starts at all."

"There's more to it than that," I said. "It's plenty dangerous. I was planning to sleep overnight in there, to make sure the buzzer things work. And other stuff. Secret stuff."

"That's stupid," she said. "What could you do if they didn't work? And what do you mean 'secret stuff?'"

"Non-logical stuff. This isn't all about logic, Megan. I just have to be there, that's all. Accept the dangers of the forest. And there will be plenty of dangers. Wild arrows, stray bullets, crazed deer—"

"Crazed deer?" she said with a little laugh.

"Scared or wounded deer can be very dangerous," I said.

She laughed. "I hardly think that our poor scared creatures are going to be a major worry, Sam."

"What if I'm out in the forest pretending to be a hunter," I said, getting to my feet in a half-standing half-crouching position. "Let's say a crazed buck—wounded, let's say. They get meaner when they're wounded. Comes flying out at me. Charging me." I wrestled the imaginary buck's horns. This was not easy, even in an expensive tent.

"Sam, this is the Wirth, remember? The scariest things those deer have encountered is a stray Frisbee or a mountain biker with blue hair."

I shook my head. "Deer are funny, Megan. I've read about it in Jeff's magazines. Well, I only read the magazines as part of my undercover role. They're all over the house since Elissa took off. In the bathroom, everywhere. Anyway, they have this cartoon feature—'It Happened to Me.' Half of the stories I swear are about crazed bucks attacking hunters. I have to be ready to defend myself."

"Don't even joke about that," she said. "That's not funny." She began shaking her head back and forth. "Why are we even talking about this? This is grossing me out. None of that is going to happen. Why are you torturing me with this?"

I sat down on the tent floor again and drifted off into myself. What was I doing? If I needed to kill a deer—even one that wanted to be killed—sure I'd be a hero with Jeff, but how could I claim that it was an accident? Would I plead self-defense? This mishmash in no way added up to a master spy's plan. I suddenly felt stupid and childish.

Megan took my hand and moved nearer to me. She smelled good, like the bouquets of dead flowers people put in bathrooms.

"Sam, you've been quiet a long time. Are you torturing yourself? I think you're just confused. I don't know what you thought you were doing with all this, but it's obviously getting to you. I'm not sure what you want. Maybe you do want to hunt. Maybe you need to make a decision."

She dropped my hand and pulled away from me. It was an oddly dramatic, like something she'd seen in a movie.

In the dim light, she looked better than usual: an old-fashioned, black-and-white movie woman. Her lips were parted and wet. I pictured her saying, "Kiss me, Sam," in a barely audible voice. I moved toward her.

"Sam?"

"What, Megan?"

"How come you've never tried to kiss me? I mean Ryan's tried. Lots of people have tried. Even some girls."

"Girls?" I said, and I backed off to evaluate what she was saying.

She placed her hand over mine. It felt weird, like some bad announcement was coming.

"It's okay if you're gay, Sam," she said.

"Gay?" All my breath went out of me.

"I mean, it's Ryan's theory—why this hunting thing is so important to you. He says most of the hunters are probably closet cases and just don't know it. They have this need to work out the male part of themselves in killing because they hate their gayness."

"Ryan said that?" I said. Then it hit me. She said Ryan and girls and other people had tried to kiss her. I remembered how Ryan had left me out of the firecracker thing at the community meeting. How he was cooking up things with Holly, all without me. Ryan was betraying me or setting me up or both, all of the time. A surge of anger rushed through me.

"I could kill him," I said.

"Who—Ryan?" she said. She gave me a look with a cock of her head. "You know what they say about that kind of anger. It's usually defensive."

I stood up, bouncing my head off the tent ceiling. The nylon fabric around us quivered.

"Can't you see what Ryan's doing?" I said. "Ryan's after you. He's undermining me."

She laughed. "Ryan? No way. Maybe he's trying to help you. Did you ever think of that?"

"That's not it," I said rather weakly, sinking down to my knees. "Megan. I respect you. A ton. Maybe too much. But you scare me a little. Sometimes you're so tough and—"

"Bossy?"

"Yes, bossy."

I looked at her. I hadn't expected to see her getting on the Train of Tears. It was my moment. On my knees, I was at least a foot taller than she was. I leaned over, grabbed her, and kissed her. I'd seen this done a million times in the movies, but this was me doing it. I couldn't believe the feeling of pressing faces together and wet lips touching wet lips. We kissed for quite a while, and finally my thighs began to quiver from the exertion, so I had to shift positions, which seemed to break the magic.

"You're supposed to ask before you do that," she said.

"I know," I said. "Can I kiss you?"

"No," she said playfully, "you can't." She squeezed my hand. "But I'm glad you did it. Maybe you're just bi."

I writhed like a leaping salmon.

Not letting go of my hand, she said, "Bi's cool. Practically everyone in Hollywood's bi. I might be bi."

Just then I heard someone—a man—whisper outside the tent. "Hey, you guys. Can I come in?"

CHAPTER TWENTY-SIX

WHO IS IT?" MEGAN WHISPERED, looking at me with wide eyes.

I moved toward the inner flap and lifted it. It was dark, so all I could see was a big hairy face.

"Jeff?" I said.

The face laughed. "It's Stewart. Spiranga. Your great and wild leader? C'mon, Sam, let me in. We got business."

I glanced back at Megan, who looked younger and more scared than she had.

"Ask him why he wants to come in," she whispered.

Stewart unzipped the flap and crawled into the tent. Like a large wet dog, he reeked of all kinds of smells—alcohol, bonfire smoke, pot, body odor.

"I heard you kids needed a chaperone," he said. "What are you doing in here, smoking pot?"

"Free City doesn't allow it," Megan said. "No drugs, no alcohol."

Stewart chuckled. "Not the way we used to run a revolution." His hair seemed bigger and furrier in the lamplight.

"Where's your . . ." I said—I couldn't remember the word.

"He means your costume," Megan said. "The Aztec thing?"

"You guys caught that? Great, then you're up to speed. We got work to do here. Jesus, Sam, how come you haven't contacted me? Didn't you forget something?" He produced a ziploc bag and shook it at me. It was a one-gallon size filled with the little buttons he had shown us at Megan's so long ago.

"Right," I said. I didn't want to try to defend myself because I feared it might backfire.

I reached for the bag and lifted them toward Megan's camp light. The buttons looked darker than I had remembered. They clumped together as if they were sticky. I gave Stewart a questioning look.

"I spray-painted them myself," he said. "I was trying for a camo look. Whaddaya think? They're not entirely dry yet."

"I can see that," I said.

"So you're going to stay overnight in the reserve as we discussed? You leaving soon?"

"Yeah," I said. "Soon."

Stewart got out a topographical map of the preserve. I was pretty good at reading topos, thanks to Jeff.

"Go in tonight after most people are asleep. Go to the far edge of the reserve. Here." He pointed at the map, but in the dim light, it looked like Japanese wallpaper. "Start sowing the buttons back here first, then work forward, toward the main encampment. This back area's where all the deer will go once the action starts tomorrow. I've got about fifty of these for you. Use them all. Don't get caught with any on you. It'll take you a while if you do it right."

I gave him the old cowboy nod. "I know the area," I said. "I've been there."

"Very good," he said. I couldn't tell if he was being sarcastic or respectful.

"I'm having a little trouble with this," Megan said. "Doesn't the shooting do the same thing as the buzzers—scare the deer to the back of the reserve? Why go to all this trouble to scare the deer before the guns start?"

"Bow hunters go in first, Megan," I said like a know-it-all.

"Oh," she said. "I guess I knew that. I'm just nervous."

"That," Stewart said. "And we don't want any deer killed at all. Zero tolerance—that's our goal. Now, let's review. Sam places the buzzers. Me and my guys activate them from remote controls to startle the deer and mess with the hunters. Hopefully, we can drive the herd to the far side of the park and have them break for freedom. People have messed with the fencing on the far side and tipped off some alternative news people to catch the escape of the deer. Like people breaking out of Auschwitz or something. It'll look great on national news."

"Like Bambi," I said. "The forest fire scene?"

Stewart said, "Yeah. Man is in the forest. And he's gonna blow you away." He broke into a cackling laugh.

"Well, nothing like waiting till the last minute to clarify all of this," Megan said.

"Hopefully, the herd won't run onto a freeway," Stewart said.

He tried to look both of us in the eye, but we looked at each other instead. He shrugged and went on.

"Even though most of these bow hunter guys couldn't sneak up on a dead squirrel, some of them have a few skills. They'll have a few hours jump on the rifle people. We want to mess things up good, especially those so-called Hunters of Men." He laughed scornfully. "Things should be pretty much over by the time any rifles get in there."

"So, we're done then," I said.

"One last thing," he said. "Sam, I just want you know what you're getting involved in. I mean, in case something happens, something bigger than just scaring the deer."

"What else could happen?" Megan said.

"I don't know," he said. "But should anything happen to me, I want you to know that I've got all my arguments written down here." He reached inside his shirt and pulled out a ratty spiral notebook, the two-for-a-dollar kind. He handed it to Megan. "I want you to make sure this gets to the press, Megan. I think it falls into your area of expertise, am I right?"

"What is it?" she said.

"My manifesto," he said. "It's all there. Don't try to read it now. I'm sure there are things in it you won't like. Just give it to the press." He paused and raised his eyebrows. "In case anything should happen to me."

"Aren't you being a little dramatic?" she said. "I mean it's highly unlikely—"

He raised his hand. "I'm no psychic or anything," he said. "But I've had a feeling all along—call it an intuition—that a hunter is going to die. At least one, maybe more. I don't know. I just feel like the gods want blood on this one. I'm sorry for the asshole that buys it. I don't want anyone to die—but like I said: Aikido. They started this violence thing. If it gets out of control, it gets out of control. Karma."

"I don't think it will," Megan said. "This is Minnesota."

"Yeah," he laughed. "Not a place where people accidentally shoot their sons on pheasant hunts, or get decapitated by phone wire while driving drunk in their snowmobiles."

"Okay, you made your point," she said. "It could happen."

"I hate to say it, but it wouldn't hurt our cause if it does," Stewart said. He winked, unzipped the tent flap, and disappeared.

I quickly zipped up the flap. Megan and I didn't speak for a long time.

"Whoa," I said finally.

"Double whoa," she said. "Do you think he's dangerous?"

"It's just talk," I said. "Maybe he doesn't want to admit that this isn't Seattle. That we're small potatoes."

"I'm not sure I trust him," Megan said.

"It's too late to back out, you said so yourself," I said. "I'm not going to defend him, but I am going to do what I promised. Anyway, it'll all be over this time tomorrow."

"Shit, I wish I smoked," she said.

"Cigarettes? You?" I laughed.

"Not real smoking, stupid. Fake smoking. Movie smoking. I wish I could smoke and make long exhales or those puffy smoke rings. I would do it too. Maybe even for real."

"I'd like to see you," I said.

"I'm such a goody-goody. So perfect and PC. I try to loosen up sometimes, but I always snap right back to serious. The last one who would ever smoke."

I snapped my fingers, pretending I was lighting a Bic. She immediately leaned into it with her pretend cigarette. I lit mine afterwards. We fake-smoked for a while.

"So, baby," I said, "ya wanna mess around?"

She half-closed her eyes. "I dunno, big boy," she said, looking me up and down. "My noives is a little jaggly and all dat."

"I know somethin' that might calm 'em down."

"Yeah?" she said. "You and what army?"

"Dis might be my last night, doll, before I go off to sea. Ta fight da big one," I said. "You might never see me again, doll."

She moved closer to me. "I like it when you talk about dying, Sam. It scares me to like it. Like, what does that mean?" She looked at the tent flap nervously. "It is sexy, thinking this is the last night we might ever have together. I mean, I've got things to lose," she said. "You." She moved in and gave me a soft kiss.

"I thought you were going to say your virginity."

"Nope. Too late for that."

"Megan!" I said, shocked.

"Don't start," she said. "Don't ask."

"That sounds like the Army," I said.

"It's a new world, Sam. Girls even call boys now."

"Megan, quit messing with me."

"I'm not messing with you. Yet." She smiled and moved so close I was forced to concentrate on her smell. It was better than anything you could find in an aerosol or a pump-spray, better than flowers.

"Why don't we drop all our worries about what's supposed to happen next?" she said. "Girls can be in charge."

She reached over and grabbed my belt. She stopped talking and looked down at it to see what she was doing. All thought instantly left me.

I stared down as she unwrapped me, folding my pants back and reaching through the hole of my bunched-up but rapidly expanding jockey shorts. My erection stood out straight and white, as if a third person had entered the tent. I was embarrassed and proud at the same time.

But I couldn't get over that she'd done this before.

"Who was it?" I said.

She gave me a disapproving look, then waved a finger at me. "No, no, no," she said. "Nice girls don't tell."

Then she touched my erection. She ran her finger over it, and I was hers.

"Nice," she said. She sounded way too experienced for my taste, but I wasn't about to quarrel about it. She quickly and expertly began undressing herself. I've seen naked women in movies and magazines, but she looked completely different.

Then she blew it by trying to step out of her underwear and falling over. Her knee hit me in the chest, and the lamp fell on its side. But I was sitting there staring at her thing, her vagina. I was embarrassed that my reaction was embarrassment.

As I helped her sit upright, she giggled, "This doesn't happen in the movies, does it?"

"Only in comedies," I said.

Finally I reached over and touched one of her breasts. She trembled and closed her eyes, and things began going the way they were supposed to. I felt power surge through me, not from my mind, but from all over and through me. I wanted the bare skin of my chest to touch the bare skin of hers. I quickly wriggled out of my shirt and pulled off my pants, then tried to pull off my underwear. I had some trouble poking my erection back through its fly to get my underwear off.

"That's funny," she said, watching me closely. "Is that why guys wear boxers?"

After that it was all wonderful. All soft lights, music, intensity, heat, urgency, and feeling as if we were one. What were the gods thinking?

Afterwards, we crawled into Megan's sleeping bag, and she fell asleep, her body clammy with sweat. I buzzed with hormones and couldn't sleep. I wanted to do it again. Was this what it felt like to be a man? Surely men didn't buzz like this all the time.

Chapter Twenty-Seven

MY WATCH ALARM WOKE ME AT 2:00 A.M. I fumbled for Megan's camping light, carefully extracted myself from the sleeping bag, found my pack, and began dressing in my hunter clothes.

"Sam?" she said sleepily. "What's happening?" She made a halfhearted attempt to pull the sleeping bag over her breast. "You're dressed already? Sam, what time is it? Say something."

"My disguise?" I said. "Remember?"

"Oh," she said. Her hair looked like small animals had nested in it. "I feel naked."

"You are," I said, smiling.

She caught me staring at her hair, then started patting it down. "I must look horrible."

"Your hair looks great. I love it like that."

"You're doing it again," she said.

"What?"

"Acting like the men in those old war movies. The romantic guys. I love that. Come here."

Lying half-naked out of the sleeping bag, she gave me a lovely wet going-off-to-war kiss.

"Meg, it's time. I've really got to get going."

"I had nightmares," she said. "About deer dying and people dying. Stewart creeps me out."

I heard voices from outside coming from the direction of the bonfire. "People must be staying up all night," I said.

"Sam, stay. I'm scared. You don't have to do this."

"I'll be okay out there," I said.

"I'm scared about someone getting killed. Is that crazy? Maybe we should tell someone."

"Tell who what?" I said. "Which side do we tell? He's on our side. Plus, he's the adult. What are we going to say? Some stoned guy babbled on about someone maybe dying in a hunting accident?"

"Maybe it's like joking about bombs at the airport—something you're not supposed to do. We might be accomplices. Maybe we could sneak the information to the other side. I don't know. You're the spy. Think of something."

"I can't believe you're being like this," I said. "What about my mission? We have to try. We owe it to them."

"Owe it to who?" she said.

"The deer," I said. "The herd, all of them. The university deer too."

Megan got out of her sleeping bag. I couldn't help but watch her breasts as she moved closer to me. She pulled me down to a kneeling position, put her hand on the back of my neck, and kissed me. I suddenly felt as if I could fight Custer.

"Here, take this," she said, fumbling with her stuff. She put a granola bar into my hand.

Not too far outside Megan's tent, I heard footsteps on the path behind me. I turned to see a large guy in a one-piece bunny outfit standing behind me. I stared at his bunny feet when I should have run. He looked me up and down.

"Who the hell are you?" he said. "And what are you doing here?"

"It's not what you think," I said haltingly. "I'm part of the—"

"Stay where you are," he said. He bent his knees and moved his feet apart, adopting a martial arts stance as he yelled over his shoulder, "Travis! Sebastian!"

"You don't understand," I said. I tried to back away from him, but the underbrush pushed against my back. "Ask Megan," I said.

"We got Megans up the butt here, pal," he said, and Travis and Sebastian showed up. The one I took to be a Travis wore regular clothes and looked tired and mean; the other wore the smeared remains of what looked like green face paint. They were old dudes, maybe in their twenties.

"Spying on us, huh, you little hunter shit," the guy in the bunny suit said.

"Get him!" Travis said, and I took off and ran ahead on the narrow path. I had no idea where I was going, but it seemed I wasn't going out the way I'd come in. I was on an odd high, in a Capture the Flag game for real. I felt intensely alive. I heard footsteps and swearing behind me, and then there was yelling, but that faded. I slowed my pace to allow myself one backward look—and a huge guy jumped out of the bushes and grabbed me. He lifted me off my feet, crushing the air out of me. Suddenly the pursuers I thought had given up were all over me.

"I'm working with Stewart Spiranga," I said, but I didn't have enough breath to project my words.

"What did he say?"

"Something about spraining his ankle?"

"Good. Let's break it."

"Leave him alone, gentlemen," a voice said, a familiar male voice. At first I couldn't place it. It sounded firm and commanding like a radio announcer's voice. "I'll take it from here. I'll walk him back to the other side."

"Who the hell are you?" Travis said to the man.

"A marshal," the voice said. "I've been deputized. I can arrest you."

"You DNR?"

The big guy let go of me, and I saw who the marshal was: Rosen.

"Marshals are from both sides, if you must know," Rosen said.

A whiney voice said, "Hunters aren't supposed to be on our side."

"So that means you can beat him up?" Rosen said. "What kind of pacifists are you?

Slowly and suspiciously, the group made an opening for us on the path. I glanced at the big guy who had been squeezing the life out of me. His beefy arms looked blue they were so thick with tattoos.

When they were out of earshot Rosen said, "Hey, there, Sam-I-am. Come up the wrong rabbit hole? Enlighten me. Which side did you end up on?"

"Are you really deputized?" I said.

"People want authority," he shrugged. "I give them authority. What the hell are you doing over here dressed as a hunter?"

"Visiting," I said. "I'm hunting tomorrow."

"Let me guess," he said, "you're visiting your girlfriend." He clucked his tongue.

I was calculating madly. How much did he know? Was he dangerous to my plan? I had to be careful.

"I like it," he said. "Intermarriage. It's already solving our racial crisis."

There were lights ahead, from the hunters' camp.

"Why don't you just stay away from Free City until after the hunt?" Rosen asked. "I'm sure you can handle being away from your girlfriend for—what—one day? Remember the Lakota tradition that, before your first deer kill, you should fast and abstain."

"Abstain?" I said.

"Oh, right," he said. "I forgot that word's been removed from the dictionary."

"What happens if you don't? I mean, don't abstain."

"You give your power to whatever you are hunting," he said. "You may change the animal's decision to allow you to kill it. You lose your advantage. You anger the gods of the forest."

"But I'm not doing that book. I'm not into that anymore."

"Right, that's just Indian shit," he said. "What do they know, they lost the war, right?"

"Something like that."

"So, you're going out tomorrow? Bow hunters or rifles?"

"Uh, bow," I said.

"Good choice."

"Gonna get me a buck. Maybe that Big Buck," I said.

"If he lets you," Rosen said.

I wanted to answer with words, but I shrugged.

"Final bit of wisdom, Sam-I-am," he said. "I don't know what you're up to, but I have a feeling it's getting a little too complicated."

In the distance I could see the main DNR tent, and we headed toward it.

"Things might get a little crazy out there," he said. "We've heard some anti-hunt kids in deer outfits are going to do a kamikaze run and call it street theater. Can you imagine? I hope your girlfriend isn't that nuts. Sam?"

Little flags told us we'd arrived at the border separating Free City from the hunter encampment. Someone in uniform was walking toward us.

"Whatcha got here, Doc?" It was Lenny. "Jeff was wondering where you were, boy. You need your sleep, Sam. Gotta be fresh in the morning."

The three of us walked toward the lighted tent as if it weren't 2:30 a.m.

"Doc, you got a tag?" Lenny asked.

It took me a minute to put it together. Rosen was hunting.

"What, Sam, you think it's nuts for an eco-psychologist to hunt?"

"You can do anything you want, I guess," I said.

"I thought you guys didn't say nuts anymore," Lenny said.

"I still use it," Rosen said. "For anyone who disagrees with me."

Lenny chuckled. "Call me a nut then."

We got to the tent. Jeff stared at me, and said, "Where the hell have you been?"

"Sam, you may not like this, but I have to tell your dad something," Rosen said.

"What are you talking about?" Jeff said.

"Mr. O'Brien, I think Sam's been deceiving you."

"How so?" Jeff said, and I could tell from his tone that he didn't want to hear this from Rosen.

"He's playing some kind of a game here, pretending he wants to hunt, but actually he's working with the other side."

I sent Rosen a serious scowl. "No way, Jeff. He's making this up. I was just visiting Megan over there. And some jerks chased me away. He's making this up."

"Sam," Jeff said, "you're making a serious accusation."

"He might be confused," Rosen said. "Mixed loyalties, common in the initiate. You've heard some kids are planning some kind of sabotage?"

"I've heard lots of rumors," Jeff said. "They don't mean much."

"What do you think's happening here?" Rosen said.

"Nothing," Jeff said. "Nothing other than your ongoing attempt to influence my boy. An attempt that appears to have failed, I might add." Jeff turned to me. "What about this, Sam?"

I desperately conjured up James Bond, GreenSWAT—anything that could help me maintain.

"This is for real," I said. "I'm going to kill Big Buck. Bambi's dad, the Prince of the Forest."

"Atta boy," Lenny said, clapping me on the back.

Rosen shrugged. "I'm not against hunting. I think I've proven that. I wouldn't say anything unless I thought this might be a dangerous situation."

"Hunting is dangerous, man," Lenny said. "That's essential to the game. Why the hell are you going out there anyway, Rosen? You don't really want to kill a deer. Maybe *you're* the one of the antis undercover, huh?"

"Listen, big guy, you don't know squat about me," Rosen said. "Sam's been my client and has been reading my book on initiation, so I feel some responsibility here."

"I thought you were done with that book," Jeff said quietly.

"Is this that pagan Native American crap again?" Lenny asked Jeff. "I told you it's a virus."

"Why do you still have his book, Sam?" Jeff said, his voice rising.

"I don't know, I forgot . . ."

"What he's trying to say—" Rosen said.

"I'm not talking to you," Jeff yelled at Rosen.

"It's my book, on loan to Sam," Rosen persisted. "As I told you—or maybe I told your wife—I think Sam's going through some sort of classic initiation. I thought reading about the Lakota—"

"Spare us the PBS documentary," Lenny said.

"It's unusual, Mr. O'Brien," Rosen said. "But this sort of initiation still happens. It's a gift, really."

Jeff wiped his face vigorously with both hands.

"What I want to know," Lenny said. "Is where do you people get your moral superiority to preach to everyone else? Tell me where the hell you get that. I'm curious."

"Same place you do, friend. The Judeo-Christian tradition."

"Only you've outgrown all that now, right?" Lenny said.

Jeff sat down and rubbed his forehead vigorously. "I can't believe I let this happen. The guy had us talking to a rock."

"Sam," Rosen said, "please be careful. Remember to watch for signs. You'll know what to do."

"We've heard about enough brainwashing mumbo-jumbo, Rosen," Jeff said.

"So now it's your turn to brainwash him?" Rosen said.

"It's called parenting," Jeff said. "Sam, go back to your tent."

I stared at Rosen. I felt as if it were the last time I'd ever see him. As he turned to leave, he said to me. "Watch for answers, Sam. The universe provides."

"Here we go," Lenny said and Rosen halted. "The universe? Is that the best you can do? A warped continuum of rapidly expanding nothingness is going to help us out? You might be waiting a while for a message from that black hole, Sammy boy."

Rosen chuckled. "Don't tell me. *Marvel Comic's CliffsNotes On Cosmology?*" He tisked. "Adios, gentlemen."

I cowboy nodded at him, but I didn't feel like a cowboy. I felt like a little kid. I couldn't help thinking that I was losing everyone, that I was completely alone. I'd lost Elissa, my idiot brother, my Game Boy, Holly, and Ryan. Ditto for Jeff, Lenny, and Stewart—after I'd botched everything up. I was sure I'd lose Megan too after I did or did not do whatever it was I would end up doing or not doing in the forest.

CHAPTER TWENTY-EIGHT

I DIDN'T GO TO MY TENT RIGHT AWAY LIKE JEFF told me to. For a while I sat alone at the nearest campfire, a tame and orderly thing compared to Free City's bonfire. I was starving. There was a cooler nearby with a sign on it: "Help Yourself." I opened it and took a hot dog out of an opened package floating on a melting sea of ice. I shoved it in my mouth without cooking it or anything. The hot dog raft in the cooler reminded me of melting polar caps, and I heard Megan's voice in my head say, "My god, Sam. How can you do that to yourself?"

Maybe Megan was right. At some level, I was confused. Maybe I had been eating too many death tubes of ground-up cow's ears mixed with steroids and antibiotics. The buildup was undoubtedly affecting my brain, dulling my edge, putting me into a sweet, consumerist sleep. Anyway, I was not among friends. The killers around me were as innocent as Nazis.

When I finally did get back to my tent, it smelled too much of mildew. I thought about curling up in my sleeping bag and sleeping through the rest of my life. The temptation was so strong I had to force myself to do something to keep moving. I rummaged through my pack for Stewart's ziploc. I took out the bag and weighed it in my hand. It was the only evidence someone was expecting me to do something.

I tried to remember what he'd told me. How much ground to cover, how far apart he expected me to put them—all the little details I should have memorized. I couldn't remember half as much as I'd thought I would.

I put on a bulky hunter's coat Jeff had given me. It was Mossy Oak camo with giant pockets. For what? I slipped Stewart's bag in the pocket, took my arrow pack and my bow out of their case. I threaded the Buck knife sheath through my belt, realizing I had never really used it. Jeff had given it to me for Christmas a long time before he'd given up on me. I remembered my canteen but didn't fill it. I shut my eyes, took a huge breath, opened the tent flap, took a few steps off the path, and it was done. I was illegally in the Wirth; I was a criminal; I felt alive again.

Light from the half-moon filtered through the forest canopy, making it easy to see. I tried to avoid paths, but the leaves crinkled loudly underfoot, and the undergrowth snagged my every step. After a while, I switched to a deer trail and picked up my pace. On foot, Wirth was much larger than I'd remembered it.

I heard the rustling of a large animal and crouched low, my senses instantly alert. I imagined it was Big Buck coming to talk to me again. Then I imagined it was a spy deer, running to tell the others about me, or a talking raccoon or fox like they have in Native American stories.

Eventually I came to an area of small hills and bumps, a secret bike jumping area Ryan and I had used a very long time ago. I heard another rustle, but I told myself the forest was doing things to me. I began stalking the sound this time instead of running from it. My heart pumped loud enough to hear in my ears. As I stalked, feeling on task, I began to review my mission. What I found was a jumble of missions, some contradicting others.

There was the mission of panicking the deer with Stewart's buzzers. That mission was for Megan, the Council, and Stewart. Then: be in the forest alone for my initiation. For Rosen and the ghosts of the Lakota. Then there was hunting—for Jeff and Lenny—a faux mission, but one that at the moment felt as real and perhaps more real than any of the others. There was that strange message from Big Buck.

I thought back to the night of my vision of Big Buck. He'd asked me to kill him. If he still wanted that, he would give me a sign. If he did give me a sign, I would know what to do. I found a hollow in a small hill. I sat down and waited.

I woke up shivering and disoriented. It was still dark, but the sky was beginning to lighten. I was also thirsty and hungry. I felt for my watch, then remembered I'd left it on the floor of Megan's tent. At least I'd remembered to put my blaze-orange vest on over my camo. At least no one would mistake me for a deer.

I shook my Cub Scout canteen. I swore at myself for not refilling it after Megan's tent. Stupid. I found the granola bar she gave me, peeled back the paper carefully, as if someone were listening for me. It was the best granola bar I ever had.

My mind was sluggish, my limbs tired. I felt like giving up. Maybe it was over. Maybe I'd slept through it. I tried to think of a way out that would vaguely satisfy everyone.

As I stuffed the crumpled granola wrapper into my pocket, I thought about Experimental Deer Station #47. If I gave up my mission, the deer would have died in vain, just like Stewart said. I felt for the Ziploc full of Stewart's buzzers. Through my sluggish brain, the thought hit me that even if I had my watch, I had no idea when his buzzers were scheduled to go off—they could go off any minute.

I felt dizzy when I stood. I was on the edge of hallucinating. I couldn't tell where my head ended and the world began. I heard voices. Images fell over each other in my mind. The illustrations from the Lakota book mixed with the memory of meeting Big Buck in the forest. Was there such a thing as the voice of the forest? Big Buck morphed into Bambi's father, a wise deer speaking in a deep voice: "Get moving, you jerk! You must kill the king—me!"

I picked up my bow, eased an arrow out of my quiver, and fitted it into the string. Like a karate guy, I shifted weight to my legs and began stalking. My still hands quivered; I walked like this for a long time. Steps quiet, senses alert, I was free of thoughts and worries. I could have walked for hours, right out of that place to— Canada, or Montana, or anywhere.

Then a twig broke up ahead. I froze, then glided behind a tree. A batch of does walked out from under a huge Red Pine. They sniffed the air and trotted away. I felt like their enemy, armed and dangerous, hiding behind a tree. I could release an arrow and kill one so easily.

But they were does. I wasn't hunting does. Jeff had worked hard to get me a buck tag. I stayed where I was, waiting and watching.

Then Big Buck walked out from under boughs of a pine. He seemed larger than before. He looked around. For a second, he looked at me. Then he shook his antlers and snorted as if to say, "I know what you're here to do, and I approve."

He bent his head and nibbled a fern.

First my breath stopped, then my heart. But I was ready. All I had to do was slowly pull back on the bow and let my arrow fly. My shaking hands grew worse. Buck fever. Jeff told me how even experienced hunters shake when they get close to a shot. He said it was nature's way of evening up the odds. Then I remembered what he'd said to do about it:

Breathe.

Moving more slowly than I'd ever moved while practicing, I inhaled, then pulled back my bow. Big Buck was less than twenty yards away. I had shot accurately at this distance before, but at a stationary target. I pulled back the string and closed one eye to find the fiberscope Lenny had added to my bow. It took me a second or two to focus through the high-tech gizmo, and I saw the fern—but Big Buck was gone.

I looked up and scanned nervously. He was still there, but had turned sideways, making for a difficult shot. His head was up now, suspicious, looking directly at me. Then something exploded at my hip with a horrible buzzing sound; Stewart's buzzers were vibrating against my leg. I danced and jumped, swatting the pocket that held the buzzers.

I pulled the bag of them from my pocket and threw them to the ground. I stomped on them, then crouched and stuffed the bag under a log. I built a bank around it with moss and leaf humus. Only after I stood up, I realized that I was holding a slack bow. The arrow was gone. I didn't remember releasing it and looked around as if I dropped it when I was jumping around. Stupidly, I looked for Big Buck as if he would still be there, laughing. It also dawned on me that the buzzers going off meant the hunters had already entered the forest. That meant I was in danger; I had to get out.

Then I saw a kicking hoof near the fern the deer had been eating. I ran forward and saw the shaft of an arrow sticking out of Big Buck's right shoulder. I looked around to see who else was on an illegal hunt, but with a sinking feeling in my stomach I realized: it was my arrow. He was lying on his side and it was in there deep, but had missed vital organs. It would have been a perfect shot if it had been a few inches to the right.

I knew I was supposed to do something, take responsibility for my actions or something. He was struggling to get up. A trickle of blood dribbled from his mouth. His dark eyes tracked me. They looked more scared than angry. I knew I couldn't let him go limping off into the woods. If I'd had a gun, I would have shot him.

He was kicking, trying to stand. I decided to shoot him again with a bow, close-up. But I had dropped my bow on the ground near the buzzers. I didn't want to turn my back on him. I could still hear the buzzers, which still reminded me of angry hornets.

What would Jeff do? Go up to the wounded deer, put your boot on his neck, and cut his throat. I eased over to Big Buck. He was a huge, magnificent creature. He was trying to put weight on his wounded leg and get up, but he fell back to the ground panting. His head lay sideways, his eyes closed. His black tongue, now covered in blood, stuck out a few inches from his open mouth. I hoped he was dying, but I knew it would take a long time.

I knelt down, then carefully took a firm grip on his antlers. He didn't jump when I put my hand on his warm neck.

"This is what you wanted, right?" I asked him. I unsheathed my knife, but I hesitated. It was as if I were killing a pet.

"Sam!" Jeff's voice cried out behind me.

I turned to see Jeff running toward me. He disappeared for a moment; I realized I was on a small hill. I saw his DNR cap, then his face, then his blaze-orange hunting vest over his brown uniform. He slipped backwards, grabbing a birch or support. "God, I'm glad I found you. When did you—I was so—"

Big Buck jerked to life. I put my knee down more firmly. The deer twisted his neck and tried to look at Jeff. While covering the short distance between us, he took his rifle off his shoulder and leaned it against a tree.

"My God, Sam. You shot this?" Then he frowned. "You snuck in here. When? You know you're in a lot of trouble." Then, looking at Big Buck: "He's magnificent! I had no idea he was this big! I bet it'll measure out at 180, maybe 190 points. But Sam, you—"

Big Buck let out a huge exhalation. I lessened the weight on my knee, thinking I was choking him.

"Sam, he's not dead. You got to take care of him. Got your knife? Good. You got to do this now."

"I can't," I said. "You do it."

He shook his head firmly. "He's your responsibility, Sam. Just finish this."

I noticed his rifle leaning against a tree. I was about to ask for it when Big Buck made a serious effort to rise. His muscular necked whacked me in the midsection and I fell backwards against Jeff. At the same moment something exploded in the tree beside us. I heard the noise and saw the bark fly. Jeff grabbed my coat pocket and pulled me to the ground, shielding me with his body.

"Some idiot's shooting at us," he said. He looked at his watch. "It's too early for the rifle people. Might be a poacher." He whipped off his orange vest and waved it as he yelled, "Cease-fire! Cease-fire! DNR officer here!" He whispered to me, "Stay down. You never know about these guys. They might be drunk."

I strained to see around Jeff, expecting a worried hunter to run out of the forest any second. Nothing happened, and after a minute or so, Jeff rose carefully, half hiding behind a tree trunk. He waved his vest as he pulled a walkie-talkie out of his jacket.

"Ten four. This is Jeff O'Brien. I found Sam."

He walked over to the tree the bullet hit and put his finger in the hole. Then we heard a rifle crack and a thud. I looked at Big Buck to see if he got hit. He was up on all fours, my arrow still sticking out of his shoulder. He coughed, lowered his head, and charged Jeff.

"Dad!" I yelled.

Jeff turned at exactly the wrong time. Big Buck lunged, and I couldn't tell what was happening because Jeff's coat flopped open, but I saw his smashed walkie-talkie fall to the ground. Then Big Buck had Jeff pinned to the tree. Jeff gripped the antlers with both hands, and he groaned as his eyes rolled.

I tried to get my arms around Big Buck's neck. Jeff's face looked ghostly white as he attempted to turn the deer's head sideways. "Knife," he hissed.

Not remembering when I'd opened it, I was surprised to see my scout knife in my hand. The blade looked pathetic, but I stabbed Big Buck in the neck. It didn't go in very far, and then I heard a third rifle crack, then felt searing pain in my leg. I screamed and fell, clutching my leg.

Jeff screamed, "Sam!"

I put it together: I'd been shot, but I had to help Jeff.

"Your knife," he said a second time.

I crawled forward and held out the knife to Jeff handle first. He shook his head with his eyes closed and nodded at the deer.

"Do it!"

I struggled to an upright position. Big Buck was slashing at Jeff with his hooves and keeping the pressure on his forward attack. I steadied myself by grabbing one side of his antlers. Then I buried the blade past his fur on the far side of his neck, tensed my arm, and drew the blade across his throat. Blood poured, and he collapsed, pulling Jeff and me down with him. Big Buck shuddered, jerking convulsively. Jeff and I sort of went down with him and crouched, partly hidden from the direction of the shots by his body.

I put both hands over my leg wound, which pulsed with blood, soaking my hands. Jeff pulled my hands away and inspected the bullet hole.

"We both gotta get help fast." His voice was sounding weirder. "I think I'm hurt bad." He rummaged on the ground and picked up his blood-smeared walkie-talkie. "It's up to you, Sam, to get us out of here. I might pass out on you, but don't panic. I'm not dying."

I yelled, "Help!" as loud as I could as if I expected the idiot hunter to step out of the forest and help us.

"Get my rifle and fire some warning shots," Jeff said. "Three in a row, very fast." He closed his eyes.

"Don't die," I said. "Please don't die."

A smile played on his lips, but he didn't open his eyes. "I'll be okay," he said. "Don't panic. First take off your belt and tie it around your leg above the wound."

I did what he said then looked around for his rifle. I saw it ten feet away leaning against the tree trunk where he'd left it. It seemed like a long distance at the moment. My leg was starting to throb, my pant leg wet with blood.

"They know we're here, right?" I said. "Maybe that hunter went to get help." Even as I said this it didn't feel right. I yelled "Help" over and over again. My voice echoed through the woods. I couldn't understand it. The buzzers had gone off. There was at least one hunter in the woods. Where were the others?

"Dad?" I said.

Jeff didn't respond, and he didn't look good. I forced myself to crawl toward his rifle. Then I saw two camo-clad legs and heavy-duty boots heading right toward me. "Help us!" I said. "We're wounded! We need help!"

"You little fucker," the voice said. "I knew I should never have trusted a DNR kid."

I looked up at Stewart's face. "This is serious," I said. "The deer wounded my dad and I got shot in the leg."

Stewart walked over and prodded Big Buck with his rifle. "You shot Big Buck? I should never have trusted you kids."

"What are you talking about? We're in a crisis here!"

"What happened to my buzzers? The big plan you agreed to? Was that all bull-shit that you were helping us?"

"You don't understand," I said. "We're hurt. Shot. I'm shot. Jeff got gored by the deer."

"You were with them after all. You double-crossed us."

"You've go to help us," I said. "My dad's hurt. Maybe dying."

"That'll make a good story. The Prince of the Forest gores the brains of the DNR operation to death. I like it."

"It's a crime not to help us. You'll go to jail."

"Oh, yeah? Who's the witness? Idiot son gets shot by stray bullets of drunk hunters eager to kill anything that moves. Works for me." He aimed his rifle at me.

I felt a chill as I realized I was talking to a madman and like madmen in all the movies he was still talking. Speech-giving. But what was I supposed to do? Thinking about the movies helped me realize I still held my scout knife in my hand. Covered with deer blood, he hadn't seen it.

"You'll never get away with this," I said as if playing the trapped hero. "This wound isn't fatal—and they'll catch you."

"Maybe that one isn't," he said then shrugged. "Doesn't matter, one way or an-other. I'm ready. I want a trial. I'll be famous either way," he said. "There'll be books, movie rights—"

"Help!" I yelled. "Over here!"

"Punk," he said, and he raised his gun at me.

The rest I did without planning it. I lunged at him and plunged my knife into his calf. He stumbled backward and dropped his rifle. It went off as he fell into a thicket of buckthorn.

"Shit!" he screamed. "My balls!"

"Cease firing! DNR!" a voice boomed, and Lenny broke through the brush running straight at us. "I found them," he yelled into his walkie-talkie. "Get my coordinates. Quick. Men down. We need paramedics in here—fast."

He crouched beside me.

"Sam?" he said. "What the hell happened here? Who's hit?"

He hopped over to Jeff, opened Jeff's jacket, and said, "Jesus Christ and all his saints." He shook Jeff gently, and Jeff moaned.

"The buck mauled him," I said.

"What the—?" Lenny glanced at Big Buck. "Spiranga? What happened to him?" He ran over to Stewart, who was clutching his bloody crotch. Lenny whipped off his backpack and took something out. "Gotta stop the bleeding, fella. Let me look at it."

Stewart continued to howl. I felt like throwing up.

With one hand on Stewart's groin, Lenny yelled into his walkie-talkie, "Where the hell are you guys? Men are down here! Officer down! Serious injuries. I repeat—injuries! Send three ATV's to these coordinates." He read numbers from another device he held in his hand.

"What the hell happened here?" Lenny said, more or less to himself.

"The . . . kid," Stewart said. "He tried to kill me."

"Ouch," Lenny said to Stewart with his hand on his bloody crotch. He looked at me. "Yeah?" he said rather casually. "What about it, Sam?"

I shook my head firmly.

"He . . . tried," Stewart said.

"Quiet down, fella," Lenny said. "We'll sort it all out later. Right now we got to make sure none of you bleeds to death."

CHAPTER TWENTY-NINE

I WOKE AND SAW THAT THE OTHER BED IN THE HOSPITAL room was empty. Then a nurse came in and told me my mother was there. I took this as a bad sign and asked, "Where's my dad?" She was gone before I yelled, "I know he's dead!"

Elissa walked in. She wore a light blue sweatshirt with sleeping kittens on it. "Jeff's dead, isn't he?" I asked.

"No, Sam, he's not, " she said calmly. "But he is in intensive care."

"He's dying then, right? It was all my fault. It's like I killed him. He was only there to protect me, and—"

"He's bad, but not *bad* bad," she said. "The antlers pierced his lung on one side and poked a small hole in his liver. It adds up to pretty serious stuff, but far from fatal. He's strong. He'll be fine."

"I think I'm gonna puke," I said. Elissa raised a banana-shaped dish to my chin, but I pushed it away. "When can I see him?"

"You'll see him," she said. "As soon as either of you can move. You aren't going anywhere for a while."

"I have to see him," I said. "I have to tell him I'm sorry." I lifted myself up with my arms—sharp pain shot through my injured leg. "Jesus!"

Elissa gripped my forearm. "Calm down, Sam. What do you have to apologize for?"

"It was my fault he nearly got killed."

"What, you commanded the big deer to attack him?"

I searched her face for mockery but found none. "It wasn't like that," I said, looking away. "How bad is my leg anyway?"

"The bullet went through your thigh," she said. "It did some damage to the greater trochanter, where the thighbone turns toward the pelvis. It looks worse than it is. They call this traction. They just wanted to make sure it set properly. It'll heal fine."

The image of my own bone splintering nauseated me again, and that feeling reminded me of what had happened to Stewart. Despite everything, I felt sorry for him. Getting shot in the crotch wasn't something you'd wish on your worst enemy.

"What happened to Stewart?" I asked.

Elissa shook her head. "You know as much as anyone. Nobody seems to know exactly what happened. Apparently he shot himself."

"He's here? In this hospital?" I asked, craning my neck to look into the hallway.

"He's at County General. He's under arrest for something. I don't know what the charges are." She shrugged. "There's a number of things they could get him on. Ask Megan when she comes. She always seems to know everything."

"Megan's coming?" I asked. "Soon?"

"Soon enough. Get some rest."

I did, and when I woke up, Elissa was still sitting on the plastic guest chair in my room. I looked at the kittens on her sweatshirt; they looked more awake now. She was knitting, and I couldn't remember the last time I saw her do that. Perry was sitting on the floor with his chin on the seat of another plastic chair. He smashed two action figures together, saying "Bam" each time they hit.

"How long have I been asleep?" I asked.

Elissa smiled and leaned toward me. "Not so long. It's still Sunday."

"Were you in a coma?" Perry said.

"You wish," I said.

"Sam," Elissa said warningly. "Lenny stopped by. He brought you *these*." She tossed an envelope at me.

I spilled the contents, a bunch of photographs, over my stomach. They were pictures, mostly of Big Buck's rack. An anonymous hand from outside the frame held his head up for the photographer. In some of the backgrounds I could see paramedics and DNR people walking about.

"You opened my envelope?" I said.

"I'm still your mom. I can't believe he'd think you'd want trophy shots." She started knitting again with a pinkish-colored yarn. I hoped it wasn't a sweater or scarf for me. "I suppose Jeff will like them, but don't think they're getting framed for our walls."

I eyed her suspiciously, suspecting a trap. "*Our* walls?" I said.

"I'm back in the house. Just like I said I'd be," she said.

Megan burst in with rustling packages and a purple heart-shaped balloon. She looked dressed up. I stared at her new hairstyle. It was its own presence, as if she had brought a friend.

"Hello, Megan," Elissa said in a tone that wasn't exactly friendly.

"Hello, Mrs. O'Brien," Megan said. She beamed at me as if I were a war hero. I wanted Elissa to leave, but she kept knitting. Megan looked at Elissa and then threw me a little kiss. She tied the heart-shaped balloon to the bed.

"It's a Purple Heart," she said. "For bravery."

"They're not going to want it tied to the bed," Elissa said without looking up.

For the second time I noted tension between Megan and Elissa. I figured I must have missed something. The balloon came loose and floated to the ceiling. Megan and I exchanged smiles as it bounced around before it came to rest in the corner. "You're the first person I know who's ever been shot," she said. "You're so . . ." Her eyes searched for a word. "Action-y."

Elissa snorted but didn't look up.

"Just how action-y-am-I?" I said. "Tell me everything you know. Elissa said you know everything."

"I said she *thinks* she knows," Elissa said.

"You were so brave," Megan said, ignoring Elissa. "You mean what happened after you saved your father from that deer?"

And then it hit me: nobody knew exactly what happened except me and Stewart, who was an unreliable convict now. I decided to hold my cards close and see what the others played. I gave Elissa a look I hoped would convince her to leave.

"Perry, honey, go buy yourself something," Elissa said. She foraged through her purse and gave Perry a handful of jingling coins, and looking fully alive for the first time, he disappeared into the hallway. She went back to knitting.

"Bring me some action-figure food," I yelled after him. Turning back to Megan, I said, "So tell me what you know."

"Okay," she said. She took a breath and closed her eyes for a second. "You saw your dad—well, this is hard to say but—he was aiming at Big Buck. You know, for the trophy?" She glanced nervously at Elissa.

Elissa rolled her eyes, but kept knitting.

"When your dad missed and the deer charged him, you tried to save him. Unfortunately, you weren't able to stop the deer, so you had to . . ."

"What?" I said.

"Kill him. You cut his throat, actually. But you only did it to save your dad's life!"

I took this in with narrowed eyes. "And Stewart?" I asked.

Perry appeared at the door with a grimace. "The machine ate my money," he whined. An old trick I'd taught him.

Elissa stood. "I'll come help you," she said. She walked toward the door and then turned around. "I think you should know, Sam, there are a many versions of what happened floating around."

"Versions?" I said, shaking my head as if this was a confusing concept.

"Yes, versions. It'll get sorted out." Elissa changed her tone to an unconvincing sweetness: "You kids probably want to catch up without me. I'll go help Perry. No hanky-panky now." She waved a possibly playful finger at us but failed to smile.

"Hanky-panky?" I said in exaggerated aggravation. "I'm practically dying here," I yelled after her.

Megan watched her balloon bump around the ceiling, pushed around by air currents.

"Why are you guys fighting?" I asked Megan. "Last I heard, you were on the same side."

Megan shrugged. "I don't know. Maybe she's just being a mom. Or maybe it's the thing with Stewart—well, the way the whole hunt ended. It's got people . . ." she looked at the balloon again, "polarized."

"What happened at the hunt? I mean, after the Stewart thing."

"No one told you?" she asked. "You don't know *anything*?"

"I know *some* things. I know my dad's in intensive care. I know Stewart is still alive, but under arrest. And—" I sighed. "Big Buck's dead."

"So—*nothing*." She leaned toward me, wide-eyed. "Ryan got a bunch of kids to dress in those Die-In deer costumes. They were going to run into Wirth, until . . ." She looked up at the balloon as if distracted. "Until the thing with Stewart. The whole hunt's been postponed. Well, that's what they're saying. We're hoping for a death row pardon for that poor herd." She brightened. "I saw your shrink. I wasn't sure what side he was on but he told me you fought off a bunch of hunters."

"He said that?"

"He said he saved you from . . . somebody."

"It's not important," I said. "But I never had a chance to fight them. I was running and Rosen sort of saved me."

"Hunters caught you crossing over from our side?"

"It wasn't the hunters," I said. For a moment I was back facing the guy in the bunny suit, listening to the voice of my rescuer. Then something hit me: when I couldn't see his face the voice reminded me of Michael Blaine, the right-wing radio guy. Rosen's voice, the general weirdness of his politics, even his humor—it might fit. I made a brief calculation about how I might be able to use this to my advantage. But what did I want from Rosen? I thought of Britt, then shook my head rather violently.

"What's wrong, Sam?" Megan said. "Should I call a nurse?"

I shook my head. "Sorry, I just had sort of a flashback."

She touched my hand sympathetically. "It must have been awful," she said. Switching to a bright smile that reminded me she probably had a future in politics, she said, "Where were we? Talking about your brave adventure in the woods, saving the deer. You're a hero, Sam."

"Hero," I said, feeling stupid repeating it, but I didn't know what else to do. I didn't want her to know how mixed that word suddenly felt. Did being a hero mean you had secrets to tell that would undermine your heroic status? Did being a hero mean people misinterpreted your actions, or interpreted them in ways that made them look good? Was this what all the superhero comics were trying to say: Being a hero is a drag?

I realized I missed some of what Megan was rambling on about. "All except Big Buck, of course, he was the only deer who actually died. I guess he was sort of a hero too." She looked up at the balloon again, and I could see the wheels turning. Sam, hero, Big Buck, hero. I saw a poster drawn in a crude style of me and Big Buck standing on two legs, arms over each other's shoulders. Then I thought of Jeff frowning, pretending he couldn't understand it, like he did to Janine's Prop19 poster. I felt like I was being swept up into a program, incomprehensible and unstoppable. Hero-dom.

I felt hungry. Weird reaction, but I looked around for something to eat. "Got any granola bars?" I asked.

I hadn't meant it as a coded message, but Megan winked and began rummaging through her purse. It seemed surreal that it was the same Guatemalan bag Elissa had.

"There's something else," she said, unwrapping a good one for me, one with real nuts and honey. She looked around conspiratorially.

"The police were asking around," she said. "About the . . ."

I was supposed to know. "What?"

"The, um, university thing?" she whispered, barely audibly. It took me a minute to get it. She was signaling with her eyes that the room might be bugged.

"Oh," I said, nodding as if thinking heroic thoughts about how to straighten out this mess.

In fact, it was hard to imagine anyone caring about something so long ago. I wondered if it would harm my new status if it all came out now. Did I care? Again I thought about the possibility of blackmailing Rosen if I was right about his secret identity. Perhaps I could force him to allow me to take Britt to the Angry Cup instead of talking to his dumb rock. Thinking of Britt twice while I sat in front of Megan was unnerving. I forced myself to look at her. Something had changed, but I wasn't sure what it was.

"It's possible they'll go after Stewart for that," she said in a soft voice, continuing to scan the room in an exaggerated fashion. "He might send them our way. We'll have to go over our stories again about that. We can't let anything mess with our chance to stop the hunt."

I felt a rush of excitement. Perhaps in her mind Operation GreenBond wasn't the complete failure I thought it was. What did I accomplish inside the enemy camp? Was I brainwashed like those guys from the Vietnam War who said they weren't responsible for the statements they made on behalf of the North? Or was it more complicated than that, not a failure so as being forced to see that both sides had good arguments, that no one was completely right?

"In any case," she said, squeezing my hand. "We have lots to do. We have to revive the Council of Nations, maybe even Mary Langsford—"

I tried to draft on her excitement, but all I could see was Megan and Mary arguing where to have our meetings. I couldn't see Mary on the broken-down playground equipment.

"The future is ours," Megan said, her eyes glistening.

For a few innocent moments, we just held hands and said nothing. I had a strange feeling we were finally crossing over into coupleness. I desperately wanted to be more excited.

"If," Megan said, suddenly lurching for the string dangling from the purple balloon. "If we do get together. You and I, I mean. We shouldn't ever get married."

"Or have kids," I said. "I mean, even if we don't marry. No kids."

"Yes!" she said, clapping her hands. "That could be a rule."

"A rule?" I asked. All I could think of were Unitarians.

"We need rules," she said, slipping into her old lecturing tone. "To prevent what happened to your parents from happening to us."

"Or what happened to yours," I said.

"What happened to mine?"

"Let's just say we never want to drive two white minivans," I said.

She smiled. "Okay. Rule Number Two: if we disagree on stuff. Like your parents? We leave it at the door so we can have a good sex life."

"Rule," I said. "Absolutely a rule." I put my hands on my lap, suddenly self-conscious about the thinness of my hospital frock.

"And if we fight," she said, "we do it like lesbians."

I waited for an explanation. When she said nothing, I asked, "Which would be?"

"We discuss," she said. "We involve the community. Like how Patti and Janine work things out."

"Okay," I said. "But then there's the most important rule."

"Yes?"

"If we ever decide to have kids," I said. "I mean if there's a plague that wipes out half the planet and it becomes a good thing to do again. The right thing to do. And if we do it—"

"Yeah?" she asked.

"Our kids do not, I repeat, do *not* call us by our first names!"

She laughed, but merely a polite laugh.

"Also, we get to eat whatever we want," I said. "Even if the other person thinks it's like full of pesticides or chemicals or bad for the planet."

"You're getting a little too into this rule thing," she said. "I think it was my turn." She frowned. "Eat *anything?*"

I reached out, grabbed her hand, and squeezed hard.

"Okay," she said. "But I have one: we don't have to like all the rules we make."

I nodded, not letting go of her hand. I thought it a good idea to summarize: "Disagreements left at door, good sex life."

Perry wandered into the room alone. He came over to my bedside and wedged himself between Megan and me. He handed me a package of Peanut M&M's and a Diet Coke.

"Here, Sam," he said. "I bought these for you. I was gonna eat them in the hallway, but I changed my mind."

I looked at Megan, who had tears in her eyes.

This was a snack I used to love years ago it seemed, before Megan taught me how bad Diet Coke was for you—how it burns holes in memory neurons and turns stomach acid to vinegar. Megan had also explained to me how the peanut farmers' toxic run-off was filling in the Mississippi delta and how the big chocolate conglomerates was forcing cocoa farmers to destroy the rainforest.

"Thanks," I said to Perry. "You're a good brother." I tousled his hair and opened the M&M's. I poured a few into Perry's outstretched hand and some into a larger hand next to his. I knew the larger hand was attached to Megan, but I had to check out her eyes. This time, there was no doubt: they were filling with tears.

Simultaneously, all of our hands shot to our faces and tossed the candies into our mouths. I snapped open the Diet Coke and filled my mouth with its stinging sweetness. My teeth mashed peanuts and chocolate together into a potent sugary concoction. I felt as if I were eating America.

"What made you change your mind about stealing my snack?" I asked Perry, my mouth full.

"I don't know," he said. "Because—you're a hero?" He picked up his two action figures and began smashing them together again. "Bam. Ow. Bam," he said, smiling at the toys.

"And what do you think I did?" I said to him, looking at Megan over the top of his head.

"You saved the earth . . . or something?" he said, not too interested. His smile was dark with chocolate, as if he had been eating mud.

"Something like that, I guess," I said.

"Bam!" he said, and his little action figures continued killing each other, but Megan and I—and whoever else cared—knew they would never die.